THE CYCLE

Phoenix sinks into decay
Haughty dragon yearns to slay.
Lyorn growls and lowers horn
Tiassa dreams and plots are born.
Hawk looks down from lofty flight
Dzur stalks and blends with night.
Issola strikes from courtly bow
Tsalmoth maintains though none knows how.
Vallista rends and then rebuilds
Jhereg feeds on others' kills.
Quiet iorich won't forget
Sly chreotha weaves his net.
Yendi coils and strikes, unseen
Orca circles, hard and lean.
Frightened teckla hides in grass
Jhegaala shifts as moments pass.
Athyra rules minds' interplay
Phoenix rises from ashes gray.

The Adventures of Vlad Taltos

THE BOOK OF TALTOS

Contains the complete text of
Taltos and Phoenix

Steven Brust

ACE BOOKS, NEW YORK

This is a work of fiction. Names, characters, places, and incidents either are the product of the author's imagination or are used fictitiously, and any resemblance to actual persons, living or dead, business establishments, events, or locales is entirely coincidental.

THE BOOK OF TALTOS

An Ace Book / published by arrangement with
the author

ISBN 0-441-00894-1

ACE®
Ace Books are published by The Berkley Publishing Group,
a division of Penguin Putnam Inc., 375 Hudson Street,
New York, New York 10014.
ACE and the "A" design are trademarks
belonging to Penguin Putnam Inc.

PRINTED IN THE UNITED STATES OF AMERICA

Author's Note

One of the questions I'm most often asked is: "In what order would you recommend reading these books?" Unfortunately, I'm just exactly the wrong guy to ask. I made every effort to write them so they could be read in any order. I am aware that, in some measure at least, I have failed (I certainly wouldn't recommend starting with *Teckla*, for example), but the fact that I was trying makes me incapable of giving an answer.

Many people whose opinion I respect believe publication order is best; this volume reflects that belief. For those who want to read the books in chronological order, it would go like this: *Taltos, Yendi, Dragon, Jhereg, Teckla, Phoenix, Athyra, Orca, Issola*.

The choice, I daresay, is yours. In any case, I hope you enjoy them.

Steven Brust
Minneapolis
March 1999

Pronunciation Guide

Adrilankha	ah-dri-LAHN-kuh
Adron	Ā-drahn
Aliera	uh-LEER-uh
Athyra	uh-THĪ-ruh
Baritt	BĀR-it
Brust	brūst
Cawti	KAW-tee
Chreotha	kree-O-thuh
Dragaera	druh-GAR-uh
Drien	DREE-en
Dzur	tser
Iorich	ī-Ō-rich
Issola	î-SŌ-luh
Jhegaala	zhuh-GAH-luh
Jhereg	zhuh-REG
Kiera	KĪ-ruh
Kieron	KĪ-rahn
Kragar	KRAY-gahr
Leareth	LEER-eth
Loiosh	LOI-ōsh
Lyorn	LI-orn
Mario	MAH-ree-ō
Mellar	MEH-lar
Morrolan	muh-RŌL-uhn
Norathar	NŌ-ruh-thahr
Rocza	RAW-tsuh
Serioli	sar-ee-Ō-lee
Taltos	TAHL-tōsh
Teckla	TEH-kluh
Tiassa	tee-AH-suh
Tsalmoth	TSAHL-mōth
Verra	VEE-ruh
Valista	vuhl-ISS-tuh
Yendi	YEN-dee
Zerika	zuh-REE-kuh

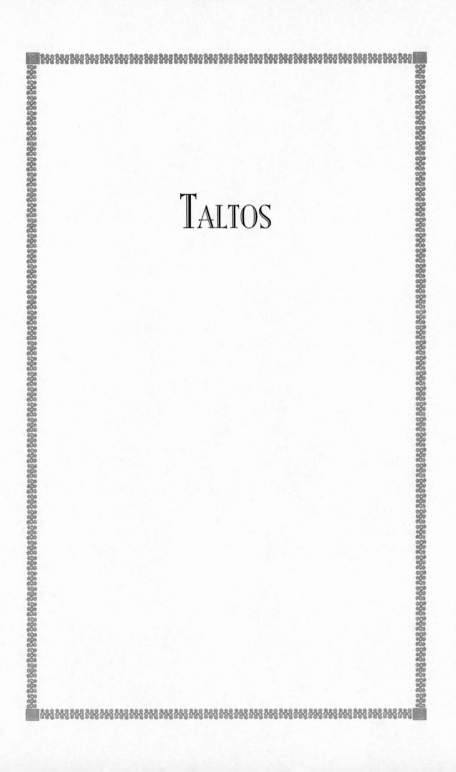

TALTOS

1

The Cycle: Dragon, dzur, and chreotha; athyra, hawk, and phoenix; teckla and jhereg.

They danced before my eyes. The Dragaeran Empire, its population divided into seventeen Great Houses, each with its animal representation, seemed to unfold in my hands. Here was the Empire of Dragaerans, and here was I, the Easterner, the outsider.

It wouldn't get any easier.

The eyes of no gods upon me, I began.

SOME TWO HUNDRED MILES to the north and east of Adrilankha there lies a mountain, shaped as if by the hand of a megalomaniacal sculptor into the form of a crouching grey dzur.

You've seen it, I'm sure, in thousands of paintings and psiprints from hundreds of angles, so you know as well as I that the illusion of the great cat is as perfect as artifice or nature could make it. What is most interesting is the left ear. It is fully as feline as the other, but is known to have been fabricated. We have our suspicions about the whole place, but never mind that; we're *sure* about the left ear.

It is here, say the legends, that Sethra Lavode, the Enchantress, the Dark Lady of Dzur Mountain, sits like a great spider in the center of an evil web, hoping to snare the true-hearted hero. Exactly why she would wish to do this the legends don't make clear; as is their right, of course.

I sat in the center of my own evil web, jiggled a strand, and caused it to bring forth more particulars about mountain, tower, and lady. It seemed likely that I was going to have to visit the place, webs being the fragile things that they are.

Of such things are legends made.

I was going over a couple of letters I'd received. One was from a human girl named Szandi, thanking me for a wonderful evening. On reflection, I decided it had been pretty nice at that. I made a mental note to write back and ask if she'd be free sometime next week. The other was from one of my employees, asking if a certain customer could have an extension on a loan he'd taken out to cover gambling losses to another of my employees. I was thinking about this and drumming my fingertips when I heard Kragar clear his throat. Loiosh, my familiar, flew off his coat rack and landed on my shoulder, hissing at Kragar.

"I wish he'd stop doing that, boss," said Loiosh psionically.

"Me, too, Loiosh."

I said to Kragar, "How long have you been sitting there?"

"Not long."

His lean, seven-foot-tall Dragaeran frame was slouched in the chair opposite me. For once, he was not looking smug. I wondered what was bothering him, but didn't ask. If it was any of my business, he'd tell me. I said, "Do you remember a Chreotha named Fyhnov? He wants to extend his loan from Machan, and I don't know—"

"There's a problem, Vlad."

I blinked. "Tell me about it."

"You sent Quion to collect the receipts from Nielar, Macham, Tor—"

"Right. What happened?"

"He scooped them up and ran."

I didn't say anything for a while, I just sat and thought about what this implied. I'd only been running this area for a few months, since the unfortunate death of my previous boss, and this was the first time I'd had this sort of problem.

Quion was what I call a button-man; an ambiguous term which in this case meant he was responsible for whatever I wanted him responsible for from one day to the next. He was old, even for a Dragaeran—I guess close to three thousand years—and had promised when I hired him that he'd stopped gambling. He was quiet, as polite as Dragaerans ever are to humans, and very experienced at the sorts of operations I was running—untaxed gambling, unlicensed brothels, making loans at illegal rates, dealing in stolen goods . . . that sort of thing. And he'd seemed really earnest when I'd hired him, too.

Shit. You'd think, after all these years, I'd know better than to trust Dragaerans, but I keep doing it anyway.

I said, "What happened?"

"Temek and I were protecting him. We were walking by a shop and he told us to wait a minute, went over to the window like he wanted to look at something, and teleported out."

"He couldn't have been snatched, could he?"

"I don't know of any way to teleport someone who doesn't want to be teleported. Do you?"

"No, I guess not. Wait a minute. Temek's a sorcerer. Didn't he trace the teleport?"

"Yeah," said Kragar.

"Well? Why didn't you follow him?"

"Ummm, Vlad, neither of us has any interest in following him where he went."

"Yeah? Well?"

"He teleported straight to Dzur Mountain."

"Dzur Mountain," I repeated a long moment later. "Well, I'll be dragon fodder. How could he have known the teleport coordinates? How could he have known he'd be safe from what's-her-name? How—?"

"Her name is Sethra Lavode, and I don't know."

"We'll have to send someone after him."

"No chance, Vlad. You won't convince anyone to go there."

"Why not? We've got money."

"Vlad, it's *Dzur Mountain*. Forget it."

"What's so special about Dzur Mountain?"

"Sethra Lavode," said Kragar.

"All right, what's so special about—"

"She's a vampire, a shape-shifter, holds a Great Weapon, is probably the most dangerous wizard living, and has the habit of killing people who get near her, unless she decides to turn them into norska or jhereg instead."

"There are worse fates than being a jhereg boss."

"Shut up, Loiosh."

I said, "How much of this is fact and how much is just rumor?"

"What's the difference if everyone believes the rumors? I know I won't go near the place."

I shrugged. Maybe if I were Dragaeran I'd have understood. I said, "Then I'll have to go myself."

"You want to die?"

"I don't want to let him get away with—how much did he take?"

"More than two thousand imperials."

"Shit. I want him. See what you can learn about Dzur Mountain that we can count on, all right?"

"Huh? Oh, sure. How many years do you want me to put in on this?"

"Three days. And see what you can find out about Quion, while you're at it."

"Vlad—"

"Go."

He went.

I settled back to contemplate legends, decided it was pointless, and began composing a letter to Szandi. Loiosh returned to his perch on the coat rack and made helpful suggestions for the letter. If I thought Szandi liked dead teckla, I might have even used some of them.

Sometimes I almost think I can remember my mother.

My father kept changing his story, so I don't know if she died or if she left him, and I don't know if I was two, four, or five at the time. But every once in a while I get these images of her, or of someone I think is her. The images aren't clear enough to describe, but I'm sort of happy I have them. They aren't necessarily my earliest memories. No, if I push my mind back, I can recall endless piles of dirty dishes, and dreams of being made to wash them forever, which I suppose comes from living above a restaurant. Don't get me wrong; I wasn't really worked all that hard, it's just that the dishes made an impression that has stayed with me. I sometimes wonder if my entire adult life has been spent in an effort to avoid dirty dishes.

One could, I suppose, have worse goals.

My OFFICE IS LOCATED in back of a psychedelic herb shop. There's a room between the shop and the office that houses an almost continuous shereba game, which would be legal if we paid taxes, and would be shut down if we didn't bribe the Phoenix Guards. The bribes are less than the taxes would be, and our customers don't have to pay taxes on their winnings. The office portion consists of a set of several small rooms, one of which is mine, another of which is Kragar's. I have a window that will give me a wonderful view of an alley if I ever decide to unboard it.

It was about an hour after noon three days later when Kragar came in, and a few minutes after that, I suppose, when I noticed him sitting there.

I said, "What did you find out about Dzur Mountain?"

He said, "It's big."

I said, "Thank you. Now, what did you find out?"

He pulled out a notebook, flipped through it, and said, "What do you want to know?"

"Many things. To start with, what made Quion think he'd be safe going to Dzur Mountain? Was he just getting old and desperate and figured what the hell?"

Kragar said, "I've reconstructed his movements for the past year or so, and—"

"In three days?"

"Yeah."

"That's fast work for a Dragaeran."

"Thanks too much, boss."

Loiosh, perching on his coat rack, sniggered into my mind.

"So, what were you saying about his movements?"

"The only really interesting thing I found was that about a month before he started working for you he was sent on an errand to a certain Morrolan."

I chewed this over, then said, "I've heard of Morrolan, but I can't remember how."

"Big-shot wizard of the House of the Dragon and a friend of the Empress. Lives about a hundred and fifty miles inland, in a floating castle."

"Floating castle," I repeated. "That's it. The only one since the Interregnum. Bit of a show-off, then."

Kragar snorted. "To say the least. He calls the place 'Castle Black.' "

I shook my head. Black is, to a Dragaeran, the color of sorcery. "Okay. What does Morrolan have to do with—"

"Technically, Dzur Mountain is part of his fief. It's about fifty miles from where his castle usually is."

"Interesting," I said.

"I wonder how he collects taxes," said Loiosh.

"It's the only thing that stands out," said Kragar.

I nodded. "Mountains have a way of doing that. But all right, Kragar. It's a connection, anyway. What else do you know about Morrolan?"

"Not much. He spent a good portion of the Interregnum out East, so he's supposed to be tolerant of Easterners." Easterner means human, like me. But Dragaerans call themselves human, which is plainly ridiculous, so it can get confusing.

I said, "Well, I could start with visiting Morrolan, if he'll consent to see me. What did you find out about Dzur Mountain?"

"Bits and pieces. What do you want to know?"

"Mostly, does Sethra Lavode really exist?"

"She certainly did before the Interregnum. There are still accounts of when she was a regular at court. Deathgate, boss, she was Warlord more than once."

"When?"

"About fifteen thousand years ago."

"Fifteen thousand years. I see. And you think she might still be alive? That's, what, five or six times a normal life span?"

"Well, if you believe the rumors, fledgling heroes from the House of the Dzur like to chase up the mountain every so often to fight the evil enchantress, and they're never heard from again."

"Yeah," I said. "But the question is, do we believe the rumors?"

He blinked. "I don't know about you, Vlad, but I do."

I ruminated on moldy legends, enchantresses, dishonest button-men, and mountains.

"You just can't trust anyone anymore," said Loiosh who flew down onto my right shoulder.

"I know. It's a sad state of affairs." Loiosh snorted psionically. *"No, I mean it,"* I said. *"I trusted the son of a bitch."*

I took out a dagger and started flipping it. After a while I put it away and said, "All right, Kragar. Send a message to the Lord Morrolan, asking him if he'd deign to receive me. Whenever he wishes, of course; I'm not—say! How do you get there, anyway? I mean, if it's a floating castle—"

"You teleport," said Kragar.

I groaned. "Okay. Try to set it up, all right? And get the coordinates to Narvane. I don't feel like spending the money on the Bitch Patrol, so I'll just live with a rough ride."

"Why don't you do it yourself, then?"

"Not *that* rough."

"You getting cheap, boss?"

"What do you mean, getting?"

"Will do, Vlad."

Kragar left the room.

Now that I have a few years' perspective, I have to say that I don't think my father was cruel to me. The two of us were alone, which made everything difficult, but he did as well as he could for who he was. And I do mean we were alone. We lived among Dragaerans, rather than in the Eastern ghetto, so our neighbors didn't associate with us, and our only other family was my father's father, who didn't come to our side of town, and my father didn't like bringing me to Noish-pa's when I was an infant.

You'd think I'd have gotten used to being alone, but it hasn't worked that way. I've always hated it. I still do. Maybe it's an instinctive thing among Easterners. The best times were what I now think must have been slow days at the restaurant, when the waiters had time to play with me. There was one I remember: a big fat guy with a mustache and almost no teeth. I'd pull his mustache and he'd threaten to cook me up for a meal and serve me with an orange in my mouth. I can't think why I thought that was funny. I wish I could remember his name.

On reflection, my father probably found me more a burden than a pleasure. If he ever had any female companionship, he did a good job of keeping it hidden, and I can't imagine why he would. It wasn't my fault, but I guess it wasn't his, either.

I never really liked him, though.

I suppose I was four years old before my father began taking me regularly to visit my grandfather. That was the first big change in my life that I remember, and I was pleased about it.

My grandfather did his job, which was to spoil me, and it is only now that I'm beginning to realize how much more he did. I must have been five or six when I began to realize that my father didn't approve of all the things Noish-pa was showing me—like how to make a leaf blow slightly askew of the wind just by willing it to. And, even more, the little slap-games we'd play that I now know to be the first introduction to Eastern-style fencing.

I was puzzled by my father's displeasure but, being a contrary little cuss, this made me pay all the more attention to Noish-pa. This may be the root of the problems between my father and me, although I doubt it. Maybe I look like my mother, I don't know. I've asked Noish-pa who I resemble, and all he ever says is, "You look like yourself, Vladimir."

I do know of one thing that must have hurt my father. One day when I was about five I received my first real beating, which was delivered by, I think, four or five punks from the House of the Orca. I remember that I was at the market running an errand of some sort, and they surrounded me, called me names I can't remember, and made fun of my boots, which were of an Eastern style. They slapped me a few times and one of them hit me in the stomach hard enough to knock the wind out of me; then they kicked me once or twice and took the money I had been given to make the purchases. They were about my own size, which I guess means they were in their late teens, but there were several of them, and I was pretty banged up, as well as terrified of telling my father.

When they were finished with me, I got up, crying, and ran all the way to South Adrilankha, to my grandfather's house. He put things on the cuts that made me feel better, fed me tea (which I suspect he spiked with brandy), brought me home, and spoke to my father so I didn't have to explain where the money had gone.

It was only years later that I actually got around to wondering why I'd gone all the way to Noish-pa's, instead of going home, which was closer. And it was years after that when I got to wondering if that had hurt my father's feelings.

About twenty-two hours after Kragar left to set things up, I was leaning back in my chair, which has a strange mechanism that allows it to tilt, swivel, and do other things. My feet were up on the desk, crossed at the ankles. The toes of my boots pointed to opposite corners of the room, and in the gap between them Kragar's thin face was framed. His chin is one that a human would call weak, but Kragar isn't—that's just another one of his innate illusions. He is built of illusions. Some natural, others, I think, cultivated. For example, when anyone else would be angry, he never seems to be; he usually just appears disgusted.

The face that was framed in the V of my boots looked disgusted. He said, "You're right. You don't have to take anyone with you. What interest could a Dragonlord possibly have in hurting a poor, innocent Jhereg, just because he's an Easterner? Or should I say, a poor, innocent Easterner, just because he's a Jhereg? Come on, Vlad, wake up. You have to have protection. And I'm your best bet for avoiding trouble."

Loiosh, who had been swooping down on stray lint, landed on my right shoulder and said, *"Just point out that I'll be there, boss. That should keep him from worrying."*

"You think so? What if it doesn't?"

"I'll bite his nose off."

I said aloud, "Kragar, I could bring every enforcer who works for me, and

it wouldn't make any difference at all if Morrolan decides to shine me. And
this is a social call. If I show up with protection—"

"That's why I think I should come. He'll never notice I'm there."

"No," I said. "He's permitted me to visit. He said nothing about bringing
a shadow. If he did notice you—"

"He'd understand that it's policy in the Jhereg. He must know something
about how we operate."

"I repeat: no."

"But—"

"Subject closed, Kragar."

He closed his eyes and emitted a sigh that hung in the air like an athyra's
mating call. He opened his eyes again. "Okay. You want Narvane to do the
teleport, right?"

"Yeah. Can he handle the coordinates?"

"Morrolan said one of his people would put them straight into the mind
of whoever we want to do the spell."

I blinked. "How can he do that? How can one of his people achieve that
close a psionic link with someone he doesn't know?"

Kragar yawned. "Magic," he said.

"What *kind* of magic, Kragar?"

He shrugged. "How should I know?"

"Sounds like witchcraft, boss."

"That's exactly what I was thinking, Loiosh."

"You think he might be employing a witch?"

"Remember, he spent a lot of time out East, during the Interregnum?"

"Yeah. That's right."

I flexed my fingers. "In any case," I said, "I do want Narvane to do the
teleport. I'll want him here tomorrow an hour ahead of time."

Kragar nodded and looked bored, which meant he was unhappy. Loiosh
was going to be unhappy, too, pretty soon.

Them's the breaks.

2

I began laying out what I would need for the spell. I concentrated only on my goal and tried not to think about how silly it was to arrange tools, objects, and artifacts before I had any idea how I intended to use any of them. I let my hands pull from the pack various and sundry items and arrange them as they would.

I couldn't know what I'd need, because the spell I was about to attempt had never been performed before; didn't even exist—except that I had to do it now.

I ARRIVED AT THE office too early the next day. I'm good at waiting patiently when I have to, but I don't like it. It would be hours before I was due at Castle Black, and there was nothing at the office that required my attention. I puttered around for a while, pretending to be busy, then said, "Screw it," and walked out.

The orange-red sky was low today, mixed with grey, threatening rain, and the wind was in from the sea. I walked, or actually strolled, through my area. These few blocks of Adrilankha were mine, and a certain satisfaction came with that knowledge. I stopped in to see a guy named Nielar, my first boss and then one of my first employees.

I said, "What's new?"

He gave me kind of a warm smile and said, "Business as usual, Vlad."

I never know how to take Nielar. I mean, he could have had the position I hold if he'd been willing to fight a bit, but he decided he'd rather stay small and healthy. I can respect that, I guess, but, well, I'd respect him more if he'd decided to take the chance. What the hell. Who can figure out Dragaerans, anyway?

I said, "What have you heard?"

"About what?"

"Don't give me that."

If he'd played dumb a little longer I'd have bought it, but he said, "Just that you got burned by one of your button-men. Who was it?"

"It doesn't matter, Nielar. And it'll matter even less in a little while."

"Right."

"See you."

I walked out of Nielar's shop and headed toward South Adrilankha, the Easterner's ghetto.

Loiosh, sitting on my left shoulder, said, *"Word is getting around, boss."*

"I know. I'm going to have to do something about it. If everyone thinks I can be taken, I will be."

I kept walking, thinking things over. With any luck at all, Morrolan would be able to steer me toward Quion. Would he be willing to? I didn't know.

"Going to visit your grandfather, boss?"

"No, I don't think so. Not today."

"Then where? No, don't tell me. A brothel or an inn."

"Good guess. An inn."

"Who's going to carry you home?"

"I'm only going to have one or two."

"I'll bet."

"Shut up, Loiosh."

"Boss, you are going to Castle Black, aren't you?"

"If I can work up the nerve. Now let me think."

It started drizzling about then. I drew on my link to the Imperial Orb and created an invisible shield, setting it up over my head. It was an easy spell. Most passersby I saw had done the same. The few exceptions, mostly of the House of the Teckla, headed for doorways to wait it out or else got wet. The streets became very muddy, and I made a mental note to allow time to clean my boots. There must be sorcery that can do that. I'll have to learn it one of these days.

By the time I had crossed Twovine and entered South Adrilankha the rain had stopped, which was just as well. Very few Easterners are sorcerers, and I didn't want to call that kind of attention to myself. Of course, I was wearing the grey and black of House Jhereg, and Loiosh riding on my shoulder was enough to proclaim, "Here is a witch!" but there was no need to make matters worse.

About then, Loiosh caught something of my thoughts and said, *"Wait a minute, boss. Just who do you think you're leaving behind?"*

"You, chum. Sorry."

"Crap. You can't—"

"Yes I can. One does not bring a Jhereg to visit a Dragon lord. At least not on a first visit."

"But—"

"You're not expendable, you're not stupid, and you're not going."

This gave us something to argue about until I reached the place I was looking for, which helped distract me. The thing is, I was really terrified. I very badly wanted not to go, but I couldn't think of any way out of it. I tried to picture myself showing up there and I couldn't. Yet, if I didn't follow up on Quion, my reputation would suffer, and, in the Jhereg, reputation means money and safety.

I found Ferenk's, which was right where I'd been told it would be, and I stepped inside, pausing to let my eyes adjust to the relative darkness. I'd never been there before, but my grandfather had recommended it as *the* place to find good Fenarian brandy.

One thing that shed a great deal of light on how Dragaerans think was when I realized that they had no term for brandy, even though they had the drink. They called it wine, and, I guess, just had to know the bottler to decide how strong it was and what tasted like. To me, brandy and wine aren't even close in taste, and maybe they aren't to Dragaerans, either. The thing is, Dragaerans don't care if they taste different, or that the process of making one has almost nothing to do with the process of making the other; the point is, they are alcoholic drinks made from fruit, so they must be the same thing. Interesting, no?

Easterners don't have that problem. Ferenk's especially didn't have that problem. One entire wall behind the long, dark, hardwood bar was filled with different Fenarian brandies, about half of them peach. I was very impressed. I hadn't known there were that many in existence. I was very glad that the Empire wasn't currently at war with Fenario.

The place was pretty much empty. I licked my lips and sat down at a tall, high-backed chair right at the bar. The host glanced at Loiosh, then wiped the counter in front of me and looked an inquiry.

I glanced at the peach brandies and said, "A glass of Oregigeret."

He nodded. "Dead bodies and seaweed, eh?"

I said, "Is that what you call it?"

He shrugged. "Well, it isn't what I'd call gentle."

I said, "What do you recommend?"

He glanced at the wall and picked out a short, round bottle and showed it to me. The label was faded, but I could see the lettering, which read "Barackaranybol."

I said, "Okay. I'll try a glass of that."

He pulled out a glass, reached under his counter, and put some ice into it. My first reaction was to be impressed that he could afford to buy the ice, not to mention the spells to keep it cold. Such things aren't cheap around here. But then I realized what he was doing and I said, "No, no. I don't want ice in it."

He looked disgusted. He pulled out a pitcher, filled the glass with water, and pushed it in front of me. Then he poured some brandy into another glass and set that next to the water. He said, "I'm just giving you some water to clear your mouth out before you drink the brandy. You know how to drink 'em; I know how to pour 'em, okay?"

I said, "Right," to the host, and started to sip the brandy. I heard Loiosh giggling. *"Shut up,"* I told him. I put the brandy down, took a sip of water, then drank some of the brandy. The brandy was very good.

"I'll have the same," came from right behind me. The voice was low in pitch, velvety, and very familiar. I turned and felt a smile growing on my face.

"Kiera!"

"Hello, Vlad."

Kiera the Thief sat down next to me.

I said, "What are you doing around here?"

"Tasting Fenarian brandies."

The host was staring at her, half hostile and half fearful. I was a Jhereg but at least I was human. Kiera was a Dragaeran. I took a look around and saw that the three other customers in the place were staring at Kiera with expressions that held different mixtures of fear and hatred. I turned back to the host and said, "The lady asked for a drink."

He glanced at the table where the other three humans sat, at Kiera, then back at me. I held his gaze, waiting. He licked his lips, hesitated, then said, "Right," and poured her the same thing he'd given me. Then he wandered over to the other end of the bar. I shrugged, and Kiera and I moved to a table.

"So," I said. "Come here often?"

She smiled. "I've heard that you're having some troubles."

I shook my head. "Someday I'll find out how you learn these things."

"Maybe you will. Do you need help, Vlad?"

"Just courage, I think."

"Oh?"

"You probably know one of my button-men has been stealing the eggs."

"Yeah. And mama hen isn't happy."

"Papa rooster if you don't mind."

"Right. What are you doing about it?"

"Going somewhere I don't want to go, for starters."

"Where?"

"Have you ever heard of Castle Black?"

Her eyes widened appreciatively. "A Dragonlord named Morrolan, I believe," she said.

"Right."

She cocked her head to the side. "I'll tell you what, Vlad. You go ahead and follow him there. If Morrolan kills you, he won't live out the month."

I felt a lump rise in my throat. After a moment I said, "Going into another line of work, Kiera?"

She smiled. "We all have friends."

"Well, thanks," I said. "That's yet another one I owe you."

She nodded, still smiling. Then she got up, said, "Good wine," and walked out of the place.

And it's funny. Revenge is rather silly. I mean, I'd be dead, why should I care? Yet, somehow, her saying that was just what I needed to reassure me. I still can't figure out why.

I had another drink after she left and, just to prove Loiosh wrong, stopped at two. I called on my link to the Orb once more, and found I still had a couple of hours before I had to be back at the office. I paid the host, told him I'd be back sometime, and headed for home.

MY GRANDFATHER HAS A white cat named Ambrus, who is the most intelligent cat I've ever met, as well as the oldest. I never actually played with him, the way people usually play with cats, but sometimes, when a child, I would sit and talk to him while my father and grandfather were in the other room, talking. I used to pretend that he could understand me, and either he really could, or my memory is playing tricks on me, because a normal cat couldn't have responded the way Ambrus did: meowing *exactly* in answer to questions, purring when I told him I liked him, and extending his claws and swiping at the air behind him when I'd point that way and say, "Look out, a dragon."

Knowing what I know now, I don't think my memory is playing tricks on me.

In any case, one day when I was, I don't know, maybe seven, my father saw me talking to him and scowled.

I said, "You don't like cats, papa?"

He said, "It isn't that. Never mind."

I think I remember seeing Noish-pa standing behind him, watching the scene, and maybe smiling just a little.

*   *   *

H UMANS DO WITCHCRAFT, DRAGAERANS do sorcery. I do both, which is unusual, so I'm in a good position to compare them. The one difference that keeps hitting me is that witchcraft is more *fun*. If a witch could teleport (a thing that seems impossible, but I could be wrong), it would involve hours of preparation, rituals, chanting, and filling all the senses with the desired result until the spell would work in a blinding explosion of emotional fulfillment.

Narvane, one of my enforcers and an excellent sorcerer, just said, "Ready?"

I said, "Yeah."

He casually raised his hand, the office vanished around me, and I felt a lurch in my gut.

T HERE WAS A DAY when I did something, I don't remember what, and my father slapped me for it. I probably deserved it. It wasn't the first time he'd slapped me, but this occasion I recall specifically. I think I must have been about seven or eight.

What I remember is that I looked up at him curiously and shook my head. His eyes grew wide, and maybe a little fearful, and he stood there staring at me for a moment before turning and walking into the other room. I guess he wanted to ask about the look on my face, but he didn't, and I didn't say anything. You must understand, I was very young, so I'm reconstructing a lot of this from memory, but I retain the impression that my reaction frightened or puzzled him a little. But what was going through my mind was something like, "You call that hitting someone? That hardly hurt. I get beat worse than that every time you send me to the market for bay leaves."

I DIDN'T NOTICE WHERE I was at first, because I was too busy feeling sick to my stomach. Dragaerans don't have this reaction to teleports but I do, and every other human I know does, too.

I kept my eyes closed and resolved not to throw up. Maybe the brandy had been a mistake. I risked a quick look and saw that I was in an open courtyard; then I realized that I was standing on air and closed my eyes again.

Whatever was holding me up felt solid. I took a deep breath and opened my eyes again.

The great double doors of the castle were about fifty yards in front of me. High, high walls were all around. Why did Morrolan have walls around a castle that floated? I risked a look down and saw orange-red clouds. Above me was more of the same. There was a cool breeze on my face bringing a faint smoky smell. I saw no one else in the courtyard.

I glanced around the walls and saw towers placed at the corners. Towers, walls, and the castle itself were of the same black stone—obsidian, I think— much of it carved into figures battling or hunting or just lounging on the walls.

Pretentious bastard.

I saw a pair of guards in one tower. They both wore the black and silver of the House of the Dragon. One carried a spear, the other a staff.

Wizards, employed as guards.

Well, he'd certainly convinced me that he was rich, if nothing else. The guard with the spear saw me looking at him and saluted. I nodded back, wishing Loiosh were with me, and started walking toward the great double doors of Castle Black.

IF I LOOK BACK on my life as if it were that of a stranger, I'd have to say that I grew up around violence. That sounds peculiar to me, because I've never really thought of it that way, but as far back as I can remember I had a fear of Dragaerans. Home was above father's restaurant, which was in an area where Easterners—humans—didn't live. I spent most of my time in the restaurant even before I started helping around the place. And I can still remember the thrill of fear every time I left it, and long chases through alleys, and beatings at the hands of Dragaerans who didn't like humans, or other humans who thought we were getting above ourselves. This latter—being beaten up by other Easterners—didn't happen often. The first time I think I was about eight. My father presented me with an outfit in the colors of House Jhereg. I remember that day because it was one of the few times I can recall seeing my father happy. I picked up his mood and went strutting around in my new clothes and was found by a few human kids about my own age who, well, you can guess. I'll spare you the details.

The funny thing is that I remember feeling sorry for them, because I'd been beaten by Dragaerans, and was thinking that these poor, puny Easterners couldn't even beat me up as well as Dragaerans could.

My BOOTS WENT *CLACK clack* against thin air, which was a bit unnerving. Things became even more unnerving as I got closer to the doors and recognized marks around them as witchcraft symbols. I licked my lips.

I was about ten feet away when both doors swung open with great, silent majesty. They didn't even squeak. This was *very* unnerving. I immediately ran one hand through my hair and adjusted the clasp of my cloak with the other. This allowed my arms to brush over various goodies that I conceal about my person because it's better to give than to receive surprises.

But I didn't spend much time thinking about the doors, as there was someone standing in the doorway, framed like a picture by the tall arch. She had the fine, fair skin of the House of the Issola, and wore the white and green of that House in the form of a half gown, half sari. Her eyes were clear blue, her hair a light brown, and she was beautiful even by human standards.

Her voice was low and sweet. "Greetings, noble Jhereg," she said (apparently deciding the term was less insulting than "Easterner"), "to Castle Black. I am Teldra. We have been awaiting you, and it is our hope that you will allow us to make your stay pleasant. I hope the teleport was not too discomforting?"

As she finished this amazing speech, she bowed in the manner of the Issola. I said, "Ummm, no, it was fine."

She smiled as if that actually mattered to her. In fact, I really think it did. She said, "Please, come in at once, and I'll send for the Lord Morrolan." She extended her hand for my cloak, and I'll be damned if I didn't almost give it to her, just out of reflex.

My reflexes don't generally work that way.

"Ummm, that's all right," I said. "I'll keep it."

"Of course," she said, smiling. "Please follow me."

It crossed my mind then that she hadn't called me by name, which probably meant she didn't know how to pronounce my patronymic, which meant that Morrolan probably didn't know a lot about me. That was most likely good.

I crossed the threshold of Castle Black. I was in a vast hall, with white marble stairways curling up to my right and left, a large arched exit before me, smaller ones to the sides, balconies above me, and a few landscape paintings—no psiprints—on the walls. At least everything wasn't done in black.

Then one of the landscapes caught my attention. It had a huge yellow sun at the upper right and the wisp of white clouds in the sky. I'd seen such sights before, through my grandfather's eyes. It was a scene done in the East.

Teldra escorted me through the tall arched doorway in the center, down about twenty paces of wide, unadorned but well-lit hallway into what was clearly a sitting room. The predominant color here was pale yellow, and the room was filled with overstuffed chairs, buffets, liquor cabinets, and tables. I gave up looking for potential traps in the first ten seconds. I wished Loiosh were with me.

Teldra indicated a chair that looked comfortable and afforded a view of the door. I sat down. She said, "The Lord Morrolan is expected in a moment. Would you allow me to serve you wine?"

"Um, yeah," I said. "Thanks."

She brought a bucket of ice with a bottle in it, which told me something else; it is the Easterners who serve wine chilled. She removed the bottle, took the wine tongs from the coals, expertly circumscribed the neck, dipped the feather in the ice, and lifted off the top of the neck. All of her movements were fluid and graceful, as if she were dancing with her hands. She poured and I drank. It was really very good, which was another surprise. I studied the bottle, but didn't recognize the label.

"Is there anything else I can get for you, my lord?"

"No, no," I said. "I'm fine. Thank you."

"Until later, then, my lord."

I rose as she left, although I wasn't sure if it was proper. Teldra nodded as if it was, but I suspect that if I'd remained seated, that would have been proper, too.

Dragonlords don't use poison; I drank some more wine. Presently, unannounced save by the rap-rap sound of his footfalls, the Lord Morrolan entered the room.

He was tall and dressed in black, with bits of silver lace on his blouse and on the epaulettes that peeked out under the full cloak he wore thrown back.

His hand rested on the hilt of a longsword. His face had the angularity of the House of the Dragon. His forehead was high, and his hair was very dark, straight, and long enough to cover his ears. I gave the sword a second look and realized, even though it was sheathed, that it was a Morganti blade, and powerful. I repressed a shudder as I felt it ringing in my mind.

It was only as an afterthought that it hit me: Why was he wearing a blade—and a Morganti blade at that—to greet a guest inside his home? Could he be afraid of me? Could it be the custom of Dragonlords to go wandering around armed in their own homes, or when greeting guests?

Or was he planning to just haul off and kill me?

You can believe what you like about the existence of the soul, or the Dragaeran's faith in reincarnation. But even if you don't believe any of that, there is no question that if I were killed by a Morganti weapon, that was it for me. I froze for a moment, then realized that I ought to acknowledge his presence, since he, at least, hadn't attacked me yet.

I rose and gave him a half bow. "Lord Morrolan, I am Vladimir Taltos. I am honored that you should consent to see me." I'm a good liar.

He nodded coolly and indicated with his head that I should sit. Teldra returned and poured him a glass of wine as he sat opposite me. As she left, he said, "Thank you, Lady Teldra." Lady? I wondered at their relationship. Meanwhile, Morrolan was appraising me as I'd appraise a jewel. His eyes never left me as he drank. I returned the favor. His complexion was fairly dark, though lighter than a Hawk's or a Vallista's. His hair was black and shoulder-length and curly and just a bit neglected. He sat rather stiffly, as if he were wound too tight. The movements of his head were quick, feral.

Eventually he set his glass down and said, "Well, Jhereg" (apparently deciding the term was more insulting than "Easterner"), "do you know why you are here?"

I licked my lips. "I thought I did. I may have been deceived, of course."

"It is likely," said Morrolan.

"That being the case," I said, falling into his speech patterns, "perhaps you would be so kind as to enlighten me."

"I intend to," he said. He studied me some more, and I began to get the impression that he was doing that just to irritate me, or perhaps to test me— which works out to the same thing.

If you're a Jhereg and an Easterner, you have to expect to be insulted from time to time. If you want to live, you have to learn not to take offense at every slur and sneer. But this was beginning to get annoying. I said, "It seems to me, most noble Dragon, that you were about to tell me something."

A corner of his mouth twitched. "Yes." Then, "A certain employee of yours was traced to Dzur Mountain. You have learned that, some time ago, he paid me a visit as part of negotiating a small land transaction. You are anxious as to his whereabouts. It seems he has run off with the family silver, as the saying goes."

"It turns out," I said, "that I knew that much already."

"Quite. Now, however, you wish to find him to kill him. You can find no one willing to travel to Dzur Mountain, so you thought to visit me, perhaps to learn what I know of the truth behind the legends of Sethra Lavode."

I was beginning to get downright irritated, as well as frightened, by how close his guesses were. I mean, what a pompous, supercilious jongleur. But the thought came to me that he was a pompous, supercilious jongleur with a very powerful Morganti blade, and he was a sorcerer, and I was in his keep. I resolved to stay polite. I said, "It is certainly the case that I am curious about Dzur Mountain, and I would appreciate any information you can give me on it, and its inhabitants."

Morrolan, by this time, was giving me a look that couldn't decide if it was a mild sneer or an attempted scowl. He said, "Very well, Jhereg, a question: Would you like to find this straying employee of yours?"

I spent a moment trying to find verbal traps in the question, then gave up and said, "Yes."

He said, "Very well. Let us go to him."

He stood up. I did the same. He took a step closer to me and seemed to concentrate for just a moment. I realized what he was doing almost at once. I thought about resisting, but made a split-second decision; I might never have another chance. You have to take some risks in any business. I allowed the teleport to take effect. My stomach lurched and the walls vanished around me.

3

The knife went near my right hand, various herbs and things went near my left hand. I didn't yet know precisely which of my supplies I'd pulled out, nor did I want to, but I noted the string with nine knots, the ash twig shaped like a bull's head, the miniature copper kettle, the toe bone of an elk, the piece of braided leather, and a few other things.

I wondered what I'd do with them.

MORROLAN SAID, "WELCOME TO Dzur Mountain."

My stomach said, *Why do you keep doing this to me?*

My knees felt weak and I braced myself against a damp stone wall. We were on a small landing, surrounded by stone, with a single, narrow stairway leading up. High above me, diffuse light trickled in through a tiny window. There was a torch burning on the wall along the stairway, and the soot on the wall above it was old. This place, then, was not used often, but had been prepared.

I hid my discomfort as best I could and said, "Charmed." I did not want to throw up. I repeated this to myself a few times.

Morrolan set his foot on the lowest stair. "This way," he said. To gain
time, I said, "Sethra Lavode?"

"She awaits us."

"Oh," I said. I took a couple of deep breaths and began following Morrolan up the stairs, which were deep as well as narrow, designed for Dragaerans rather than humans. There were many steps. The stairway curved
gently to our left. At one point we passed a window and I took the opportunity to look out. We were, indeed, high up in the mountains. If I'd had
more time, I think I could have enjoyed just looking, as I caught a glimpse
of pine trees and a green valley. There was also snow, however, as well as a
cold, sharp breeze that struck me through the window. The chill from it
continued up the stairs with us. But my stomach was settling down, so I
couldn't complain.

Morrolan continued two steps ahead of me. I decided he must be pretty
trusting to walk with his back to me. On the other hand, my eyes were on
a level with the hilt of his longsword. This kept my tongue in check for some
time. Eventually, however, I risked saying, "With all respect, my Lord Morrolan."

He stopped and turned. "Yes, my good Jhereg?"

"Would you mind giving me some idea as to what, by all the Demons of
Terlocha, is going on?"

He smiled an enigmatic smile and resumed his climb. I followed. Over his
shoulder, he said, "What do you wish to know, my lord?" There was, I think,
a bit of ironic emphasis on the last two words.

I said, "For instance, why did you agree to see me?"

I saw rather than heard a chuckle at that. "It would have been foolish not
to, after going to all that trouble."

I'd be lying if I said this didn't send shivers down my back. A few steps
more and I was able to say, "So you planned to bring me to you."

"Of course, if we couldn't convince you to come directly to Dzur Mountain."

"Oh. Of course. Foolish of me."

"Yes."

I clenched my teeth and said nothing. The hilt of his blade was still before
my eyes, and I could feel its hunger. I shivered.

Then, "All right, Lord Morrolan, you have me here. Why?"

Over his shoulder he said, "Be patient, my lord. You will know soon."

"All right."

I said nothing for another turn of the stairs, thinking about Sethra Lavode. In all probability, I would soon be meeting her. Why? These people had no cause to kill me, and they could have done so already if they'd wanted. What were they after?

I said, "What about Quion, then?"

"Who?"

"The button-man—the employee of mine who vanished in Dzur Mountain."

"Ah. Yes. He was set up, of course. He came across certain information implying that he could expect sanctuary here. The information was incorrect."

"I see."

Another turn of the stairs. "How much farther up are we going, Lord Morrolan?"

"Not far, I think. Are you getting tired?"

"A bit. But never mind." He'd said "I think." I pondered that and said, "So, are you a regular visitor to this place?"

"Oh, yes," he said. "Sethra and I see each other often."

That set me a pretty mystery, with which I was able to occupy myself for another turn or two of that endless stairway. Why was he unsure of the length of the stair if he was often at Dzur Mountain? Obviously because he didn't usually come this way. We passed a heavy wooden door on the left side but didn't stop. Why was he coming this way now? In order to tire me out, or else to size me up, or both.

This realization, which ought to have put me more on guard, actually did nothing except make me more angry. But, with some difficulty, I kept my voice even as I went back to an earlier subject of conversation.

"Lord Morrolan, I think I can understand how it was that you knew Quion would come to Dzur Mountain with the gold."

"I am pleased for you."

"But what I don't understand is how you knew he was going to grab the money in the first place."

"Oh, that part was easy. You see, I am something of a witch. As are you, I believe."

"Yes," I said.

"Well, then, as you know, with witchcraft it is possible to plant an idea in someone's head. We let it occur to him that it would be a good and safe thing to do, and he did it."

"You bastard!" This burst out of me before I could stop it. I regretted it at once, but it was too late.

Morrolan stopped and turned toward me. His hand rested easily on the hilt of that sword. He looked down at me, and the expression on his face was not pleasant. He said, "I beg your pardon?"

I watched his eyes and didn't answer. I allowed my shoulders to relax and mentally fingered my nearest weapon, a stiletto with a four-and-one-eighth-inch blade, located in my left sleeve and set to draw with my right hand. My best chance was to lunge for his throat. I estimated my chance of killing him to be fairly good if I drew first.

On the other hand, looking at the way he stood—the lack of tension in his neck, shoulders, and arms, and the balanced power of his stance—I guessed that he had very good odds of giving me a cut as I nailed him. And, with a Morganti blade, one cut would do the job.

"Let me put it this way," I said. "If you mess with one of my people again, I'm going to cut your heart out." I let my breathing relax and watched him.

"Are you really," he said, making it more a statement than a question. His face took on a sardonic expression, and with no warning he took a step backward, up another step. Damn, he was fast! His blade wasn't yet drawn, but now I'd have to either try to draw my rapier or throw the knife. Killing someone with a thrown knife, even if you're as good as I am, is more a matter of chance than skill.

I said nothing, waiting for him to draw. He also waited. His knees were slightly bent and his balance was perfect, left foot on the higher stair, right hand on the hilt of that weapon. I felt the coolness of the dagger's hilt press against my left wrist and decided it was my only chance. My rapier may as well have been back home; he was faster than me. I continued to wait.

Finally, he smirked and bowed slightly. "All right, my lord Jhereg, we'll settle this later." He presented his back to me and continued up the stairs.

The idea of nailing him came and went. Even if I got away with it, that would leave me in Dzur Mountain, alone except for a very irate Sethra Lavode, who could probably prevent me from teleporting out. Besides, there was still the matter of Quion and two thousand gold imperials.

I took a helping of nonchalant and followed him. My knees were steady, which took all of my concentration for the next few moments. We passed a couple more doors on the left, then emerged into a narrow hallway. We followed the hallway through an arch, after which it widened. The walls were black and unadorned save by torches. I didn't recognize the stone here, but it wasn't obsidian, in any case. It was rough and seemed to absorb light. Where the black at Morrolan's keep seemed to work hard to be ominous, the black at Dzur Mountain was naturally gloomy and hinted, almost as an aside, at insidious power and dark strength.

Yes, I know that to a Dragaeran black means sorcery. But to me black is gloomy. Dragaerans are warped; I've said so before.

I noted in passing that the torches were placed seventeen feet apart.

Morrolan opened a door, behind which was a tight spiral staircase made of iron. I followed him up into a yet wider hall that seemed to slope upward, and that held more lamps and more ornate doorways. The walls were still black.

At one point I said, "There was no better way of getting me here?"

He said, "We could have kidnaped you."

He stopped before a large wooden door, upon which a crouching dzur was pictured. Morrolan pushed the door and it swung open.

The room was thirty feet on a side. Candles and torches provided the light. The chairs looked comfortable. All done in black. I've stated my opinion on that. Shadows flickered back and forth, making it hard to pick out objects . . .

. . . Someone was in one of the chairs. I took a wild guess as to who she might be. I stared at her. No one moved. She was gaunt, with a smooth, ageless aquiline face with hollowed-out cheeks, framed by straight hair that was black black black. Gods, but I was growing tired of black.

Perhaps she would have looked appealing to a Dragaeran, I don't know. She was very pale; in fact, it was startling that I hadn't seen her at once, there was such a contrast between her face and her surroundings. She wore black as well, of course. Her gown had high lace ruffles, coming to her chin. Below it, at her breast, was a large ruby. Her hands were long, and seemed even longer since her nails were done to a point. On the middle finger of her left hand was a ring that held what I think was a very large emerald. She stared at me with eyes that were deep and bright and old.

She stood up, and I saw that there was one splash of blue at her side, which I recognized as a jewel on the hilt of a dagger. Then I felt the dagger and knew it for at least as powerful a weapon as Morrolan's sword. As she stood, it vanished in a swirl of her cloak, which made her disappear entirely except for the dead white of her face, with those eyes gleaming at me like a wolf's.

I guess she'd decided to make me feel at home, because as she stood there the room brightened. That was when I saw, on the floor in front of me, face up, the lifeless body of Quion. His throat had been cut and the red of his blood was almost invisible against the black carpet.

"Welcome," she said in a voice that rolled from her tongue, as smooth as glass and as soft as satin. "I am Sethra."

No shit.

AMONG THE CUSTOMS PECULIAR to Easterners is the one involving the anniversary of one's birth. To the Easterners, this is a day for the person born to celebrate, rather than for him to honor and thank those who brought him into the world.

I spent my tenth birthday with my grandfather, mostly watching him work and enjoying it. I asked him questions whenever there wasn't a customer in the place, and learned about the three types of love potions, which herbs the witch should grow himself instead of buying, which incense should be used for which sorts of spells, why to make certain there are no mirrors or reflective surfaces nearby when doing magic, how to ensure an easy labor, cure cramps and headaches, prevent infection, and where to find spell books along with some idea of how to tell worthwhile spells from nonsense.

When he closed up shop, he said, "Come on back, Vladimir. Sit down." I went into his living area and sat in a big comfortable chair. He pulled up another chair and sat facing me. His cat, Ambrus, jumped onto his shoulder. I could hear it purring.

"Look at me, Vladimir." I did, wondering. He said, "Sink back into the chair now. Pretend you grow heavy, yes? Feel that you are getting heavy, and joining with the chair now. Can you do this? Keep looking at my face now, Vladimir. Think of me. Close your eyes. Try to still see me, even though your eyes are not open. Can you do this? Can you feel warm, now? Don't speak yet. Feel that you float in water, and you are warm. Think of my voice, see how it fills your head? Listen to how my voice rings in your head. Listen to nothing else. My voice is everything, all you know. Now, tell me this: How old are you?"

That puzzled me a little; I mean, did he think I'd fallen asleep, or what? I tried to answer him and was surprised at the effort it took. But I finally said, "Ten," and my eyes snapped open. My grandfather was smiling. He didn't say anything, because he didn't have to. As I'd said it, I had realized that the word "ten" had been the first word actually spoken aloud in the room for some few moments.

I STEPPED OVER THE body as carefully as I could because it would have been embarrassing to slip. The Dark Lady of Dzur Mountain indicated a chair for me. I sat in another one only partly to be contrary—the one I chose wasn't as soft, and thus easier to get out of quickly. In case you haven't figured it out yet, I was, like, scared.

And I'll tell you another thing that surprised me: I felt bad about Quion. Sure, I'd been planning to kill him as soon as I caught up with him, but seeing him lying there dead like that, I don't know . . . I remembered how he'd been when he'd pleaded with me to let him work, and how he'd stopped gambling and all that, and it didn't seem as important that he'd stabbed me in the back by running off with my money. I suppose the fact that Morrolan had set him up for it made some difference.

But yeah, I was scared; I was also mad as a dzur in a chreotha net.

The Lord Morrolan sat facing me, working his chin and jaw. When I do that it means I'm nervous. I was inclined to think it meant something else in Morrolan, but I couldn't say what. A servant came in, dressed in black livery with a dragon's head on the left breast. I wondered what sort of man would be a servant to Sethra Lavode. From the roundness of his eyes and fullness of his face, I would have guessed him to be a Tsalmoth. He walked with his face cast down and his eyes squinting out from beneath tufts of hair sticking out from his brows. He seemed old. His tongue kept flicking out of his mouth, and I wondered if he were of sound mind. There was just the slightest bend to his waist. His walk was mostly a shuffle.

He presented us with aperitif glasses half filled with something the color of maple floors. He somehow managed to step over the body without appearing to notice it. He served me first, then Morrolan, then Sethra. His hands were splotched with white and shook with age. After serving us, still holding the tray, he stood behind Sethra and to her left, his eyes flicking around the room, never resting. His shoulders seemed permanently hunched. I wondered if he coordinated his eye motions with his tongue, but I didn't take the time to check. The drink turned out to be a liqueur that was sweet and tasted just a little like fresh mint.

I didn't want to stare at Sethra or Morrolan, so I found myself staring at Quion's body. I don't know about you, but I'm not used to having a quiet, social drink with a corpse on the floor. I wasn't sure what appropriate behavior was. After a couple of sips, however, I was relieved of the worry by Sethra taking charge. She whispered to the servant and put a purse on his tray. He shuffled over and, making eye contact with everything in the room except my face, delivered the purse to me.

Sethra Lavode said, "We had cause to borrow some of your funds."

How nice.

I chewed on the inside of my lip and tried to think about things that would distract me before I lost my temper completely and got myself killed. I hefted the bag while the servant bowed and returned to his place behind Sethra. On reflection, I decided that the hunching of his shoulders occurred when he stopped; rather like a runner sets himself to spring off the starting line. I signaled to him. He hesitated, glanced at his mistress, blinked about twelve times, and returned to me.

"Hold out the tray," I told him. He did, still not looking at me, and I slowly counted out fifteen hundred gold imperials in fifties and tens. "Give this to the Lady," I said. His mouth worked for just an instant, as if he had to think about it, and I noticed that he was missing some teeth. But then he brought the tray over to her. The entire scenario felt like a poorly blocked play.

Sethra stared at me. I held her gaze. She said, "This is . . . ?"

"Standard rates for the job you did," I explained, glancing at the body. "You do good—"

At which point the tray with the money went flying as Sethra Lavode struck it. She stood and her hand went to the hilt of her weapon. Morrolan also stood, and I swear he *growled*. I widened my eyes and did my innocent inquiring act, though my pulse was racing from that delicious mix of anger and fear that usually means someone is about to become damaged.

But Sethra stopped and raised her hand, which stopped Morrolan. Some portion of a smile came to Sethra's lips and she barely nodded. She sat down and looked a look at Morrolan. He also sat down, giving me a glare that said "That's another one." The servant went about methodically picking up the gold and putting it back on the tray. It took him quite a while. I hoped he'd be able to palm some of it.

Sethra said, "All right, Jhereg. You've made your point. Can we get down to business now?"

Business. Right.

I cleared my throat. I said, "You wanted to talk business. You want to buy a title in the Jhereg? Sure, I can set that up. Or maybe you want to buy into—"

"*Enough,*" said Morrolan.

I'll admit it: Push me far enough and anger overcomes self-preservation. I said, "Shove it, Dragonlord. I don't know what 'business' you think you have with me, but you have interfered with my work, murdered my employee, tricked me, and threatened me. Now you want to talk business? Shit. Talk away." I sat back, crossed my legs, and folded my arms.

They exchanged glances for a moment. Perhaps they were communicating psionically, perhaps only by expression. After a minute or so I sipped some more liqueur. The servant finished gathering the spilled money onto the tray. He started to offer it to Sethra again, but she glared at him. He gave some sort of grimace of resignation and set it down on a nearby table.

Sethra turned to me and said, "I don't know what to say. We thought you'd be pleased that we had killed this man and saved you the trouble—"

"Saved me the trouble? Who says I was going to kill him?" Well, sure, I was, but I wasn't going to admit to these two, was I? "And I wouldn't have needed to find him if you two hadn't—"

"Lord Taltos, please," said Sethra. She seemed genuinely contrite, and I guess the shock of that realization stopped me as much as her words. She said, "I assure you that all we did was help him choose the time for his theft. Morrolan's spell wouldn't have worked if he hadn't been planning to steal from you anyway." She paused, glanced at Morrolan, and shrugged. "We knew you to be a Jhereg as well as an Easterner, and had been expecting you to respond as a Jhereg only. Most of those in your House would have been happy to discuss a business deal no matter how they were brought into it. It seems we don't know Easterners. We have erred. We are sorry."

I bit my lip and thought about it. I would have felt better if Morrolan had expressed an apology, but there's something to be said for extracting one from the Enchantress of Dzur Mountain, isn't there? All right, I'll be honest. I still don't know if she was making all that up as she went along or if she was telling the truth, but believing her salved my pride a little. It allowed me to continue talking to them, at any rate.

I said, "Would you mind explaining to me why you went through all this in the first place?"

Sethra said, "Very well, then. Tell me this: Can you think of any other way we could have gotten you here?"

"Paying me would have worked."

"Would it have?"

I reflected. No, I suppose if they'd offered me enough to convince me to come, it would have just made me suspicious. I said, "If you'd wanted to see me, you could have come to me," I smirked. "The door to my office—"

"It is impossible for me to leave Dzur Mountain at the moment."

I gestured toward Morrolan. "And him?"

"I wanted to see you myself." She smiled a little. "Which is just as well, since I might have had some trouble convincing him to walk into a Jhereg's place of business."

Morrolan snorted. I said, "All right, I'm convinced that you're clever." I felt silent, but they seemed to be waiting for me to continue. What was there to say? I felt my jaw clenching with anger that hadn't yet died down. But, as I said, my best chance of getting out of there alive was cooperation. If they wanted me for something, they at least weren't going to kill me out of hand. I let out my breath and said, "Business, then. You have business in mind. Tell me about it."

"Yes." She sent Morrolan a glance that was impossible to read, then turned back to me. "There is a thing we'd like you to do."

I waited.

She said, "This is going to take some explanation."

D<small>URING MY ENTIRE TENTH</small> year it was almost impossible to keep me away from my grandfather's. I felt my father's growing dislike of this, and ignored it. Noish-pa was delighted at my interest in witchcraft. He taught me to draw things that I only saw in his mind, and gave me tours of his memories of his homeland. I still remember how it felt to see clear blue sky, with white puffy clouds and a sun so bright I couldn't look directly at it, even through the eyes of his memory. And I remember the stars as vividly as if I were there. And the mountains, and the rivers.

Finally my father, in an effort to distract me, hired a sorcerer to teach me. He was a snide young Jhegaala whom I hated and who didn't like me, but he taught me anyway and I learned anyway. I hate to think of what that cost my father. It was interesting, and I did learn something, but I resented it, so I didn't work as hard as I could have. In fact, I think I was working not to like it. But, on the other hand, I enjoyed the closeness with my grandfather much more than I enjoyed making pretty flashing lights in the palm of my hand.

This process continued for quite some time—until my father died, in fact. My grandfather had started teaching me fencing, in the one-handed, side-stance Eastern rapier style. When my father learned of it, he hired a Dragaeran sword teacher to show me the full-forward cut and slash sword and dagger method, which turned out to be a fiasco since I hadn't the strength to use even the practice sword of the Dragaerans.

The funny thing is, I suspect that if my father had ever actually told Noish-pa to stop, he would have. But my father never did; he only glowered and sometimes complained. I think he was so convinced that everything Dragaeran was better than everything Eastern, he expected me to be convinced of it, too.

Poor fool.

SETHRA LAVODE STUDIED THE floor, and the expression on her face was the one I wear when I'm trying to figure out a delicate way to say something. Then she nodded, almost imperceptibly, and looked up. "Do you know the difference between a wizard and a sorcerer?"

I said, "I think so."

"There aren't many who can achieve the skill in sorcery, necromancy, and other disciplines to combine them effectively. Most wizards are of the House of the Athyra or the House of the Dzur. Loraan is an Athyra."

"What was the name?"

"Loraan."

"I've never heard of him."

"No. You wouldn't have. He's never done anything remarkable, really. He is a researcher of magic, as are most Athyra wizards. If it means anything to you, he discovered the means by which the last thoughts of the dying may be preserved temporarily in fluids. He was attempting to find more reliable means of communicating with the dead by introducing a means of . . ."

After a few minutes of getting lost in a description of strange sorcery that I'll never need to know, I interrupted. "Fine," I said. "Let's just say he's good at what he does. What do you want from me?"

She smiled a little. Her lips were very thin and pale. She said, "He has in his possession a certain staff or wand, containing a necromantic oddity—the soul of a being who is neither alive nor dead, unable to reach the Plane of Waiting Souls, unable to reach the Paths of the Dead, unable to—"

"Fine," I said. "A staff with a soul in it. Go on."

Morrolan shifted and I saw his jaw working. He was staring at me hard but I guess exercising restraint. It occurred to me for the first time that they wanted me pretty badly.

Sethra said, "We have spoken to him at great length, but he is determined to keep this soul imprisoned. The soul is a wealth of information for him, and his work is all he cares about. He happened to acquire it shortly after the end of the Interregnum, and has no interest in giving it up. We have been trying to convince him to sell or trade it for several weeks now, ever since we discovered where it was. We have been looking for it for more than two hundred years."

I began to get the picture, and I didn't like it at all. But I said, "Okay, go on. How do I fit in?"

"We want you to break into his keep and steal the staff."

I said, "I'm trying to find a polite way of saying 'drop dead,' and not having much luck."

"Don't bother being polite," said Sethra with a smile that sent chills up and down my spine. "I died before the Interregnum. Will you take the job?"

4

I took hold of the knife I'd carried for so long and used so seldom. The one with the ebony hilt and embedded rubies, and the thin, dull blade of pure silver. It wasn't as expensive as it looked, but then, it looked very expensive. I held it near the point, holding it firmly between my thumb and forefinger, then I knelt down, so slowly I felt tremors in my legs. Just as slowly, I touched the point of the dagger to the ground. I stopped for a moment, studying the dirt. It was black and dry and fine, and I wondered why I hadn't noticed it before. I touched it with my left hand. I rubbed it between my fingers. It was powdered and very cold.

Enough. I concentrated on the knife again, and very slowly drew the rune for the verb "to receive." The rune, of course, was in the language of sorcery, which was meaningless at this time and in this place. But it gave me a spot to concentrate my attention on, and that was what I wanted. I drew a circle around the rune then, and set the knife aside. I knelt and studied the drawing, waiting for the moment to begin again.

I was very much aware of Loiosh, claws hard on my right shoulder, a pressure more than a weight. It was as if none of the events of the last few days had affected him, which I knew wasn't the case; he was the wall of *calm, the pillar of ice, the ground that would hold me steady. If you think that isn't important, you're a bigger fool than I am. Moments went by in contemplation, and I began the next step.*

THERE WERE NO WINDOWS in the room, yet we must have been near the outside, because I could hear distant cries of ravens, and the occasional roar of a hunting dzur. I wondered if there were dragons on the mountain, present company excepted, of course. Why have a room with a wall to the outside and not put a window in it? Who knows? I like windows, but maybe Sethra Lavode doesn't. It is true that windows enable others to see in as well as allow you to see out.

A candle flickered and shadows danced.

"All right," I said. "Let's back up a little. If you want this staff so badly, why don't you and the Lord Morrolan here just blast into his keep and take it?"

"We'd like to," said Morrolan.

Sethra Lavode nodded. "One doesn't just 'blast into' the keep of an Athyra wizard. Perhaps if I were able to leave—but never mind."

I said, "Okay, fine. But look: I don't know what you know about me or what you think you know about me, but I'm not a thief. I don't know anything about breaking into places and stealing things. I don't know what made you think I could do it in the first place—"

"We know a great deal about you," said the Enchantress.

I licked my lips. "All right, then you know I'm not—"

"Close enough," said Morrolan.

"The point is," said Sethra Lavode before I could respond, "the particular nature of Loraan's alarm system."

"Ummmm, all right," I said. "Tell me about it."

"He has spells over the entire keep that keep track of every human being in the place, so any intruder, no matter how good, will be instantly detected. Neither Morrolan nor I have the skill to disable these alarms."

I laughed shortly. "And you think I do?"

"You weren't listening," said Morrolan. "His spells detect human beings—not Easterners."

"Oh," I said. Then, "Are you sure?"

"Yes," said Sethra. "And we also know that he has sufficient confidence in these alarms that he has little else that could detect you."

I said, "Do you know what the place looks like on the inside?"

"No. But I'm sure you have the resources—"

"Yeah, maybe."

Sethra continued. "Morrolan will be ready to aid you once you are inside."

A voice inside my head pointed out that Sethra appeared to be assuming I was going to do this crazy thing, and that she might be irritated when she learned I wanted no part of it. But I was curious; perhaps fascinated would be a better word.

Morrolan said, "Well?"

I said, "Well what?"

"Will you do it?"

I shook my head. "Sorry. I'm not a thief. As I said, I'd just bungle it."

"You could manage," said Morrolan.

"Sure."

"You are an Easterner."

I paused to look over my body, feet, and hands. "No. Really? Gosh."

Sethra Lavode said, "The individual whose soul lives in that staff is a friend of ours."

"That's fine," I said. "But it doesn't—"

"Seven thousand gold imperials," she said.

"Oh," I said after a moment. "A *good* friend of yours, eh?"

Her smile met my own.

"In advance," I said.

MY GRANDFATHER IS RELIGIOUS, though he never pressed the issue. My father rejected the Eastern gods as he rejected everything else Eastern. Naturally, then, I spent a great deal of time asking my grandfather about the Eastern gods.

"But Noish-pa, some Dragaerans also worship Verra."

"Don't call her that, Vladimir. She should be called the Demon Goddess."

"Why?"

"If you speak her name, she may become offended."

"She doesn't get angry at the Dragaerans."

"We aren't elfs. They don't worship as we do. Many of them know of her, but think she is only a person with skills and power. They do not understand the concept of a goddess the way we do."

"What if they're right and we're wrong?"

"Vladimir, it isn't a right and a wrong. It is a difference between those of our blood and those of the blood of Faerie—and those of the blood of gods."

I thought about that, but couldn't make it make sense. I said, "But what is she like?"

"She is changeable in her moods, but responds to loyalty. She may protect you when you are in danger."

"Is she like Barlan?"

"No, Barlan is her opposite in all ways."

"But they are lovers."

"Who told you that?"

"Some Dragaerans."

"Well, perhaps it is true, but it is not my concern or yours."

"Why do you worship Ver—the Demon Goddess and not Barlan?"

"Because she is the patron of our land."

"Is it true that she likes blood sacrifice? The Dragaerans told me that."

He didn't answer for a moment, then he said, "There are other ways to worship her and to attract her attention. In our family, we do not commit blood sacrifice. Do you understand this?"

"Yes, Noish-pa."

"You will never sacrifice a soul to her, or to any other god."

"All right, Noish-pa. I promise."

"You swear on this, on your powers as a witch and on your blood as my grandson?"

"Yes, Noish-pa. I swear."

"Good, Vladimir."

"But why?"

He shook his head. "Someday you will understand."

That was one of the few things about which my grandfather was wrong; I never have understood.

*   *   *

THE TELEPORT BACK TO my office was no more fun than any of the others. It was early evening, and the shereba game in the room between the fake storefront and real office was in full swing. Melestav had left, so I thought the office was empty until I noticed Kragar sitting behind Melestav's desk. Loiosh flew onto my shoulder and rubbed his head against my ear.

"*You okay, boss?*"

"Well . . ."

"*What is it?*"

"*It's hard to explain, Loiosh. Want to become a thief?*"

"How'd it go, Vlad?"

"The good news is that no one hurt me."

"And?"

"And Sethra Lavode is certainly real."

He stared at me but said nothing.

"*Well, what happened, boss?*"

"*I'll get to it, Loiosh.*"

"Kragar," I said, "this is going to get complicated." I paused and considered. "All right, sit back and relax; I'll tell you about it."

IT WOULD BE NICE if I could identify the point when I stopped fearing Dragaerans and started fighting back, but I can't. It certainly was before my father died, and that happened when I was fourteen. He'd been wasting away for quite a while, so it was no surprise, and, in fact, it didn't really bother me. He'd picked up some sort of disease and wouldn't let my grandfather perform the cures, because that was witchcraft and he wanted to be Dragaeran. He'd bought a title in the Jhereg, hadn't he?

Crap.

Anyway, I can't really pinpoint when I started hating Dragaerans more than I feared them, but I do remember one time—I think I was twelve or thirteen—when I was walking around with a lepip concealed in my pants. Lepip? It's a hard stick or piece of metal covered with leather. The leather keeps it from cutting; it's for those occasions when you don't want to leave scars, you just want to hurt someone. I could have used a rapier effectively, but my grandfather insisted that I not carry it. He said it was asking for trouble, and that drawing it would signal a fight to the death when otherwise someone would only be hurt. He seemed to feel that life should never be taken unless necessary, not even that of an animal.

In any case, I remember that on this occasion I deliberately walked through some areas where toughs of the House of Orca liked to hang out, and yeah, they started harassing me, and, yeah, I creamed them. I think they just didn't expect an Easterner to fight back, and a heavy stick can make a big difference in a fight.

But that wasn't the first time, so I don't know. What's the difference, anyway?

I LEANED BACK IN my chair and said, "Kragar, I have another research project for you."

He rolled his eyes skyward. "Great. Now what?"

"There is a wizard named Loraan, of the House of the Athyra."

"Never heard of him."

"Get busy then. I need a complete drawing of his keep, including a floor plan, and a guess as to where he'd do his work."

"Floor plan? Of an Athyra wizard's keep? How am I supposed to get that?"

"You never let me in on your methods, Kragar; how should I know?"

"Vlad, why is it that whenever you get greedy, I have to risk my hide?"

"Because, in this case, you get ten percent."

"Of what?"

"Lots and lots."

"Say, that's even more than 'quite a bit,' isn't it?"

"Don't be flippant."

"Who, me? Okay, when do you want it? And if you say 'yesterday,' I'll—"

"Yesterday."

"—have to hurry. Spending limit?"

"None."

"I thought it might be one of those. I'll get back to you."

* * *

I DON'T REALLY KNOW when I killed a Dragaeran for the first time. When I'd fight them I was pretty casual about where and how hard I'd hit them, and I know that, more than once, there would be one or two of them stretched out on the ground when we were done. Thinking back on times I'd crack them on the top of the head with my lepip, I'd be surprised if none of them died. But I never found out for sure.

Every once in a while that bothers me. I mean, there's something frightening, in retrospect, in not knowing whether you killed someone. I think of some of those fights, and I remember most of them quite clearly, and I wonder where those people are today, if anywhere. I don't spend a lot of time wondering, though. What the hell.

The first time I knew that I had killed someone was when I was thirteen years old.

THERE IS AN INTERESTING story in how Kragar managed to get the information I wanted, but I'll leave it to him to tell. He has peculiar friends. In the two days it took, I finished closing a deal on a gambling operation I'd been hungry for, convinced someone who owed money to a friend of mine that paying it was the gentlemanly thing to do, and turned down a lucrative proposal that would have taken three weeks and a Morganti dagger.

I hate Morganti weapons.

When Kragar returned with the drawings we spent a whole day going over them and coming up with stupid ideas. We were flatly unable to think up an intelligent one. We put the whole thing off for a day and tried again with the same results. Finally Kragar said, "Look, boss, the idea of breaking into an Athyra's keep is stupid. Naturally, any idea for how to do it is also going to be stupid."

I said, "Ummm, yeah."

"So just close your eyes and pick one."

"Right," I said.

And that's pretty much what I did.

We spent a few hours polishing it down to the point of least possible idiocy. When Kragar went off to make some of the arrangements, I closed my eyes and thought about Sethra Lavode. I called up a picture of her face, tried to "hear" her voice, and sent my mind out, questing. *Sethra Lavode? Where are you, Sethra? Hello? Vlad, here . . .*

Contact came remarkably easily.

She said, *"Who is it?"*

"Vlad Taltos."

"Ah. What do you want?"

"I have a plan for getting in. I need to make arrangements with you and Morrolan for timing and backup and stuff like that."

"Very well," she said.

It took about an hour, at the end of which I was no more confident than I'd been before speaking with her. But there you are. Orders went out, arrangements were made, and I reviewed my will. The stuff of life.

5

I felt very close to Loiosh, in tune with him. I discovered I was sitting cross-legged before the sorcery rune I'd drawn. I still had no idea why I'd drawn it in the first place, but it felt right.

It was quiet here. The wind, though almost still, whispered secret thoughts in my ear. I could clearly hear the rustle of fabric as Loiosh shifted slightly on my shoulder.

I began to feel something then—a rhythmic pulsing, disconcerting in that I was feeling it, not hearing it. I tried to identify its source, and could only conclude that it was coming from within me.

Strange.

I could try to ignore it, or I could try to understand it, or I could try to incorporate it. I opted for the latter and began to concentrate on it. A Dragaeran would have been impatient with its simplicity, but to me it was a rather attractive rhythm, soothing. My grandfather had told me that drums were often used in spells, back in his homeland. I could believe that. I allowed myself to fall into it, waiting until my skin seemed to vibrate in sympathy.

Then I reached out my right hand, slowly, gently, toward the herbs and charms I'd laid out on that side. My hand touched something and I picked it up, brought it before my eyes without moving my head. It was a sprig of *parsley. I set that in the center of the rune. I repeated the process with my left hand, and it brought back a clod of dirt from the Eastern home of my ancestors.*

The dirt would reinforce arrival and safety; I had no idea what the parsley could represent in this context. I broke the dirt over the parsley. Behind the rune I placed a single white candle, which I also retrieved without looking. I kindled it, gently, with flint and a scrap of paper. A single candle burns brightly when it is the only source of light save the faint glow from the night sky.

It was then that I noticed the horizon before me, which had begun to flicker and waver, dancing, it seemed, in time to the pulsing of nonexistent drums. I decided not to let this disturb me unduly.

I contemplated my next action, waiting.

THE VERY WEALTHY MAN drove his wagon up the hill toward the keep. This keep was actually a single, reddish stone structure, half of it underground, the other half in the form of a single tower.

It is a common misconception that those in the House of the Athyra have no doors into or out of their homes—the idea being that if one doesn't know how to teleport, one doesn't belong there. This is almost true, except that they don't require their servants to know how to teleport. There is almost always a door or two for deliveries of those goods the wizards and sorcerers of the keep consider too demeaning to fetch for themselves. Trivial things such as food, drink, and assassins. These items are delivered by wagons to a special receiving area in the rear, where they are received, each in its own way.

Of course, the assassins aren't usually expected and, one hopes, not noticed. Theirs is a sad lot, to be sure, with no servant within who knows to announce them. Nor, in fact, are they able to announce themselves, being hidden in a cask marked "Greenhills Wine, '637."

They are most certainly not going to be announced by the very wealthy and equally terrified Teckla who delivers them and who, presumably, wishes to live to enjoy his newly acquired wealth.

No one was around to witness the various indignities I suffered during the unloading and storing process, so I shall refrain from mentioning them. It is sufficient to say that by the time I was able to break out of the stupid cask I was, fortunately, neither drunk nor drunk, if you take my meaning.

So . . . out. Stretch. Check my weapons. Stretch again. Look around. Do not make any rustling noises by getting out the floor plan, because you have it memorized. You *do* have it memorized, don't you? Think now—this is either *that* room or *that* room. Either way, the door lets out into a hall that leads . . . don't tell me now . . . oh, yes. Good. Shit. What, by all the gods of your ancestors, are you doing here, anyway?

Oh, yeah: money. Crap.

"You okay, boss?"

"I'll live, Loiosh. You?"

"I think I'll live."

"Good."

First step is getting the door open. Loraan may not be able to detect it when someone uses witchcraft within his keep, but I'm not going to bet *my* life on it; at least not unless I have to.

So I pulled a vial of oil from within my cloak, opened it, smeared its contents on the hinges, and tested the door. No, it wasn't locked, and yes, it opened silently. I put the oil away, sealing it carefully. Kiera had taught me that. This, you understand, is how assassins are able to sneak around so quietly: we cheat.

There was no light in the hall, and there shouldn't be any random boxes, either, according to Kragar's source. My favorite kind of door (an unlocked one) guarded the room where I chose to spend the remaining hours until the early morning hour I had selected. More oil, and I was inside. There was about a ten-to-one chance against anyone disturbing me in this room. If anyone did, Loiosh would wake me up and I'd kill the intruder. No sweat. Assuming no trouble, Loiosh would keep track of time for me and wake me at the right hour. I spread out my cloak, closed my eyes, and rested. Eventually I slept.

T̲HE CITY OF ADRILANKHA is most of County Whitecrest, which is a thin strip of land along the southern seacoast. The name "Adrilankha" means "bird of prey" in the secret language of the House of the Orca, which no one speaks anymore. The story is that the mariners who first sighted the area along the red cliffs thought it looked like such a bird, with bright red wings held high, head down at the sea level where the Sunset River cut through the land.

The low area around the river is where the docks were built, and the city grew up from it, until now most of the city is high above the docks and a long way inland. The two "wings" of the bird don't look much like wings anymore, since the northern wing, called Kieron's Watch, collapsed into the sea a few hundred years ago.

The southern wing has many good places from which to watch the waves crashing, and ships coming and going, and like that. I remember sitting there doing that sort of watching and not thinking about anything in particular when a Dragaeran—an Orca and probably a seaman—came staggering up next to me.

I turned and looked him over and decided he was drunk. He was pretty old, I think. At least, his face had turned into a prune, which doesn't usually happen to Orcas until they're at least a couple thousand years old.

As he came up, his eyes fell on me and I backed up a couple of steps from the cliff edge out of an instinctive mistrust of Dragaerans. He noticed this and laughed. "So, whiskers, you don't want to go swimming today?"

When I didn't say anything, he said, "Answer me. You want to go swimming or not?" I couldn't think of anything to say so I remained quiet, watching him. He snarled and said, "Maybe you ought to just leave, whiskers, before I send you for a swim whether you want one or not."

I don't know for sure why I didn't leave. Certainly I was frightened—this man was much older than the punks I usually had to deal with, and he looked tougher, too. But I just stood there, watching him. He took a step toward me, perhaps just to frighten me away. I took my lepip from my pants and held it at my side. He stared at it, then laughed.

"You think you're going to hit me with that, is that it? Here, I'll show you how to use one of those things." And he came at me with his hand out, to take it away.

What I remember most vividly is the cold thrill in my stomach as I realized I wasn't going to let him take my weapon. This wasn't a bunch of kids out to have a lark and vent their frustration at whatever it was they were frustrated about—this was a grown man. I knew I was committing myself to something that would have far-reaching effects, though I couldn't have put it that way then.

Anyway, as soon as he was in reach I cracked him one on the side of the head. He stumbled and fell to his knees. He looked up at me, and I saw in his eyes that there wasn't a beating at stake anymore; that he'd kill me if he had the chance. He started to stand up and I went for him with the lepip. I missed, but he fell over backward, rolled, and came to his knees again.

His back was to the cliff, about two steps behind him. The next time he tried to stand up, I stepped up and very deliberately shoved him backward with the lepip.

He screamed all the way down, and I couldn't hear the splash over the sound of the waves crashing against the cliff.

I put my lepip back in my pants and walked straight home, wondering if I should be feeling something.

"... *C'MON, BOSS, TIME TO get up. There are six Dragon warriors here, and they all want to duel with you. Let's go! There's a Dzur hero knocking on the door asking about his daughter, better get up. Okay boss, wake up! The Great Sea of Chaos has just moved into the next bedroom and it insists that you have a better view. Wakey wakey.*"

Waking up in the middle of the night, in a damp storage closet, wedged between dried kethna ribs and a tub of lard, with a wise-ass jhereg thundering smart remarks in your mind, has little to recommend it.

"*All right, stuff it, Loiosh.*"

I got up and stretched, worrying about the sound my joints were making, though that was silly. I buckled on this and checked that. I moved over to the door and spent a few minutes listening to make sure there was no one out there. I opened the door, which was still lubricated. Then left down the hall, eighteen paces, oil the door, open it.

I was in the back of the kitchen. The morning cook wouldn't be started for another couple of hours, and there were no guards here. I moved across the kitchen and found the door I wanted. Oil, open, walk. If the bastard had been a little poorer, he would have had leather hinges on his doors, which are easier to deal with. Or even empty doorways with curtains. Oil, open, walk. First checkpoint.

This door led down into the sublevels, and there were a pair of Dragaeran guards here, in addition to sorcerous alarms. The sorcery was simple and straightforward; mostly token, and I had what the Left Hand of the Jhereg calls a "device" and an Eastern witch would call a "charm" for dealing with it. The guards would be more difficult. They were more or less facing me and, unfortunately, awake.

I kill people for money; I don't like doing it when I don't have to. But sometimes there just isn't any other way. I studied the guards standing there and tried to think of a way to avoid killing them.

I did not succeed.

Some time before this I had assassinated a certain moneylender who, it turned out, had been skimming more than his share out of the profits. His employer had been very upset and wanted me to "make a 'xample outta the sonufabitch." The boss arranged to meet the guy in a big, crowded inn at the busiest time. The boss didn't show; instead, I did. When my target sat down, I walked straight up to him, put a dagger into his left eye, and walked out of the place.

One thing I remember about that is the wave of reaction that followed me out the door, as the patrons of the inn noticed the blood, the body, the event. None of them were able to describe me, though many of them saw me.

What I'm getting at is the advantage of surprise—of the attack that comes with no warning whatsoever. One moment all is peaceful, the next there is an Easterner in your face, knives flashing.

I hauled the bodies of the guards into the kitchen so they wouldn't be quite so obvious, then I picked the lock and headed down into the dungeon.

I GUESS IT WAS my grandfather who really helped keep me going after my father died. It was funny how he did it. I mean, I've always hated being alone, but my grandfather felt that, at fourteen, I had to be independent, so he never responded to my hints that I could move in with him. Instead, he

spent even more hours teaching me witchcraft and fencing, to give me something to do in my spare time.

It worked, too, in that I turned into a quite passable witch, a very good
swordsman in the Eastern style, and that I learned to live alone.

I learned many things during that time, but it's taken the perspective of
years to understand all of them. Like, I learned that to be not alone was
going to take money. I had none, nor any means to acquire any (the restaurant I'd inherited from my father kept me alive and that was about it), but
the lesson stuck with me, for the future.

I think practicing witchcraft was what did the most for me during that
time. I could do things and *see* the results. Sometimes, in the peculiar trance
state that witches fall into when performing, I'd see the entire thing as a
metaphor of my life, and wonder if I'd ever be able to take control of my
world and just *make* it be what I wanted.

Later, when I'd recovered from my attempt to take the salt out of seawater,
or something equally useful, I'd take my lepip and go beat up a few Orca.

The other thing my grandfather did was insist—as did my father—that I
have a good grounding in Dragaeran history. My grandfather found an Eastern tutor for me (he made me pay for it, too) who was quite good at those
things, but who also knew something of the history of Fenario, the Eastern
kingdom of my ancestors. I learned some of the language, too.

I would occasionally wonder what use these things would have for me,
but then I'd start wondering about the rest of my life, and I just didn't want
to think about that.

Oh, well.

So I WENT DOWN. Real quiet, now. My eyes were already adjusted to the
dark and there was a dim light from below; I was able to move quickly. The
steps were narrow and deep, but solid stone. There was no railing. I concentrated on silence.

I reviewed The Plan: get down to the level where Loraan would—I hope—
keep such things as souls contained in staffs, unlock the door (breaking any
spells necessary without alerting Loraan), and have Morrolan launch his sur-

prise (we hoped) attack on the keep's defenses just hard enough and long enough to teleport us both out of there.

It occurred to me again that I'd never before depended on any form of magic to get me out of something. I didn't like it. I reviewed the various ways I could ditch and run at this point, which took no time at all.

Ah! The bottom!

There was one guard here. Unlike the two upstairs, he was dozing, which saved his life. I made sure he wouldn't wake any time soon, and continued. Left for twenty-five paces, and to a door. This one was big and strong, and the lock, I'd been told, was serious. I studied it, and it was. But then I'm pretty good.

My fingers twitched as I studied the dead-bolt and the hinges. Frankly, though, I was more worried about the spells that sealed it, as well as any that might trigger alarms. I estimated the door itself to weigh about forty pounds. It was composed of thick wooden planks with iron bands around them. It wasn't perfectly sealed, though, since light was coming from the other side of it. I didn't know what that meant; this was where my information ended. I licked my lips and started working.

Kiera the Thief had not only found a set of burglar tools for me, but had trained me in their use. I'm not a thief, but I get by. I hoped the "device" was up to overcoming the alarms, because I wasn't; defeating the lock was the most I could hope for.

A good lock combines a fine mechanism with a heavy bolt. This one had, indeed, a very fine mechanism, and three separate dead-bolts. So the pick had to be strong enough to turn the bolts, but light enough to go into the lock. It turned out to be a three-tumbler system, requiring a spring-pick and three rods, all of which had to be pressed against tumblers going in different directions while being turned in yet a fourth direction. If my fingers had been much smaller and I'd had an extra pair of arms, it would have been much easier. As it was, it took me twenty minutes, but I got it, and no alarms went off as far as I could tell.

I would have forgotten to oil the hinges but Loiosh reminded me. On the other side was a landing with several lamps blazing and stairs leading down to a set of three doors, all of which looked—from up here—to be rather flimsy.

I spent about fifteen minutes locking the heavy door again. This may have been a waste of time; I couldn't decide. Then I took a couple of deep, silent breaths, closed my eyes, and—

"What is it, Vlad?" One is always on a first-name basis in psionic communication, because magic transcends courtesy.

"I'm past the big door."

"All right. I'll inform Morrolan. We'll stay in contact. As soon as you have the staff in your hand, we'll break the teleport block. It won't be down for long."

"So you've said."

"And I repeat it. Be careful."

"Yeah."

Once at the bottom, I had to pick a door. None of them were locked or enchanted, so I chose the middle one. I oiled the hinge and slipped it open. Forty-five minutes later I was back in front of the three doors, and I had a much better idea of the sorts of seashells Loraan liked to collect, and a very good idea of his taste in art, but no better idea of where the staff was.

I wondered how long it would be until someone discovered the bodies in the kitchen, or noticed that the guards weren't at their posts.

I really hated this. I tried the left-hand door.

The room was lit, though I couldn't see the light source. It was about forty paces square, with another door opposite me. A large table, say ten feet long, dominated the middle of the room. There were globes suspended from the ceiling, emitting narrow beams of light that were concentrated on a single point at one side, and near this point was a stack of thick, heavy tomes. There was another tome on the table, open, with a quill pen next to it and half a page written in. Small, glittering stones were scattered on the table. Three wands—none of which matched the description of what I was looking for—stood against the wall to my left, and a pedestal at the end of the table held what seemed to be a chain made of gold, suspended in air except for the end that touched the pedestal. A broadsword leaned against the table, and it would have looked incongruous save that from where I stood I could see that it was covered with runes and symbols. Against another wall was a large basin, probably holding something unnatural to which unmentionable things had been done.

In case you haven't figured it out yet, this was Loraan's work area.

I studied the floor in front of me for a long time, checking the path to the door opposite. It seemed to be clear. I let my observations flow back to Sethra. She acknowledged but didn't comment. I crossed very carefully and reached the other door without making a sound.

I studied this door for quite a while. No spells, no bolts, no alarms. I oiled the hinges just to be safe, then opened it. I was in a slightly smaller room, not as cluttered. The only thing of note was what seemed to be a cube made of orange light, about six feet on a side, in the middle of the room. In the center of the glowing cube was a white, five-foot-long staff. At one end I could almost make out the rusty star I'd been told to look for.

That was not, however, the only thing in the room.

Next to the cube of light, facing it, was a Dragaeran. He stared at me and I stared at him. He is frozen that way in my mind—all of seven and a half feet tall, big, thick eyebrows on a florid face, with long, tangled reddish hair that stuck out at improbable angles. He was old, I guess, but he certainly wasn't infirm. He stood straight, and his stance reminded me of Morrolan just before he had almost attacked me. I saw the lines of muscles beneath his tight, white blouse, and the blood-red cloak he wore was drawn back, held by a ruby clasp that reminded me of Sethra's. His brown eyes were clear and unblinking, yet his expression seemed mildly curious, neither frightened nor angry.

Only his hands seemed old—long fingers that were twisted and bent, with what might have been tiny scars all over the backs of his fingers. I have no idea what could have caused that. In his hands was a dark, thin tube, about four feet long, that was pointed at the staff inside the orange cube.

The bastard was working late tonight.

I would almost certainly have beaten him to the draw, as it were, if he hadn't noticed me coming in. He gestured vaguely in my direction and I discovered I couldn't move. A black fog swam before my eyes. I said, *"Sorry, Sethra, not this time."* And nothing held me as I sagged against nothing, fell in, and was buried.

6

I stared at the flickering, weaving dance of the horizon and tried to decide if I liked it, or if it mattered. The thought that I was losing my mind came, and I pushed it aside. It is a not uncommon fear in such circumstances, largely because it sometimes happens. But I just didn't have time to deal with it then.

My eyes were drawn from the wavering landscape to the sorcery rune I had, for whatever reason, drawn on the ground before me. I blinked and it didn't go away. I licked my lips.

The rune was glowing. I hadn't asked it to, but I guess I hadn't asked it not to, either.

I brought my palms together in front of me, fingers pointing out, and in the air I drew another rune, this one the verb "to summon." I considered what nouns I might hang from it, shuddered, and almost lost control of the spell. Loiosh pulled me back and I dropped my hands back to my lap.

The rhythm was still with me and the landscape still wavered and the rune on the ground still glowed.

I think the other sound was my teeth grinding.

I WAS UNCONSCIOUS FOR about twenty seconds, near as I can figure it. The side of my face still stung from slapping the floor, as did my right hand.

I awoke slowly, and swirls of black dissipated before me. I know better than to shake my head under such circumstances; my eyes cleared.

Loraan was leaning up against the far wall, staring past me, both his arms raised. I turned my head and saw Morrolan, who seemed to be fighting something invisible that was trying to entangle him. Sparks flashed in the air between them—that is, directly over my head.

I was being rescued. Oh, rapture.

I was about to try to convince my body to function—at least enough to get out from between the two of them—when Loraan gave a kind of cry, struck the wall behind him, bounced, and came careening at me. I would have put a knife into him then and there but he fell on top of me before I could go into action.

This is called "not being in top form."

Loraan was quite agile, though, especially for a wizard. After landing on me he kept rolling until he ended up in the room with Morrolan, as well as the table, the sword, the staves, and all that stuff. He came smoothly to his feet and faced Morrolan.

There was a bit of confused action lasting maybe ten seconds, including smoke and sparks and fire and loud noises, and when it was over Morrolan had his back to me and Loraan was too far away for any of my goodies to be effective.

Loiosh, who had been so quiet I'd all but forgotten him, said, *"Should we get the staff now?"*

Oh, yeah. Right. The staff. What we came for.

I got to my feet, a little surprised that they worked, and moved toward the cube of orange light. I began studying the enchantment on it and muttering curses to myself. I didn't know what it was or how it had been accomplished, but I could tell it wouldn't be safe to put my hand in there; I could also tell that breaking it would be *way* over my head. I wondered if Morrolan would be open to taking a job. I turned back to the fight to ask him.

*   *   *

I WAS ALMOST SIXTEEN when I decided I was old enough to ignore my grandfather's advice, and started carrying my rapier. It wasn't a very good one, but it had a point, an edge, and a guard.

I'd been carrying it for less than a week before I learned that my grandfather was right. I was heading back to the restaurant from the market at the time. On reflection, an Easterner with a sword at his hip carrying a basket full of fish, meat, and vegetables must have looked a bit absurd, but at the time I didn't think about that.

I heard laughter as I was near the door and saw two kids, roughly my age (taking different growth rates into account), dressed in the livery of the House of the Hawk. They were clearly laughing at me. I scowled at them.

One laughed harder and said, "Think you're pretty dangerous, don't you?" I noticed he was also wearing a blade.

I said, "Could be."

He said, "Want to show me how dangerous?"

I set the basket down and walked into the alley, turned, and drew, my pulse racing. The pair of them walked up to me and the one with the weapon shook his head in mock sadness. He was quite a bit taller than I, and may have had good reason to be confident.

He took his sword in his right hand and a long fighting knife in his left. I noted that he probably wasn't going to use sorcery, or his left-hand weapon would have been different. My grandfather's words came back to me, and I put a little more mental emphasis on the word "probably."

He faced me, full forward, both arms extended, right arm and right leg a bit more. I came into a guard position, presenting only my side, and a look of puzzlement came over his features.

I said, "Get on with it."

He took a step toward me and began an attack. At that time, I had no idea of just how much of an advantage in speed and technique there was to the Eastern style of fencing. I actually wondered why he was taking such big actions, and wondering prevented me from stop-cutting his exposed forearm. However, I still had time to shift backward, which I did, and his cut missed.

He came at me again, in the same slow, stupid way, and this time I did put a cut on his arm before pulling back out of the way. He made a sound of some sort and dropped his knife out of line.

His heart was wide open, with absolutely no protection. How could I resist? I nailed him. He gave out a yell, dropped both of his weapons, fell over backward, and began rolling on the ground. Before he hit the ground I was pointing my weapon at his companion, who was staring at me, wide-eyed.

I approached the uninjured one then and, as he stood there, cleaned my blade on his garments, still staring him in the eye. Then I sheathed my rapier and walked out of the alley, picked up my basket, and continued home.

On the way, I decided that my grandfather had certainly known what he was talking about: Wearing a weapon is asking for trouble.

I continued to wear it.

EVERYONE SHOULD, AT LEAST once, have the chance to witness a fight between two wizards. I'd have preferred to watch this one from more of a distance, though. The air between them seemed to dance, and my eyes had trouble focusing. Loraan held a staff with his right hand, in front of him. The tip of it was glowing with a sort of gold, and images behind the glow were blurred and out of focus. His other hand continually made motions in the air, and sometimes my ears would pop—from what I'm not sure.

I could see that Morrolan was hard-pressed. He had lost whatever advantage he had gained, and was leaning against a wall. There was a black mist in front of him, pushing against something invisible that was trying to get through to him. From thirty feet away I could make out the sweat on his forehead.

Loraan took a step forward. Morrolan raised his hands. The black mist in front of him grew thicker. I recalled an old maxim: Never attack a wizard in his keep. The black mist dissipated completely, and Morrolan seemed to shrink against the wall. Loraan took another step forward and raised his hands. I recalled another old maxim, this one concerning wizards and knives. Loraan's back was to me now, more or less.

My dagger caught him high on his back next to his backbone, though it didn't quite hit his spine. He stumbled. Morrolan straightened and took a step forward. He turned to Loraan. Loraan promptly vanished; one of the fastest teleports I've ever seen. Morrolan gestured at him as he was going, and there was a flash of bright light, but I didn't think it had accomplished anything. I entered the room and approached Morrolan.

He turned to me. "Thank you, Lord Taltos."

I shrugged. "I can't figure out how to get the staff out of whatever it is he's got it in."

"Okay. Let's—"

Clang. The door burst open and Dragaerans started pouring through. About a zillion of them, give or take a few. Most of them had the sharp chins and high foreheads of the House of the Dragon, though I thought I saw a Dzur or two. They all wore the red and white of the Athyra. I looked at their broadswords and longswords as I drew my cute little rapier. I sighed.

"No, Vlad," said Morrolan. "Get the staff. I'll hold them."

"But—"

Morrolan drew his sword, which assaulted my mind by its very presence, and the room seemed to darken. I'd known it was Morganti the first time I'd seen it, but he hadn't actually drawn it in my presence before. Now . . .

Now I suddenly knew it for a Great Weapon, one of the Seventeen. A blade that could break kingdoms. Its metal was as black as its pommel, and its heart was grey. It was small for a longsword, and it seemed to absorb the light from the room. The demons of a thousand years came and sat upon my shoulder, crying, "Run, as you value your soul."

Our eyes locked for a moment. "I'll hold them," he repeated.

I stood there, staring, for perhaps a second, then snapped back. "I can't get it out of—"

"Right," he said and glanced around the room. If you're wondering about the guards during this whole exchange, they were stopped in the doorway, staring at Morrolan's sword and, I suppose, trying to work up courage to attack. Morrolan's eyes came to rest on the pedestal on which one end of the golden chain rested, the other end hanging, coiled, in midair.

"Try that," said Morrolan.

Right. Just the sort of thing I wanted to play with.

I raced over and, trying hard not to think, grabbed the end of the chain near where it touched the pedestal. It wasn't fastened, coming away easily in my hand, still coiling in midair like a snake about to strike. I crossed over to the door beyond which was the cell. I paused long enough to look at the tableau of guards and Morrolan. All of their eyes were riveted on that blade. Perhaps their courage would have failed them and they wouldn't have attacked, I don't know. But while they were considering, Morrolan charged. One sweep of that blade and one fell, his body almost cut in half from right shoulder to left hip. Morrolan lunged and took the next through the heart and he screamed. A stream of what I can only describe as black fire came from Morrolan's left hand and more cries rose.

I turned away, not doubting that he could hold them off—as long as Loraan didn't show up again.

I hurried to the glowing cube.

The chain looked like it was made of gold links, each link about half an inch long, but as I held it, it seemed much harder than gold. I wished I'd had the time to study it, at least a little. I ran my left hand over it, in a kind of petting motion. It wasn't held in the air rigidly, so I pushed it down. There was a bit of resistance, then it hung free, like a chain is supposed to. I felt worlds better. I took a moment to reflect and to allow my life to pass before my eyes if it chose to (it didn't), and then, for lack of any other ideas, struck the chain against the orange glow, bracing myself to take whatever kind of backlash it generated. A light tingling ran up my arm. The glow became a flare and was gone.

A white staff with a rusty star at the end lay on the floor. I swallowed and picked it up. It felt a bit cold, and was perhaps heavier than it ought to have been, but nothing happened to me when I touched it. I turned, holding my trophies, toward the sounds of mayhem.

As I walked back into the room, I was nearly blinded by a flash of light. I managed to blink and duck my head enough to avoid most of it, so I was able to look up and see perhaps two dozen bodies lying on the floor. Morrolan was standing, feet braced, his sword acting as a shield to hold off a barrage of white light coming from—

Loraan!

I cursed softly to myself. He now held both a red staff and a small rod or wand. The light was coming from the staff, and, as I entered, I saw him look at me and look at the staff in my hand; his eyes grew wide. Then he saw the chain and they grew wider, and I even saw him mouthing a curse which I recognized and won't repeat. He turned the rod toward me. I fell over backward as a blue sheet of . . . something came rolling toward me. I might have screamed. I threw my hands up in front of my face.

The golden chain was still in my right hand. As I threw my hands up, it swung out in front of me and struck the sheet of blue, which promptly evaporated. All I felt was a tingling in my arm.

It's all in the wrist, see.

By this time I was flat on my back. I raised my head in time to see Morrolan step toward Loraan, stop, curse loudly, and begin to gesture with his left hand. Loraan was still looking at me, which I didn't like at all. Then he turned the staff so it was pointed at me, which I liked even less.

I felt as if I'd been kicked in the head and stomach at the same time, lying there on my back, waiting for him to do whatever it was he was going to do. Somehow he was holding off Morrolan, who would have killed him then if it were possible, so the wizard must have had some sort of sorcerous defense against physical attacks.

"*Suggestions, Loiosh?*"

"*I'll bet he doesn't have any defense against witchcraft, boss.*"

"*Sure. Now just give me an hour or two to set up a spell, and—*" No, wait. Maybe it wasn't such a bad idea after all. Witchcraft is controlled psychic energy. Maybe I could—

I sat up, setting the chain to spinning in front of me, hoping that would prevent whatever Loraan wanted to do to me. I saw him gnash his teeth and turn back and gesture with the rod at Morrolan, who gave a cry and fell against the far wall.

I allowed my psychic energy to flow into a dagger I pulled, and I think I chanted something, too. Then I let the chain fall and threw the dagger. Loraan waved his arms and something hit me and I fell backward, cracking my head against the floor. I wondered which one of us would get it. Maybe both.

I heard a scream from what seemed to be the right direction, and then Morrolan was hauling me up. I shied away from his sword, but he held me. My left hand still gripped the chain.

"Come on, dammit! Stand up. He summoned help, and I've been holding them off for the last minute. We have to get out of here."

I managed to support myself, and saw Loraan. My knife was in his stomach, and there was a large cut, as from a sword, in his chest, directly over the heart. He seemed to be rather dead. Morrolan was holding the white staff. Just about then figures began to appear all around us. Morrolan gestured with his free hand. The walls vanished.

We were lying on hard stone. I recognized the place where I had first arrived at Dzur Mountain. Morrolan collapsed onto the floor. The staff went rolling off to the side. I threw up.

7

I began to feel a slight giddiness, but that was to be expected, and I could ignore it if it didn't get any worse. I dropped my eyes from the empty spot in front of me and studied the glowing rune. If the rune was here, then the object of my desire was—there.

I touched the spot, making a small impression with my forefinger. I picked up one of the knives I'd laid out—the small, sharp one—and made a cut in the palm of my left hand. It stung. I held it over my right hand until I'd cupped a few drops of blood; then I let the blood dribble into the impression in the dirt. It was soaked up immediately, but that was all right.

I picked up the stiletto with my right hand, then wrapped my left hand around it, too. There would be blood on the handle, but that wouldn't hurt this; might even help. I raised the stiletto high and focused on the target. It was every bit as important to strike dead on as it was when striking at a person. This was easier, though, as I could take my time.

The moment was right; I plunged the weapon into the ground, the depression, the blood.

I saw, for just an instant, a sheet of white before my eyes, and my ears were filled with an incomprehensible roar, and there was the smell of fresh parsley. Then it was all gone, and I was left with the rhythm, the glowing

rune, and the queer landscape. And, in addition, a certain feeling of fulfill-
ment.

The link was forged.

I began composing my mind for the next step.

W E MADE IT BACK up to the library and found seats. I closed my eyes and leaned back. Loiosh spent his time hissing at Morrolan and being generally jumpy. I was feeling a bit weak-kneed, but not too bad, all in all. Morrolan kept glancing at Loiosh, as if he didn't quite know what to make of him. I rather enjoyed that.

Sethra Lavode joined us. She nodded to each of us, glanced at Loiosh without remarking on his presence, and sat down. Her servant, whose name turned out to be Chaz, came in and was sent out again. While he was getting refreshments, Loiosh was staring at the Dark Lady of Dzur mountain.

"That's her, boss? Sethra Lavode?"

"Yeah. What do you think?"

"Boss, she's a vampire."

"I'd wondered about that. But is she a good vampire or a—"

"Have we ever run into her before?"

"Ummm, Loiosh, I think we'd remember if we had."

"Yeah, I guess."

While this was going on, the lady under discussion held out her hand toward Morrolan. He gave her the staff. She studied it for a moment, then said, "Someone is, indeed, inside of it." As she was saying it, Chaz walked back in. He glanced quickly at the staff and went on with serving us. Well, if he can step over bodies, he can ignore people inside wizard staffs, I guess.

Morrolan said, "Is it she?"

"I will tell you anon."

She sat there for a moment longer, her eyes closed. At one point Chaz stepped up behind her with a cloth and wiped her forehead, which I hadn't noticed had become sweaty. He still never looked up. Then Sethra announced, "It passes the tests. It is she."

"Good," said Morrolan.

"I will begin work on it then. Chaz, open up the west tower."

As the servant left, without answering or acknowledging, Morrolan said, "Shall I ask the Necromancer to come by?" I didn't know to whom Morrolan referred here, but I heard the capital letter.

"No," said the Enchantress. "Perhaps later, if there are problems."

Morrolan nodded and said, "How have things been here?"

"Difficult." I noticed then that she seemed a little harried and worn out, as if she'd just been through a rough experience of some kind. None of my business.

Her eyes fell on the chain I was still holding in my left hand. "Is that yours?"

I said, "Yes."

"Where did you find it?"

"An Athyra wizard gave it to me."

She maybe smiled a bit. "How kind of him." She stared at it for a moment longer, then said, "Have you named it?"

"Huh? No. Should I?"

"Probably."

"Care to tell me about it?"

"No."

"All right."

She took the staff and walked out of the room. I wrapped the chain around my left wrist and asked Morrolan if he'd be good enough to teleport me back to my home. He said he'd do this, and he did.

I'D FIRST MET KIERA when I was eleven years old, during an altercation in my father's restaurant, and she'd been inordinately kind to me—the first Dragaeran who ever was. We'd been in touch off and on since then. Once I asked her why she liked me, when every other Dragaeran I'd met hated me. She'd just smiled and tousled my hair. I didn't bother asking a second time, but I wondered quite a bit.

She wore the grey and black of the House into which my father had purchased orders of nobility, but I eventually learned that she actually worked for the organization—that she was a thief. Far from being disturbed by this, I always found it fascinating. Kiera taught me a few things, too, like picking locks, disabling sorcery alarms, and moving through crowds without being noticed. She offered to teach me more, but I was just never able to picture myself as a thief.

I don't want to talk about all the boring business stuff associated with running a restaurant, but there was one time—I think I was fifteen—when it looked like I'd have to sell the place due to some weird tax thing. In the midst of trying to decide how to deal with this, the pressure let up, and the imperial tax man stopped coming around.

I've never been one to let well enough alone, so I started looking for him, to find out what was going on. Eventually I saw the guy harassing another merchant in the area and asked him about it.

"It's been taken care of," he said.

"How?"

"It was paid."

"Who paid it?"

"Didn't you?"

"Maybe."

"What do you mean, maybe?"

I thought fast. "I'm missing some money," I said, "and there was someone who should have taken care of it, and I just want to make sure it was done."

"A Jhereg paid it off. A lady."

"Wearing a grey cloak with a big hood? Long hands, a low voice?"

"Right."

"Okay, thanks."

A week or so later I noticed Kiera in an alley, leaning against a building. I walked up to her and said, "Thanks."

She spoke from out of her hood. "For what?"

"Paying off my taxes."

"Oh, that," she said. "You're welcome. I want you to owe me a favor."

I said, "I already owe you about a hundred. But if there's something I can do for you, I'd be happy to."

She hesitated, then said, "There is."

I got the vague impression that she was making this up as she went along, but I said, "Sure. What is it?"

She pushed the cowl back and stared at me. She chewed her lip, and it suddenly startled me that Dragaerans did that, too.

It always surprises me how young she seems, if you don't look into her eyes. She made a slow careful scan of the alley. When she turned back to me, she was holding something in her hand. I took it. It was a small, clear vial with a dark liquid inside; perhaps an ounce. She said, "Can you hold this for me? I don't think it will be dangerous to you. It *is* dangerous for me to hold it just now."

I studied the vial to see how breakable it was. It wasn't very. I said, "Sure. How long do you think you'll want me to hang on to it?"

"Not long. Twenty, thirty years maybe."

"Huh? Kiera—"

"Oh. Yes. I guess that is a long time to you. Well, perhaps it won't be that long. And, as I say, it shouldn't be dangerous for you."

She handed me a small pouch on a cord. I slipped the vial into it and put it around my neck.

I said, "What's in the vial?"

She paused, appearing to consider, then covered her head again. "The blood of a goddess," she said.

"Oh." And, "I don't think I'll ask."

I WOKE UP THE night after my altercation with Loraan feeling a peculiar half-thought growing in the back of my head and realized that someone was trying to reach me psionically. I woke up more fully, saw that it was almost dawn, and allowed the contact to occur.

"Who is it?"

"Sethra Lavode."

"Oh. Yes?"

"We need your help."

Several remarks came to mind, but I didn't make any of them. *"Go on,"* I said.

"We'd like to bring you here."

"When?"

"Right away."

"*Mind if I break my fast first?*"

"*That will be fine. Would you like us to have a bucket ready for you to throw up in?*"

Bitch. I sighed. "*All right. Give me ten minutes to wake up and become human.*"

"*What?*"

"*Become Eastern, then. Never mind. Just give me ten minutes.*"

"*All right.*"

I rolled over and kissed Szandi's neck. She mumbled something incomprehensible. I said, "I have to run. Help yourself to breakfast and I'll see you later, okay?"

She mumbled again. I got up and took care of necessary things, including wrapping the gold chain around my left wrist and putting various weapons in place. Loiosh landed on my shoulder as I was finishing.

"*What is it, boss?*"

"*Back to Dzur Mountain, chum. I don't know why.*"

I walked down to the street and around a corner and waited. Sethra reached me again right on time, and then I was at Dzur Mountain.

I WONDERED ABOUT THE vial Kiera had given me, holding what she claimed to be the blood of a goddess. When I got back home, I took it out of its pouch and studied it. It was dark and could have been blood as easily as anything else, I suppose. I shook it, which was perhaps foolish but no harm came of it. Yeah, maybe it was blood. Then again, maybe not. I put the vial back in the pouch. I chose not to open it. I wondered if I would ever learn the story behind why Kiera had it but didn't want to hold onto it and couldn't sell it and like that. I realized that it made me feel good to do something for her for a change.

I put it in a chest where I kept my few precious objects and didn't think about it again for some time. I had other things to keep me occupied. My grandfather had decided that, as part of my ongoing training in witchcraft, it was time for me to acquire a familiar.

*   *   *

TEN MINUTES AFTER I got there, I was deciding that I could come to like Sethra, after all. They brought me straight into the library this time, and, after giving me ten minutes to recover from the teleport, Chaz showed up with hot, good klava (klava is a strange Dragaeran brew made from Eastern coffee beans. It tastes like Eastern coffee but without the bitterness). She had thick cream and honey to put into it, and hot biscuits with butter and honey. Morrolan and I sat around eating and sipping for a good, long while. Chaz stood behind Sethra, occasionally eating bits of the crumbs off the tray and flicking his eyes around the room.

I studied Morrolan because he still fascinated me. He seemed to be working to keep any expression off his face, which probably meant that he was pretty concerned about something. I speculated idly but came up with no good guesses, so I concentrated on eating and drinking.

I have to say I was quite surprised by the food and even more surprised, and pleased, when the servant brought Loiosh a fresh dead teckla. He presented it to me and indicated Loiosh with a sort of half-flick of his head, as if he thought I might not know for whom it was intended. He set the tray down, and Loiosh started in on it, displaying his best table manners. Neither Sethra nor Morrolan seemed put off at eating with him.

"These people are okay, boss."

"I was just thinking that."

What shocked me even more, however, was the sight of Lord Morrolan, wizard and witch, duke of the House of the Dragon, licking honey off his fingers. It's a shame Dragaerans don't have facial hair, because Morrolan ought to have had a black goatee to get honey in.

If the whole thing was a scheme to put me in a better mood for helping them, I can only say it worked. I found it, at least, far preferable to the last idea they'd come up with. When the bowls of warm water with the steamed towels came around, I was pretty much willing to listen to any crazy idea they'd come up with.

It was plenty crazy, too.

*   *   *

THE SPELL TO ACQUIRE a familiar is as old as witchcraft, and has as many variations as there are types of familiars and families of witches. It is a simple spell by the standards I'm used to, but has some risks beyond those inherent in performing any ritual to which you are committing your mental energy. For instance, it meant wandering alone through the jungle. I'd asked my grandfather why I couldn't simply find one of the jhereg that fly about the city, and he asked me if I'd ever seen any of them close up.

My grandfather gave me a pack and stern lectures on what to put in it, and only general comments on hazards to avoid. I asked him why he couldn't be more specific, and he said it was because he didn't know. That scared me. I said, "Are you sure this is safe, Noish-pa?"

He said, "Of course not, Vladimir. I will tell you that it has much danger. Do you wish to not do it?"

"Ummm, no. I guess I'll go ahead with it."

Then I spent many hours in study of the wildlife of the jungles west of Adrilankha. I think my grandfather knew I'd do that, and, in fact, that was why he'd phrased things the way he did. I learned a great deal as a result. The most important thing was to study carefully anything that might hurt you.

This lesson has held me in very good stead.

"WAIT A MINUTE," I said. "Start over. Just exactly *why* am I supposed to pack up and trundle off to the Paths of the Dead?"

REMEMBER HOW YOU FELT the first time you buckled on a sword and went stomping around town? Remember the scabbard clanking against your leg? Remember touching the hilt with your off hand every now and then, just to reassure yourself it was there? If you've never done it, try to imagine the feeling. There's nothing quite like it; a little voice in the back of your head goes, "I'm dangerous now. I matter."

If you can remember that, or imagine it, think about how you'd feel the first time you slipped a dagger into your sleeve and another into your boot, and concealed a few shuriken in the folds of your cloak. All of a sudden you feel, I don't know, like a force to be reckoned with. Does that make sense? Now, in point of fact, you don't want to show this at all. I never had to be told this; it's obvious. Even in subtle ways, you don't want to project the feeling of danger; you'd rather disappear. But there it is, anyway. Walking around with lethal surprises about your person changes the way you look at life; especially if you're a sixteen-year-old Easterner in a city of Dragaerans. It feels great.

Why was I walking around carrying concealed weaponry? Because I'd been advised to by someone who ought to know. She'd said, "If you're going to work for the Organization—and don't kid yourself, Vlad, that's what you're doing—it's always best to have a few surprises about you."

That's what I was doing: working for the Organization. I'd been given a job. It wasn't clear exactly what my job was, except that it could involve violence from time to time, starting with today. I was human, hence smaller and weaker than the Dragaerans I lived among. Yet I didn't fear violence from them, because I knew I could hurt them. I'd done so. More than once.

Now, for the first time, I was going to be paid for it, and I sure didn't mind. Whatever becomes of me, I'm going to hold the memory of walking from my tiny little flat to the shoemaker's where I was to meet my partner for the first time. A newly hatched jhereg whom I was going to make my familiar nestled against my chest, reptilian head lying just below my neck, wings tucked in, claws gripping the fabric of my jerkin. Occasionally I would "hear" him in my mind: "*Mama?*" I'd send back comforting thoughts that somehow didn't conflict with the rather violent frame of mind I was in.

It was the sort of day you look back on later and see as a pivotal point in your life. Thing is, I knew it at the time. It was a day when magic things were happening. Every time I swung my left arm, I'd feel the hilt of a dagger press against my wrist. With every step, my rapier would thump against my left leg. The air was cool and smelled of the sea. My boots were new enough to look good, yet old enough to be comfortable. My half-cloak was old and worn, yet it was Jhereg-grey and I could feel it dance behind me. The wind blew my hair back from my eyes. The streets were midafternoon quiet. The buildings were mostly shut, and—

There was a shadow that stood out unnaturally from the tall apartment complex on my left. I paused and saw that the shadown was beckoning me.

I approached it and said, "Hello, Kiera."

MORROLAN LOOKED DISGUSTED; IT was something he was good at. He said, "Sethra, you try."

She nodded; brisk, businesslike. "Morrolan has a cousin; her name is—"

"Aliera. Right; I got that."

"Aliera was caught in the explosion in Dragaera City that brought down the Imperium."

"Okay. I'm with you so far."

"I managed to save her."

"That's where you lose me. Didn't Morrolan say she was dead?"

"Well, yes."

"All right, then."

She drummed her fingers on the arm of her chair.

"You getting any more of this than I am, Loiosh?"

"Yeah, boss. I've already figured out that you're messed up with a couple of nut cases."

"Thanks loads."

At last Sethra said, "Death isn't as simple and straightforward as you may think it is. She is dead, but her soul has been preserved. It's been lost since the Interregnum, but we have located it, with your help, as well as the help of . . . well, some others. Yesterday, it was finally recovered."

"Okay, fine. Then why the trip to Deathgate Falls?" I had to suppress a shudder as I said the words.

"We need to have a living soul to work with, if not a living body. The body would be better, but the Necromancer can supply us with . . . well, never mind." Her voice trailed off, and consternation passed over her face.

"There you go again," I said. "First you say you have her soul, then you say—"

"The soul," said Sethra Lavode, "isn't as simple and straightforward as you may think it is."

"Great," I said. I'm not sure, but I think Chaz might have smiled a bit. "Well, okay, how did it end up in the staff?"

"It's complicated. Loraan put it there, though. He found it right after the Interregnum, in a peasant's field somewhere. Now—"

"How did you know what the staff looks like?"

She gave me a scornful glance. "I can manage elementary divination, thank you."

"Oh. Well, excuse me for living, all right?"

"I might."

"So what is the state of her soul at the moment?"

She was silent for a few moments. Then she said, "Have you ever had cause to use a Morganti weapon?"

I held my face expressionless. "Maybe."

"In any case, you are familiar with them?"

"Yeah."

"Are you aware that Morganti weapons cannot destroy the soul of some-one who is already dead?"

"Hmmm. I guess I've never thought about it. I've never had cause to go sticking Morganti weapons into corpses. It makes sense, though, I suppose."

"It's true. And yet the soul is still there, or else revivification would not be possible."

"Okay. I'll buy that."

"And are you aware that sometimes the bodies of those highly respected by their House are sent over Deathgate Falls, there to walk the Paths of the Dead?"

"I've heard that, too."

"So you can understand—"

"I understand that Easterners aren't allowed to enter the Paths of the Dead, and that, in any case, no one except the Empress Zerika has emerged alive."

"Both true," said Sethra. "But those two facts, taken together, may indi-cate that an *Easterner* would be allowed to—"

"May?"

She hesitated. "I think it likely."

"Great. And, for doing this, I get exactly what?"

"We can pay—"

"I don't want to hear. Certain amounts of money are so high they become meaningless. Any less than that and I won't do it."

The two of them exchanged looks.

Morrolan said, "We'd very much like to convince you. It means a great deal to us, and there is no one else who can do it."

"This conversation sounds really familiar." I said. "You two had this in mind from the beginning, didn't you?"

"We considered it a possibility," said the Dark Lady of Dzur Mountain.

"And now you're saying that you'll kill me if I don't do it."

"No," said Morrolan. "Only that we'll be very grateful if you do."

They were learning how to deal with me. This could be good or bad, I suppose. I said, "Your gratitude would be nice, but if I'm already dead—"

"I think you can survive," said Sethra.

"How?"

"I've been there. I can tell you which paths to take and which to avoid, and warn you of dangers you are likely to encounter and how to protect yourself. That will leave you with only one danger, and I think the fact that you are an Easterner, who doesn't belong there, will be enough to—"

"What danger is that?"

"From those who run the place. The Lords of Judgment."

I didn't like the sound of that. There was a sharp intake of breath from Chaz, who'd been standing in his usual position during the whole interchange. I said, "The Lords of Judgment?"

"You know," said Sethra. "The gods."

8

I noticed that the stiletto I'd stuck in the ground was vibrating, and I wondered what that meant. After a moment, I detected a low-pitched hum. I concentrated on it until I could pick out the beats.

Beats . . .

Now, there was an idea.

I concentrated on the rhythm and held out my left hand, palm up. I concentrated on the humming and held out my right hand, palm up. I brought my hands together, turning them over so the palms met. Behind me, I felt Loiosh spreading his wings and collapsing them. My eyes closed as if of their own accord. I realized I was starting to feel fatigued, which frightened me, and I still had a great deal to do.

I don't know which changed, but now the humming worked with the rhythm I'd established.

I wondered how I'd write this up in a spell book, if I ever chose to do so.

"FINE," I SAID. "NO problem. You mean I have nothing at all to worry about except a few gods? Well, in that case I don't see how it could go wrong. Sure, sign me up."

I was being sarcastic, in case it escaped you. I found myself glancing over at Chaz to see if he appreciated it, but I couldn't tell.

Sethra said, "I don't think it's quite as gruesome as that."

"Oh."

Morrolan said, "Show him the staff."

"I can see it from here," I said, looking at it next to Sethra's hand. Sethra ignored my comment and picked it up, held it out to me.

I said, "This person's soul is in there?"

"Yes," said Sethra. "Take it."

"Why?"

"To see if you feel anything."

"What am I supposed to feel?"

"Perhaps nothing. You won't know unless you hold it."

I sighed and took the thing. Since she'd spoken about feeling something, I was very much aware of the smooth finish, and that the thing was slightly cold. I'd held it before, but I'd been rather busy at the time. It was a light-colored wood, probably diamond willow.

"Feel anything, Loiosh?"

"I'm not sure, boss. Maybe. I think so."

Then I became aware of it, too. Yes, there was some sort of presence, seemingly dwelling at my fingertips. Strange. I was even getting a vague sense of personality; fiery, quick-tempered. A Dragon, certainly.

Also, to my surprise, I felt an instant sympathy; I'm still not sure why. I handed the staff back to Sethra and said, "Yeah, I felt something."

She said, "Well?"

"Well, what?"

"Will you do it?"

"Are you crazy? You've said no one except Zerika has—"

"I've also explained why I think you'll live through it."

I snorted. "Sure. All right, I'll do it—if you'll go along to protect me."

"Don't be absurd," snapped Sethra. "If I could go, there would be no need for you in the first place."

"Fine," I said. "Then I'll take Morrolan." I smirked, which I'm beginning to think is always an error when dealing with Dragonlords. I think I caught Chaz smirking, but I can't be sure.

Sethra and Morrolan exchanged glances. Then, "Very well," said Morrolan. "I agree."

I said, "Wait a minute—"

Sethra said, "Morrolan, the Lords of Judgment won't let you leave."

"Then so be it."

Sethra said, "But—"

I said, "But—"

"We'll leave tomorrow," Morrolan told me. "We'd best get you back at once to prepare for the journey."

KIERA THE THIEF'S LONGISH face was mostly concealed by a cowl as she towered over me, and her voice was low, not quite a whisper. "Hello, Vlad."

"Thank you."

She said, "So you know."

"I know it must have been you who spoke to Nielar about me. Thanks."

"I hope I'm doing you a favor," she said.

"Me, too. Why do you think you might not be?"

"Working for the Jhereg can be dangerous."

"I beat up Dragaerans anyway, every chance I get. Why not get paid for it?"

She studied my face. "Do you hate us so much?"

"Them, not you."

"I am Dragaeran."

"You still aren't one of them."

"Perhaps not."

"In any case, I need to make money if I'm going to stay out of the Easterners' ghetto."

"I know." I saw the flash of her teeth. "It wouldn't be proper for you to live there. You are a nobleman, after all."

I smiled back.

She said, "There are things I can teach you that will help."

"I'd like that," I said. "You're very kind."

"I like you."

She'd said that before. I often wondered why. I wondered how old she was, too. But these were questions I didn't ask.

I said, "Well, wish me luck."

"Yes. There are a few things I should tell you now, though."

I was anxious to get going, but I'm not stupid. Kiera the Thief doesn't waste words. I said, "All right."

"The important thing is this, Vlad: Don't let your anger get the best of you. Dead men can't pay, and you won't earn if you don't deliver. And if you can get what you want without hurting someone, your employer will appreciate it. You may not realize it, but every time a Jhereg has to use violence, he's taking chances. They don't like that. Okay?"

"Okay." As she spoke, it struck me that in less than an hour, probably, I was going to be facing down and perhaps attacking someone I'd never met before. It seemed awfully cold-blooded. But, well, tough. I said, "What else?"

"Do you know anything about the Left Hand of the Jhereg?"

"Ummm . . . the what?"

"You don't, then. Okay. The Organization as you know it makes its money by providing goods and services that are either illegal or highly taxed, right?"

"I guess so. I'd never thought of it that way, but sure."

"Think of it that way. Now, the one exception is sorcery. There are sorcerous activities that are, as you know, illegal. Sorcerously aiding another illegal act, bending someone's will, and so forth." She spread her palms. "As the Demon says, 'Whenever they make a new law, they create a new business.' "

"Who said that?"

"The Demon."

"Who's he?"

"Never mind. In any case, the Left Hand of the Jhereg is mostly made up of women—I'm not sure why. They deal in illegal magic."

"I see."

"Stay away from them. You aren't up to fighting them, and you don't know enough to protect yourself from their machinations."

I said, "Yeah. I'll remember. Thanks, Kiera."

Her cowl nodded. She peered at me from within, then said, "Good luck, Vlad." She merged with the shadow of the building and was gone.

Hʟᴏᴡ ᴏᴜɢʜᴛ ᴏɴᴇ ᴛᴏ prepare for a journey to the land of the dead? I mean, I know how to get ready to go out on the town, and I know how to get ready to kill someone, and I even have some idea of how to prepare for a night spent in the jungle. But if you're going to visit the shades of the once living, the servitors of the dead, and the gods, what do you want to bring with you? How ought you to dress?

I wore my Jhereg colors, with a stylized jhereg on the back of the grey cloak I wear when I want to carry concealed this and that with me, and black Eastern riding boots that are comfortable, even if I wasn't going to be doing any riding—which was just as well. I've been on horseback before and if I never am again, that'll be fine. Just don't tell my grandfather I said that. He thinks Fenarians are supposed to be naturally great horsemen.

I wondered at Morrolan's agreement to accompany me. From everything I understood, his chances of emerging alive were worse than mine, and mine didn't seem to be all that good. I mean, Sethra had never actually *said* I'd be safe from the gods.

The gods. This was silly. I had occasionally joined my grandfather in our private family rituals, asking for the protection of Verra, the Demon Goddess, but I'd never been more than half convinced of her existence. Many Easterners I knew believed in one or more of the gods, and even those who didn't dropped their voices when naming them. But *all* Dragaerans seemed to believe in them, and spoke about them in such matter-of-fact tones that I wondered if, to a Dragaeran, the term "god" was all but meaningless. Someday, I decided, I'd have to investigate this.

Or perhaps I was going to find out during this journey. Which thought reminded me that I ought to be preparing. Morrolan had said the journey there should only take a few days, as we would teleport to a point fairly close to Deathgate Falls. Water would be available as we walked, as would food. The weather was unpredictable, but my cloak was fairly warm when pulled around me, fairly cool when thrown back, and waterproof.

"Any thoughts about what I should bring along?"

"*An enchanted dagger, boss. Just in case.*"

"*I always carry one. What else?*"

"*That chain thing.*"

"*Hmmm. Yeah. Good idea.*"

"*Witch supplies?*"

"*I don't know. That's what I'm asking you.*"

"*No, I mean, are you going to bring supplies for spells?*"

"*Oh. I guess so.*"

So I got these things together, threw in some eddiberries in case I needed to sleep, some kelsch leaves in case I needed to stay awake, then reached out for contact with Morrolan. It took quite a while since I didn't know him terribly well, but at last we were in touch.

"*I'll be ready in an hour,*" I told him.

"*That will be fine,*" he said. "*Where should we meet?*"

I thought about this, then told him, "*There's this tavern called Ferenk's in South Adrilankha.*"

EVERY TIME I VISIT a shoemaker I'm given to wonder how anyone's shoes can come out well. That is, I've never seen a shoemaker's place that wasn't as dark as Verra's Hell, nor a shoemaker who didn't squint as if he were half blind.

The remains of the clothing on this particular shoemaker claimed him for the House of the Chreotha, as did his longish face and stubby fingers. The amount of grime under his nails would have been sufficient for a garden. The hair on his head was thin and grey; his eyebrows were thick and dark. The room smelled heavily of leather and various oils and I can't say what it looked like save that it was dark and gloomy.

The Chreotha gave me a silent grunt (I can't describe it any better that that) and indicated a spot of gloom that turned out to contain a chair made of pieces of leather stretched across a wooden frame. I sat down in it carefully, but it didn't seem about to collapse, so I relaxed. It was a bit small for a Dragaeran, which was pleasant since Dragaerans are taller than humans and it's annoying to sit in a chair designed for someone larger.

The shoemaker shuffled out of the room, presumably to let Nielar know

I was there. Nielar was the guy who had hired me, after an unpleasant introduction involving a game of shereba that ran in the back of his building.
Kiera had, I had gathered, intervened on my behalf, so I was showing up to
work for him. I was also supposed to be meeting a partner.

"You must be Vlad Taltos," he said.

I jumped and almost drew the dagger from my sleeve.

"Mama?"

"It's all right, Loiosh."

He was sitting right across from me, and I'd somehow missed him in the
dim light. He had a bit of a smirk on his face, probably from seeing me jump,
but I resolved not to hate him right away. "Yes," I said. "I believe your name
is Kragar?"

"I believe so, also. Since we both believe it, we might as well assume it's
true."

"Ummm . . . right."

He watched me, still with the same sardonic expression. I wondered if he
was trying to make me mad enough to attack him, to see if I could control
myself. If so, I resented being tested. If not, he was just a jerk.

He said, "There's a guy who owes Nielar some money. Not all that much;
forty imperials. But he's being stubborn. If we can get it, we split four imperials." I kept my face blank, while being amazed that my co-worker didn't
think forty imperials was much money. This, I decided, might bode well for
my future.

He continued, "Shall we go?" As he said this, he handed me what turned
out to be a smooth, round stick, maybe an inch and a half in diameter and
two feet long. I wrapped my hand around it. It was heavy enough to hurt
someone. He continued, "Nielar said you already know how to use this."

"I guess so," I said, hefting the thing. "It is rather like a chair leg."

"What?"

"Never mind." I smirked back at him, feeling a bit cocky all of a sudden.
"Let's go."

"Right."

As we headed out the door I said, "You'll do the talking, right?"

"No," he said. "You will."

* * *

"How long will you be gone, Vlad?"

"I don't know, Kragar. You're just going to have to take care of things as best you can. If I'm lucky, I'll be back in three or four days. If I'm not, I won't be back at all."

He chewed on his lip, a gesture I think he picked up from me. "I hope you're getting something for this."

"Yeah," I said. "Me, too."

"Well, good luck."

"Thanks."

Loiosh and I made our way to Ferenk's. The host recognized me at once and managed to keep a scowl off his face. When Morrolan came in, however, I could see that he drew his lips back and almost hissed. I smiled and said, "Two, please. We want dead bodies and seaweed. I'm sure you still know how to pour them."

He did, and I was pleased that Morrolan liked Fenarian peach brandy, but a little disappointed that he already knew about it, and even called it by its Fenarian name. However, he hadn't known that Ferenk's existed. I think he enjoyed being the only Dragaeran in the place, too. I remembered meeting Kiera there (by chance? Ha!) and wondered how the regulars would take to having Dragaerans drop by, and what sort of reputation I'd acquire at the place. At any rate, Morrolan enjoyed the experience more than Ferenk did.

Tough.

We walked out the door after a couple of glasses each. Then Morrolan stopped. I stood next to him. He closed his eyes and held himself still, then nodded to me. I braced myself, and South Adrilankha vanished. I expected to feel nauseous, and I was.

I hate that.

The target lived about half a mile away. To kill time as we walked, I asked Kragar to tell me about him.

"I don't know much, Vlad. He's an Orca, and he's owed Nielar the money for quite a while."

"An Orca? That's nice to hear."

"Why?"

"Nothing," I said. He glanced at me quickly but didn't comment. "Is he big?"

Kragar shrugged. "What's the difference? Hit him hard enough and he'll go down."

"Is that what we want to do?" I asked, remembering Kiera's advice. "Start swinging?" I discovered I was feeling nervous. When I'd taken to beating up the Dragaerans who'd been beating me up, it always happened suddenly. I'd never actually set out to get one. It makes a difference.

Kragar said, "Up to you."

I stopped. "What is this? You've done this before; I haven't. Why am I making all the decisions?"

"That was my deal when I agreed to work for Nielar—that I never have to give an order."

"Huh? Why?"

"None of your business."

I stared at him. Then I noticed that the House of the Dragon was so clearly marked on his face I couldn't understand how I'd missed it before. There was almost certainly a story there.

As we resumed our walk, I pondered Kragar. He was almost exactly seven feet tall, had medium straight brown hair, brown eyes, and, well, really nothing else to distinguish him. Questions buzzed around my head, without attending answers. Where had he come from? How had he found himself in the Jhereg?

He touched my shoulder and pointed to a building. It bore the insignia of a wolf howling and seemed to be a pretty nice place from the outside. The inside was also in good repair. We walked through the main room, earning some scowls from patrons who didn't like Easterners, Jhereg, or both. We went up the stairs. As we climbed the three flights and turned to the left, I was still wondering about Kragar, and I continued to wonder until we had clapped outside the door and it had opened.

The Orca looked at me and blinked. He said, "Yeah, whiskers?"

Oh. Here I was. I'd been so distracted thinking about Kragar that I hadn't considered how to approach the Orca. Well, since I didn't know what to say, I hit him in the stomach with the stick. He said something like "Oooph" and buckled over. I think I might have cracked a couple of ribs; my aim wasn't all that good. I wondered if he was the right guy.

In any case, the top of his head was right below me. I almost brought the club down, but I remembered Kiera's words and didn't. Instead I put my foot against him and pushed. He fell over backward and it occurred to me how easy it had been to take the guy when he wasn't expecting an attack.

He rolled over onto his stomach, coughing. I'd gotten him pretty good, but Orca are tough. I put my foot on his back. Kragar came up next to me and put a foot on the guy's neck. I removed my foot and walked around, then knelt down in front of him. He seemed startled and craned his neck, looking around. I guess he hadn't realized there were two of us. Then he glared at me.

On impulse I reached into my cloak, pulled out my jhereg, and held him in front of the guy. I said, "Hungry, Loiosh?"

"Mama?"

"It's okay."

Loiosh flicked a tongue out toward the Orca, whose eyes were now wide with fear. I said to him, "You owe people money."

"Let me up," he croaked. "I'll give it to you."

"No. I don't want it. I want you to pay it. If you don't, we'll come back. You have twenty-four hours. Do you understand?"

He managed to nod.

"Good." I stood up and put Loiosh away. I headed out to the stairs, Kragar behind me.

Once we'd left, Kragar said, "Why didn't you take the money?"

I said, "Huh? I don't know. I guess it would have felt like robbing him."

Kragar laughed. Well, I suppose on reflection it was funny. I was trembling a bit. If Kragar had commented on it I would have smashed his face in, but he didn't.

I had settled down by the time we were back where we'd started. The shoemaker wasn't around when we returned, but Nielar was. He studied me, ignoring Kragar, and said, "Well?"

I said, "I don't know."

"You don't know?"

"Does the guy have dark hair that he wears plastered straight back, kind of a wide face, big shoulders, a short neck, and a little white scar across his nose?"

"I've never noticed the scar, but, yeah, that sounds right."

"Then we talked to the right guy."

"That's good. What did you talk about?"

"We asked him if he wouldn't mind paying what he owes."

"What did he say?"

"He seemed to consider the matter carefully."

Nielar nodded slowly. "Okay. Where's Kragar?"

"Right here," said Kragar, sounding amused.

"Oh. What do you think?"

"He'll pay. We gave him a day." He paused, then, "Vlad does good work."

Nielar studied me for a moment. "Okay," he said. "I'll be in touch with you guys."

I nodded and walked out of the shop. I wanted to thank Kragar, but I couldn't find him. I shrugged and went home to feed Loiosh and wait.

I got home feeling a bit exhausted, but good. I was pretty pleased with life for a change. I fed Loiosh some cow's milk and fell asleep on the couch with him on my stomach. Perhaps I was smiling.

THE FIRST THING I noticed was the sky. It was still the ugly reddish, orangish thing that hangs over the Empire, but it was higher and somehow cleaner. We were surrounded by grasses that reached my waist. There was not a tree or a mountain or a building in sight.

We stood there for a few minutes, Morrolan politely remaining silent while I took several deep breaths, trying to recover from the aftereffects of the teleport. I looked around, and something occurred to me. I tried to figure it out, then said, "All right, I give up. How did you get a teleport fix on a spot with absolutely no distinguishing features?"

He smiled. "I didn't. I just fixed on approximately where I wanted to go, visualized the area, and hoped nothing would be there."

I stared at him. He smiled back at me. "Well," I said after a while. "I guess it worked."

"I guess so. Shall we begin walking?"

"What direction?"

"Oh. Right." He closed his eyes and turned his head slowly from side to side. He finally pointed off in a direction that looked like any other. "That way," he said.

Loiosh flew overhead. The breeze was cool but not chilly. Morrolan cut back on the length of his strides so he wouldn't keep getting ahead of me.

I tried not to think of the whithers or the wherefores of the journey, but the staff in Morrolan's left hand kept reminding me.

9

The object of my desire was there, and I needed it here. I had forged most of those links already: there was represented by a quivering knife, here was the glowing rune. But more, I had to break a spatial barrier and cause a thing to exist that did not, while destroying a thing that did, yet in fact do neither of these, merely cause a spatial readjustment.

If that sounds confusing to listen to, try doing it.

I had become a thing of rhythm and wave, sight and sound, of a wavering landscape and a humming knife and a glowing rune and a pulse.

They were united in my will and in the symbols before me. Think of it as a cosmic juggling act in the mind, and you'll have about the right idea.

I was getting to the hard part.

W E RESTED UNDER THE open sky that night, which sounds romantic but wasn't, and ought to have been chilly but Morrolan fixed that. I don't like the hard ground, but it was better than it could have been. Morrolan doesn't snore, and if I do he never mentioned it.

We didn't have any cooking gear with us, but we didn't need any, what with Morrolan being along. I drank tea from an invisible glass and ate bread that hadn't been with us the night before and berries that were growing all around us, nice and ripe.

I stared at the slowly diminishing cylinder of liquid in my hand and said, "Now, that's the sort of magic I'd like to be able to do."

Morrolan didn't deign to answer. The good stuff is always difficult. We resumed our walk. It was a nice warm day, and I saw the distant peaks of mountains.

I said, "Is that our destination?"

Morrolan nodded.

I said, "How long a walk would you say that is?"

"It doesn't matter. When we get close enough to make out a few details, we'll teleport again."

"Oh."

It was, I have to say, hard to stay hostile to the man next to me, if only because the day was nice and the walk so pleasant. Birds sang, the wind rustled, and all that sort of thing.

Loiosh flew above me and occasionally disappeared for brief intervals when he found something to scavenge. I could feel that he was enjoying himself. From time to time I would catch sight of wild jhereg, flying high above us, but Loiosh and I ignored them.

We stopped around midday, and Morrolan conjured more food for us. I don't know whether he was creating it from thin air or teleporting it from somewhere. I suspect the former because it tasted pretty bland. As we ate, Morrolan studied the mountains that were slowly growing before us as we walked. As we stood up, he announced, "Not yet. We need to be closer."

That was fine by me. We resumed our walk, and all was well with the world.

I wondered if I'd be dead by this time tomorrow.

I GOT A MESSAGE the next day to see Nielar. This time I was to meet him at his office—in back of the shereba game, which was in turn in back of a small sorcery supply shop. I was admitted at once, without having to identify myself ("When the Easterner shows up, let him in"), and Nielar nodded me to a chair.

He said, "Let's wait for Kragar."

Kragar said, "I'm here already."

We both did double takes, then Nielar cleared his throat. "Right," he said. "Well, here's four imperials for you two to split. And, Vlad, here's another four for your first week's pay. You work for me now, all right? I want you here tomorrow evening to keep an eye on the shereba game."

I took the eight coins and gave Kragar two of them. I had just earned, in one day, more than I would have taken in at the restaurant in several weeks. I said, "Right, boss."

MORROLAN STOPPED SUDDENLY, WITH no warning, and he stood still, staring off ahead and a little to his left. I looked in that direction and saw nothing except unbroken plain, with more mountains in the distance.

"*Check it, Loiosh.*"

"*Right, boss.*"

We stood there for most of a minute, Morrolan continuing to stare, Loiosh flying off in the indicated direction. Then Loiosh said, "*Boss, you've got to see this.*"

"*Very well. Show me.*" I closed my eyes and let Loiosh fill my brain.

Yeah, it was quite a sight.

There were these beings, maybe two dozen of them, and I've never seen anyone or anything run so fast. They had four legs and from the waist down appeared to be feline, smaller than the dzur, perhaps the size of the tiassa but without wings. From the waist up they appeared human. They carried spears.

"*Cat-centaurs, Loiosh?*"

"*I guess so, boss. I hadn't known they were real.*"

"*Nor had I. Interesting.*"

"*I think they're heading toward us.*"

"*Yeah.*"

I broke the connection, and by now I could see them with my own eyes, as a gradually resolving blur in the distance. Verra, but they were fast. I noted that Morrolan had not touched his sword, and I took some comfort from that. I began to hear them then; a very low rumble that made me realize

I ought to have heard them some time ago. They were awfully quiet for their size.

They were suddenly stopped before us. The butt ends of their spears rested on the ground as they looked at us through human faces with expressions of mild curiosity. The spears had worked metal heads, which I decided was significant. I had the impression that they ran just because they wanted to. None of them were breathing hard. They stared at us, unblinking, like cats. They wore no clothing, but many of them carried pouches, tied around their backs and hanging down the sides. The muscles around their back legs were impressive as hell.

I said, "So, what else do you do for fun?"

Morrolan turned and glared at me. The cat-centaur who was at their head, and who was emphatically female, looked at me and smiled a little. "Chase things," she said. She spoke Dragaeran without any trace of accent.

Loiosh landed on my shoulder, and the leader's eyes widened. I said, "My name is Vlad Taltos."

Morrolan said, "I am Morrolan."

She said, "I am called Mist."

A cat-centaur with red eyes said, "That's because when she throws her spear—"

"Shut up, Brandy." There was some laughter, which included Loiosh, though only I was aware of that.

Mist said, "The jhereg on your shoulder—he is your friend?"

I said, "Yeah."

"Jhereg feed on dead cat-centaurs."

I said, "Dead men, too," which seemed to satisfy her.

She said, "What brings you to the Forever Plains?"

Morrolan said, "We journey to Deathgate Falls," and the entire collection of cat-centaurs took a step back from us. I stooped down and picked and ate a strawberry, waiting.

After a moment, Mist said, "I assume you have good reason."

Morrolan started to answer, but another cat-centaur said, "No, they're just out on a lark."

Mist said, "Keep still, Birch."

I said, "Say, are those *real* spears?"

Morrolan said, "Shut up, Vlad."

Loiosh seemed about to have hysterics. Some of the cat-centaurs appeared to be in the same situation. Me, too. Morrolan and Mist caught each other's eyes and shook their heads sadly.

Mist said, "If you wait here, we're following a very large wild kethna. When we bring it down, we'll share it with you."

"We shall get a fire going," said Morrolan. Then, "Um, you *do* cook your meat, do you not?"

Brandy said, "No, we prefer to let the raw, fresh blood of our kill drip down our—"

"Shut up, Brandy," said Mist. "Yes, a fire would be nice."

"See you soon, then," said Morrolan.

"Quite soon, I expect," said Mist, and they turned and sped off the way they'd come.

THERE WAS A GOOD tailor who lived near my flat. I went to see him late in the afternoon of the next day and ordered a full, grey cloak. I also ordered a new jerkin, with ribbing parallel to the collarbone. I lusted after a hat with a tall plume, but didn't get it.

The tailor said, "Come into some funds, eh?"

I didn't know what to say so I just gave him a terse nod. I don't know what he read into that, but his eyes widened just a bit, showing what could have been fear. A small thrill passed through me as I turned away and said, "I'll expect them in a week."

He said, "Yes, they'll be done." He sounded just a bit breathless.

I went a bit farther down the street and bought a brace of throwing knives. I resolved to start practicing with them.

Then I reported in to Nielar. He nodded to me and sent me to the room with the shereba game. Two days before, I'd been playing there, and a large Jhereg had thrown me out after I'd gotten into a tussle with another customer. Now I was sitting where the Jhereg had sat. I tried to look as relaxed and unconcerned as he'd been. I guess I was partially successful.

But, hell, I enjoyed it.

* * *

WE LOST MOST OF the day eating and socializing with the cat-centaurs and enjoying it, although it got us no closer to our goal. I don't usually gamble, but these poor, uncivilized creatures didn't even know how to play S'yang Stones, so I had to show them, didn't I? We had a good medium of exchange, too, as there are certain cuts of kethna that are better than others. The cat-centaurs were fairly dexterous, so I quit when they were starting to catch on.

Mist said, "I suspect that I won't be thanking you for teaching us this game, in another few weeks."

"It's just harmless fun," I said between bites of my fresh-roasted winnings. As they say, gambling isn't fun; winning is fun.

It was fun exchanging banter with them, and I learned to know when I was pushing one too far by watching the tail, which would have been very strange if I'd stopped to think about it. Morrolan did some healing spells on three of the cat-centaurs whose left legs had been injured in one way or another. "There's been a rash of that lately," said Mist after thanking him.

"A curse?" said Morrolan.

"Just bad luck, I think."

"There's a lot of that going around," said Morrolan.

"Especially where you're going."

Morrolan shrugged. "I don't imagine you know much more about the place than we do."

"I usually avoid it."

"We would, too, if we could," said Morrolan.

Mist stared at the ground, her tail flicking. "Why are you going there?"

Morrolan said, "It's a long story."

Mist said, "We have time for long tales. Shut up, Brandy."

Morrolan seemed disinclined to talk about it, so a silence fell. Then a male I didn't recognize approached Mist and handed her something. She took and studied it. I hadn't noticed before how long and sleek her hands were, and her fingernails made me wince, recalling a girl I once knew. What Mist held seemed to be a piece of bone. After some study she said, "Yes. This will do." She handed it to Morrolan.

He took it, puzzled, while I went around behind him and stared at it over his shoulder. It probably had been broken from the skull of the kethna. It was very roughly square, about two inches on a side, and I could see some thin tracings on it. I could make nothing whatsoever of the markings.

Morrolan said, "Thank you. What—"

"Should you come across Kelchor in the Paths of the Dead, and show her this token, it may be that she'll protect you." She paused. "On the other hand, she may not."

"Gods are like that," said Morrolan.

"Aren't they, though," said Mist.

I had my doubts about whether either of them actually knew anything.

HERE'S SOMETHING YOU CAN do, if you ever get the mood. Find a Dragaeran who isn't inclined to beat you up, and start talking about magic. Watch the curl of his lip when he hears about witchcraft. Then start discussing numbers associated with the art. Talk about how, with some spells, you want two black candles and one white one, other times you want two white ones and no black. Mention that, for instance, in one of the simpler love spells you must use three pinches of rosemary. The size of a "pinch" doesn't matter, but the number three is vital. In another spell you can tell him, you must speak in lines of nine syllables, although what you say doesn't matter.

Long about this time, he'll be unable to hide his contempt and he'll start going on about how silly it is to attach significance to numbers.

That's when you get to have your fun. Cock your head to the side, stare at him quizzically, and say, "Why is the Dragaeran population broken up into seventeen Great Houses? Why are there seventeen months in the Dragaeran year? Why is seventeen times seventeen years the minimum time for a House to hold the throne and the Orb, while the maximum is three thousand something, or seventeen times seventeen times seventeen? Why are there said to be seventeen Great Weapons?"

He will open his mouth and close it once or twice, shake his head, and say, "But seventeen is the mystical number."

Now you can nod wisely, your eyes twinkling, say, "Oh, I see," and walk away.

I mention this only because I have a little nagging feeling that the Dragaerans may be right. At least, it does seem that the number seventeen keeps popping up when I least expect it.

At any rate, I was seventeen years old the first time I was paid to kill a man.

W E MADE OUR FAREWELLS to the cat-centaurs the next morning. Mist and Morrolan exchanged words that struck me as a bit formal and pompous on both sides. Brandy and I enjoyed making fun of them, though, and Loiosh had a few remarks as well.

Then Mist came up to me, her tail swishing, and she seemed to be smiling. She said, "You are a good companion."

I said, "Thanks."

She paused, and I was afraid she was gathering herself together for some speech that I'd have trouble keeping a straight face for, but then she lowered her spear until its point was a few inches from my breast. Loiosh tensed to spring. Mist said, "You may touch my spear."

Oh. Peachy. I had to restrain myself from glancing over at Brandy to see if he was sniggering. But what the hell. I touched it, then drew my rapier. I said, "You may touch my sword."

She did so, solemnly. And you know, all sarcasm aside, I was moved by the whole thing. Mist gave Morrolan and me a last nod, then she led her friends or tribe or companions, or whatever, back into the plain. Morrolan and I watched them until they were out of sight, then got our things together and set off for the mountains.

After walking a few more hours, Morrolan stopped again and stared straight ahead, toward the base of the mountains. He said, "I think I can make out enough details to teleport us safely."

I said, "Better be sure. Let's walk another few hours."

He glanced at me. "I'm sure."

I kept my moan silent and merely said, "Fine. I'm ready."

He stared hard at the mountains ahead of us as I drew next to him. All was still except for our breathing. He raised his hands very slowly, exhaled loudly, and brought his arms down. There was the sickening lurch in my stomach and I closed my eyes. I felt the ground change beneath my feet, opened my eyes again, looked around, and almost fell.

We were on a steep slope and I was facing down. Loiosh shrieked and dived into my cloak as I fought to recover my balance. After flailing around for a while I did so.

The air was cool here, and very biting. Behind us was an incredible expanse of green. All around us were mountains, hard and rocky. I managed to sit without losing my balance. Then, using my backpack as a pillow, I lay on my back on the slope, waiting for the nausea to pass.

After a few minutes, Morrolan said, "We're about as close as we can get."

I said, "What does that mean?"

"As you approach Greymist Valley, sorcery becomes more difficult. From the time you reach the Deathgate, it is impossible."

I said, "Why is that?"

"I don't know."

"Are you certain it's true, or is it just rumor?"

"I'm certain. I was at the top of the falls with Zerika, holding off some local brigands while she made her descent. If I could have used sorcery, I would have."

I said, "Brigands?"

"Yes."

"Charming."

"I don't see any at the moment."

"Great. Well, if they return, they may recognize you and leave us alone."

"None of those will return."

"I see."

"There are far fewer now than during the Interregnum, Vlad. I wouldn't worry. Those were wilder times."

I said, "Do you miss them?"

He shrugged. "Sometimes."

I continued looking around and noticed a few jhereg circling in the distance. I said, *"Loiosh, did you see the jhereg?"*

He said, *"I saw them."* He was still hiding inside my cloak.

"What's the matter, chum?"

"Boss, did you see them?"

I looked up at them again but couldn't figure out the problem until one of them landed on a cliff far above us. Then, suddenly, the scale made sense.

"By the Phoenix, Loiosh! Those things are bigger than I am."

"I know."

"I don't believe it. Look at them!"

"No."

I stood up slowly, put my pack on, and nodded to Morrolan. We continued up the slope for another couple of hours, then it leveled off. The view was magnificent, but Loiosh couldn't appreciate it. From time to time, the giant jhereg would come close enough to us to give me the creeps, so I couldn't blame him. After another hour or so, we came to a wide, fast stream coming from up a slope we didn't take.

Morrolan turned with the stream, and in a couple more hours it had become a small river. By dark it was a big river, and we found a place to make our last camp.

As we were settling in for the night, I said, "Morrolan, does this river have a name?"

He said, "Blood River."

I said, "Thought so," and drifted off to sleep.

After walking for an hour or so the next morning, we had followed it to Deathgate Falls.

10

I suppose I would have composed a chant if I'd had time, but I'm not very good at that. No chance for it now, though. Loiosh lent me strength, which I poured into the enchantment, creating more tension. The rhythm became stronger, and the candle suddenly flared before me.

Scary.

I concentrated on it, turning the flare into a shower of sparks, which exploded into a globe of flickering nothing. I brought it together again, surrounding the candle flame with a rainbow nimbus. I didn't have to ask Loiosh to pick up and control it; I wanted him to and he did.

My breathing stilled; I felt my eyes narrow. I was relaxed, easy and part of things, no longer on the edge. This was a stage and it would pass, but I could use it while it lasted. Now was the time to forge the connection between source and destination, to establish the path along which reality would bend.

The knife quivered, saying, "Start here." All right, fine. Start there and do what? I looked from knife to rune and back. I reached forward with my right hand, forefinger extended, and traced a line. I repeated the process. And again.

*I kept it up, always going from knife to rune. After a while there was a
line of flame connecting them.*

*It felt right. I raised my eyes. The landscape still wavered, as if I were
surrounded by unreality, ready to close in on me. That could be pretty frightening, if I let it.*

D EATHGATE FALLS HAS AN exact geographical location; therefore, so do the
Paths of the Dead, only they don't. Don't ask me to explain that because I
can't. I know that somewhere in the Ash Mountains is a very high cleft called
Greymist Valley. There is a possibly legendary assassin named Mario Greymist
who was named after the place, for the number of people he sent there.

To this valley are brought the corpses of any Dragaeran deemed important
(and rich) enough for someone to make the arrangements. The Blood River
flows into the valley, and over a waterfall, and that is the end of the matter
as far as the living are concerned.

The height of the waterfall has been reported by those undead who have
returned from the Paths. The reports say it is a mere fifty feet, that it is a
thousand feet, and any number of distances in between. Your guess is as
good as mine, and I mean that.

No one has ever come to the foot of the falls by any route except the cliff,
though many, especially Hawks and Athyra, have tried. For all intents and
purposes, the foot of the falls isn't in the same world as the lip. Volumes
have been written in the debate over whether this was set up by the gods, or
whether it is a naturally occurring phenomenon. To show how futile it is,
several of the gods have participated in the debate on various sides.

Those few who leave the Paths of the Dead (undead such as Sethra, and
the Empress Zerika who got a special dispensation) do not leave by means
of the falls. Instead they report finding themselves walking out through a
long cave they can never find later, or waking up at the foot of the Ash
Mountains, or lost in the Forbidden Forest, or even walking along the seacoast a thousand miles away.

It isn't supposed to make sense, I suppose.

I stood next to the lip of the waterfall and looked out at an orangish horizon interrupted by the occasional jutting of rocky peaks. Below me grey fogs swirled and rose, obscuring the bottom hundreds of feet below. The din of the falls made talking all but impossible. The Blood River somehow turned white on its thundering way down.

I stepped back from the brink. Morrolan, next to me, did the same at almost the same instant. We walked away from it. The sound dropped off rapidly, and, just as quickly, the river widened and slowed, until only fifty feet from the falls it seemed like you could wade in it, and we could hear ourselves breathe.

This did not seem normal, but I saw no reason to ask about it.

Morrolan was glancing around him, an odd look on his face. I would have said wistful if I could have believed it of him. I noticed him staring at a pedestal set back about twenty feet from the water. I came up next to him, expecting, I guess, to see the name of some dead guy, and to ask Morrolan if it was a relative. Instead, I saw a stylized dzur head.

I looked a question at Morrolan: He pointed back toward the river, where I noticed a flat spot. "It is here where the remains of those of the House of the Dzur are sent onto the river to go over the falls."

"Splash," I said. "But at least they're dead already. I doubt it bothers them."

He nodded and continued to stare at the pedestal. I said, trying to sound casual, "Know any Dzurlords who've come this way?"

"Sethra," he said.

I blinked. "I thought she was a Dragon."

Morrolan shrugged and turned away, and we continued walking away from the falls. We came upon another flat spot against the river, which was starting to curve now, and I saw a stylized chreotha, then later a hawk, then a dragon. Morrolan paused there for some moments, and I backed up and gave him room for whatever he was feeling. His hand was white where he gripped the staff that contained some form of the soul of his cousin, in some condition or another.

Loiosh still hid inside my cloak, and I realized that the giant jhereg still circled above us, and we could hear their cries from time to time. Presently, Morrolan joined me in staring at the dark swirling waters. Birds made bird sounds, and the air was clear and very sharp. It was a somber, peaceful place, and it seemed to me that this was a calculated effect, achieved I'm not sure how. Yet, certainly, it worked.

Morrolan said, "Dragons usually use boats."

I nodded and tried to picture a small fishing boat, then a skip like they use along the Sunset River above the docks, and finally a rowboat, which made the most sense. I could see it floating down the stream until it reached the waterfall, and over, lost.

I said, "Then what happens?"

Morrolan said, "Eventually the body comes to rest along the shore, below the falls. After a few days, the soul awakens and takes whatever it finds on the body that it can use, and begins the journey to the Halls of Judgment. The journey can take hours or weeks. Sometimes it lasts forever. It depends on how well the person has memorized the Paths for his House while he is alive, and on what he meets on the way, and how he handles it." He paused. "We may meet some of those who have been wandering the Paths forever. I hope not. I imagine it would be depressing."

I said, "What about us?"

"We will climb down next to the falls."

"Climb?"

"I have rope."

"Oh," I said. "Well, that's all right, then."

I HAD BEEN IN the Organization nearly a year and it was getting to where I was feeling quietly good at what I did. I could threaten people without saying a word, just with a raised eyebrow or a smile, and they'd feel it. Kragar and I functioned well together, too. If the target started getting violent I'd just stand there while Kragar hit him, usually from behind. Then I'd inflict some minor damage on him and give him a lecture on pacifism.

It was working well, and life was going smoothly, until we heard about a guy named Tiev being found in an alley behind a tavern. Now, it is sometimes possible, although expensive, to return a corpse to life. But in this case Tiev had been cut in the back of the neck, severing his spine, which is something sorcerers can't deal with. He was carrying about twenty imperials when he was killed, and the money was still on his body.

Tiev, I heard, was working for a guy named Rolaan, and rumors had it that Tiev had been known to do assassinations. Rolaan was a powerful kind of guy, and Kragar mentioned hearing a rumor that another powerful kind of guy, named Welok the Blade, had ordered Tiev's killing. This was important to me because my boss worked for Welok—or, at least, he supposedly paid Welok a percentage of everything he earned.

A week later a guy named Lefforo was killed in a manner similar to Tiev. Lefforo worked directly for Welok and was, furthermore, someone I'd actually met, so that was hitting pretty close to home. People I'd see at my boss's place started looking nervous, and my boss implied to me that it would be a good idea not to wander around alone. I couldn't imagine what anyone had to gain from killing me, but I started staying home a lot. That was okay. I wasn't making so much money that I was anxious to go and spend it, and Loiosh was by now almost full grown, so it was fun to spend time training him. That is, I'd say, *"Loiosh, find the red ball in the bedroom,"* and he'd go off and come back with it in his claws. He'd stopped calling me *"Mama"* by then, but had picked up the habit of calling me "boss," I guess from the way I addressed my superior.

Anyway, a couple of weeks later, my boss asked to see me. I went over to his office, and he said, "Shut the door." I did. We were alone, and I started getting nervous.

He said, "Sit down, Vlad."

I sat down and said, "Yeah, boss?"

He licked his lips. "Any interest in doing some work for me?" There was just a bit of emphasis on the word "work."

My mouth went dry. After close to a year, I'd picked up enough of the slang to know what he meant. I was surprised, startled, and all that. It had never occurred to me that anyone would ask me to do that. On the other hand, saying no never crossed my mind. I said, "Sure."

He seemed to relax a little. "Okay. Here's the target." He handed me a drawing of a Dragaeran. "Know him?"

I shook my head.

He said, "Okay. His name is Kynn. He's an enforcer for, well, it doesn't matter. He's tough, so don't take any chances. He lives on Potter's Market Street, near Undauntra. He hangs out in a place called Gruff's. Know it?"

"Yeah."

"He bounces for a brothel three doors up from there most Endweeks, and he does collecting and bodyguard work pretty often, but he doesn't keep to a schedule. Is that enough?"

I said, "I guess so."

"He isn't traveling alone much these days, so you may have to wait for a chance. That's okay. Take as much time as you need to get it right, and don't let yourself be seen. Be careful. And I don't want him revivifiable, either. Can you handle that?"

"Yeah."

"Good."

"Is he going to have alarms in his flat?"

"Huh? Oh. Stay away from his flat."

"Why?"

"You don't do that."

"Why not?"

He looked at me for a moment, then said, "Look, he's a Jhereg, right?"

"Right."

"And you're a Jhereg, right?"

"Right."

"You don't do that."

"Okay."

"You also don't go near him while he's in or around a temple, an altar, or anywhere like that."

"All right."

"He's married, too. You don't touch him while his wife's around."

"All right. Do I get to use both hands?"

"Don't be funny."

"I don't get to do that, either, huh?"

Loiosh, who'd taken to wandering around on my shoulder, stared at the drawing and hissed. I guessed he was picking up on more than I thought. My boss started at this, but didn't comment. He handed me a purse. I took it and it seemed very heavy.

I said, "What's this?"

"Your payment. Twenty-five hundred imperials."

When I could speak again, I said, "Oh."

W E BUILT A FIRE considerably back from the river and cooked the last of the meat from the kethna. We ate it slowly, in silence, each busy with his own thoughts. Loiosh sneaked out of my cloak long enough to grab a morsel and dived back in.

We rested and cleaned up after eating, then Morrolan suggested we rest some more.

"Some have said it is bad luck to sleep while in the Paths. Others have said it is impossible. Still others have said nothing on the subject." He shrugged. "I see no reason to take chances; I should like to be as well rested as possible before we begin."

Later I watched Morrolan as he fashioned a harness to hold the staff to his back, so he could have both hands free for climbing. I unwrapped my chain from around my left wrist and looked at it. I swung it around a few times. It was behaving just like any other chain, which was either because of where we were or because it hadn't anything else to do. I put it away again, considered testing what Morrolan had said by attempting sorcery, changed my mind.

I caught Morrolan staring at me. He said, "Have you named it?"

"The chain? No. What's a good name?"

"What does it do?"

"When I used it before, it worked like a shield against whatever that wizard was throwing at me. How about Spellbreaker?"

Morrolan shrugged and didn't answer.

"*I like it, boss.*"

"*Okay. I'll stick with it. I have trouble being all that serious about giving a name to a piece of chain.*"

Morrolan said, "Let's be about it, then."

I nodded, put Spellbreaker back around my wrist, and stood up. We walked back to the falls, our voices once again drowned by proximity to the falls. I noticed there was a pedestal quite close to the edge, and saw an athyra carved on it. Morrolan tied one end of his rope around this pedestal which some might think in poor taste, I don't know.

The rope seemed thin and was very long. He threw the other end down the cliff. My mouth was dry. I said, "Is the rope going to be strong enough?"

"Yes."

"Okay."

"I'll go first," said Morrolan.

"Yeah. You go down and hold 'em off while I set up the ballista."

He turned his back to the falls, wrapped his hands around the rope, and began to lower himself. I had this momentary urge to cut the rope and run, but instead I gripped the rope tightly and got ready to go over. I turned and yelled down over the roar of the falls, "Any last-minute advice on this, Morrolan?"

His voice was barely audible, but I think he said, "Be careful, it's wet here."

I LEFT MY PAYMENT for the work in my flat and wandered toward Gruff's. On the way over, I wondered what I'd do there. My first thought had been to find him there, wait for him to leave, and kill him. In retrospect, this wouldn't have been that bad a plan, as the sight of death tends to make witnesses confused about those who cause it. But I was worried that, as an Easterner, I was likely to stand out in the crowd, which meant he'd notice me, which I knew wasn't good. By the time I got there, I still hadn't figured out what to do, so I stood in the shadow of a building across the street from it, thinking.

I hadn't come up with anything two hours or so later, when I saw him leave in the company of another Dragaeran in Jhereg colors. Just because it seemed like the thing to do, I concentrated on my link to the Imperial Orb and noted the time. I waited for them to get a block ahead of me, then set out after them. I followed them to a building which I assumed was the home of my target's friend.

My target.

The words had peculiar echo in my head.

I shook off the thought and noted that Kynn and his friend seemed to be saying good-bye. Then the friend went upstairs, leaving Kynn alone on the street. This could be good luck for me, because now Kynn had to walk back to his own place alone, which gave me several blocks to come up behind him and kill him.

I fingered the dagger next to my rapier. Kynn seemed to waver for a moment, then he became transparent and vanished.

He teleported, of course. Now that was just plain rude.

Teleports can be traced, but I'm not a good enough sorcerer to do so. Hire someone to do it? Who? The Left Hand of the Jhereg had sorcerers good enough, but they charged high, and Kiera's warning about them still echoed in my ears. And it would involve standing out there waiting for him on another occasion, as no sorcerer can work from a trail that cold.

I settled on cursing as the appropriate action, and did so silently for a moment. I'd wanted to get it done today, which on reflection was stupid, but I had the feeling that the money wasn't really mine until I'd done the work, and I could use that money. I could move to a nicer flat, I could pay for fencing lessons from an Eastern master, and sorcery lessons from a Dragaeran, which never came cheap, and—

No, not now. Now I had to think about how to earn it, not how to spend it. I returned to my flat and considered the matter.

THE NEXT TIME I climb down from somewhere on a rope I think I'm going to try to arrange for it to be somewhere dry. I also want to be able to see the bottom.

Come to think of it, I'd rather not do it at all.

I don't care to guess how long the way down was. I suspect it was different for Morrolan than for me, and I don't want to know that. I'll admit I'm curious about what would have happened if we'd marked the rope, but we didn't.

The climb down was no fun at all. I tended to slip on the wet rope, and I was afraid I'd land on Morrolan, sending us both crashing down. First my hands stung from gripping the thing, then they ached, then I couldn't feel them, which scared me. Then I noticed that my arms were getting sore. We won't even mention the bruises and contusions my legs and body were sustaining from hitting the rocks on the side. I managed not to bang my head too hard or too often, which I think was quite an accomplishment.

Crap. Let's just say I survived.

The thing is, it was impossible to really determine where the bottom was, because not only was the first place my feet landed slippery, it seemed to be the point of a massive slab of rock tilted sideways, so I kept going.

It was a bit easier after that, though, and eventually I found myself in water, and Morrolan was next to me. The water was very cold. My teeth started chattering, and I saw that Morrolan's were, too, but I was too cold to be pleased about it. Loiosh angrily climbed onto my shoulder. The noise was still deafening, every inch of me was soaked, and my hands hurt like blazes from gripping the rope.

I put my mouth next to Morrolan's ear and yelled, "What now?"

He gestured a direction with his head and we struck out for it. After having developed a symbiotic relationship with that rope, it was hard to let go of it, but I did and started splashing after him. Loiosh took wing and flew just over my head. The mist kicked up by the waterfall made it impossible to see more than a couple of feet ahead of me. The current was strong, though, and tended somehow to keep Morrolan and me together, so I never lost sight of him.

I was too busy fighting the current and keeping track of Morrolan to be as scared as I ought to have been, but it wasn't actually all that long before my feet felt the bottom of the river, and then we were crawling up onto the bank, and then we collapsed, side by side.

11

My left hand froze, and some part of me was aware that it hovered over the rune. My right hand continued to drift without direction; then it, too, stopped. It was directly over the vibrating knife.

Time for one deep breath, which I let out slowly.

I DON'T THINK I'LL ever again see so many corpses in one place. I don't especially want to, either. And they were all in different and interesting stages of decomposition. I'll forego the details, if you don't mind. I'd seen bodies before, and sheer number and variety makes them no more pleasant to look at.

I should mention one odd thing, though: there was no odor of decay. In fact, as I thought about it, I realized that the only smell I could detect was faint and sulfurous and seemed to come from the river, which was now fast and white-capped. The river also provided the only sounds I could hear as it sloshed its way over greyish rocks and up onto sandy banks, doing carvings in slate.

I felt Loiosh shivering inside of my cloak.

"You okay?"

"I'll live, boss."

I sat up and looked at Morrolan; he seemed even more exhausted than I. He was also very wet, as I was, and he was shivering as much as I, which I took a perverse pleasure in noting.

Presently he caught me looking at him. I suppose he guessed some of my thoughts, because he scowled at me. He sat up and I noticed his hands twitching as another scowl crossed his features. "Sorcery doesn't work here," he remarked. His voice sounded a bit odd, as if he was speaking through a very thin glass. Not really distant, yet not really close either. He said, "It would be nice to dry off."

"Not much wind, either," I said. "I guess we stay wet for a while." My voice sounded the same way, which I liked even less. I still felt cold, but it was warmer here than in the river.

"Let us proceed," said Morrolan.

"After you," I said.

We worked our way to our respective feet and looked around. The river behind us, corpses to the sides, and mists ahead.

"This place is weird, boss."

"I've noticed."

"Have you noticed that the corpses don't stink?"

"Yeah."

"Maybe it's the soul that gives off the stink, and since these guys don't have any soul, there isn't any smell."

I didn't ask Loiosh if he was serious, because I didn't want to know. Morrolan touched the hilt of his sword and checked to be sure the staff was still with him, reminding me of why we were here. He nodded to a direction off to his right. I girded my loins, so speak, and we set off.

I SAT IN MY favorite slouch-chair at home and considered how I was going to kill Kynn. What I wanted to do was just walk up and nail him, wherever he was; whoever was around. As I've said, this is not, in general, a bad policy. The trouble was that he knew there was a war going on, so he was being careful not to be alone.

I don't know how I got so fixed on Gruff's as the place to nail him, and in thinking about the whole thing later I decided that had been a mistake and made sure to avoid such preconceptions. I knew I could take him in a public setting if I wanted to, because when I was a kid I'd seen someone assassinated in a public place—my father's restaurant. That was how I first met Kiera, too, but never mind that now.

I chewed the whole thing over for a while, until Loiosh said, *"Look, boss, if it's just a distraction you want, I can help."*

I said, *"Like hell you can."*

W E WERE WALKING THROUGH swirling fog, which was merely annoying until I realized that there was no perceptible air movement to cause the fog to swirl. I pointed this out to Morrolan, who said, "Shut up."

I smiled, then smiled a little more as the end of a bare tree branch smacked him in the face. He deepened his scowl and we kept walking, albeit more slowly. Fog was the only thing to look at except the ground, which was soft and sandy and looked as if it couldn't contain growing things. As I'd reached this conclusion, a sudden shadow appeared before us which turned out to be a tree, as bare as the first.

"Boss, why are the trees bare in the summer?"

"You're asking me? Besides, if it were summer, it wouldn't be this chilly."

"Right."

More and more trees appeared as if they were sprouting in front of us, and we moved around them, keeping more or less to a single direction. Morrolan stopped shortly thereafter and studied what seemed to be a path running off diagonally to our left. His jaw worked and he said, "I don't think so. Let's keep going."

We did, and I said, "How can you tell?"

"The book."

"What book?"

"I was given a book to guide me through the Paths. Sethra helped, too."

"Who gave you the book?"

"It's a family inheritance."

"I see. How accurate is it?"

"We will find out, won't we? You may have been better off without me, for then Sethra would have been able to tell you of safer paths."

"Why couldn't she have told you the safer paths?"

"I am Dragaeran. I'm not allowed to know."

"Oh. Who makes up all these rules, anyway?"

He gave me one of his looks of disdain and no other answer. We came to another path leading off at a slightly different angle. Morrolan said, "Let's try this one."

I said, "You've memorized this book?"

He said, "Let us hope so."

The fog was thinner now, and I asked Morrolan if that was a good sign. He shrugged.

A bit later I said, "I take it there's a good reason for not bringing the book along."

He said, "It's not permitted."

"This whole trip isn't permitted, as I understand it."

"So why make things worse?"

I chewed that over and said, "Do you have any idea what's going to happen?"

"We will appear before the Lords of Judgment and ask them to restore my cousin."

"Do we have any good reasons why they should?"

"Our nerve for asking."

"Oh."

Shortly thereafter we came to a flat greyish stone set into the middle of the path. It was irregulary shaped, maybe two feet wide, four feet long, and sticking up about six inches out of the ground. Morrolan stopped and studied it for a moment, chewing his lip. I gave him silence to think for a while, then said, "Want to tell me about it?"

"It indicates a choice. Depending on which way we go around it, we will be taking a different way."

"What if we walk directly over it?"

He gave me a withering look and no other answer. Then he sighed and passed around the right side of it. I followed. The path continued among the naked trees, with no difference that I could detect.

Shortly thereafter we heard wolves howling. I looked at Morrolan. He shrugged. "I'd rather deal with an external threat than an internal one at this point."

I decided not to ask what he meant. Loiosh shifted nervously on my shoulder. I said, "I'm getting the impression that these things have been set up deliberately, like a test or something."

He said, "Me, too."

"You don't know?"

"No."

More howling, and, *"Loiosh, can you tell how far away that was?"*

"Around here, boss? Ten feet or ten miles. Everything is weird. I'd feel better if I could smell something. This is scary."

"Feel like flying around for a look?"

"No. I'd get lost."

"Are you sure?"

"Yeah."

"Okay."

I caught a flicker of movement to my right and, as the adrenaline hit me, I realized that Morrolan had his sword out and that I did, too. Then there were greyish shapes appearing out of the mist and flying through the air at us, and there was a horrible moment of desperate action and it was over. I hadn't touched anything, and nothing had touched me.

Morrolan sighed and nodded. "They couldn't reach us," he said. "I'd hoped that was the case."

I sheathed my blade and wiped the sweat from my hands. I said, "If that's the worst we have to fear, I'll be fine." Loiosh came back out of my cloak.

Morrolan said, "Don't worry, it isn't."

LOIOSH EXPLAINED TO ME that he was now more than a year old. I allowed as to how this was true. He went on to say that he was damn near full grown, and ought to be allowed to help. I wondered in what way he could help. He suggested one. I couldn't think of a good counterargument, so there we were.

The next day, early, I returned to Gruff's. This time I went inside and found an empty corner. I had a mug of honey-wine and left again. When I left, Loiosh wasn't with me.

I walked around to the back of the place and found the back door. It was locked. I played with it, then it was unlocked. I entered very carefully. It was a storeroom, filled with casks and barrels and boxes with bottles, and it could have kept me drunk for a year. Light crept past a curtain. So did I, finding myself in a room filled with glasses and plates and things one needs to wash dishes. I decided the area wasn't arranged very efficiently. I would have put the shelves to the left of the drying racks and . . . never mind.

There were no people in this room, either, but the low noise from the inn's main room came through the brown wool curtain. I remembered that curtain from the other side. I returned to the storeroom, moved two barrels and a large box, and hid myself.

Five aching, stiff, miserable hours later, Loiosh and I decided Kynn wasn't going to show up. If this continued, I was going to start taking a dislike to him. I massaged my legs until I could walk again, hoping no one would come through the door. Then I let myself out the back way, even managing to get the door locked behind me.

W E WERE ATTACKED TWICE more; once by something small and flying, and once by a tiassa. Neither of them could touch us, and both went away after one pass. We also came across several diverging or crossing paths, which Morrolan chose among with a confidence I hoped was justified.

We came to another grey stone, and Morrolan once more took the right-hand path, once again after some thought. I said, "Is it pretty much the way you remember it?" Morrolan didn't answer.

Then a thick old tree covered with knots appeared just off to our right, with a branch hanging across the path, about ten feet off the ground. A large brown bird that I recognized as an athyra studied us with one eye.

"*You live,*" it said.

I said. "*How can you tell?*"

"*You don't belong here.*"

"*Oh. Well, I hadn't known that. We must have made a wrong turn on Undauntra. We'll just leave, then.*"

"*You may not leave.*"

"*Make up your mind. First you say—*"

"Let's go, Vlad," said Morrolan. I assume that he was having his own little conversation with the athyra while I was having mine, but maybe not. We ducked under the branch and continued on our way. I looked back, but tree and bird were gone.

A little later Morrolan stood before another grey stone. This time he sighed, looked at me, and led us around to the left. He said, "We are going to have to, sooner or later, or we will never arrive at our destination."

"That sounds ominous."

"Yes."

And, a little later, "Can you give me a hint about what to expect?"

"No."

"Great."

And then I was falling. I started to scream, stopped, and realized that I was still walking next to Morrolan as before. I turned to him as I stumbled a bit. He stumbled at the same moment and his face turned white. He closed his eyes briefly and shook his head, looked at me, and continued down the path.

I said, "Were you falling there, just for a moment?"

"Falling? No."

"Then what happened to you?"

"Nothing I care to discuss."

I didn't press the issue.

A little later I took a step into quicksand. For a moment I thought it was going to be a repeat of the same kind of experience, because I was aware that, at the same time, I was still walking, but this time it didn't let up. Morrolan faltered next to me, then said, "Keep walking."

I did, though to one part of my mind it seemed that every step took me deeper. I also felt panic coming from Loiosh, which didn't help matters, as I wondered what he was seeing.

It occurred to me that Loiosh could feel my fear, too, so I tried to force myself to stay calm for his sake, telling myself that the quicksand was only an illusion. It must have worked, because I felt him calm down, and that helped me, and the image let up just as it was covering my mouth.

Morrolan and I stopped for a moment then, took a couple of deep breaths, and looked at each other. He shook his head once more.

I said, "Aren't there any clear paths to the Halls of Judgment?"

He said, "Some books have better paths than others."

I said, "When we get back, I'll steal one of the better ones and go into business selling copies."

"They can't be copied," said Morrolan. "There are those who have tried."

"How can that be? Words are words."

"I don't know. Let's continue."

We did, and I was quite relieved when we came to another grey stone and Morrolan took the right-hand path. This time it was a wild boar who couldn't touch us, and later a dzur.

Morrolan chose among more paths, and we came to another stone. He looked at me and said, "Well?"

I said, "If we have to."

He nodded and we went around it to the left.

I RETURNED TO MY flat, my legs feeling better, my disposition sour. I decided I never wanted to see Gruff's again. I was beginning to get positively irritated at Kynn, who kept refusing to let himself be set up. I poured myself a glass of brandy and relaxed in my favorite chair, trying to think.

"So much for that idea, Loiosh."

"We could try it again tomorrow."

"My legs won't take it."

"Oh. What next, then?"

"Dunno. Let me think about it."

I paced my flat and considered options. I could purchase a sorcery spell of some sort, say, something that worked from a distance. But then someone would know I'd done it, and, furthermore, there are too many defenses against such things; I was even then wearing a ring that would block most attempts to use sorcery against me, and it had cost less than a week's pay. Witchcraft was too chancy and haphazard.

Poison? Once again, unreliable unless you're an expert. It was like drop-

ping a rock on his head: It would probably work, but if it didn't he'd be
alerted and it would be that much harder to kill him.

No, I was best off with a sword thrust; I could be certain what was going
on. That meant I'd have to get close up behind him, or come on him unex-
pectedly. I drew my dagger from my belt and studied it. It was a knife-
fighter's weapon; well made, heavy, with a reasonably good point and an
edge that had been sharpened at about eight degrees. A chopping, slicing
weapon that would work well against the back of a neck. My rapier was
mostly point, suitable for coming up under the chin, and thus into the brain.
Either would work.

I put the knife away again, squeezed my hands into fists, and paced a little
more.

"Got something, boss?"

"I think so. Give me a minute to think about it."

"Okay."

And, a little later, *"All right, Loiosh, we're going to make this idiot-simple.
Here's what I'll want you to do . . ."*

THERE WERE TIMES WHEN we were howling maniacs, times when we were
hysterical with laughter.

Keep walking.

We were dying of hunger or thirst, with food or drink just to the side, off
the path.

Keep walking.

Chasms opened before us, and the monsters of our nightmares bedeviled
us, our friends turned against us, our enemies laughed in our faces. I guess
I shouldn't speak for Morrolan, but the strained look of his back, the set of
his jaw, and the paleness of his features spoke volumes.

*Keep walking. If you stop, you'll never get out of it. If you leave the path
you'll become lost. Walk into the wind, through the snowstorm, into the
landslide. Keep walking.*

Paths crisscrossing, Morrolan choosing, gritting our teeth and going on.
Hours? Minutes? Years? I dunno. And this despite the fact that anytime we
took a right-hand path we were safe from the purely physical attacks. Once

we were attacked by a phantom sjo-bear. I have a clear memory of it taking a swipe through my head and being amazed that I didn't feel it, but I still don't know if that was the product of a right-hand or a left-hand choice.

Frankly, I don't see how dead people manage it.

There came a point when we had to stop and rest and we did, taking food and drink, directly before another grey stone. I'd given up asking stupid questions. For one thing, I knew Morrolan wouldn't answer, and for another, I had the feeling that the next time he shrugged I was going to put a knife in his back. I suppose by that time he was feeling equally fond of me.

After a rest, then, we stood up again and Morrolan chose a left-hand path. I gritted my teeth.

"You holding up all right, Loiosh?"

"Just barely, boss. You?"

"About the same. I wish I knew how long this was going to go on. Or maybe I'm glad I don't."

"Yeah."

But, subjectively speaking, it wasn't long after that when the path before us suddenly widened. Morrolan stopped, looked up at me, and a faint smile lightened his features. He strode forward with renewed energy, and soon the trees were swallowed in mist, which cleared to reveal a high stone arch with a massive dragon's head carved into it. Our path led directly under the arch.

As we walked through it, Morrolan said, "The land of the dead."

I said, "I thought that's where we've been all along."

"No. That was the outlying area. Now things are likely to get strange."

12

I squeezed my right hand into a fist and slowly began to bring it toward my
left. There was a resistance against my right hand that wasn't physical. It
was as if I knew what I had to do, and wanted to do it, yet actually making
the motion required fighting an incredible lassitude. I understood it—it was
the resistance of the universe to being abused in this fashion—but that was
of little help. Slowly, however, there was motion. I'd bring my hands to-
gether, and then the break would come, and I'd commit everything to it.

Failure was now, in a sense, impossible. My only options were success, or
else madness and death.

My right fist touched my left hand.

A Dragaeran was approaching us at a nice, leisurely pace. His colors,
black and silver, spoke of the House of the Dragon. He wore some sort of
monster sword over his back. While we waited for him, I looked up at the
sky, wondering whether it would be the typical orange-red overcast of the
Dragaeran Empire. No, there wasn't any sky. A dull, uniform grey, with no
break at all. Trying to figure out how high it was and what it was made me
dizzy and queasy, so I stopped.

When the new arrival got close enough for me to see his face, his expression seemed not unpleasant. I don't think it could actually be friendly even if he wanted—not with a forehead that flat and lips as thin as paper. He came closer and I saw that he was breathing, and I couldn't decide whether to be surprised or not.

Then he stopped and his brow furrowed. He looked at me and said, "You're an Easterner." Then his gaze traveled to Morrolan and his eyes widened. "And you're living."

I said, "How can you tell?"

Morrolan snapped, "Shut up, Vlad." Then he inclined his head to the Dragonlord, saying, "We're on an errand."

"The living do not come here."

Morrolan said, "Zerika."

The Dragaeran's mouth twitched. "A Phoenix," he said. "And a special case."

"Nevertheless, we're here."

"You may have to bring your case to the Lords of Judgment."

"That," said Morrolan, "is what we came to do."

"And you will be required to prove yourselves."

"Of course," said Morrolan.

"Say what?" said I.

He turned a sneer toward me. "You will be required to face and defeat champions of—"

"This has got to be a joke," I said.

"Shut up, Vlad," said Morrolan.

I shook my head. "Why? Can you give me one good reason for making us fight our way to the Lords of Judgment, just so they can destroy us for being here?"

The stranger said, "We are of the House of the Dragon. We fight because we enjoy it." He gave me a nasty smile, turned, and walked away.

Morrolan and I looked at each other. He shrugged and I almost belted him. We looked around again, and we were surrounded by Dragonlords. I counted twelve of them. One of them took a step forward and said, "E'Baritt," and drew her sword.

Morrolan said, "E'Drien," and drew his. They saluted.

I backed away a step and said, "Are you sure we can touch them, and they us?"

"Yes," said Morrolan as he faced his opponent. "It wouldn't be fair otherwise."

"Oh. Of course. How silly of me."

They came within a few steps of each other, and Morrolan's opponent looked at the sword and licked her lips nervously.

"Don't worry," said Morrolan. "It does what I tell it to."

The other nodded and took a sort of guard position, her left hand in front holding the dagger. Morrolan drew a dagger and matched her. He struck first with his sword, and she blocked it. She tried to strike with her dagger for his stomach, but he slipped around the blow and, pushing her off balance with his sword, struck her soundly in the chest with his dagger.

She bled. Morrolan stepped back and saluted.

After a moment I said to Morrolan, "Am I next, or are you doing all of them?"

One of the waiting Dragonlords said, "You're next, whiskers," as he stepped out, drew his sword, and faced me.

"Fine," I said, whipped out a throwing knife from my cloak, and threw it into his throat.

"Vlad!" called Morrolan.

"I've covered mine," I said, watching the guy writhe on the ground about six feet from Morrolan's victim. There came the sound of blades being drawn. Loiosh took off toward someone as I drew my rapier. It occurred to me that I might have committed some sort of social blunder.

Morrolan cursed and I heard the sound of steel on steel. Then there were two of them right in front of me. I feinted cuts toward their eyes, *flick flick*, spun to get a look at what was behind me, spun back, and threw three shuriken into the nearest stomach. Another Dragonlord almost took my head off, but then I sliced up his right arm bad enough that he couldn't hold his sword. He actually threatened me briefly with his dagger after that, which threat ended when my point took him cleanly through the chest, and that was it for the other one.

I had another throwing knife in my left hand by then, this one taken from the back of my collar. I used it to slow down the one nearest me, then charged another and veered off into a feint just outside of his sword range. His attack missed, then Loiosh flew into his face, then I cut open his chest and throat with my rapier.

I caught a glimpse of something moving, so I took a step to the side and lunged at it, then wondered if I were about to skewer Morrolan. But no, I skewered someone else instead, and was past him before he hit the ground. I got a glimpse of Morrolan fighting like a madman, then Loiosh screamed into my mind and I ducked and rolled as a sword passed over my head.

I came up, faced my enemy, feinted twice, then cut open her throat. Morrolan was dueling with a pair of them, and I thought about helping him, but then someone else was coming at me, and I don't remember how I dispatched him but I must have because I wasn't hurt.

I looked around for more targets but there weren't any; just the injured dead and the dead dead, so to speak. I wondered what happened to those who died here when they were already dead, as well as those who died here when they were alive.

Morrolan was glaring at me. I ignored him. I cleaned my rapier and sheathed it, trying to recover my breath. Loiosh returned to my shoulder, and I picked up my own belligerence reflected in his mind. Morrolan started to say something and I said, "Drop dead, asshole. You may think this multiple duel business is some sort of cute game, but I don't care to be tested. They wanted to kill me. They didn't manage. That's the end of it."

His face went white and he took a step toward me. "You never learn, do you?" He raised his sword until it was pointed at me.

I held my hand out. "Killing a man who isn't even holding a weapon? That would hardly be honorable, would it?"

He glared at me a moment longer, then spat on the ground. "Let's go," he said.

I left my various weapons in whatever bodies they happened to have taken up residence and followed him farther into the land of the dead.

I hoped the rest of the dead we met would be more peaceful.

THERE ARE TIMES, I guess, when you have to trust somebody. I would have chosen Kiera, but I didn't know where she was. So I gave Kragar some money and had him purchase, discreetly, a stiletto with a seven-inch blade. It took him an afternoon, and he didn't ask any questions.

I tested the balance and decided I liked it. I spent an hour in my flat sharpening the point. I shouldn't have taken an hour, but I was used to sharpening edges for vegetables or meat, not sharpening points for bodies. It's a different skill. After sharpening it, I decided to put a coat of dull black paint on the blade and, after some thought, on the hilt, too. I left the actual edge of the blade unpainted.

When I was done it was already evening. I went back to Gruff's and positioned Loiosh in the window of the place. I took up a position around the corner and waited.

"*Well, Loiosh? Is he there?*"

"*Ummm . . . yeah. I see him, boss.*"

"*Is he with his friend?*"

"*Yeah. And a couple of others.*"

"*Are you sure you're out of sight?*"

"*Don't worry about it, boss.*"

"*Okay. We'll wait, then.*"

I went over my plan, such as it was, a couple of times in my head, then settled back to do some serious waiting. I amused myself by thinking up fragments of bad poetry for a while, which put me in mind of an Eastern girl named Sheila whom I'd gone out with for a few months a year before. She was from South Adrilankha, where most humans live, and I guess she was attracted to me because I had money and seemed tough. I suppose I *am* tough, come to think of it.

Anyway, she was good for me, even though it didn't last long. She wanted to be rich, and classy, and she was an argumentative bitch. I was working on keeping my mouth shut when Dragaeran punks insulted me, and she helped a lot because the only way to get along with her was to bite my tongue when she made her outrageous statements about Dragaerans or the Jhereg or whatever. We'd had a lot of fun for a while, but she finally caught a ship to one of the island duchies where they paid well for human singers. I missed her, but not a lot.

Thinking about her and our six-hour shopping sprees when I had money was a good way to waste time. I went through the list of names we'd called each other one afternoon when we were trying to see who could get cute enough to make the other ill. I was actually starting to get melancholy and teary-eyed when Loiosh said, *"They're leaving, boss."*

"Okay. Back here."

He came back to my shoulder. I stuck my head around the corner. It was very dark, but in the light escaping from the inn I could see them. It certainly was my target. He was walking right toward me. As I ducked back behind the building, my heart gave one quick thud, there was a drop in my stomach, and I felt I was perspiring, just for an instant. Then I was cool and relaxed, my mind clear and sharp. I took the stiletto from its sheath at my side.

"Go, Loiosh. Be careful."

He left my shoulder. I adjusted the weapon to an overhand grip because Dragaerans are taller than we are. Eye level for Kynn was just a bit over my head. No problem.

Then I heard, "What the—Get that thing away from me!" At the same time, there was laughter. I guess Kynn was amused by his friend's dance with a jhereg. I stepped around the corner. I can't tell you what Loiosh was doing to Kynn's friend because I had eyes only for my target. His back was to me, but he turned quickly as I emerged from the alley.

His eyes were on a level with the blade, but the knife and my sleeve were dark, so his eyes locked with my own, in the tiny instant when the world froze around me and all motion slowed down. He appeared slightly startled.

It wasn't as if I hesitated. The motion of my knife was mechanical, precise, and irresistible. He had no time to register the threat before the stiletto took him in the left eye. He gave a jerk and a gasp as I twisted the knife once to be sure. I left it in him and stepped back into the alley as I heard his body fall. I crouched between two garbage cans and waited.

Then I heard cursing from around the corner.

"I'm away, boss, and he's found the body."

"Okay, Loiosh. Wait."

I saw the guy come around the corner, sword out, looking. By this time I had another knife in my hand. But I was hoping that, knowing there was an assassin around, the guy wouldn't be interested in looking too closely for him. I was right, too. He just gave a cursory glance up the alley, then probably decided that I'd teleported away.

He took off at a run, probably to inform his boss of what had happened. As soon as Loiosh told me it was safe, I continued through the alley and, walking quickly but not running, made my way back to my flat. By the time I arrived I wasn't trembling anymore. Loiosh joined me before I got there. I stripped off all of my clothing and checked for bloodstains. My jerkin was stained, so I burned it in the kitchen stove. Then I bathed, while thinking about how to spend my money.

O̲UR FRIEND FROM THE gate—the Dragonlord with the flat forehead—joined us again. He glared at me and I sneered back. Loiosh hissed at him, which I think unnerved him just a bit. We won the exchange, though it was close. He turned to Morrolan, who actually seemed a little embarrassed. Morrolan said, "My companion—"

"Do not speak of it," said the other.

"Very well."

"Follow."

Morrolan shot me one more glare for good luck and we set off behind him. The area seemed empty of trees, rocks, or buildings. Every once in a while, off in the distance, we would see figures moving. As I continued looking, trying to avoid looking at the sky, it seemed that things were shifting a bit, as if our steps were taking us over more ground than just a footstep ought to, and the position of landmarks would change out of proportion to our rate of movement. Well, this shouldn't surprise me. I went back to concentrating on our friend's back.

Then someone else came toward us—a woman dressed in a robe of bright purple. Our guide stopped and spoke quietly to her, and she turned and went off again.

"Boss, did you get a look at her eyes?"

"No, I didn't notice. What about them?"

"They were empty, boss. Nothing. Like, no brain or something."

"Interesting."

The landscape began changing. I can't be precise about when or to what, because I was trying not to watch. The changes didn't make sense with how we were moving, and I didn't like it. It was almost like a short teleport, except I didn't get sick or feel any of the effects. I saw a grove of pine trees and then they vanished; there was a very large boulder, big and dark grey, directly in front of us, but it was gone as we started to step around it. I'm sure there were mountains not too far away at one point, and that we were walking through a jungle at another, and next to an ocean somewhere in there. In a way, this was more disconcerting than the attacks we'd endured earlier.

It started raining just as I was getting dry again after the soaking we'd started this journey with. I hate being wet.

The rain lasted only long enough to annoy me, then we were walking among sharp, jutting rocks. Our path seemed to have been cut through the stonework, and I'd have guessed we were in a mountain.

It was then that a dragon appeared before us.

I RAN INTO KRAGAR the next day. He cleared his throat and looked away in the particular way he has and said, "I heard that one of Rolaan's enforcers went for a walk last night."

I said, "Yeah?"

He said, "No one saw who did it, but I heard a rumor that the assassin used a jhereg to distract the guy he was with."

I said, "Oh."

He said, "I'd almost think of you, Vlad, except you're so well known for having a pet jhereg that you couldn't possibly be stupid enough to do something that obvious."

I suddenly felt queasy. Loiosh said, *"Pet?"*

I said, *"Shut up,"* to Loiosh, and "that's true," to Kragar.

He nodded. "It was interesting, though."

I said, "Yeah."

My boss sent for me a little later. He said, "Vlad, you should leave town for a while. Probably a month. You have anywhere to go?"

I said, "No."

He handed me another bag of gold. "Find somewhere you'll like. It's on me. Enjoy yourself and stay out of sight."

I said, "Okay. Thanks." I got out of there and found a commercial sorcerer with no Jhereg connections to teleport me to Candletown, which is along the seacoast to the east and is known for food and entertainments. I didn't even stop home first. It didn't seem wise.

IT IS REALLY HARD to conceive of just how big a dragon is. I can tell you that it could eat me, perhaps without the need for a second bite. I can mention that it has tentaclelike things all around its head, each of which is longer than I am tall and as big around as my thigh. I could let you know that, at the shoulders, it was around eighteen feet high and much, much longer than that. But, until you've seen one up close, you just can't really imagine it.

Loiosh dived under my cloak. I'd have liked to have followed. Morrolan stood stiffly at my side, waiting. His hand wasn't resting on his sword hilt, so I kept my hands away from my rapier.

Anyway, just what good is a rapier going to do against a dragon?

"WELL MET, STRANGERS."

What can I say? It wasn't "loud" as a voice is loud, but, ye gods, I felt the insides of my skull pounding. Earlier, when the athyra had spoken to us, I had the impression that it was carrying on simultaneous but different conversations with Morrolan and me. This time, it seemed, we were both in on it. If I ever actually come to understand psychic communication I'll probably go nuts.

Morrolan said, *"Well met, dragon."*

One of its eyes was fixed on me, the other, I assume, on Morrolan.

It said, *"YOU ARE ALIVE."*

I said, *"How can you tell?"*

Morrolan said, *"We are on an errand."*

"FOR WHOM?"

"The lady Aliera, of the House of the Dragon."

"OF WHAT IMPORTANCE IS THIS TO ME?"

"I don't know. Does the House of the Dragon matter to you, Lord Dragon?"

I heard what may have been a chuckle. It said, *"YES."*

Morrolan said, *"Aliera e'Kieron is the Dragon heir to the throne."*

That was news to me. I stared at Morrolan while I wondered at the ramifications of this.

The dragon turned its head so both its eyes were on Morrolan. After a moment it said, *"WHERE STANDS THE CYCLE?"*

Morrolan said, *"It is the reign of the Phoenix."*

The dragon said, *"YOU MAY BOTH PASS."*

It turned around (not a minor undertaking) and walked back out of sight. I relaxed. Loiosh emerged from my cloak and took his place on my right shoulder.

Our guide continued to lead us onward, and soon we were back in a more normal (ha!) landscape. I wondered how much time had actually passed for us since we'd arrived. Our clothing had pretty much dried before the rain and we'd had a meal. Four hours? Six?

There was a building ahead of us, and there seemed to be more people around, some in the colors of the House of the Dragon, others in purple robes.

"Morrolan, do you know the significance of those dressed in purple?"

"They are the servants of the dead."

"Oh. Bitch of a job."

"It is what happens to those who arrive in the Paths of the Dead but don't make it through, or who die here."

I shuddered, thinking of the Dragonlords we'd killed. "Is it permanent?"

"I don't think so. It may last for a few thousand years, though."

I shuddered again. "It must get old, fast."

"I imagine. It is also used as punishment. It is likely what will happen to us if our mission fails."

The building was still quite some distance in front of us, but I could see that it would have compared well to the Imperial Palace. It was a simple, massive cube, all grey, with no markings or decorations I could distinguish. It was ugly.

Our guide gestured toward it and said, "The Halls of Judgment."

13

I held the world in my hands. There was a moment of incredible clarity, when the horizon stopped wavering, and I was deaf to rhythms and pulses. Everything held its breath, and my thought pierced the fabric of reality. I felt Loiosh's mind together with mine as a perfectly tuned lant, and I realized that, except for my grandfather, he was the only being in the world that I loved.

Why was I doing this?

The scent of pine needles penetrated my thoughts, and everything seemed clean and fresh. It brought tears to my eyes and power to my hands.

As WE APPROACHED THE building, it didn't get any smaller. I think the area around me continued to change, but I wasn't noticing. We came to an arch with another stylized dragon's head, and our guide stopped there. He bowed to Morrolan, studiously ignoring me. I said, "It's been a pleasure. Have a wonderful time here."

His eyes flicked over me and he said, "May you be granted a purple robe."

"Why, thanks," I said. "You, too."

We passed beneath the arch. We were in a sort of courtyard in front of doors I suspect our friend the dragon could have gone through without ducking. I saw other arches leading into it, about twenty of them.

Oh. No, of course. Make that exactly seventeen of them. There were several purple robes standing around in the courtyard, one of whom was approaching us. He made no comment, only bowed to us both, turned, and led us toward the doors.

It was a long way across the courtyard. I had a chance to think about all sorts of possibilities I didn't enjoy contemplating. When we were before the doors they slowly and majestically swung open for us, with an assumed grandeur that seemed to work on me even though I was aware of it.

"Stole one of your tricks," I told Morrolan.

"It is effective, is it not?"

"Yeah."

Back when the doors of Castle Black had opened, Lady Teldra had stood there to greet me. When the doors of the Halls of Judgment opened before us, there was a tall male Dragaeran in the dress of the House of the Lyorn— brown ankle-length skirt, doublet, and sandals—with a sword slung over his back.

He saw me and his eyes narrowed. Then he looked at the pair of us and they widened. "You are living men."

I said, "How could you tell?"

"Good Lyorn," said Morrolan, "we wish to present ourselves to the Lords of Judgment."

He sort of smiled. "Yes, I suppose you do. Very well, follow me. I will present you at once."

"I can hardly wait," I muttered. No one responded.

I SPENT THE TWO weeks following Kynn's death in Candletown, discovering just how much fun you can have while you're worried sick; or, if you wish, just how miserable you can be while you're living it up.

Then, one day while I was sitting on the beach quietly getting drunk, a waiter came up to me and said, "Lord Mawdyear?" I nodded, as that was close enough to the name I was using. He handed me a sealed message for which I tipped him lavishly. It read "Come back," and my boss had signed it. I spent a few minutes wondering if it was faked, until Loiosh pointed out that anyone who knew enough to fake it knew enough to send someone to kill me right there on the beach. This sent a chill through me, but it also convinced me the message was genuine.

I teleported back the next morning, and nothing was said about what I thought must have been a miserable blunder. I found out, over the course of the next few months, that it hadn't really been that bad a mistake. It was pretty much the policy to send the assassin out of town after he shined someone, especially during a war. I also found out that going to Candletown was a cliché; it was sometimes referred to as Killertown. I never went back there.

But there was something I noticed right away, and I still don't really understand it. My boss knew I'd killed the guy, and Kragar certainly guessed it, but I don't think many others even suspected. Okay, then why did everyone treat me differently?

No, it wasn't big things, but just the way people I worked with would look at me; it was like I was a different person—someone worthy of respect, someone to be careful of.

Mind you, I'm not complaining; it was a great feeling. But it puzzled me then and it still does. I can't figure out if rumors got around, or if my behavior changed in some subtle way. Probably a little of each.

But you know what was even more strange? As I would meet other enforcers who worked for someone or other in the strange world of the Jhereg, I would, from time to time, look at one and say to myself, "That one's done 'work.' " I have no idea how I knew, and I guess I can't even guarantee I was right, but I felt it. And, more often than not, the guy would look at me and give a kind of half nod as if he recognized something about me, too.

I was seventeen years old, a human in the Dragaeran Empire, and I'd taken a lot of garbage over the years. Now I was no longer an "Easterner," nor was I Dragaeran or even a Jhereg. Now I was someone who could calmly and coldly end a life, and then go out and spend the money, and I wasn't going to have to take any crap anymore.

Which was a nice feeling while it lasted.

* * *

I WONDERED, WALKING THROUGH the Halls, if there were ever any dragons brought there for judgment. I mean, not only were the doors large enough to admit one, but the halls were, too. At any rate, the scale made me feel small and insignificant, which was probably the reason behind the whole thing.

Reason?

"Loiosh, who designed this place, anyway?"

"You're asking me, boss? I don't know. The gods, I suppose."

"And if I just knew what that meant, I'd be fine."

"Have you noticed that there isn't any decoration? Nothing at all."

"Hmmm. You're right, Loiosh. But, on the other hand, what sort of mood would you pick if you were decorating this place?"

"A point."

The place was nearly empty, save for a few purple robes coming or going, all with that same blank look. Seeing them made me queasy. I didn't notice any side passages or doors, but I don't think I was at my most observant. It was big and it was impressive. What can I say?

"Good day," said someone behind us. We turned and saw a male Dragaeran in the full splendor of a Dragonlord wizard, complete with shining black and silver garb and a staff that was taller than he was. His smile was sardonic as he looked at Morrolan. I turned to see my companion's expression. His eyes were wide. I'd now seen Morrolan wet, embarrassed, and startled. If I could just see him frightened, my life would be complete.

I said, "Are you certain it's day?"

He turned his sardonic expression to me and sent me the most withering glare I've ever experienced. Several comments came to mind, but for once I couldn't manage to get them out. This may have saved my life.

Morrolan said, "I salute you, Lord Baritt. I had thought you were yet living, I grieve to know—"

He snorted. "Time flows differently here. Doubtless when you left, I hadn't been. . . ." He scowled and didn't complete the sentence.

Morrolan indicated the surrounding wall. "You live within this building, Lord?"

"No, I merely do research here."

"Research?"

"I suppose you wouldn't be familiar with the concept."

By this time I'd recovered enough to appreciate someone being contemptuous of Morrolan. Morrolan, on the other hand, didn't appreciate it at all. He drew himself up and said, "My lord, if I have done something to offend you—"

"I can't say much for your choice of traveling companions."

Before Morrolan could respond, I said, "I don't like it either, but—"

"Don't speak in my presence," said Baritt. As he said it, I found that I couldn't; my mouth felt like it was filled with a whole pear, and I discovered that I couldn't breathe. I hadn't thought it possible to perform sorcery here. The Lyorn who was guiding me took a step forward, but at that moment I found I could breathe again. Baritt said "Jhereg" as if it were a curse. Then he spat on the floor in front of me and stalked away.

When he was gone I took a couple of deep breaths and said, "Hey, and here I'd thought he hated me because I'm an Easterner."

Morrolan had no witty rejoinder for that. Our guide inclined his head slightly, from which I deduced that we were to follow him. We did.

A few minutes later he had led us to a big square entrance way, which was where the hall ended. He stopped outside it and indicated that we should continue through. We bowed to him and stepped forward into another world.

AFTER KYNN'S DEATH, AND its aftermath, I learned slowly. I trained in sorcery in hopes of being able to follow someone teleporting, but that turned out to be even harder than I'd thought.

I never again used Loiosh as a distraction, but he got better at other things, such as observing a target for me and making sure an area was free of Phoenix Guards or other annoyances.

The war between Rolaan and Welok lasted for several months, during which everyone was careful and didn't go out alone. This was an education for me. I "worked" several more times during that period, although only once was it a direct part of the war as far as I know.

The mystery, though, is where, by all the gods, my money went. I ought to have been rich. The fee for assassination is high. I was now living in a nice comfortable flat (it was *really* nice—it had this great blue and white carpet and a huge kitchen with a built-in wood stove), but it didn't cost all that much. I was eating well, and paying quite a bit for sorcery lessons, as well as paying a top fencing master, but none of these things comes close to accounting for all the income I was generating. I don't gamble a whole lot, which is a favorite means of losing money for many Jhereg. I just can't figure it out.

Of course, some of it I can trace. Like, I met an Eastern girl named Jeanine, and we hung out together for most of a year, and it's amazing how much you can spend on entertainment if you really put your mind to it. And there was a period when I was paying out a lot for teleports—like two or three a day for a couple of weeks. That was when I was seeing Jeanine and Constance at the same time and I didn't want them finding out about each other. It ended because all the teleports were making me too sick to be of much good to either of them. I guess, in retrospect, that could account for quite a bit of the money, couldn't it? Teleports don't come cheap.

Still, I can't figure it out. It doesn't really matter, I suppose.

My FIRST REACTION WAS that we'd stepped outside, and in a way I was right, but it was no outside I'd ever seen before. There were stars, such as my grandfather had shown me, and they were bright and hard, all over the place, and so *many* of them. . . .

Presently I realized that my neck was hurting and that the air was cold. Morrolan, next to me, was still gawking at the stars. I said, "Morrolan."

He said, "I'd forgotten what they were like." Then he shook his head and looked around. I did the same at just about the same time, and we saw, seated on thrones, the Lords of Judgment.

Two of them were right in front of us; others were off to the sides, forming what may have been a massive circle of thrones, chairs, and like that. Some of them were grouped close together, in pairs or trios, while others seemed all alone. The creature directly before me, perhaps fifty feet away, was huge and green. Morrolan began walking toward it. As we came closer, I saw that it was covered with scalelike hide, and its eyes were huge and deep-set. I recognized this being as Barlan, and an urge to prostrate myself came over me; I still have no idea why. I resisted.

Next to him was one who looked like a Dragaeran, dressed in a gown of shifting colors, with a haughty face and hair like fine mist. I looked at her hands, and, yes, each finger had an extra joint. Here was the Demon Goddess of my ancestors, Verra. I looked to her right, half expecting to see the sisters legends claimed she had. I think I saw them, too—one was small and always in shadow, and next to her was one whose skin and hair flowed like water. I avoided looking at either of them. I controlled my shaking and forced myself to follow Morrolan.

There were others, but I hardly remember them, save one who seemed to be dressed in fire, and another who seemed always to be fading into and out of existence. How many? I can't say. I remember the few I've mentioned, and I know there were others. I retain the impression that there were thousands of them, perhaps millions, but you'll forgive me if I don't trust my senses fully.

Morrolan seemed to be steering us to a point between Verra and Barlan. As we neared them, it seemed that their gigantic size was illusory. We stopped when we were perhaps fifteen feet from them, and they appeared large, but hardly inhuman. At least in size. Barlan was covered with green scales and had those frightening huge pale green eyes. And Verra's hair still shimmered, and her clothing refused to stop changing color, form, and material. Nevertheless, they seemed more like beings I might be able to talk to than some of the others in the area.

They acknowledged us at the same moment.

Morrolan bowed, but not as low as he had to Baritt. I didn't try to figure it out; I just bowed myself, very low indeed. Verra looked back and forth between the two of us, then over at Barlan. She seemed to be smiling. I couldn't tell about him.

Then she looked back at us. Her voice, when she spoke, was deep and resonating, and very odd. It was as if her words would echo in my mind, only there was no gap in time between hearing them in my mind and in my ears. The result was an unnatural sort of piercing clarity to everything she said. It was such a strange phenomenon that I had to stop and remember her words, which were: "This is a surprise."

Barlan said nothing. Verra turned to him, then back to us. "What are your names?"

Morrolan said, "I am Morrolan e'Drien, Duke of the House of the Dragon."

I swallowed and said, "Vladimir Taltos, Baronet of the House of the Jhereg."

"Well, well, well," said Verra. Her smile was strange and twisted and full of irony. She said, "It would seem that you are both alive."

I said, "How could you tell?"

Her smile grew a bit wider. She said, "When you've been in the business as long as I have—"

Barlan spoke, saying, "State your errand."

"We have come to beg for a life."

Verra's eyebrows went up. "Indeed? For whom?"

"My cousin," said Morrolan, indicating the staff.

Barlan held his hand out, and Morrolan stepped forward and gave him the staff. Morrolan stepped back.

"You must care for her a great deal," said Verra, "since by coming here you have forfeited your right to return."

I swallowed again. I think Verra noticed this, because she looked at me and said, "Your case is less clear, as Easterners do not belong here at all."

I licked my lips and refrained from comment.

Verra turned back to Morrolan and said, "Well?"

"Yes?"

"Is she worth your life?"

Morrolan said, "It is necessary. Her name is Aliera e'Kieron, and she is the Dragon heir to the throne."

Verra's head snapped back, and she stared straight into Morrolan's face. There is something terrifying about seeing a god shocked.

After a little while, Verra said, "So, she has been found."

Morrolan nodded.

Verra gestured toward me. "Is that where the Easterner comes in?"

"He was involved in recovering her."

"I see."

"Now that she has been found, we ask that she be allowed to resume her life at the point where—"

"Spare me the details," said Verra. Morrolan shut up.

Barlan said, "What you ask is impossible."

Verra said, "Is it?"

"It is also forbidden," said Barlan.

"Tough cookies," said Verra.

Barlan said, "By our positions here we have certain responsibilities. One of them is to uphold—"

"Spare me the lecture," said Verra. "You know who Aliera is."

"If she is sufficiently important, we may ask to convene—"

"By which time the Easterner will have been here too long to return. And his little jhereg, too." I hardly reacted to this at the time, because I was too amazed by the spectacle of the gods arguing. But I did notice it, and I noted that Verra was aware of Loiosh even though my familiar was inside my cloak.

Barlan said, "That is not our concern."

Verra said, "A convocation will also be boring."

"You would break our trust to avoid boredom?"

"You damn betcha, feather-breath."

Barlan stood. Verra stood. They glared at each other for a moment, then vanished in a shower of golden sparks.

IT IS NOT ONLY the case that Dragaerans have never learned to cook; it is also true, and far more surprising, that most of them will admit it. That is why Eastern restaurants are so popular, and the best of them is Valabar's.

Valabar and Sons has existed for an impossibly long time. It was here in Adrilankha before the Interregnum made this city the Imperial Capital. That's hundreds of years, run by the same family. The same family of humans. It was, according to all reports, the first actual restaurant within the Empire; the first place that existed as a business just to serve meals, rather than a tavern that had food, or a hotel that supplied board for a fee.

There must be some sort of unwritten law about the place that those in power know, something that says, "Whatever we're going to do to Easterners, leave Valabar's alone." It's that good.

It is a very simple place on the inside, with white linen tablecloths and simple furnishings, but none of the decoration that most places have. The waiters are pleasant and charming and very efficient, and almost as difficult to notice as Kragar when they are slipping up on you to refill your wine glass.

They have no menus; instead your waiter stands there and recites the list of what the chef, always called "Mr. Valabar" no matter how many Valabars are working there at the moment, is willing to prepare today.

My date for the evening, Mara, was the most gorgeous blonde I'd ever met, with a rather nasty wit that I enjoyed when it wasn't turned on me. Kragar's date was a Dragaeran lady whose name I can't remember, but whose House was Jhereg. She was one of the tags in a local brothel, and she had a nice laugh.

The appetizer of the day was anise-jelled winneoceros cubes, the soup was a very spicy potato soup with Eastern red pepper, the sorbet was lemon, the pâté—made of goose liver, chicken liver, kethna liver, herbs, and unsalted butter—was served on hard-crusted bread with cucumber slices that had been just barely pickled. The salad was served with an impossibly delicate vinegar dressing that was almost sweet but not quite.

Kragar had fresh scallops in lemon and garlic sauce, Kragar's date had the biggest stuffed cabbage in the world, Mara had duck in plum brandy sauce, and I had kethna in Eastern red pepper sauce. We followed it with dessert pancakes, mine with finely ground walnuts and cream chocolate brandy sauce topped with oranges. We also had a bottle of Piarran Mist, the Fenarian dessert wine. I paid for the whole thing, because I'd just killed someone.

We were all feeling giggly as we walked the meal off; then Mara and I went up to my flat and I discovered that a meal at Valabar's is one of the world's great aphrodisiacs. I wondered what my grandfather would make of that information.

Mara got tired of me and dumped me a week or so later, but what the hell.

I SAID, "FEATHER-BREATH?"

Loiosh said, *"Sheesh."*

"I think," said Morrolan judiciously, "that we've managed to get someone in trouble."

"Yeah."

Morrolan looked around, as did I. None of the other beings present seemed to be paying us any attention. We were still standing there a few minutes later when Verra reappeared in another shower of sparks. She had a gleam in her eye. Barlan appeared then, and, as before, his expression was unreadable. I noticed then that Verra was holding the staff.

Verra said, "Come with me."

She stepped down from her throne and led us around behind it, off into the darkness. She didn't speak and Morrolan didn't speak. I certainly wasn't going to say anything. Loiosh was under my cloak again.

We came to a place where there was a very high wall. We walked along it for a moment, passing another purple robe or two, until we came to a high arch. We passed beneath it, and there were two corridors branching away.

Verra took the one to the right and we followed. In a short time, it opened to a place where a wide, shallow brick well stood, making water noises.

Verra dipped her hand into the well and took a drink; then, with no warning, she smashed the staff into the side of the well.

There was the requisite cracking sound, then I was blinded by a flash of pure white light, and I think the ground trembled. When I was able to open my eyes again, there was still some sort of visual distortion, as if the entire area we were in had been bent at some impossible angle, and only Verra could be seen clearly.

Things settled down then, and I saw what appeared to be the body of a female Dragaeran in the black and silver of the House of the Dragon stretched out next to the well. I noticed at once that her hair was blonde— even more rare in a Dragonlord than in a human. Her brows were thin, and the slant of her closed eyes was rather attractive. I think a Dragaeran would have found her *very* attractive. Verra dipped her hand in again and allowed some of the water to flow into the mouth of her whom I took to be Aliera.

Then Verra smiled at us and walked away.

Aliera began to breathe.

14

My grandfather, in teaching me fencing, used to make me stand for minutes at a time, watching for the movement of his blade that would give me an opening. I suspect that he knew full well that he was teaching me more than fencing.

When the moment came, I was ready.

HER EYES FLUTTERED OPEN, but she didn't focus on anything. I decided that she was better looking alive than she'd been dead. Morrolan and I stood there for a moment, then he said softly, "Aliera?"

Her eyes snapped to him. There was a pause before her face responded; when it did she seemed puzzled. She started to speak, stopped, cleared her throat, and croaked, "Who are you?"

He said, "I'm your cousin. My name is Morrolan e'Drien. I am the eldest son of your father's youngest sister."

"Morrolan," she repeated. "Yes. That would be the right sort of name." She nodded as if he'd passed a test. I took in Morrolan's face, but he seemed to be keeping any expression off it. Aliera tried to sit up, failed, and her eyes fell on me; narrowed. She turned to Morrolan and said, "Help me."

He helped her to sit up. She looked around. "Where am I?"

"The Halls of Judgment," said Morrolan.

Surprise. "I'm dead?"

"Not anymore."

"But—"

"I'll explain," said Morrolan.

"Do so," said Aliera.

"Those two must be related," I told Loiosh. He sniggered.

"What is the last thing you remember?"

She shrugged, a kind of one-shoulder-and-tilt-of-the-head thing that was almost identical to Morrolan's. "It's hard to say." She closed her eyes. We didn't say anything. A moment later she said. "There was a strange whining sound, almost above my audible range. Then the floor shook, and the ceiling and walls started to buckle. And it was becoming very hot. I was going to teleport out, and I remember thinking that I couldn't do it fast enough, and then I saw Sethra's face." She paused, looking at Morrolan. "Sethra Lavode. Do you know her?"

"Rather," said Morrolan.

Aliera nodded. "I saw her face, then I was running through a tunnel—I think that was a dream. It lasted a long time, though. Eventually I stopped running and lay on what seemed to be a white tile floor, and I couldn't move and didn't want to. I don't know how long I was there. Then someone shouted my name—I thought at the time it was my mother. Then I was waking up, and I heard a strange voice calling my name. I think that was you, Morrolan, because then I opened my eyes and saw you."

Morrolan nodded. "You have been asleep—dead, actually—for, well, several hundred years."

Aliera nodded, and I saw a tear in her eye. She said very quietly, "It is the reign of a reborn Phoenix, isn't it?"

Morrolan nodded, seeming to understand.

"I told him it would be," she said. "A Great Cycle—seventeen Cycles; it had to be a reborn Phoenix. He wouldn't listen to me. He thought it was the end of the Cycle, that a new one could be formed. He—"

"He created a sea of chaos, Aliera."

"What?"

I decided that "he" referred to Adron. I doubted that he was to be found in these regions.

"Not as big as the original, perhaps, but it is there—where Dragaera City used to be."

"Used to be," she echoed.

"The capital of the Empire is now Adrilankha."

"Adrilankha. A seacoast town, right? Isn't that where Kieron's Tower is?"

"Kieron's Watch. It used to be there. It fell into the sea during the Interregnum."

"Inter—Oh. Of course. How did it end?"

"Zerika, of the House of the Phoenix, retrieved the Orb, which somehow landed here, in the Paths of the Dead. She was allowed to return with it. I helped her," he added.

"I see," she said. Morrolan sat down next to her. I sat down next to Morrolan. Aliera said, "I don't know Zerika."

"She was not yet born. She's the only daughter of Vernoi and, um, whoever it was she married."

"Loudin."

"Right. They both died in the Disaster."

She nodded, then stopped. "Wait. If they both died in the explosion, and Zerika wasn't born when it happened, how could . . . ?"

Morrolan shrugged. "Sethra had something to do with it. I've asked her to explain it, but she just looks smug." He blinked. "I get the impression that, whatever it was she did, she was too busy doing it to rescue you as thoroughly as she'd have liked. I guess you were the second priority after making sure there could be an Emperor. Zerika is the last Phoenix."

"The last Phoenix? There can't be another? Then the Cycle is broken. If not now, for the future."

"Maybe," said Morrolan.

"Can there be another Phoenix?"

"How should I know? We have the whole Cycle to worry about it. Ask me again in a few hundred thousand years when it starts to matter."

I could see from Aliera's expression that she didn't like this answer, but she didn't respond to it. There was a silence, then she said, "What happened to me?"

"I don't understand entirely," said Morrolan. "Sethra managed to preserve your soul in some form, though it became lost. Eventually—I imagine shortly after Zerika took the Orb—an Athyra wizard found you. He was studying necromancy. I don't think he realized what he had. You were tracked down, and—"

"Who tracked me down?"

"Sethra and I," he said, watching her face. He glanced at me quickly, then said, "And there were others who helped, some time ago."

Aliera closed her eyes and nodded. I hate it when they talk over my head. "Did you have any trouble getting me back?"

Morrolan and I looked at each other. "None to speak of," I said.

Aliera looked at me, then looked again, her eyes narrow. She stared hard, as if she were looking inside of me. She said, "Who *are* you?"

"Vladimir Taltos, Baronet, House Jhereg."

She stared a little longer, then shook her head and looked back at Morrolan.

"What is it?" he asked.

"Never mind." She stood up suddenly, or, rather, tried, then sat down. She scowled. "I want to get out of here."

"I believe they will let Vlad leave. If so, he will help you."

She looked at me, then back at Morrolan. "What's wrong with you?"

"As a living man, I am not allowed to return from the Paths of the Dead. I shall remain here."

Aliera stared at him. "Like hell you will. I'll see you dead first."

IT'S HARD FOR ME to pin down the point at which I stopped considering myself to be someone's enforcer who sometimes did "work" and started considering myself a free-lance assassin. Part of it was that I worked for several different people during a short period of time during and after the war, including Welok himself, so this made things confusing.

Certainly those around me began to think of me that way before it occurred to me, but I don't think my own thinking changed until I had developed professional habits and a good approach to the job.

Once again, it's unclear just when this occurred, but I was certainly functioning like a professional by the time I finished my seventh job—assassinating a little turd named Raiet.

W<small>HILE</small> I <small>WAS THINKING</small> over this announcement and wondering whether to laugh, I realized that Verra had left us; in other words, we had no way of knowing where to go from here.

I cleared my throat. Morrolan broke off from his staring contest with Aliera and said, "Yes, Vlad?"

"Do you know how we can find our way back to where all the gods were?"

"Hmmm. I think so."

"Let's do that, then."

"Why?"

"Do you have a better idea?"

"I suppose not."

As I stood, I was taken with a fleeting temptation to take a drink from the well. It's probably fortunate that it was only fleeting. We helped Aliera to stand, and I discovered that she was quite short—hardly taller than me, as a matter of fact.

We began walking back the way we'd come, Morrolan and me each supporting one of Aliera's arms. She looked very unhappy. Her teeth were clenched, perhaps from anger, perhaps from pain. Her eyes, which I'd first thought were green, seemed to be grey, and were set straight ahead.

We made it back to the archway and rested there for a moment.

Morrolan suggested that Aliera sit down and rest her legs. Aliera said, "Shut up."

I saw that Morrolan's patience was wearing thin. So was mine, for that matter. We bit our lips at the same moment, caught each other's eyes, and smiled a little.

We took her arms and started moving again, in what Morrolan thought was the right direction. We took a few tentative steps and stopped again when Aliera gasped. She said, "I can't . . ." and we let her sink to the ground.

Her breath came in gasps. She closed her eyes, her head up toward the sky; her brow was damp and her hair seemed soaked with sweat. Morrolan and I looked at each other, but no words came.

A minute or so later, as we were still standing there wondering if we would mortally insult Aliera if we offered to carry her, we saw a figure approach us out of the darkness and gradually become visible in the light of those incredible stars.

He was very tall and his shoulders were huge. There was a massive sword at his back, and his facial features were pure Dragon, as were the colors of his clothing, though their form—a peculiar formless jacket and baggy trousers tucked into darrskin boots—were rather strange. His hair was brown and curly, his eyes dark. He was—or, rather, had died at—late middle age. He had lines of thought on his forehead, lines of anger around his eyes, and the sort of jaw that made me think he kept his teeth clenched a lot.

He studied the three of us while we looked at him. I wondered what Morrolan thought of him, but I couldn't take my eyes off the Dragonlord's face to check Morrolan's expression. I felt my pulse begin to race and my knees suddenly felt weak. I had to swallow several times in quick succession.

When he finally spoke, he was addressing Aliera. "I was told I'd find you here."

She nodded but didn't say anything. She looked miserable. Morrolan, who I guess wasn't used to being ignored, said, "I greet you, lord. I am Morrolan e'Drien."

He turned to Morrolan and nodded. "Good day," he said. "I am Kieron."

Kieron.

Kieron the Conqueror.

Father of the Dragaeran Empire, elder of the proudest of lines of the House of the Dragon, hero of myth and legend, first of the great Dragaeran butchers of Easterners, and, well, I could go on, but what's the point? Here he was.

Morrolan stared at him and slowly dropped to one knee. I didn't know where to look.

P EOPLE SHOULD KNOW BETTER.

I don't know of any case of a Jhereg testifying to the Empire against the Jhereg and surviving, yet there are still fools who try. "I'm different," they say. "I've got a plan. No one will be able to touch me; I'm protected." Or maybe it isn't even that well thought out, maybe it's just that they're unable to believe in their own mortality. Or else they figure that the amount of money the Empire is paying them makes it worth the risk.

But never mind, that isn't my problem.

I was hired through about four layers, I think. I met with a guy in front of a grocer, and we talked as we strolled around the block. Loiosh rode on my left shoulder. It was early morning, and the area we were in was empty. The guy was called "Feet" for some reason or other. I knew who he was, and when he proposed an assassination I knew it had to be big, because he was placed pretty high in the Organization. That meant that whoever had told him to get this done must be *really* important.

I told him, "I know people who do that kind of thing. Would you like to tell me about it?"

He said, "There was a problem between two friends of ours." This meant between two Jhereg. "It got serious, and things started getting very uncomfortable all around." This meant that one or both of these individuals was very highly placed in the Organization. "One of them was afraid he'd get hurt, and he panicked and went to the Empire for protection."

I whistled. "Is he giving official testimony?"

"He already has to an extent, and he's going to give more."

"Ouch. That's going to hurt."

"We're working on burying it. We may be able to. If we can't, things will get nasty all over for a while."

"Yeah, I imagine."

"We need serious work done. I mean, *serious* work. You understand?"

I swallowed. "I think so, but you'd better state it clearly."

"Morganti."

"That's what I thought."

"Your friend ever done that?"

"What's the difference?"

"None, I suppose. Your friend will have the full backing of many people on this; all the support he needs."

"Yeah, I'll need some time to think about it."

"Certainly. Take as much time as you need. The price is ten thousand imperials."

"I see."

"How much time do you need to think it over?"

I was silent for a few minutes as we walked. Then I said, "Tell me his name."

"Raiet. Know him?"

"No."

We walked for a while as I thought things over. The neighborhood did neighborhood things all around us. It was a peculiar, peaceful kind of walk. I said, "All right. I'll do it."

"Good," he said. "Let's walk over to my place. I'll pay you and give you what information we have to start with. Let us know as you need more and we'll do what we can."

"Right," I said.

I FOUND MYSELF TAKING a step backward from the father of the Dragaeran Empire, while conflicting thoughts and emotions buzzed around my brain faster than I could note them. Fear and anger fought for control of my mouth, but rationality won for a change.

We held these positions for a moment. Kieron continued to look down at Aliera. Something in how they looked at each other seemed to indicate they had met before. I don't know how that could be, since Kieron was as old as the Empire and Aliera was less than a thousand years old, however you measured her age.

Kieron said, "Well, will you stand up?"

Her eyes flashed. She hissed, "No, I'm going to lie right here forever." Yes, I know there are no sibilants in what she said. I don't care; she hissed it.

Kieron chuckled. "Very well," he said. "If you ever do decide to stand up, you may come and speak to me." He started to turn away, stopped, looked right at me. For some reason I couldn't meet his eyes. He said, "Have you anything to say to me?"

My tongue felt thick in my mouth. I could find no words. Kieron left.

Morrolan stood up. Aliera was quietly sobbing on the ground. Morrolan and I studied our belt buckles. Presently Aliera became silent; then she said in a small voice, "Please help me to rise."

We did, Morrolan indicated a direction, and we set off on our slow, limping way. Loiosh was being strangely silent. I said, *"Something bothering you, chum?"*

"I just want to get out of here, boss."

"Yeah. Me, too."

I said to Aliera, "You seemed to recognize him."

She said, "So did you."

"I did?"

"Yes."

I chewed that over for a moment, then decided not to pursue it. Presently a pair of what seemed to be monuments appeared before us. We passed between them and found ourselves back amid the thrones of the gods. We kept going without taking too close a look at the beings we'd just blithely stepped past.

A bit later Morrolan said, "Now what?"

I said, "You're asking me? Wait a minute. I just thought of something."

"Yes?"

I looked around and eventually spotted a purple robe passing by. I called out, "You. Come here."

He did, quite humbly.

I spoke to him for a moment, and he nodded back at me without speaking, his eyes lifeless. He began leading us, adjusting himself to our pace. It was a long walk and we had to stop once or twice on the way while Aliera rested.

At last we came to a throne where was seated a female figure the color of marble, with eyes like diamonds. She held a spear. The purple robe bowed to us and turned away.

The goddess said, "The living are not allowed here."

Her voice was like the ringing of chimes. It brought tears to my eyes just to hear it. It took me a moment to recover enough to say anything, in part because I'd expected Morrolan to jump in. But I said, "I am Vladimir Taltos. These are Morrolan and Aliera. You are Kelchor?"

"I am."

Morrolan handed her the disk he'd been given by the cat-centaurs. She studied it for a moment, then said, "I see. Very well, then, what do you wish?"

"For one thing, to leave," said Morrolan.

"Only the dead leave," said Kelchor. "And that, rarely."

"There is Zerika," said Morrolan.

Kelchor shook her head. "I told them it was a dangerous precedent. In any case, that has nothing to do with you."

Morrolan said, "Can you provide us with food and a place to rest while Aliera recovers her strength?"

"I can provide you with food and a place to rest," she said. "But this is the land of the dead. She will not recover her strength here."

"Even sleep would help," said Aliera.

"Those who sleep here," said Kelchor, "do not wake again as living beings. Even Easterners," she added, giving me a look I couldn't interpret.

I said, "Oh, fine," and suddenly felt very tired.

Morrolan said, "Is there any way in which you can help us?" He sounded almost like he was begging, which in other circumstances I would have enjoyed.

Kelchor addressed Aliera, saying, "Touch this." She held out her spear, just as Mist had done for me. Aliera touched it without hesitation.

I felt the pressure of holding her up ease. Kelchor raised the spear again, and Aliera said, "I thank you."

Kelchor said, "Go now."

I said, "Where?"

Kelchor opened her mouth to speak, but Aliera said, "To find Kieron."

I wanted to say that he was the last thing I wanted to see just then, but the look on Aliera's face stopped me. She let go of our support and, though she seemed a bit shaky, walked away on her own. Morrolan and I bowed low to Kelchor, who seemed amused, then we followed Aliera.

Aliera found a purple robe and said in a loud, clear voice, "Take us to Kieron."

I hoped he'd be unable to, but he just bowed to her and began leading us off.

15

When I felt it, it was almost as if I heard Noish-pa's voice saying, "Now, Vladimir."

"Now, Vladimir."

It is much too long a phrase for that instant of time in which I knew to act, but that is what I recall, and that is what I responded to. It burst.

There was no holding back, there were no regrets; doubts became abstract and distant. Everything had concentrated on building to this place in time, and I was alive as I am never alive except at such moments. The exhilaration, the release, the plunge into the unknown, it was all there. And, best of all, there was no longer any point in doubting. If I was to be destroyed, it was now too late to do anything about it. Everything I'd been saving and holding back rushed forth. I felt my energy flow away as if someone had pulled the plug. It spilled forth, and, for the moment, I was far too confused to know or, for that matter, to wonder if my timing had been right. Death and madness, or success. Here it was.

My eyes snapped open and I looked upon bedlam.

Even if my life depended on it, I couldn't tell you how we ended up there, but the purple robe somehow led us back to the white hallway through which we'd approached the gods. There was a side passage in it, though I'd noticed none before, and we took it, following its curves and twists until we came to a room that was white and empty save for many candles and Kieron the Conqueror.

He stood with his back to the door and his head bowed, doing I don't know what before one of the candles. He turned as we entered and locked gazes with Aliera.

"You are standing on your own, I see."

"Yes," she said. "And now that I do so, I can explain how proud I am to be descended from one who mocks the injured."

"I am glad you're proud, Aliera e'Kieron."

She drew herself up as best she could. "Don't—"

"Do not think to instruct me," he said. "You haven't earned it."

"Are you sure?" she said. "I know you, Kieron. And if you don't know me, it's only because you're as blind as you always were."

He stared at her but allowed no muscle in his face to change. Then he looked right at me and I felt my spine turn to water. I kept it off my face. He said, "Very well, then, Aliera; what about him?"

"He isn't your concern," said Aliera.

I leaned over to Morrolan and said, "I love being spoken of as if—"

"Shut up, Vlad."

"Polite bastards, all of them."

"I know, boss."

Kieron said to Aliera, "Are you quite certain he isn't my concern?"

"Yes," said Aliera. I wished I knew what this was about.

Kieron said, "Well, then, perhaps not. Would you care to sit?"

"No," she said.

"Then what would you like?"

Her legs were still a bit unsteady as she approached him. She stopped about six inches away from him and said, "You may escort us out of the Paths, to make up for your lack of courtesy."

He started to smile, stopped. He said, "I do not choose to leave again. I have done—"

"Nothing for two hundred thousand years. Isn't that long enough?"

"It is not your place to judge—"

"Keep still. If you're determined to continue to allow history to pass you by, give me your sword. I'll fight my own way out, and put it to the use for which it was intended. You may be finished with it, but I don't think it has finished its task."

Kieron's teeth were clenched and the fires of Verra's hell burned in his gaze.

He said, "Very well, Aliera e'Kieron. If you think you can wield it, you can take it."

Now, if some of this conversation doesn't make sense to you, I can only say that it doesn't make sense to me, either. For that matter, judging from the occasional glances I took at Morrolan's face, he wasn't doing much better at understanding it than I. But I'm telling you as best I can remember it, and you'll just have to be as satisfied with it as I am.

Aliera said, "I can wield it."

"Then I charge you to use it well, and to return to this place rather than give it to another or let it be taken from you."

"And if I don't?" she said, I think just to be contrary.

"Then I'll come and take it."

"Perhaps," said Aliera, "that's what I want."

They matched stares for a little longer, then Kieron unstrapped swordbelt and sword and scabbard and passed the whole thing over to Aliera. It was quite a bit taller than she was; I wondered how she'd even be able to carry it.

She took it into her hand without appearing to have difficulty, though. When she had it she didn't even bow to Kieron, she merely turned on her heel and walked out the door, a bit shakily, but without faltering. We followed her. "Come on," she said. "We're going home. All of us. Let him stop us who can."

It didn't sound practical, but it was still the best idea I'd heard that day.

*   *   *

Τ HE INFORMATION FEET HAD "to start with" consisted of fourteen pages of parchment, all tightly written by, apparently, a professional scribe, though that seemed unlikely. It consisted of a list of Raiet's friends and how often he visited them, his favorite places to eat out and what he liked to order at each, his history in the Organization (which made this an amazingly incriminating document itself), and more like that. There was much detail about his mistress and where she lived (there's no custom against nailing someone at his mistress's place, unlike his own home). I'd never had any interest in knowing so much about someone. Toward the end were several notes such as, "Not a sorcerer. Good in a knife fight; very quick. Hardly a swordsman." This stuff ought not to matter but was good to know.

On the other hand, this made me wonder if, perhaps, this wasn't the sort of thing I should be trying to find out about all of my targets. I mean, sure, killing someone with a Morganti weapon is as serious as it gets, but any assassination is, well, a matter of life and death.

In addition to the parchment, Feet gave me a large purse containing more money than I'd ever seen in my life, most of it in fifty-imperial coins.

And he gave me a box. As soon as I touched it, I felt for the first time, albeit distantly, that peculiar hollow humming echo within the mind. I shuddered and realized just what I'd gotten myself into.

It was, of course, far too late to back out.

Τ ROMP TROMP TROMP. HEAR us march, ever onward, onward, doom uncertain, toward the unknown terrors of death, heads high, weapons ready . . .

What a load of crap.

We made our way through the corridors of the Halls of Judgment as well as we could, which wasn't very. What had been a single straight, wide corridor had somehow turned into a twisty maze of little passages, all the same. We must have wandered those halls for two or three hours, getting more and more lost, with none of us willing to admit it. We tried marking the walls with the points of our swords, keeping to the left-hand paths, but nothing worked. And the really odd thing was that none of the passages led anywhere except to other passages. That is, there were no rooms, stairways, doors, or anything else.

The purple robes we asked to lead us out just looked at us blankly. Aliera had buckled Kieron's greatsword onto her back and was grimly not feeling the weight. Morrolan was equally grim about not feeling anything. Neither Loiosh nor I felt like talking. No one else had any good suggestions, either. I was getting tired.

We stopped and rested, leaning against a wall. Aliera tried to sit down on the floor and discovered that the greatsword on her back made this impossible. She looked disgusted. I think she was close to tears. So was I for that matter.

We talked quietly for a while, mostly complaining. Then Morrolan said, "All right. This isn't working. We are going to have to find the gods and convince them to let us go."

"No," said Aliera. "The gods will prevent you from leaving."

"The gods do not have to prevent me from leaving; these halls are doing a quite sufficient job of that."

Aliera didn't answer.

Morrolan said, "I suspect we could wander these halls forever without finding a way out. We need to ask someone, and I, for one, can think of no better expert than Verra."

"No," said Aliera.

"Are you lost, then?" came a new voice. We turned, and there was Baritt once again. He seemed pleased. I scowled but kept my mouth shut.

"Who are you?" asked Aliera.

Morrolan said, "This is Baritt."

Baritt said, "And you?"

"I am Aliera."

His eyes widened. "Indeed? Well, this is, indeed, droll. And you are trying to return to living lands, are you not? Well then, I crave a favor. If you succeed, and I am still alive, don't visit me. I don't think I could stand it."

Aliera said, "My Lord, we are—"

"Yes, I know. I cannot help you. There is no way out except the one you know. Any purple robe can guide you back there. I am sorry."

And he did actually seem to be sorry, too, but he was looking at Aliera as he said it.

Aliera scowled and her nostrils flared. She said, "Very well, then," and we left Baritt standing there.

Finding a purple robe in that place was about as difficult as finding a Teckla in the market. And, yes, the purple robe was willing to escort us back to see the gods. She seemed to have no trouble finding the large passage. The thought crossed my mind that we could just turn around and take this passage out the way we'd come. I didn't suggest it because I had the feeling it wouldn't work.

We passed through the gate once more, the purple robe leaving us there, and we came once more before the throne of Verra, the Demon Goddess. She was smiling.

The bitch.

I COULD HAVE DONE most of my planning without ever leaving my flat, and I almost decided to. But I was getting more and more nervous about this whole Morganti business, so I decided to take the precaution of verifying some of the information on the fact sheets.

I'll make a long, dull story short and say it all checked out, but I was happier seeing it myself. His imperially assigned protection consisted of three Dragonlords who were always with him, all of whom were very good. None of them spotted me while I was following them around, but they made me nervous. I eventually sent Loiosh to trail him while I studied the information, looking for a weakness.

The problem was the fact that the bodyguards were of the House of Dragon. Otherwise, I could probably bribe them to step out of the way at the crucial time. I wondered if the Dragons might have other weaknesses.

Well, for the moment, assume they did. Was there a good, obvious place to take him? Sure. There was a lady he liked to visit in the west of Adrilankha, past the river. If there is a better time and place to nail someone than his mistress's, I don't know what it is. Loiosh checked the area out for me and it was perfect—rarely traveled in the early morning hours when he left her place, yet with a fair share of structures to hide near. All right, if I were going to take him there, what would I do? Replace the cabman who picked him up? That would involve bribing the cabman, who'd then know about the assassination, or else killing or disabling him, which I didn't like.

No, there had to be a better way.

And there was, and I found it.

Sʜᴇ ꜱᴀɪᴅ, "I ɢʀᴇᴇᴛ you again, mortals. And you, Aliera, I give you welcome. You may leave this place, and the Easterner may accompany you, on the condition that he never return. The Lord Morrolan will remain."

"No," said Aliera. "He returns with us."

The goddess continued to smile.

"All right," said Aliera. "Explain to me why he has to stay here."

"It is the nature of this place. The living are simply unable to return. Perhaps he can become undead, and leave that way. There are those who have managed this. I believe you know Sethra Lavode, for instance."

"That is not acceptable," said Aliera.

Verra smiled, saying nothing.

Morrolan said, "Let it lie, Aliera."

Aliera's face was hard and grim. "That's nonsense. What about Vlad, then? If it was the nature of the place, he couldn't leave either. And don't tell me it's because he's an Easterner—you know and I know there's no difference between the soul of an Easterner and the soul of a Dragaeran." Indeed? Then why weren't Easterners allowed into the Paths of the Dead, assuming we'd want to be? But this wasn't the time to ask.

Aliera continued, "I couldn't leave either, for that matter. And didn't the Empress Zerika manage? And for that matter, what about you? I know what being a Lord of Judgment means, and there's nothing that makes you so special that you should be immune to these effects. You're lying."

Verra's face lost its smile, and her multijointed hands twitched—an odd, inhuman gesture that scared me more than her presence. I expected Aliera to be destroyed on the spot, but Verra only said, "I owe you no explanation, little Dragon."

Aliera said, "Yes, you do," and Verra flushed. I wondered what it was that had passed between them.

Then Verra smiled, just a little, and said, "Yes, perhaps I do owe you an explanation. First of all, you are simply wrong. You don't know as much about being a god as you think you do. Easterners hold gods in awe, denying us any humanity. Dragaerans have the attitude that godhood is a skill, like sorcery, and there's nothing more to it than that. Neither is correct. It is a combination of many skills, and many natural forces, and involves changes in every aspect of the personality. I was never human, but if I had been, I wouldn't be now. I am a god. My blood is the blood of a god. It is for this reason that the Halls of Judgment cannot hold me.

"In the case of Zerika, she was able to leave because the Imperial Orb has power even here. Still, we could have stopped her, and we nearly did. It is no small thing to allow the living to leave this place, even those few who are capable.

"Your Easterner friend could never have come here without a living body to carry him. No, the soul doesn't matter, but it's more complicated than that. It is the blood. As a living man he could bring himself here, and as a living man he can leave." She suddenly looked at me. "Once. Don't come back, Fenarian." I tried not to look as if I were shaking.

Verra went on, "And as for you, Aliera . . ." Her voice trailed off and she smiled.

Aliera flushed and looked down. "I see."

"Yes. In your case, as perhaps your friends told you, I had some difficulty in persuading certain parties to allow you to leave. If you weren't the heir to the throne, we would have required you to stay, and your companion with you. Are you answered?"

Aliera nodded without looking up.

"What about me, boss?"

Shit. I hadn't thought of that. I screwed up my courage and said, "Goddess, I need to know—"

"Your familiar shares your fate, of course."

"Oh. Yes. Thank you."

"Thanks, boss. I feel better."

"You do?"

Verra said, "Are you ready to leave, then? You should depart soon, because if you sleep, none of you will live again, and there are imperial rules against the undead holding official imperial positions."

Aliera said, "I will not leave without my cousin."

"So be it," snapped Verra. "Then you will stay. Should you change your mind, however, the path out of here is through the arch your friends know, and to the left, past the Cycle, and onward. You may take it if you can. The Lord Morrolan will find his life seeping away from him as he walks, but he can try. Perhaps you will succeed in bringing a corpse out of this land, and denying him the repose of the Paths as well as the life which is already forfeit. Now leave me."

We looked at each other. I was feeling very tired indeed.

For lack of anywhere else to go, we went past the throne until we found the archway beneath which we'd first met Kieron the Conqueror. To the right was the path to the well, which was still tempting, but I still knew better. To the left was the way out, for Aliera and me.

I discovered, to my disgust, that I really didn't want to leave Morrolan there. If it had been Aliera who had to stay, I might have felt differently, but that wasn't one of my options. We stood beneath the arch, no one moving.

I OPENED THE BOX. The sensation I'd felt upon touching it became stronger. It contained a sheathed dagger. Touching the sheath was very difficult for me. Touching the hilt was even more difficult.

"*I don't like this thing, boss.*"

"*Neither do I.*"

"*Do you have to draw it before—*"

"*Yes. I need to know I can use it. Now shut up, Loiosh. You aren't making this any easier.*"

I drew the dagger and it assaulted my mind. I found my hand was trembling, and forced my grip to relax. I tried to study the thing as if it were just any weapon. The blade was thirteen inches, sharp on one side. It had enough of a point to be useful, but the edge was better. It had a good handguard and it balanced well. The hilt was nonreflective black, and—

Morganti.

I held it until I stopped shaking. I had never touched one of these before. I almost made a vow never to touch one again, but careless vows are stupid, so I didn't.

But it was a horrible thing to hold, and I never did get used to it. I knew there were those who regularly carried them, and I wondered if they were sick, or merely made of better stuff than I.

I forced myself to take a few cuts and thrusts with it. I set up a pine board so I could practice thrusting it into something. I held it the whole time, using my left hand to put the board against a wall on top of a dresser. I held my right hand, with the knife, rigidly out to the side away from my left hand. I must have looked absurd, but Loiosh didn't laugh. I could tell he was exercising great courage in not flying from the room.

Well, so was I, for that matter.

I thrust it into the board about two dozen times, forcing myself to keep striking until I relaxed a bit, until I could treat it as just a weapon. I never fully succeeded, but I got closer. When I finally resheathed the thing, I was drenched with sweat and my arm was stiff and sore.

I put it back in its box.

"Thanks, boss. I feel better."

"Me, too. Okay. Everything is set for tomorrow. Let's get some rest."

As we stood, I said to Aliera, "So tell me, what's so special about you that you can leave here and Morrolan can't?"

"It's in the blood," she said.

"Do you mean that, or is it a figure of speech?"

She looked at me scornfully. "Take it however you will."

"Ummm, would you like to be more specific?"

"No," said Aliera.

I shrugged. At least she hadn't told me she owed me no explanation. I was getting tired of that particular phrase. Before us was a wall, and paths stretched out to the right and to the left. I looked to the right.

I said, "Morrolan, do you know anything about that water Verra drank and fed to Aliera?"

"Very little," he said.

"Do you think it might allow us to—"

"No," said Aliera and Morrolan in one voice. I guess they knew more about it than I did, which wasn't difficult. They didn't offer any explanations and I didn't press the issue. We just stood for a long moment, then Morrolan said, "I think there is no choice. You must go. Leave me here."

"No," said Aliera.

I chewed on my lower lip. I couldn't think of anything to say. Then Morrolan said, "Come. Whatever we decide, I wish to look upon the Cycle."

Aliera nodded. I had no objection.

We took the path to the left.

16

The horizon jumped and twisted, the candle exploded, the knife vibrated apart, and the humming became, in an instant, a roar that deafened me.

On the ground before me, the rune glowed like to blind me, and I realized that I was feeling very sleepy. I knew what that meant, too. I had no energy left to even keep me awake. I was going to lose consciousness, and I might or might not ever regain it, and I might or not be mad if I did.

My vision wavered, and the roar in my ears became a single monotone that was, strangely, the same as silence. In the last blur before I slipped away, I saw on the ground, in the center of the rune, the object of my desire—that which I'd done all of this to summon—sitting placidly, as if it had been there all along.

I wondered, for an instant, why I was taking no joy in my success; then I decided that it probably had something to do with not knowing if I'd live to use it. But there was still somewhere the sense of triumph for having done something no witch had ever done before, and a certain serene pleasure in having succeeded. I decided I'd feel pretty good if it didn't kill me.

Dying, I've found, always puts a crimp in my enjoyment of an event.

I'D LOVE TO SEE a map of the Paths of the Dead.

Ha.

We followed the wall to the left, and it kept circling around until we ought to have been near the thrones, but we were still in a hallway with no ceiling. The stars vanished sometime in thee, leaving a grey overcast, yet there was no lessening in the amount of light I thought had been provided by the stars. I dunno.

The wall ended and we seemed to be on a cliff overlooking a sea. There was no sea closer than a thousand miles to Deathgate Falls, but I suppose I ought to have stopped expecting geographical consistency some time before.

We stared out at the dark, gloomy sea for a while and listened to its roar. It stretched out forever, in distance and in time. I can't look at a sea, even the one at home, without wondering about who lives beyond it. What sorts of lives do they have? Better than ours? Worse? So similar I couldn't tell the difference? So different I couldn't survive there? What would it be like? How did they live? What sorts of beds did they have? Were they soft and warm, like mine, safe and—

"Vlad!"

"Uh, what?"

"We want to get moving," said Morrolan.

"Oh. Sorry. I'm getting tired."

"I know."

"Okay, let's—Wait a minute."

I reached around and opened my pack, dug around amid the useless witchcraft supplies I'd carried all this way, and found some kelsch leaves. I passed them around. "Chew on these," I said.

We all did so, and, while nothing remarkable or exciting happened, I realized that I was more awake. Morrolan smiled. "Thanks, Vlad."

"I should have thought of it sooner."

"I should have thought of it, boss. That's my job. Sorry."

"You're tired, too. Want a leaf? I've got another."

"No, thanks. I'll get by."

We looked around, and far off to our right was what seemed to be a large rectangle. We headed toward it. As we got closer, it resolved itself into a single wall about forty feet high and sixty feet across. As we came still closer, we could see there was a large circular object mounted on its face. My pulse quickened.

Moments later the three of us stood contemplating the Cycle of the Dragaeran Empire.

R̲AIET PICKED UP A carriage at the Imperial Palace the next day and went straight to the home of his mistress. A Dragonlord rode with him, another rode next to the driver, and a third, on horseback, rode next to the carriage, or in front of it, or behind it. Loiosh flew above it, but that wasn't part of their arrangements.

Watching them through my familiar's eyes, I had to admire their precision, futile though it was. The one on top of the coach got down first, checked out the area, and went straight into the building and up to the flat, which was on the second floor of the three-story brick building.

If you'd been there watching, you would have seen the rider dismount smartly as the driver got down and held the door for the two inside while looking up and down the street, and up at the rooftops as well. Raiet and the two Dragons walked into the building together. The first one was already inside the flat and had checked it over. Raiet's mistress, who name was Treffa, nodded to the Dragon and continued setting out chilled wine. She seemed a bit nervous as she went about this, but she'd been growing more and more nervous as this testimony business continued.

As he finished checking the apartment, the other two Dragons delivered Raiet. Treffa smiled briefly and brought the wine into the bedchamber. He turned to one of the Dragons and shook his head. "I think she's getting tired of this."

The Dragon probably shrugged; he'd been assigned to protect a Jhereg, but he didn't have to like it, or him, and I assume he didn't. Raiet walked into the bedchamber and closed the door. Treffa walked over to the door and did something to it.

"What's that, babe?"

"A soundproofing spell. I just bought it."

He chuckled. "They making you nervous?"

She nodded.

"I suppose it's starting to wear on you."

She nodded again and poured them each a glass of wine.

When he hadn't appeared after his usual few hours, the Dragons knocked on the door. When no one answered, they broke the door down. They found his lifeless and soulless body on the bed, a Morganti knife buried in his chest. They wondered why they hadn't heard him scream, or the window opening. Treffa lay next to him, drugged and unconscious. They couldn't figure out how the drugs had gotten into the wine, and Treffa was no help with any of it.

They were suspicious of her, naturally, but were never able to prove that Treffa had actually taken money to set him up. She disappeared a few months later and is doing quite well to this day, and Treffa isn't her name anymore, and I won't tell you where she's living.

It IS COMMONLY BELIEVED that if anyone had the strength to take hold of the great wheel that is the Cycle and physically move it, the time of the current House would pass, and the next would arrive. It is also commonly held that it would require enough strength to overcome all the weight contained by the forces of history, tradition, and will that keep the Cycle turning as it does. This being the case, it seems a moot point, especially when, as I stared at it, it was hard to imagine anyone with the strength to just move the bloody great wheel.

That's all it was, too. A big wheel stuck onto a wall in the middle of nowhere. On the wheel were engraved symbolic representations of all seventeen Houses. The Phoenix was at the top, the Dragon next in line, the Athyra having just passed. What a thrill it must be to be here when it actually changed, signaling the passing of another phase of Dragaeran history. At that point, either the Empress would step down, or she would have recently done so, or would soon do so, or perhaps she would refuse and blood would run in the Empire until the political and the mystical were once more in agreement. When would it happen? Tomorrow? In a thousand years?

Everyone I've asked insists that this thing *is* the Cycle in every meaningful way, not merely its physical manifestation. I can't make sense of that, but if you can, more power to you, so to speak.

I glanced at Morrolan and Aliera, who also stared at the Cycle, awe on their faces.

"Boss, the kelsch won't last forever."

"Right, Loiosh. Thanks."

I said, "All right, folks. Whatever we're going to do, we'd best be about it."

They looked at me, at each other, at the ground, then back at the Cycle. None of us knew what to do. I turned my back on them and walked back to look out over the sea again.

I WON'T SAY THAT I'm haunted by the look in Raiet's eyes in that last moment—when the Morganti dagger struck him—or his scream as his soul was destroyed. He deserved what happened to him, and that's that.

But I never got used to touching that weapon. It's the ultimate predator, hating everything, and it would have been as happy to destroy me as Raiet. Morganti weapons scare me right down to my toes, and I'm never going to be happy dealing with them. But I guess it's all part of the job.

The whole thing gave me a couple of days of uneasy conscience in any case, though. Not, as I say, for Raiet; but somehow this brought home to me a thought that I'd been ignoring for over a year: I was being paid money to kill people.

No, I was being paid money to kill Dragaerans; Dragaerans who had made my life miserable for more than seventeen years. Why shouldn't I let them make my life pleasant instead? Loiosh, I have to say, was no help at all in this. He had the instincts of an eater of carrion and sometime hunter.

I really didn't know if I was creating justifications that would eventually break down or not. But a couple of days of wondering was all I could take. I managed to put it out of my mind, and, to be frank, it hasn't bothered me since.

I don't know, maybe someday it will, and if so I'll deal with it then.

I DON'T KNOW HOW long I stood there, perhaps an hour, before Morrolan and Aliera came up behind me. Then the three of us watched the waves break for a few minutes. Behind us, the way we'd come, were the Paths of the Dead and the Halls of Judgment. To our right, beyond the Cycle, was a dark forest, through which lay the way out, for some of us.

After a time Aliera said, "I won't leave without Morrolan."

Morrolan said, "You are a fool."

"And you're another for coming here when you knew you couldn't get out alive."

"I can think of another fool, Loiosh."

"Another two, boss."

"That's as may be," said Morrolan. "But there is no need to make the venture useless."

"Yes there is. I choose to do so."

"It is absurd to kill yourself merely because—"

"It is what I will do. No one, *no one* will sacrifice his life for me. I won't have it. We both leave, or we both remain."

There was a cool breeze on the right side of my face. That way was home. I shook my head. Morrolan should have known better than to expect rationality from a Dragaeran, much less a Dragonlord. But then, he was one himself.

Aliera said, "Go back, Vlad. I thank you for your help, but your task is finished."

Yes, Morrolan was a Dragonlord and a Dragaeran. He was also pompous and abrasive as hell. So why did I feel such a resistance to just leaving him? But what else could I do? There was no way to leave with him, and I, at least, saw no value in pointless gestures.

Morrolan and Aliera were looking at me. I looked away. "Leave, Vlad," said Morrolan. I didn't move.

"You heard him, boss. Let's get out of here."

I stood there yet another minute. I wanted to be home, but the notion of just saying good-bye to Morrolan and walking away, well, I don't know. It didn't feel right.

I've spent many fruitless minutes since then wondering what would have happened if the breeze hadn't shifted just then, bringing with it the tang of salt and the smell of seaweed.

Dead bodies and seaweed. I chuckled. Yeah, this was a place where that phrase was appropriate. Where had I first heard it? Oh, yeah, the bar. Fer-enk's. Drinking with Kiera.

Kiera. Right. That. It just might do it. If there was only a way . . .

Witchcraft?

I looked at Morrolan and Aliera.

"*It's crazy, boss.*"

"*I know. But still—*"

"*We don't even know if we're on the same world as—*"

"*Maybe it doesn't matter.*"

"*What if it does?*"

"*Boss, do you have any idea how much that will take out of you?*"

"*They'll have to carry me back.*"

"*If it doesn't work, they won't be able to.*"

"*I know.*"

Loiosh shut up, as he realized I wasn't really listening to him. I dug in my pack and found my last kelsch leaf.

Aliera said, "What is it, Vlad?"

"An idea for getting Morrolan out of here. Will you two be willing to carry me if I can't walk on my own?"

Morrolan said, "What is it?"

"Witchcraft," I said.

"How—"

"I'm going to have to invent a spell. I'm not certain it can be done."

"I am a witch. Can I help?"

I hesitated, then shook my head. "I have one more kelsch leaf left. I'm going to chew on it myself in order to get the energy to do the spell. If you help, who will carry us both out?"

"Oh. What is the spell intended to do?"

I licked my lips, realizing that I didn't want to tell him.

"*Why not, boss?*"

"*He'll just say it can't be done.*"

"*Well, can it?*"

"*We'll find out.*"

"*Why?*"

"*I've always wanted to test myself as a witch. Here's my big chance.*"

"*Boss, I'm serious. If you put that much into it and it doesn't work it will—*"

"*Kill me. I know. Shut up.*"

"*And with the amount of energy you'll have to pour into it you won't be able to stay awake. And—*"

"*Drop it, Loiosh.*"

To Morrolan I said, "Never mind. Wait here. I'm going to find a place to set this up. I'll probably be near the Cycle, so stay away from there; I don't want anyone around to distract me. When I'm done, if it works, I'll find you."

"What if it doesn't work?"

"Then you'll find me."

BRIBING TREFFA HAD COST quite a bit, as had the soundproofing spells and the escape, since I dealt directly with a sorceress who worked for the Left Hand, rather than going through Feet. Why? I don't know. I mean, after hiring me, he wouldn't turn around and shine me after I did the job. If word of that got around, no one would work for him again. But on the other hand, this killing was *Morganti*. If he had the chance to cleanly dispose of me by having a teleport go wrong, he *probably* wouldn't take it, but why tempt him?

In any case, by the time all was said and done, I'd spent a great deal, but I still had a great deal left. I decided not to live it up this time, because I didn't want to call attention to myself. I didn't want to leave town for the same reason. This killing made quite a splash, and that made me nervous, but I got over it.

So far as I know, no one ever found out I'd done it. But once again, there were those who seemed to know. One of them was Welok the Blade, who was about as nasty as they come. I started working directly for him a few weeks later—doing collecting and trouble-shooting and keeping an eye on his people. I carefully set aside the money I'd earned, determined to invest it in something that would keep earning for me. Maybe even something legit-imate.

About a month after I started working for Welok, I was visiting my grand-

father in South Adrilankha, and I met a human girl named Ibronka, who
had the longest, straightest, blackest hair I'd ever seen, and eyes you could
get lost in. I still hadn't made my investment.

Oh, well.

AFTER GOING THIS FAR, I couldn't back out. The three of us were going
to leave together or not at all, and now there was a chance of success. If I'd
wanted to pray just then, I would have prayed to my grandfather, not to
Verta, because his guidance would have been more useful.

I didn't think he'd ever tried inventing a spell, though. Dammit, if sorcery
worked around here, Morrolan could have simply caused the thing to appear
from my flat. But then, if sorcery worked we could have just teleported out
of here. No point in thinking about that.

I selected a spot facing the Cycle. Why? I'm not sure. It seemed appropriate, and the apropos is a vital thing to a practicing witch.

I started chewing on the leaf while I meditated, relaxing, preparing myself.
When it had done as much for me as it was capable of, I spit it out.

I took my pack off and opened it, then sat down. I wondered if the gods
would stop me, then decided that if they were looking at me, they would
have done something as soon as I began laying out the implements of the
spell. It was amusing to be out of their sight, yet right in their backyard, so
to speak.

I studied the Cycle and tried to collect my courage.

Waiting would just make things more difficult.

I took a deep breath and began the spell.

17

I have a vague memory of a little girl shaking my shoulder, saying, "Don't fall asleep. You'll die if you fall asleep. Stay awake."

When I opened my eyes there was no one there, so it may have been a dream. On the other hand, to dream one must be sleeping, and if I was sleeping . . .

I don't know.

Flap flap, peck peck.

I knew what that was. My eyes opened. I spoke aloud. "It's all right. I'm back."

I DON'T THINK I'VE ever had to work so hard to stand up. When I'd finally managed, I felt the way Aliera must have, and I really wished I had more kelsch leaves to chew on. The world spun around and around. Don't you just hate it when it does that?

I started walking, then heard something, very distant. It gradually got more urgent in tone, so I stopped and listened. It was Loiosh, saying, *"Boss! Boss! They're back the other way."*

I got myself turned around, which wasn't as easy as you might think, and stumbled off in the direction Loiosh told me was the right one. After what seemed like hours I found them, sitting where I'd left them. Morrolan noticed me first, and I saw him moving toward me. All of his actions seemed slowed down, as did Aliera's as she rose and came toward me. I started to fall, which also seemed to happen slowly, and then the two of them were supporting me.

"Vlad, are you all right?"

I mumbled something and held on to them.

"Vlad? Did it work?"

Work? Did what work? Oh, yes. I had more to do. Wait, the vial . . . no, I had it in my hand. Good move, Vlad. I held it up. A dark, dark liquid in a clear vial with a rubber stopper.

"What is it?" asked Aliera.

Formulating an answer seemed much too difficult. I gathered my strength, looked at Morrolan, and said, "Bare your arm."

"Which one?" he asked.

I shook my head, so he shrugged and bared his left arm.

"Knife," I said.

Morrolan and Aliera exchanged looks and shrugs, and then Morrolan put a knife into my left hand. I gestured for him to come closer and, with some hesitation, he did.

I forced my hand to remain steady as I cut his biceps. I handed the vial to Aliera and said, "Open." I couldn't bring myself to watch her, though I did curse myself for not having had her open it before I cut Morrolan.

I have no idea how she managed it without letting me fall, but she did, and after a while she said, "It's done."

I grabbed Morrolan's arm and held the vial against the cut. I told him, "You're a witch. Make the liquid go into your arm."

He looked at me, puzzled, then licked his lips. I suddenly realized that he was deciding whether he trusted me. If I'd had the strength, I'd have laughed. *Him* wondering if he should trust *me*? But I guess he decided to, and he also chose to assume I knew what I was doing. More fool he on that point, I thought to myself. My eyes closed. Aliera shook me and I opened them. When I looked up, the vial was empty and Morrolan was holding it in his hand, staring at it with a mildly inquiring expression. I hoped Kiera hadn't needed it for anything important.

"Let's go home," I said.

"Vlad," asked Morrolan, "just what was that?"

"Home," I managed. There was a pause, during which they might have been looking at each other. Then, each with an arm around me, we set off for the woods.

I CAN'T RECALL MAKING a decision to set up on my own. I was in a certain situation, and I got out of it the best way I could.

The situation?

Well, when the war between Welok and Rolaan finally ended, there were a number of shakedowns. Nielar, my first boss, got rid of most of what he owned because he would have had to fight to keep it and didn't think he could manage. I respect that. Courage is all well and good, but you can't earn when you're dead, and it takes a certain kind of intelligence to know when to back off.

I had many different employers in the months after Nielar, but when everything settled down I was working for a guy named Tagichatn, or Takishat, or something like that; I've never been able to get his name exactly right.

In any case, I never liked him and he never liked me. Most of my earnings were straight commissions for collections and such, and those came pretty rarely around then. I did a few assassinations for people to whom my reputation had spread, which kept me living comfortably, but assassinations also pull in a lot of pressure; I like to have income that comes from things that aren't quite so risky.

I could have left and found employment with someone else, but I'd only been around for a few years by then and I didn't know that many people. So the best way out of the situation turned out to be killing Tagijatin.

KEEP WALKING. STAY AWAKE.

A dim glow seemed to come from the ground, or perhaps from the air around us, I don't know. It was almost enough light to see by. How long were we walking through that forest? Who can say? My time sense was completely screwed up by then.

Stay awake. Keep walking.

From time to time we'd stop, and Aliera and Morrolan would have a hushed conversation about which way to go. I think they were afraid we were walking in circles. When this happened Loiosh would say, *"Tell them that way, boss,"* and I'd gesture in the indicated direction. I guess by this time they were trusting me. The gods alone know why.

At one point Morrolan said, "I feel odd."

Aliera said, "What is it?"

"I'm not sure. Something strange."

"Vlad, what did you give him?"

I shook my head. Talking was just too much work. Besides, what had I given him? Oh, right. The blood of a goddess, according to Kiera. Why had I done it? Because the only other choice was letting Morrolan die.

Well, so what? What had he ever done for me? He'd saved my life, but that was because I was working for him. Friend? Nonsense. Not a Dragaeran. Not a Dragonlord, in any case.

Then why? It didn't matter; it was over. And I was too tired to think about it, anyway.

Keep walking. Stay awake.

Later, Aliera said, "I'm beginning to feel it, too. Want to rest?"

Morrolan said, "If we stop, Vlad will fall asleep, and we'll lose him."

That seemed like sufficient answer for Aliera, which surprised me. But then, why were they working so hard to save me? And why had I been so certain they would? They were Dragonlords and I was a Jhereg; they were Dragaerans and I was human. I couldn't make it make sense.

Aliera said, "How are you feeling?"

I couldn't answer, but it turned out she was speaking to Morrolan. He said, "I'm not certain how to describe it. It's as if I am lighter and heavier at the same time, and the air tastes different. I wonder what he gave me?"

"If we get out of this," said Aliera, "we can ask him later."

Stay awake. Keep walking.

The woods went on and on and on.

*   *   *

KILLING TADISHAT MAY HAVE been one of the easiest things I've ever done. For someone who accumulated enemies as quickly as he did, you'd think he'd have taken some sort of precaution. But he was new at running an area, and I guess he was one of those people who think, "It can't happen to me." I got news for you, sucker: It can.

He always worked late, doing his own bookkeeping so he could be sure no one was cheating him out of a copper, and I just walked in one day while he was poring over the books and crept up on him with a stiletto in my hand. He didn't notice me until I was right in front of him, by which time it was much too late. No problem.

By the time his body was found, I'd already moved into his office. Why? I don't know. I guess I just decided I'd rather work for me than for anyone else I could think of.

I CAN'T RECALL WHEN we left the woods, but I do remember being carried through a cave. Morrolan tells me I pointed the way to it, so I don't know. The next clear memory I have is lying on my back staring up at the orange-red Dragaeran sky and hearing Morrolan say, "Okay, I know where we are."

A teleport must have followed that, but I have no memory of it, which is just as well.

KRAGAR JOINED ME RIGHT away when I took over from Tagichatin and, to my surprise and pleasure, Nielar showed more loyalty to me than I would have expected from a former boss. Of course, I had some problems getting started, as there were several people in my organization who had trouble taking an Easterner seriously as a boss.

I changed their minds without killing any of them, which I think was quite an accomplishment. In fact, I didn't have any major problems running my area—until a certain buttonman named Quion had to ruin it all.

*   *   *

Sᴇᴛʜʀᴀ Lᴀᴠᴏᴅᴇ, ᴛʜᴇ Eɴᴄʜᴀɴᴛʀᴇss, the Dark Lady of Dzur Mountain, studied me from beneath her lashes. I wondered why she hadn't asked what I'd given Morrolan, and decided that she either guessed what it was or knew I wouldn't answer. I was feeling belligerent, though I'm not sure why. Maybe it had something to do with having been assisted out of the Paths of the Dead by Morrolan and Aliera, I don't know.

These two worthies were watching Sethra's face as they concluded the tale. We were sitting, quite comfortably, in the library at Dzur Mountain. Chaz served wine and blinked a lot and loudly sucked his lips.

"I am pleased," said Sethra at last. "Aliera, your presence is required by the Empire."

"So I'm given to understand," said Aliera.

"What are the rest of us, roast kethna?"

"Shut up, Loiosh," I said, though I tended to share his sentiments.

"And, Vlad," continued Sethra, "I am in your debt. And I don't say that lightly. If you think this can't help you, you are a fool."

Morrolan said, "She speaks for me, also."

I said, "That I'm a fool?"

He didn't answer. Aliera said, "I owe you something, too. Perhaps someday I'll pay you."

I licked my lips. Was there a threat in there? If so, why? They were all looking at me, except for Chaz, who seemed to be looking for insects in a corner. I didn't know what to say, so I said, "Fine. Can I go home now?"

I ʀᴇᴄᴏᴠᴇʀᴇᴅ ᴍᴏsᴛ ᴏꜰ the money Quion had taken, so I guess that worked out all right. I don't think it's hurt my reputation any. I've seen Morrolan a couple of times since then, and he's okay for a Dragaeran. He suggested getting together with Sethra and Aliera a few times, but I think I'll pass for the moment.

I told Kiera I'd lost the bottle, but, oddly enough, she didn't seem disturbed. I never *have* told Morrolan what was in it. Whenever he asks, I just smile and look smug. I don't know, maybe I'll tell him one of these days. Then again, maybe not.

PHOENIX

All the time people say to me, "Vlad, how do you do it? How come you're so good at killing people? What's your secret?" I tell them, "There is no secret. It's like anything else. Some guys plaster walls, some guys make shoes, I kill people. You just gotta learn the trade and practice until you're good at it."

The last time I killed somebody was right around the time of the Easterners' uprising, in the month of the Athyra in 234 PI, and the month of the Phoenix in 235. I wasn't all that involved in the uprising directly; to be honest, I was just about the only one around who didn't see it coming, what with the increased number of Phoenix Guards on the street, mass meetings even in my neighborhood, and whatnot. But that's when it occurred, and, for those of you who want to hear what happens when you set out to kill somebody for pay, well, here it is.

PART ONE

Technical Considerations

Lesson 1

Contract Negotiations

MAYBE IT'S JUST ME, but it seems like when things are going wrong—your wife is ready to leave you, all of your notions about yourself and the world are getting turned around, everything you trusted is becoming questionable—there's nothing like having someone try to kill you to take your mind off your problems.

I was in an ugly, one-story wood-frame building in South Adrilankha. Whoever was trying to kill me was a better sorcerer than me. I was in the cellar, squatting behind the remains of a brick wall, just fifteen feet from the foot of the stairs. If I stuck my head out the door again, it might well get blasted off. I intended to call for reinforcements just as soon as I could. I also intended to teleport out of there just as soon as I could. It didn't look like I'd be able to do either one any time soon.

But I was not helpless. At just such times as these, a witch may always take comfort in his familiar. Mine is a jhereg—a small, poisonous flying reptile whose mind is psychically linked to my own, and who is, moreover, brave, loyal, trustworthy—

"If you think I'm going out there, boss, you're crazy."

Okay, next idea.

I raised as good a protection spell as I could (not very), then took a brace of throwing knives from inside my cloak, my rapier from its scabbard, and a deep breath from the clammy basement air. I leapt out to my left, rolling, coming to my knee, throwing all three knives at the same time (hitting nothing, of course; that wasn't the point), and rolling again. I was now well out of the line of sight of the stairway—both the source of the attack and the one path to freedom. Life, I've found, is often like that. Loiosh flapped over and joined me.

Things sizzled in the air. Destructive things, but I think meant only to let me know the sorcerer was still there. It wasn't like I'd forgotten. I cleared my throat. "Can we negotiate?"

The masonry of the wall before me began to crumble away. I did a quick counterspell and held myself answered.

"All right, Loiosh, any bright ideas?"

"Ask them to surrender, boss."

"Them?"

"I saw three."

"Ah. Well, any other ideas?"

"You've tried asking your secretary to send help?"

"I can't reach him."

"How about Morrolan?"

"I tried already."

"Aliera? Sethra?"

"The same."

"I don't like that, boss. It's one thing for Kragar and Melestav to be tied up, but—"

"I know."

"Could they be blocking psionics, as well as teleportation?"

"Hmmm. I hadn't thought of that. I wonder if it's possib—" Our chat was interrupted by a rain of sharp objects, sorcerously sent around the corner behind which I hid. I wished fervently that I were a better sorcerer, but I managed a block, while letting Spellbreaker, eighteen inches of golden chain, slip down into my left hand. I felt myself becoming angry.

"Careful, boss. Don't—"

"I know. Tell me something, Loiosh: Who are they? It can't be Easterners, because they're using sorcery. It can't be the Empire, because the Empire

doesn't ambush people. It can't be the Organization, because they don't do this clumsy, complicated nonsense, they just kill you. So who is it?"

"Don't know, boss."

"Maybe I'll take a longer look."

"Don't do anything foolish."

I made a rude comment to that. I was seriously upset by this time, and I was bloody well going to do *something,* stupid or not. I set Spellbreaker spinning and hefted my blade. I felt my teeth grinding. I sent up a prayer to Verra, the Demon-Goddess, and prepared to meet my attackers.

Then something unusual happened.

My prayer was answered.

IT WASN'T LIKE I'D never seen her before. I had once traveled several thousand miles through supernatural horrors and the realm of dead men just to bid her good-day. And, while my grandfather spoke of her with reverence and awe, Dragaerans spoke of her and her ilk like I spoke about my laundry. What I'm getting at is that there was never any doubt about her real, corporeal existence; it's just that although it was my habit to utter a short prayer to her before doing anything especially dangerous or foolhardy, nothing like this had ever happened before.

Well, I take that back. There might have been once when—no, it couldn't have been. Never mind. Different story.

In any case, I found myself abruptly elsewhere, with no feeling of having moved and none of the discomfort that we Easterners, that is, humans, feel when teleporting. I was in a corridor of roughly the dimensions of the dining hall of Castle Black. All of it white. Spotless. The ceiling must have been a hundred feet above me, and the walls were at least forty feet apart, with white pillars in front of them, perhaps twenty feet between each. Perhaps. It may be that my senses were confused by the pure whiteness of everything. Or it may be that everything reported by my senses was meaningless in that place. There was no end to the hallway in either direction. The air was slightly cool, but not uncomfortable. There was no sound except my own breathing, and that peculiar sensation you have when you don't know whether you're hearing your heart beat or feeling it.

Loiosh was stunned into silence. This does not happen every day.

My first reaction, in the initial seconds after my arrival, was that I was the victim of a massive illusion perpetrated by those who had been trying to kill me. But that didn't really hold up, because, if they could do that, they could have shined me, which they clearly wanted to do.

I noticed a black cat at my feet, looking up at me. It miaowed, then began walking purposefully down the hall in the direction I was facing. All right, so maybe I'm nuts, but it seems to me that if you're in big trouble, and you pray to your goddess, and then suddenly you're someplace you've never been before, and there's a black cat in front of you and it starts walking, you follow it.

I followed it. My footsteps echoed very loudly, which was oddly reassuring.

I sheathed my rapier as I walked, because the Demon Goddess might take it amiss. The hall continued straight, and the far end was obscured in a fine mist that gave way before me. It was probably illusory. The cat stayed right at the edge of it, almost disappearing into it.

Loiosh said, *"Boss, are we about to meet her?"*

I said, *"It seems likely."*

"Oh."

"You've met before—"

"I remember, boss."

The cat actually vanished into the mists, which now remained in place. Another ten or so paces and I could no longer see the walls. The air was suddenly colder and felt a great deal like the basement I'd just escaped. Doors appeared, caught in the act of opening, very slowly, theatrically. They were twice my height and had carvings on them, white on white. It seemed a bit, well, *silly* to be having both of those doors ponderously open themselves to a width several times what I needed. It also left me not knowing whether to wait until they finished opening or to go inside as soon as I could. I stood there, feeling ridiculous, until I could see. More mist. I sighed, shrugged, and passed within.

It would be hard to consider the place a room—it was more like a court-yard with a floor and a ceiling. Ten or fifteen minutes had fallen behind me since I'd arrived at that place. Loiosh said nothing, but I could feel his tension from the grip of his talons on my shoulder.

She was seated on a white throne set on a pedestal, and she was as I remembered her, only more so. Very tall, a face that was somehow indefinably alien, yet hard to look at long enough to really get the details. Each finger had an extra joint on it. Her gown was white, her skin and hair very dark. She seemed to be the only thing in the room, and perhaps she was.

She stood as I approached, then came down from the pedestal. I stopped perhaps ten feet away from her, unsure what sort of obeisances to make, if any. She didn't appear to mind, however. Her voice was low and even, and faintly melodic, and seemed to contain a hint of its own echo. She said, "You called to me."

I cleared my throat. "I was in trouble."

"Yes. It has been some time since we've seen each other."

"Yes." I cleared my throat again. Loiosh was silent. Was I supposed to say, "So how's it been going?" What does one say to one's patron deity?

She said, "Come with me," and led me out through the mist. We stepped into a smaller room, all dark browns, where the chairs were comfortable and there was a fire crackling away and spitting at the hearth. I allowed her to sit first, then we sat like two old friends reminiscing on battles and bottles past. She said, "There is something you could do for me."

"Ah," I said. "That explains it."

"Explains what?"

"I couldn't figure out why a group of sorcerers would be suddenly attacking me in a basement in South Adrilankha."

"And now you think you know?"

"I have an idea."

"What were you doing in this basement?"

I wondered briefly just how much of one's personal life one ought to discuss with one's god, then I said, "It has to do with marital problems." A look of something like amusement flicked over her features, followed by one of inquiry. I said, "My wife has gotten it into her head to join this group of peasant rebels—"

"I know."

I almost asked how, but swallowed it. "Yes. Well, it's complicated, but I

ended up, a few weeks ago, purchasing the Organization interests in South
Adrilankha—where the humans live."

"Yes."

"I've been trying to clean it up. You know, cut down on the ugliest sorts
of things while still leaving it profitable."

"This does not sound easy."

I shrugged. "It keeps me out of trouble."

"Does it?"

"Well, perhaps not entirely."

"But," she prompted, "the basement?"

"I was looking into that house as a possible office for that area. It was
spur-of-the-moment, really; I saw the 'For Rent' sign as I was walking by on
other business—"

"Without bodyguards?"

"My other business was seeing my grandfather. I don't take bodyguards
everywhere I go." This was true; I felt that as long as my movements didn't
become predictable, I should be safe.

"Perhaps this was a mistake."

"Maybe. But you didn't actually have them kill me, just frighten me."

"So you think I arranged it?"

"Yes."

"Why would I do such a thing?"

"Well, according to some of my sources, you are unable to bring mortals
to you or speak with them directly unless they call to you."

"You don't seem angry about it."

"Anger would be futile, wouldn't it?"

"Well, yes, but aren't you accustomed to futile anger?"

I felt something like a dry chuckle attempt to escape my throat. I suppressed it and said, "I'm working on that."

She nodded, fixing me with eyes that I suddenly noticed were pale yellow.
Very strange. I stared back.

"You know, boss, I'm not sure I like her."

"Yeah."

"So," I said, "now that you've got me, what do you want?"

"Only what you do best," she said with a small smile.

I considered this. "You want someone killed?" I'm not normally this direct, but I still wasn't sure how to speak to the goddess. I said, "I, uh, charge extra for gods."

The smile remained fixed on her face. "Don't worry," she said. "I don't want you to kill a god. Only a king."

"Oh, well," I said. "No problem, then."

"Good."

I said, "Goddess—"

"Naturally, you will be paid."

"Goddess—"

"You will have to do without some of your usual resources, I'm afraid, but—"

"Goddess."

"Yes?"

"How did you come to be called 'Demon Goddess,' anyway?"

She smiled at me, but gave no other answer.

"So tell me about the job."

"There is an island to the west of the Empire. It is called Greenaere."

"I know of it. Between Northport and Elde, right?"

"That is correct. There are, perhaps, four hundred thousand people living there. Many are fishermen. There are also orchards of fruit for trade to the mainland, and there is some supply of gemstones, which they also trade."

"Are there Dragaerans?"

"Yes. But they are not imperial subjects. They have no House, so none of them have a link to the Orb. They have a King. It is necessary that he die."

"Why don't you just kill him, then?"

"I have no means of appearing there. The entire island is protected from sorcery, and this protection also prevents me from manifesting myself there."

"Why?"

"You don't have to know."

"Oh."

"And remember that, while you're there, you will be unable to call upon your link to the Orb."

"Why is that?"

"You don't need to know."

"I see. Well, I rarely use sorcery in any case."

"I know. That is one reason I want you to do this. Will you?"

I was briefly tempted to ask why, but that was none of my business. Speaking of business, however—"What's the offer?"

I admit I said this with a touch of irony. I mean, what was I going to do if she didn't want to pay me? Refuse the job? But she said, "What do you usually get?"

"I've never assassinated a King before. Let's call it ten thousand Imperials."

"There are other things I could do for you instead."

"No, thanks. I've heard too many stories about people getting what they wish for. The money will be fine."

"Very well. So you will do it?"

"Sure," I said. "I've got nothing pressing going on just at the moment."

"Good," said the Demon Goddess.

"Is there anything I should know?"

"The King's name is Haro."

"You want him non-revivifiable, I assume?"

"They have no link to the Orb."

"Ah. So that shouldn't be a problem. Ummm, Goddess?"

"Yes?"

"Why me?"

"Why, Vlad," she said, and it was odd to have her call me by my first name. "It is your profession, is it not?"

I sighed. "And here I'd been thinking of getting out of the business."

"Perhaps," she said, "not quite yet." She smiled into my eyes, and her eyes seemed to spin, and then I was once more in the same basement in South Adrilankha. I waited, but there was no sound. I poked my head out quickly, then for a longer time, then I stepped over, picked up my three throwing knives, and walked up the stairs and out of the house. I saw no sign of anyone.

"*M*ELESTAV? *I TOLD YOU to send Kragar in.*"

"*I already did, boss.*"

"*Then where—? Never mind.*" "Say, Krager."

"Hmmm?"

"I'm being called out of town for a while."

"How long?"

"Not sure. A week or two, anyway."

"All right. I can take care of things here."

"Good. And keep tabs on our old friend, Herth."

"Think he might decide to take a shot at you?"

"What do you think?"

"It's possible."

"Right. And I need a teleport for tomorrow afternoon."

"Where to?"

"Northport."

"What's up?"

"Nothing special. I'll tell you about it when I get back."

"I'll just wait to hear who dies in Northport."

"Funny. Actually, though, it isn't Northport, it's Greenaere. What do you know about it?"

"Not much. An island kingdom, not part of the Empire."

"Right. Find out what you can."

"All right. What sorts of things?"

"Size, location of the capital city, that kind of stuff. Maps would be good, both of the island and of the capital city."

"That shouldn't take long. I'll have it by this evening."

"Good. And I don't want anyone to know you're after the information. This job might cause a stir and I don't want to be attached to it."

"Okay. What about South Adrilankha?"

"What about it?"

"Any special instructions?"

"No. You know what I've been doing; keep it going. No need to rush anything."

"Okay. Good luck."

"Thanks."

* * *

I CLIMBED THE STAIRS to my flat slowly, unaccountably feeling like an old man. Loiosh flew over and began necking (quite literally) with his mate, Rocza. Cawti was wearing green today, with a red scarf around her neck that highlighted the few, almost invisible freckles on her nose. Her long brown hair was down and only haphazardly brushed, an effect I rather like. She put down her book, one of Paarfi's "histories," and greeted me without coolness, but without the pretense of great warmth, either. "How was your day?" I asked her.

"All right," she said. What could she say? I wasn't terribly interested in the details of her activities with Kelly and his band of rebels, or nuts, or whatever they were. She said, "Yours?"

"Interesting. I saw Noish-pa."

She smiled for the first time. If we had anything at all in common at that point, it was our love for my grandfather. "What did he say?"

"He's worried about us."

"He believes in family."

"So do I. It's inherited, I suspect."

She smiled again. I could die for that smile. "We should speak to Aliera. Perhaps she's isolated the gene." Then the smile was gone, leaving me looking at the lips that had held it. I looked into her eyes. I always used to look into her eyes when we made love. The moment stretched, and I looked away, sat down facing her. I said, "What are we going to do?" My voice was almost a whisper; you'd never know we had already had this conversation, in various forms, several times.

"I don't know, Vladimir. I *do* love you, but there's so much between us now."

"I could leave the Organization," I said. This wasn't the first time I'd said that.

"Not until and unless you want to for your own reasons, not because I disapprove." It wasn't the first time she'd said that, either. It was ironic, too; she'd once been part of one of the most feared teams of assassins ever to haunt the alleys of Adrilankha.

We were silent for a while, while I tried to decide how to tell her about the rest of the day's events. Finally I said, "I'm going to be leaving for a while."

"Oh?"

"Yeah. A job. Out of town. Across the great salt sea. Out past the horizon. To sail beyond the—"

"When will you be back?"

"I'm not sure. Not more than a week or two, I hope."

"Write when you find work," she said.

Lesson 2

Transportation

I CAN'T TELL YOU much about Northport (which ought to have been called Westport, but never mind) because I didn't really see it. I saw the area near the waterfront, which compared pretty poorly to the waterfront of Adrilankha. It was dirtier and emptier, with fewer inns and more derelicts. It occurred to me in the first few minutes, before I'd even recovered from the teleport, that this was because Adrilankha was still a busy port, whereas Northport had never recovered from Adron's Disaster and the Interregnum.

Yet there were, once or twice a day, ships that left for Elde or returned from there, as well as a few that went up and down the coast. Of the ships leaving for Elde, many stopped at Greenaere, which was more or less on the way, taking tides and winds into account. (Personally I knew nothing about tides or winds, but as I also knew almost nothing about where these islands could be found, I had no trouble believing what I was told.)

In any case, I located a ship in less than an hour and had only a few hours' wait. I had arrived in the early afternoon. We weighed anchor just before dusk.

I sometimes wonder if sailors don't get lessons in how to do strange and confusing things, just to impress the rest of us. There were ten of them, pulling on ropes, tying things, untying things, setting boxes down, and striding purposefully along the deck. The captain introduced herself as Baroness Mul-something-or-other-inics, but the name I caught was Trice, when they didn't call her "Captain." She was stocky for a Dragaeran, with a pinched-in face and an agitated manner. The only other officer was named Yinta, who had a long nose over a wide mouth and always looked like she was half asleep.

The captain welcomed me aboard with no great enthusiasm and a gentle request to "keep your arse out of our way, okay, Whiskers?" Loiosh, riding on my shoulder, generated more interest but no comments. Just as well. The ship was one of those called a "skip"; intended, I'm told, for short ocean jaunts. She was about sixty feet long, and had one mast with two square sails, one with a little triangular sail in front, and a third holding a slightly larger square one in back. I settled down on the deck between a couple of large barrels that smelled of wine. The wind made nice snapping sounds on the sails as they were secured, at which time some ropes were undone and we were pushed away from the dock by a couple of shore hands wielding poles I couldn't have lifted. Shore hands, crew, and officers were all of the House of the Orca. The mast held a flag which showed an orca and a spear and what looked like the tower of a castle or fort.

Before leaving, I had been given a charm against seasickness. I touched it now and was glad it was there. The boat went up and down, although, frankly, not as much as I'd been afraid it would.

"I've never been on one of these before, Loiosh."

"Me, neither, boss. Looks like fun."

"I hope so."

"Better than basements in South Adrilankha."

"I hope so."

In the setting sun, I saw the edge of the harbor. There was more activity among the sailors, and then we were in the open sea. I touched the charm again, wondering if I'd be able to sleep. I made myself as comfortable as I could and tried to think cheery thoughts.

W HEN I THINK OF the House of the Orca, I mostly think of the younger ones, say a hundred or a hundred and fifty years old, and mostly male. When

I was young I'd run into groups of them, hanging around near my father's restaurant being tough and annoying passersby; especially Easterners and especially me. I'd always wondered why it was Orca who did that. Was it just that they spent so much time alone while their family was out on the seas? Had it something to do with the orca itself, swimming around, often in packs, killing anything smaller than itself? Now I know: It was because they ate so much salted kethna.

Please understand, I don't dislike salted kethna. It's tough and rather plain, yes, but not inherently unpleasant. But as I sat in my little box on the *Chorba's Pride*, huddled against the cold morning breeze, and was handed a couple of slabs with a piece of flatbread and a cup of water, I realized that they must eat a great deal of it, and that, well, this could do things to a person. It isn't their fault.

The wind was in my face the next morning as I looked forward, making me wonder how the winds could propel the ship, but I didn't ask. No one seemed especially friendly. I shared the salted kethna with Loiosh, who liked it more than I did. I didn't think about what I was going to do, because there would be no point in doing so. I didn't know enough yet, and empty speculation can lead to preconceptions, which can lead to errors. Instead I studied the water, which was green, and listened to the waves lapping on the sides of the ship and to the conversation of the sailors around me. They swore more than Dragons, although with less imagination.

The man who'd delivered the food stood next to me, staring out into the sea, chewing on his own. I was the last to be fed, apparently. I studied his face. It was old and wrinkled, with eyes very deep set and light blue, which is unusual in a Dragaeran of any kind. He studied the sea with a detached interest, as if communing with it.

I said, "Thanks for the food." He grunted, his eyes not leaving the sea. I said, "Looking for something in particular?"

"No," he said in the clipped accent of the eastern regions of the Empire, making it sound like "new."

There is, indeed, a steady rocking motion to a ship, not unlike my own experience with horses (which I won't detail, if it's all the same to you). But, within the steady motion, no two actions of the ship are precisely the same.

I studied the ocean with my companion for a while and said, "It never stops, does it?"

He looked at me for the first time, but I couldn't read his expression. He turned back to the sea and said, "No, she never stops. She's always the same, and she's always moving. I never get tired of watching her." He nodded to me and moved back toward the rear of the ship. The stern, they call it.

Off to the left, the side I was on, a pair of orca surfaced for a moment, then dived. I kept watching, and it happened again, somewhat closer, then yet a third time. They were sleek and graceful; proud. They were very beautiful.

"Yes, they are," said Yinta, appearing next to me.

I turned and looked at her. "What?"

"They are, indeed, beautiful."

I hadn't realized I'd spoken aloud. I nodded and turned back toward the sea, but they didn't reappear.

Yinta said, "Those were shorttails. Did you notice the white splotches on their backs? When they're young they tend to travel in pairs. Later they'll gather into larger groups."

"Their tails didn't seem especially short," I remarked.

"They weren't. They were both females; the males have shorter tails."

"Why is that?"

She frowned. "It's the way they are."

There were gulls above us, many flying low over the water. I'd been told that this meant we were near land, but I couldn't see any. There were few other signs of life. Such a large body of water, and we were so alone there. The sails were full and made little sound, save for creaking of the boom every now and then in response to a slight turn of ship or wind. Earlier, they had made snapping sounds as the wind changed its mind more quickly about where it wanted us to go and how fast it wanted us to get there. During the night I had become used to the motion of the ship, so now I hardly noticed it.

Greenaere was somewhere ahead. Something like two hundred thousand Dragaerans lived there. It was an island about a hundred and ten miles long, and perhaps thirty miles wide, looking on my map like a banana, with a crooked stem on the near side. The port was located where the stem joined the fruit. The major city, holding maybe a tenth of the population, was about twelve miles inland from the stem. Twelve miles; about half a day's walk, or, according to the notes Kragar had furnished, fifteen hours aboard a pole raft.

The wind changed, sending the boom creaking ponderously over my head. The captain lay on her back, hands behind her head, smoking a short pipe with a sort of umbrella over the top of it, I suppose to keep the spray out. The change in wind direction brought me the brief aroma of burning tobacco, out of place with the sea smells I was now used to. Yinta leaned against the railing.

"You were born to this, weren't you?" I said.

She turned and studied me. Her eyes were grey. "Yes," she said at last. "I was."

"Going to have your own ship, one of these days?"

"Yes."

I turned back to the sea. It seemed smooth, the green waves painted against the orange-red Dragaeran horizon. I understood seascapes. I looked back for the first time, but, of course, the mainland had long since passed from sight.

"Not one of these, though," said Yinta.

I turned back, but she was looking past me, at the endless sea. "What?"

"I won't be captain of one of these. Not a little trading boat."

"What, then?"

"There are stories of whole lands beyond the sea. Or beneath them, some say. Beyond the Maelstrom, where no ships pass. Except that, maybe, some do. The whirlpools aren't constant, you know. And there is always talk of ways around them, even though we have charts that show only the Grey Rocks on one side, and the Spindrift Lands on the other. But there is talk of other ways, of exploring Spindrift and launching a ship from there. Of places that can be reached, where people speak strange languages and have magics of which we've never heard, where even the Orb is powerless."

I said, "I've heard the Orb is powerless in Greenaere."

She shrugged, as if this interested her not at all; nothing as commonplace as Greenaere mattered. Her hair was short and brown and curled tightly, although less so as it became wet in the spray. Her wide Orca face was weathered, so she seemed older than she probably was. The wind changed again, followed by ringing of bells that were tied high on what they called the head stay. I'd asked what that was for just before the boom hit me in the back. Funny people, Orca. This time I ducked, while someone said something about tightening the toesail, or perhaps tying it; I couldn't hear clearly over the creaking of the masts and the splashing of the waves.

I said, "So you'd like to take a ship through this Maelstrom, to see what's on the other side?"

She nodded absently, then grinned suddenly. "To tell you the truth, Easterner, what I'd really like to do is design a ship that can stand up to it. My great-great-uncle was a shipwright. He designed the steerage system for the *Luck of the South Wind,* and served on her before the Interregnum. He was aboard her when the breakwaves hit."

I nodded as if I'd heard of the ship and the "breakwaves." I said, "Have you married?"

"No. Never wanted to. You?"

"Yes."

"Mmmm," she said. "Like it?"

"Sometimes more than other times."

She chuckled knowingly, although I doubt she did know. "Tell me something: Just what are you going to Greenaere for?"

"Business."

"What sort of business has us delivering you as cargo?"

"Does the whole crew know about that?"

"No."

"Good."

"So what sort of business is it?"

"I'd rather not say, if you don't mind."

She shrugged. "Suit yourself. You've paid for our silence; we have no reason to report every passenger to the Empire, and certainly not to the islanders."

I didn't make an answer to this. We spoke no more just then. Currents and hours rolled beneath us. I ate more salted kethna, fed Loiosh, and slept as night collapsed the sea into a small lake which fed waves to the bow of *Chorba's Pride,* who excreted a narrow wake from her stern.

*   *   *

Aʀᴏᴜɴᴅ ɴᴏᴏɴ ᴏꜰ ᴛʜᴇ following day we spotted land, followed by a few scraggly masts from the cove that was our destination. The sky seemed high and very bright, with more red showing, and it was warm and pleasant. The captain, Trice, was sitting up in what I'd learned was called the fly bridge. Yinta was leaning casually against a bulwark near the bow, shouting obscure information back to the captain, who relayed orders to those of the crew who were piloting the thing, or rigging lines, or whatever they were doing.

During a pause in the yelling, I made my way up to Yinta and followed her gaze. "It doesn't look much like the stem of a banana," I remarked.

"What?"

"Never mind."

The captain yelled, "Get a sound," which command Yinta relayed to a dark, stooped sailor, who scurried off to do something or other. Greenaere, whose tip I could see quite well now, seemed to be made of dark grey rock.

I said, "It looks like we're going to miss her." Yinta didn't deign to answer. She relayed some numbers from the sailor to the captain. More commands were given, and, with a creaking of booms as the foresail shifted, we swung directly toward the island, only to continue past until it looked like we'd miss it the other way. It seemed a hell of an inefficient way to travel, but I kept my mouth shut.

"You know, boss, this could get to be fun."

"I was thinking the same thing. But I'd get tired of it, I think, sooner or later."

"Probably. Not enough death."

That rankled a bit. I wondered if there was some truth in it. I could see features of the island now, a few trees and a swath of green behind them that might have been farmland. A place that small, I supposed land would be at a premium.

"A whole island of Teckla," said Loiosh.

"If you want to look at it that way."

"They have no Houses."

"So maybe they're all Jhereg."

That earned a psionic chuckle.

An odd sense of peace began to settle over me that I couldn't figure out. No, not peace, more like quiet—as if a noise that I'd been hearing so constantly I'd come to ignore it had suddenly stopped. I wondered about it, but I had no time to figure it out just then—I had to stay alert to what was going on around me.

There was an abrupt lessening of the wave action on the ship, and we were enclosed in a very large cove. I had seen the masts of larger ships; now I saw the ships themselves—ships too large to pull up to the piers that stuck out from the strip we approached. Closer in, there were many smaller boats, and I thought to myself, *escape route.* In another minute I was able to make out flashes of color from one pier, flashes that came in a peculiar order, as if signals were being given. I looked behind me and saw Yinta now next to the captain on the fly bridge, waving yellow and red flags toward the pier.

The wind was still strong, and the sailors were quite busy taking in sails and loosening large coils of rope. I moved toward the back and wedged myself between the cartons where I'd started the journey.

"All right, Loiosh. Take off, and stay out of trouble until I get there."

"You stay out of trouble, boss; no one's going to notice me." He flew off, and I waited. I saw little of the happenings on the ship, and only heard the sounds of increased activity, until at last the sails seemed to collapse into themselves. This was followed almost at once by a hard thump, and I knew we had arrived.

Everyone was still busy. Ropes were secured, sails were brought in, and crates and boxes were manhandled onto the dock. At one point, there were several workmen on board at the same time, their backs to me. I went below with Yinta, who pointed to an empty crate.

"I'm going to hate this," I said.

"And you're paying for the privilege," she said.

I fitted myself in as best I could. I'd done something like this once before, sneaking into an Athyra's castle in a barrel of wine, but I expected this to be of shorter duration. It was uncomfortable, but not too bad except for the angle at which my neck was bent.

Yinta nailed in the top, then left me alone for what seemed to be much longer than it should have been; long enough for me to consider panicking, but then the crate and I were picked up. As they carried me, I was tempted to shout at them to try to take it easy, since each step made a bruise in a new portion of my anatomy.

"I see you, boss. They're carrying you down the dock now, to a wagon. You've got about three hundred yards of pier . . . okay, here's the wagon."

They weren't gentle. I kept the curses to myself.

"Okay, boss. Everything looks good. Wait until they finish loading it."

I'll skip most of this, okay? I waited, and they hauled me away and unloaded me in what Loiosh said was one of a row of sheds a few hundred feet from the dock. I sat in there for a couple of hours, until Loiosh told me that everyone seemed to have left, then I smashed my way out; which is easier to say than it was to do. The door to the shed was not locked, however, so once my legs worked, it was no problem to leave the shed.

It was still daylight, but not by much. Loiosh landed on my shoulder. *"This way, boss. I've found a place to hide until nightfall."*

"Lead on," I said, and he did, and soon I was settled in a ditch in a maize field, surrounded by a copse of trees. No one had noticed me coming in. Getting out, I suspected, was going to be more difficult.

THIS PARTICULAR BIT OF island was heavily farmed; very heavily compared to Dragaera. I wasn't used to a road that cut through farmland as if there were no other place for it to run. I wanted to be off the main road, too, so I wouldn't be so conspicuous, which left me walking parallel to the road about half a mile from it, through fields of brown dirt with little shoots of something or other poking out of them and feeding various sorts of birdlife. Loiosh chased a few of the birds just for fun. The houses were small huts built with dark green clapboard. The roofs seemed to be made of long shoots that went from the ground on one side to the ground on the other. They didn't look as if they would keep the rain out, but I didn't examine them closely. The land itself consisted of gentle slopes; I was always going either uphill or down, but never very much. The terrain made travel slow, and it was more tiring than I'd have thought, but I was in no hurry so I rested fairly often. The breeze from the ocean was at my back, a bit cold, a bit tangy; not unpleasant.

A few trees began to appear on both sides of the road; trees with odd off-white bark, high branches, and almost round leaves. They grew more frequent and were joined by occasional samples of more familiar oak and rednut, until I was walking in woods rather than farmlands. I wondered if this area would be cleared someday, when the islanders needed more land. Would they ever? How much farming did they do, compared to fishing? Who cared? I kept walking, checking my map every now and then just to make sure.

We stayed to the side as we walked. We caught glimpses of travelers on the road, mostly on foot, a few riding on ox-drawn wagons with wheels with square bracing. Birds sang tunes I'd never heard before. The sky above was the same continuous overcast of the Empire, but it seemed higher, as it were, and it looked like there could be times here when the sky was clear, as it was in the East.

It was late afternoon when another road joined the one we paralleled. I found the road on the map, which told me the city was near, and the map was right. It wasn't much of a city by Dragaeran standards, and was quite strange by Eastern standards. There were patches of cottage here and there: structures made of canvas on wooden frames, or even stone frames, which seemed very odd; and a couple of structures, open on two sides with tables in front of them, that could be places of worship or something else entirely. I never did find out. It looked like the sort of town that would be empty at night. Maybe it was; now was not the time to check. There weren't many people near us, in any case.

I hid in a garbage pit while Loiosh flew around and found me a better hiding place, and a safe path to it. Loiosh did some more exploring, and found one grey stone building, three stories high, set back from the road and surrounded by a small garden. There were no walls around the garden, and a path of stones and shells of various bright colors led to the unimposing doorway. It matched the location of the Palace, and the description we'd been given for it. There you have it.

Lesson 3

The Perfect Assassination

THERE ARE MILLIONS OF ways for people to die, if you number each vital organ, each way it can fail, all of the poisons from the earth and the sea which can cause these failures, all the diseases to which a man, Dragaeran or human, is subject, all the animals, all the tricks of nature, all the mischances from daily life, and all the ways of killing on purpose. In fact, looked at this way, it is odd that an assassin is ever called upon, or that anyone lives long enough to accomplish anything. Yet the Dragaerans, who expect to live two thousand years or more, generally do not die until their bodies fail, weak with age, just as we do, though not quite so soon.

But never mind that. I had taken the task of seeing to it that a particular person died, and that meant that I couldn't just take the chance of him choking on a fish bone, I had to make sure he died. All right. There are thousands of ways to kill a man deliberately, if you number each sorcery spell, each means of dispensing every poison, each curse a witch can throw, each means of arranging an accidental death, each blow from every sort of weapon.

I've never made a serious study of poisons, accidents are complicated and tricky to arrange, sorcery is too easy to defend against, and the arts of the witch are unpredictable at best, so let us limit discussion to means of killing by the blade. There are still hundreds of possibilities, some easier but less reliable, some certain but difficult to arrange. For example, cutting someone's throat is relatively easy, and certainly fatal, but it will be some seconds before the individual goes into shock. Are you certain he isn't a sorcerer skilled enough to heal himself? Getting the heart will actually produce shock more quickly, but it is harder to hit, with all those ribs in the way.

There are other complications, too: such as, does he have friends who could revivify him? If so, do you want to allow this, or do you have to make sure the wound is not only fatal but impossible to repair after death? If so, you probably want to destroy his brain, or at least his spine. Of course, you can do this after your victim is dead or helpless, but those few seconds can make the difference between getting away and being spotted. As long as the Empire is so fussy about under what circumstances one is allowed to do away with another, not being spotted will remain an important consideration. You do the job, then you get away from there, ideally without teleporting, because you're helpless during the two or three seconds while the teleport is taking place, and you can be not only identified but even traced if you get really unlucky.

So the key is to make sure all the factors are on your side: You know your victim's routine, you have the weapon ready, and you know exactly where you're going to do it and where you're going to go and how you're going to dispose of the murder weapon after you're done.

You'll notice that these methods have little in common with wandering into a strange kingdom, with no knowledge of the culture or the physical layout, and trying to kill someone whose features you don't even know, much less what sort of physical, magical, or divine protection he might have.

It was still fully night, and the darkness here was considerably darker than in Adrilankha, where there were always a few lights spilling out onto the street from inn doors or the higher windows of flats, or the lanterns of the Phoenix Guards as they made their rounds. In the East there might be a few stars—twinkling points of light that can't be seen in the Empire because they are higher than the orange-red overcast. But here, nothing, save for the tiniest sparkles that came from curtained windows high in the Palace, and a thin line from the doorway in the front. We waited there, at the edge of the city, for several long, dull hours. Four Dragaerans left the building, all holding lanterns, and one arrived. The light on the third story of the Palace went out, and we waited another hour. I wondered what time it was, but dared not do anything even as simple as reaching out to the Orb.

We returned to our hiding place before dawn. I spent most of the day sleeping, while Loiosh made sure I wasn't disturbed, scrounged for food to supplement the salted kethna, and observed the Palace and the city for me. Yes, the town was pretty much deserted at night.

After dark had fallen, I went in to town and got a better picture of the Palace and looked for guards. There weren't any that I could see. I checked the place over for windows, found a few, and then looked for various possible escape routes. This was starting to look like it might be easier than I had thought, but I know better than to get cocky.

The next night I moved into town once more, this time to sneak into the Palace so I could get the layout of the place. I sent Loiosh to look around the building once, just in case there was something interesting that he could hear or see. He returned and reported no open windows with rope ladders descending, no large doors with signs saying, "Assassins enter here," and no guards. He took his place on my shoulder and I stepped up to the door. I'm used to casting a small and easy spell at such times, to see if there is any protection on the door, but Verra had said it wouldn't work, and for all I knew it might even alert someone.

This was the first time I'd ever gone into someone's house in order to kill him. In the Organization you don't do that. But this guy wasn't in the Organization. Come to think of it, this was also the first time I'd shined someone who wasn't one of us. It felt, all in all, distinctly odd. I gently pulled on the doors. They weren't locked. They groaned quietly, but didn't squeak. It was completely dark inside, too. I risked half a step forward, didn't stumble across anything, and carefully shut the door behind me. It felt like a large room, though by what sense I knew that I couldn't say.

"Loiosh, this whole job stinks."

"Right, boss."

"Is there anyone in the room?"

"No."

"I'm going to risk some light."

"Good."

I took a six-inch length of lightrope from my cloak and set it twirling slowly. Even that dim light was painful for a moment, as it lit up about a seven-foot area. I set it going a little faster and saw that the room wasn't as big as I'd thought at first. It looked more like the entry room of a well-to-do merchant than a royal household. There were hooks on the wall for hanging coats, and even a place by the door with a couple of pairs of boots, for the love of demons. I kept looking, and saw a single exit, straight ahead of me. I slowed the lightrope and went through the doorway.

I had the feeling that, in normal daylight, this place wouldn't have been at all frightening, but it wasn't daylight, and I wasn't familiar with it, and half-forgotten fragments of the Paths of the Dead came back to haunt me as I gradually increased the speed of the lightrope.

"Can this place really be as undefended as it seems, boss?"

"Maybe." But I wondered, if these people were so unwarlike, why their King had to die. None of my business. I moved slowly and kept the light as dim as possible. Loiosh strained to catch the psychic trace of anyone who might be awake as we explored room after room. There was one room that seemed quite large, and in the Empire would have been a sitting room of some sort, but there was a large carved orca on one of the walls, with a motto in a language I couldn't read, and in front of the carving, which seemed to be of gold and coral, was a chair that was maybe a little more plush than the rest. The ceiling was about fifteen feet over my head. Assuming the other two stories to be slightly smaller, that agreed with my estimate of the total height of the building. There was some sort of thin paneling against the stone, and parts of it had been painted on, mostly in blues, with thin strokes. I couldn't make out the designs, but they seemed to be more patterns and shapes than pictures. Possibly they were magical patterns of some sort, though I didn't feel anything in them.

I made more light and studied the room fairly carefully, noting the line from that chair to the doorway, the single large window with carvings in the frame that I couldn't make out, the position of the three service trays, which appeared to be of gold. There was a vase on a stand in a corner, and flowers in it that seemed to be red and yellow, but I couldn't be certain. And so on. I passed on to the next room, still being totally silent. I can do that, you know.

The kitchen was large but undistinguished. Plenty of work space, a little low on storage space. I would have enjoyed cooking there, I think. The knives had been well cared for and most of them seemed to be of good workmanship. The cooking pots were either very large or very small, and there was plenty of wood next to the stove. The chimney ran from it out of the wall behind it to the outside. The opposite wall held a sink with a hand pump that gleamed in the dim light I was making. Whose job was it to polish it?

And so on. I went through every room, convinced myself there wasn't a basement, and decided against trying the upstairs. Then I went back out into a chilly breeze full of the salt water and dead fish, and circled the place again, this time without a light. I didn't learn much except that it is difficult to remain silent while stumbling over garden tools. By the time I returned to my hiding place, dawn was only an hour or so away. There was now enough light in the east so that I could almost see, so Loiosh and I used the time to look for a place near the Palace where we could hide. To turn an hour-long search into a sentence, we didn't find one. We left the town and walked off the main roads until we were well into a thicket that seemed safe enough. It was still chilly, but would warm up soon. I pulled my cloak tightly around me and eventually drifted off into something that passed for sleep.

I awoke late in the afternoon.

"We going to do it today, boss?"

"No. But if all goes well today, we'll do it tomorrow."

"We're almost out of salted kethna."

"Good. I'm beginning to think I'd rather starve."

Loiosh was right, however. I ate some of what was left and sneaked up to the edge of town. Yes, the Palace did seem to be completely unprotected. I could probably have gone in right then and done it if I'd known for certain where the King was. I crept a little closer, staying hidden behind a rotting, collapsed fruit stall that had been tossed aside some years before.

The sky had just begun to darken, and I decided this would be about the right time of day to do it; when there was enough light so I could still see, but when the approaching night would shield my escape. I consulted the notes I'd made about entry points and the layout of the Palace, and figured that today I'd make a test run: doing everything I could to try things out.

Getting inside was easy, since the kitchen staff didn't lock the service door, and there was no one in the kitchen after the evening meal. I listened for a long time before proceeding down the hall and into the narrow aperture below the stairs. It was nerve-racking waiting there, hearing footsteps and bits of the servants' conversation.

After half an hour I found the right time: when the king left his dining hall to go upstairs. I saw him walk by: a slinky-looking fellow, moderately old, with plastered-down hair and bright green eyes. He was dressed fairly simply, in red and yellow robes, and bore no marks of office except a heavy chain around his neck engraved with one of the symbols I'd seen in his throne room, or audience chamber, or whatever it was. He was walking with a young fellow who carried a short spear over his shoulder. I could have taken them both, but one reason I'm still alive is that I'm always very careful when my own life is on the line.

They walked by, as I said, right in front of me, not able to see me in the dark stairwell. As they were walking up the stairs over my head, I tested my escape route back through the kitchen and out, around the Palace, and back to my hiding place.

"*Well, how does it look, boss?*"

"*Everything seems fine, Loiosh. Tomorrow we do it.*"

I spent the rest of the night memorizing landmarks in the dark so I could get as far away as possible, and, as the sky was just beginning to get light, I pulled my cloak around me and slept.

O<small>NCE UPON A</small> D<small>RAGAEREN</small> time, they say, there was a Serioli smith who, at the request of the gods, built a chain of diamonds that was so long it went up past the top of the sky, and so strong the gods used it to hold the sky up when they got tired of the job. One day one of the gods took a diamond as the wedding price for a mortal she had a hankering for, and all the other diamonds went flying about the heavens, and the gods have been holding the sky up ever since. They couldn't punish the goddess who did the deed, because if they did, the sky would fall, so instead they took it out on the smith, turning him into a chreotha to walk the woods and, well, you get the idea.

I mention this because it came to mind as I sat in the woods, trying to stay alert for anyone coming near me and considering that the only reason I was on that island was that my personal goddess had sent me there. It also occurred to me again that this would be the first time I'd ever killed someone outside the Organization. Coming as it did just while I was going through the sort of moral crisis an assassin has no business having, I didn't like it much. It began to start bothering me that I was taking life for money. Why, I'm not sure.

Or maybe I am, now that I think about it, from the perspective of the other side of the ocean (metaphorically). I think everyone knows someone whose opinions especially matter to him. That is, there's this person whose image lives in the back of your head, and you sometimes find yourself saying, "Would he approve of this?" And if the answer is no, you get a kind of queasy feeling when you do it. In my case, it wasn't my wife, actually, although it hurt badly when she, in the course of two years, went from a skilled assassin to a politico with a save-the-downtrodden complex as big as my ego. No, it was my paternal grandfather. I'd suspected for a long time that he didn't approve of assassination, but in a moment of weakness I'd made the mistake of asking him directly, and he'd told me, just as all the rest of this nonsense was going on, and all of a sudden I was unsure about things that had been basic up until then.

Where did this leave me? Hiding in a thicket on a strange island and figuring how to take the life of someone I didn't know, someone who wasn't in the Organization and subject to its laws, all because my goddess told me to. We humans believe that what a god tells you to do is, by definition, the right thing. Dragaerans have no such ideas. I was a human who'd been brought up in Dragaeran society, and it made for much discomfort.

I pulled a blade of grass and chewed it. The trees in front of me bent uniformly to the right, as if from years of wind. Their bark was smooth, an unusual effect, and there were no branches on the lower fifteen or twenty feet, after which they erupted like mushrooms, full of thick green leaves that whispered as the wind stirred them. Behind me were typical cloin-burrs, about my height, bunched up like they were having a conversation, their reedy bodies standing on those silly exposed roots as if they were about to turn and walk away. Cawti had a gown made of cloin-burr thread. She'd pulled the thread herself, finding a whole grove in late summer, just when they were turning from pale green to crimson, so the gown, a sweeping, flowing thing, with white lace about the shoulder, starts as a mild green at the bottom and burns like fire where it meets at her throat. The first time I took her to Valabar's, she wore that gown with a white gem as the clasp.

I spat out the blade of grass and found another as I waited for sunset, when I could walk down the streets unnoticed. When that time came, I still hesitated, undecided, until Loiosh, my companion and familiar, spoke into my mind from his perch on my right shoulder.

"Look, boss, are you really going to explain to Verra that you had a sudden attack of conscience, so she's going to have to find someone else to shine the bum?"

I started a small fire with the bark of the trees, which turned out to burn very well, and in it I destroyed the notes I'd made. I put the fire out and scattered the ashes, then I removed a dagger from under my left arm, tested the point and edge, and made my way into town.

THERE WAS THE BLOOD of a king on the back of my right hand as I stepped out of the Palace and ducked around behind it. The few moments after the assassination are the most dangerous time, and this whole job was flaky enough already that I very badly didn't want to make any mistakes. It was early evening and would be full dark in less than an hour. Even as it was, I didn't think I'd stand out very much. I ducked behind a large wooden frame that I'd picked out earlier, and I still didn't allow myself to break into a run. I walked steadily toward the edge of town. I wrapped the knife, red with the King's blood, in a piece of cloth and stuck it in my cloak.

Loiosh had stayed outside, above the Palace, and was still flying around nearby.

"Any pursuit?"

"None, boss. Quite a bit of excitement. They're looking around for you, but they don't seem very efficient."

"Good. Anyone looking at the ground? Any signs of spells or rituals?"

"No, and no. Nothing but a lot of running around and—wait. Someone's just come out and—yeah, he's sending people off in various directions. No one going the right way."

"How many toward the dock?"

"Four."

"All right. Come back."

A minute or two later he landed on my right shoulder.

"You hanging on to the knife, boss?"

"If they catch me, the knife won't matter. I don't want to leave it lying around, because they might have witches."

"The sea?"

"Right."

Once I was well away from the city, I began to jog. This was a part of the escape plan I wasn't too happy with, but I hadn't been able to come up with anything better. I try to stay in shape, but I carry several pounds of hardware around with me, not to mention a rapier in a sheath that reaches almost to the ground and is not designed to be run with. I jogged for a while, then walked quickly, then jogged some more. A small stream met up with me, and I splashed through it for a while, and when we said our good-byes my feet were still dry; miracle provided by darrskin boots and chreotha oil.

All I had to do was get to the dock area before morning, grab one of the small boats, and sail it far enough out to sea that I could teleport. One of the interesting things was that I didn't know how far out that was, so if I was seen and pursued it could get tricky. As I figured it, though, I'd be there at least two hours before dawn. The trick was to get there well ahead of those who'd set out after me, and they were on the road. If they beat me there, and I found the dock was guarded, I'd have to hide and wait for a chance.

"There's someone around, boss. Wait. More than one. Close. We'd better—"

Something knocked into me and I suddenly realized I was lying down on my back, and then I realized I couldn't move my left shoulder, and I started to hurt. There was a roundish rock next to me, which I deduced someone had thrown at me. I lay there, hurting, until Loiosh said, *"Boss. Here they come!"*

I usually have a pretty good memory for fights, because my grandfather trained me to remember all of our practice sessions so we could go over them later to discuss my mistakes, but this one is largely a blur. I remember feeling a certain cold precision as Loiosh flew into the face of a woman dressed in light clothing of a tan color, and I noted that I could forget her for a while. I think I was already standing by then. I don't remember getting to my feet, but I know I rolled around on the ground for a while first to avoid giving them a target.

Somewhere, way back, I noticed that drawing my sword hurt quite a bit, and I remember nicking a very tall thin woman on the wrist, and poking a man in the kneecap, and spinning, and feeling dizzy. The short spear seemed to be the standard weapon, and one bald guy with amazing blue eyes, a potbelly, and great strong arms got lined up for a good thrust at my chest, which I parried easily. My automatic reaction was to nail him with a dagger, but when I tried to draw it with my left hand, nothing happened, so I slashed at his face, connected, and kept spinning.

There were three or four times when Loiosh told me to duck and I did. Loiosh and I had gotten good at this sort of thing. None of my attackers said much, except one called out, "Get the jhereg, he's warning him," and I remember being impressed that she'd figured it out. The whole fight, four of them against Loiosh and me, couldn't have lasted as long as it seemed to. Or maybe it did. I tried to keep moving so they'd get in each other's way, and that worked, and I finally got the potbellied guy a good one, straight through the heart, and he went down.

I don't know if he took my sword with him, or if I let go, but I think it was right after that I drew a dagger and dived at one of the spears. That time the man, wearing a broad leather belt from which a long horn was suspended, was too startled to keep his spear up. He backed up and fell, and I don't remember what happened next but I think I took him then and there, because later I found the dagger still in his neck.

I suspect I picked up his spear, because I remember throwing it and missing just as Loiosh told me to duck, and then there was a burning pain low in my back, to the right, and I thought, "I've had it." There was a scream behind me at almost the same moment and I mentally marked one up for Loiosh. I realized I was on my knees, and thought, "This won't do at all," as the tall woman charged straight at me.

I don't know what happened to her, because the next clear memory I have is of lying on my back as the other woman, the one in tan, stood over me holding her spear, with Loiosh attached to the side of her face. She had a dazed look in her eyes. Jhereg poison isn't the most deadly I know of, but it will get the job done, and he was giving her a lot. She tried to nail me with her spear, but I rolled away, although I'm not certain how. She took a step to follow me, but then she just sort of sighed and collapsed.

I lay there, breathing very hard, and raised my head. The tall woman was crumbled against a tree, still breathing, but with her own spear sticking out of her abdomen. I have no idea how I managed that. Her eyes were open, and she was staring at me. She tried to speak, but blood came from her mouth. Presently her breathing stopped and a shudder ran through her body.

"*We took 'em, Loiosh. All four of 'em. We took 'em.*"

"*Yeah, boss. I know.*"

I crawled over to the remains of the nearest one, the woman Loiosh had killed, and ripped at her clothing until I had enough cloth to cover the wound on my back. Getting at it hurt like—well, it hurt. I turned over and lay on it, hoping the pressure would stop the bleeding.

I got dizzy, but I didn't pass out, and after what must have been an hour I began the process of finding out if I could sit up. There were jhereg circling overhead, which might or might not lead someone to this place. Loiosh offered to get rid of them for me, but I didn't want him to leave. In any case, I needed to be away from there.

I managed to stand, which was hard, and I didn't scream, which was harder. I took a few items from my pouch of witchcraft supplies, such as kelsch leaves for energy, and a foul-tasting concoction made from moldy bread, and a powder made from kineera, oil of cloves, and comfrey. I wrapped this in more of my enemy's clothing, got it wet from my canteen, and managed to replace the cloth on my back with it. The bleeding had somehow stopped, but taking the cloth away started it again, and it hurt a lot. I took some more kineera, my last, and mixed it with oil of wormwood, more clove oil, corfina, and ground-up pine needles, got it all wet in more cloth from Loiosh's victim, and put this against my shoulder.

I spat out the kelsch leaf, decided chewing another one would probably kill me, and struggled to my feet. The cloth on my back slipped, so I had to place it again and fasten it with blue eyes' belt. I held the other one in place, gritted my teeth, and quickly, heh, plodded through the forest.

I must have made it a hundred yards before I got dizzy and had to sit down. After a few minutes I tried again and got maybe a little further. I sat there and caught up on my cursing, decided on another kelsch leaf, after all. It worked, I guess, because I think I made it most of a mile before I had to stop again.

"*Loiosh, what direction are we going?*"

"*Still toward the docks, boss. I'd have told you if you were going wrong.*"

"*Oh. Good.*"

I didn't say anything else, because even that seemed to drain me. I stumbled to my feet and resumed my brisk trudge. Every step was—but no, I don't want to think about it and you don't want to hear about it. We were less than three miles from the scene of the fight, perhaps five miles from the dock, when Loiosh said, "*There's someone up ahead, boss.*"

"Oh," I said. "*Can I die now?*"

"*No.*"

I sighed. "*How far?*"

"*About a hundred feet.*"

I stopped where I was and pulled myself behind a large tree. "*Is there some reason why you just noticed him, Loiosh?*"

"*I don't know. These people don't have much psychic energy. Maybe—he's gone.*"

"*I don't feel a teleport.*"

"*Got me, boss. He just—what's that?*"

"That" was a sound, like a low droning, gradually building in pitch. We stood listening. Were there waves, pulses within it? I wasn't sure. The tree had odd, pale green bark, and it was smooth against my cheek. Yes, there were pulses within the droning, a delicate suggestion of rhythm.

"*It's sort of hypnotic, boss.*"

"*Yes. Let's take a look.*"

"*Eh? Why? We don't want to be seen around here, do we?*"

"*If he's looking for me, we can't avoid him. If not—do you really think I'm going to be able to make it all the way to the shore? Not to mention operating a Verra-be-damned boat when I get there?*"

"*Oh. What are you going to do?*"

"*I don't know. Maybe kill him and steal whatever he has that's useful.*"

"*Do you think you're up to killing him?*"

"*Maybe.*"

He sat in a small dip in the fields, his legs drawn up under him, his back perfectly straight, yet he seemed relaxed. His eyes were open and looking more or less in our direction, but he didn't appear to see us as we approached. I couldn't guess his House; he seemed as pale as a Tiassa, as thin and gangly as an Athyra, with the slanted eyes and pointed ears of a Dzur. His facial structure, high cheekbones and pointed chin, could have been Dragon, or perhaps Phoenix. His hair was light brown, appearing darker in contrast to his skin. He wore baggy pants of dark brown, sandals, and a sort of blue vest with fringes. A large black jewel hung on a chain around his neck. I didn't think he'd be allowed into the Battles Club unless he found some other footgear.

He held a strange, round device, perhaps two feet in diameter, under his left arm. "*It's a drum, boss. Notice the skin across it?*"

"*Yes. Made out of shell, I think. I suspect he's harmless. We can ask for help, or we can kill him. Any other ideas?*"

"*Boss, I don't think you can take him in your condition.*"

"*If I can catch him when he's not expecting it —*"

The stranger stopped what he was doing, quite abruptly, and his eyes focused on us. He looked down at the drum and adjusted one of the leather cords that were sewn onto the head and appeared stretched all the way around the drum. He tapped the head with a beater of some sort, creating a rich and surprisingly musical tone. He frowned and adjusted another strap, struck the head again, and seemed satisfied. I hadn't heard any difference between the two tones.

"Good afternoon," I managed.

He nodded and gave me a vague smile. He looked at Loiosh, then back at his drum. He struck it again, very lightly, then louder.

"It sounds good," I ventured, my breath coming in gasps.

His eyes widened, but the expression seemed to mean something other than surprise, I don't know what. He spoke for the first time, his voice quiet and pitched rather high. "Are you from the mainland?"

"Yes. We're visiting." He nodded. I looked around for something else to talk about while I figured out what to do. I said, "What do you call that thing?"

"On the island," he said, "we call this a *drum*."

"Good name for it," I told him. Then I stumbled forward a few steps and collapsed.

I SAW THE TOPS of trees, swaying in a light wind. It smelled like morning, and I hurt everywhere.

"*Boss?*"

"*Hey, chum. Where are we?*"

"*Still here. With that drummer guy. Can you eat again?*"

"*Drummer guy? Oh, right. I remember. What do you mean 'again'?*"

"*He's fed you three times since you collapsed. You don't remember?*"

I thought about it, decided I didn't. "*How long have we been here?*"

"*A little more than a day.*"

"*Oh. They haven't found us?*"

"*No one's come close.*"

"*Odd. I'd have thought I left a trail a nymph jhegaala could follow.*"

"*Maybe they haven't found the bodies.*"

"*That can't last long. We should move.*"

I sat up slowly. The drummer looked at me, nodded, and went back to whatever it was he'd been doing when we got there. He said, "I changed your dressing again."

"Thanks. I'm in your debt."

He went back to concentrating on his drum.

I tried to stand up, decided early on in the process that it was a mistake, and relaxed. I took a couple of deep breaths, letting tension out of my body. I wondered how long it would be until I could walk. Hours? Days? If it was days, I might as well roll over and die right now.

I discovered I was very thirsty and said so. He handed me a flask which turned out to contain odd-tasting water. He tapped his drum again. I lay back against the tree and rested, my ears straining for sounds of pursuit. After a while he put a kettle on the fire, and a bit after that we had a rather bland soup that was probably good for me. As we drank it, I said, "My name is Vlad."

"Aibynn," he said. "How did you come to be injured?"

"Some of your compatriots don't take to strangers. Provincialism. There's no help for it."

He gave me a look I couldn't interpret, then he grinned. "We don't often see anyone from the mainland here, especially dwarfs."

Dwarfs? "Special circumstances," I said. "Couldn't be prevented. Why did you help me?"

"I've never seen anyone with a tame jhereg before."

"Tame?"

"Shut up, Loiosh."

To Aibynn I said, "I'm glad you were here, anyway."

He nodded. "It's a good place to work. You aren't bothered much—what's that?"

I sighed. "Sounds like someone's coming," I said.

He looked at me, his face blank. Then he said, "Do you think you can climb a tree?"

I licked my lips. "Maybe."

"You won't leave a trail that way."

"If they see a trail leading here, and not away, won't they ask questions?"

"Probably."

"Well?"

"I'll answer them."

I studied him. *"What do you think, Loiosh?"*

"Sounds like the best chance we're going to get."

"Yeah."

I could, indeed, climb a tree. It hurt a lot, but other than that it wasn't difficult. I stopped when I heard sounds from below, and Loiosh gave me a warning simultaneously. I couldn't see the ground, which gave me good reason to hope they couldn't see me. There was no breeze, and the smoke from the fire was coming up into my face. As long as it didn't get strong enough to make me cough, that would also help keep me hidden.

"Good day be with you," said someone male, with a voice like a grayswan in heat.

"And you," said Aibynn. I could hear them very well. Then I could hear drumming.

"Excuse me—" said grayswan.

"What have you done?" asked Aibynn.

"I mean, for disturbing you."

"Ah. You haven't disturbed me."

More drumming. I wanted to laugh but held it in.

"We are looking for a stranger. A dwarf."

The drumming stopped. "Try the mainland."

Grayswan made a sound I couldn't interpret, and there were mutterings I couldn't make out from his companions. Then someone else, a woman whose voice was as low as a musk owl's call, said, "We are tracking him. How long have you been here?"

"All my life," said Aibynn with a touch of sadness.

"Today, you idiot!" said grayswan.

"At least," agreed my friend.

Someone else, a man with a voice that sounded like a man's voice, said, "His tracks lead to this spot. Have you seen him?"

"I might have missed him," said Aibynn. "I'm tuning my drum, you see, and it requires concentration."

Grayswan demanded, "You mean he could have walked right by you? Cril and Sandy, look around. See if you can find any tracks leaving." There came the sound of feet moving near the base of the tree. I remained very still, not even waving the smoke away from my face; it wasn't very thick, anyway.

Aibynn said, "This part of preparing the drum is very difficult. I must—"

Musk owl said, "You're Aibynn of Lowporch, aren't you?"

"Why, yes."

"I heard you drum at the Winter Festival. You're very good."

"Thank you."

"That's a new drum you're making?"

Grayswan: "We don't have time to—"

Aibynn: "Why, yes. This is the shell of the sweetclam. The head is made from the skin of a nyth, as big a one as you can find. The beater is made from the jawbone, wrapped in nythskin and cloth. To prepare the head, you make a fire of langwood, and season the fire with rednut shells, drownweeds, clove, dreamgrass, silkbuds, the roots of the trapvine—"

Another voice, a man's I hadn't heard before, said, "Nothing. He must be around here somewhere."

Aibynn said, "This one is almost done. I'm just tuning it. You can also change the pitch when you play it. This knob, you see, I hold in my left hand, and when I turn it this way the head becomes tighter and the tone rises. This way lowers the pitch." He demonstrated.

"I see," said musk owl.

Grayswan said, "Look, this dwarf has killed four of the King's guards, and we have every reason to think he—"

Aibynn continued demonstrating. The sound produced by the drum was a single smooth pulse, out of which rhythms began to emerge. I noticed an odd, sweet smell drifting up to me, probably from the treatment he had given the drumhead. The pulsing became more and more complex, and I began to hear beats within it, and I became more aware of the variations in tone. The sweet smell grew stronger. As he played, he said, "You have to play the drum for a few hours after it's seasoned, to allow the head to work into the shell." His voice wove in and out of the pulses, the rhythms, sometimes riding high above them, sometimes supporting them from beneath, and I wondered idly if it was changing pitch and tone or if the drum was, and were those voices mixed in with it? "Then the straps must be moistened with an emulsion made from the sap of a teardrop elm . . . they will respond to long pulses and slow pulses . . . so the rhythm emerges from the drum itself . . . the Lecuda calls the dance, or the spell, which is really the same . . . some of the oldest drums sound the best because the shell itself begins to absorb the sound, so after many years . . . the last time I tried one of those, I had borrowed a drum. . . ."

Loiosh said, *"Boss, did he say dreamgrass? Boss?"*

Then I felt like lying down, then I was falling, and felt like I was passing right through the branches without touching them. I heard someone say, "Look!" but I don't remember hitting the ground.

Lesson 4

Handling Interrogation

To a Dzurlord, civilized means adhering to proper customs of dueling. To a Dragonlord, civilized means conforming to all the social niceties of mass mayhem. To a Yendi, civilized means making sure no one ever knows exactly what you're up to. In the land of my ancestors, civilized means never drinking a red wine at more than fifty-five or less than fifty degrees. The islands had their own notions of civilization, and I decided I liked them.

"We're civilized here, Jhereg," said my interrogator, beneath brows you could have planted maize in. "We do not beat or torture our prisoners."

Of all the responses that sprang to mind, I decided the quick nod would be safest. His mouth twitched, and I wondered if I'd get to know him well enough to know what that indicated.

"On the other hand," he continued, "you can probably expect to be executed."

On reflection, his brows weren't all that bushy; they just seemed that way because of his high, hairless forehead. He looked more like an Athyra than anything else, and acted a bit like one, too: cold, intellectual, and distant. "Executed for what?" I said.

He ignored this. We both knew for what, and if I didn't want to admit it, that was my concern. He said, "I am assuming that you are either a paid assassin or are fanatically loyal to some person, entity, or cause. It is possible that if you cooperate with us by revealing all of the circumstances which led you to take this action, you may live. Unlikely, but possible." He spoke a lot like Morrolan, a friend of mine you'll meet later.

I started in on another protestation of innocence but he gestured me to silence. "Think it over," he said, and stood up slowly. "We can give you some time to think, but not a great deal. I'll be back." He left me alone again.

Of what shall I tell you now? Time, place, or circumstance? Time, then. I'd been there three days, during which I'd been attended by various persons concerned about my health, and this was the first day I'd been able to walk the six or so steps to the slop bucket in the corner without leaning on the walls all the way. That was about the most I could do, but I was proud of it.

I could tell day from night because I could almost see the outside through a narrow window about eight feet up the brick wall. There were thick horizontal bars across the window, which I suspected had been added after the place was built—perhaps very recently, like three days ago. I noted it as a possible weakness. I didn't think the room had been originally designed to hold prisoners, but it worked. The door was very thick and, from what I could hear before it was opened, had an iron bar across it on the outside. There was a cot that was longer than it had to be, made of something soft that rustled in my ears whenever I moved. I had been given a tan-colored shapeless robe of some animal skin. I didn't know if it was their custom to remove clothing from prisoners, or if they had found so many weapons in my clothing that they'd deduced—correctly—that they'd never be able to find them all. I was also barefoot, which I've never liked, even as a kid.

I got two meals a day. The first I'm still blurry on. The second was a fish stew that was completely flavorless except for too much salt. The next was some sort of mush that tasted better than it looked, but only a little. The one after that was a squid dish that a good cook could have done fine things with. The latest one, the remains of which were on a wooden plate on the floor next to me, involved boiled vegetables and a bit of fish with a loaf of coarse, dark bread. The bread was actually pretty good.

Twice now, I had tried small spells to heal myself, but nothing had happened. This was very odd. It was one thing if they had means to cut off my access to the Orb, but witchcraft is a matter of skill and one's innate psychic energy; I didn't see any way to cut someone off from that.

On the other hand, I remembered Loiosh commenting that people around here seemed to be psionically invisible to him, which also wasn't normal, and might be related. I had also tried a few times to reach Morrolan and Sethra, but got nowhere; I wasn't certain if that was a matter of distance or something else.

Loiosh hadn't been in touch with me the entire time. I very much wanted to know if he was all right. I had the feeling that if anything had happened to him I'd know, but I'd never been out of touch with him for this long before.

To take my mind off this, I went over the conversation I'd just had with the something-or-other of the Royal Guard. His remarks about them maybe letting me live could be discounted—I'd killed four of their citizens plus the King. But he might have been telling the truth about his definition of "civilized." Good news, if true; the last time I'd tried to hold up under torture I hadn't done so well.

But the real puzzler was one of his first remarks. He'd walked in and stared down at me, given his title, and said, "We are holding you for the assassination of His Majesty King Haro Olithorvold. We want you to tell us why you killed him, for whom, where you came from—"

I interrupted him with as credible an expression of innocent outrage as I could manage. He shook his head and said, "Don't try to deny it. Your accomplice has admitted his part in it."

I said, "Oh. Well, that's different, then. If you've got my accomplice, what can I do? I confess to—what was it you said I did? And who was my accomplice?"

That was when he'd started in on being civilized, and now, lying there aching and worried about Loiosh, I wondered many things about my "accomplice." It was obvious who they meant—the drummer I'd stumbled over, so to speak, in the woods. When I'd become conscious again, and had figured out that I'd been knocked out by the smoke (he'd mentioned dreamgrass, after all), I'd assumed he'd done it deliberately. Now, though, I wondered.

It was still possible he had, but they simply didn't believe him. Or it could have been an accident, and he was just what he appeared to be. Or they could be playing some sort of deep game that hadn't made itself apparent yet.

Not that any of this mattered, since I couldn't do anything about any of the possibilities, but I was curious. I wasn't worried. They would most likely spend at least a day or two trying to get me to tell them who had hired me before they killed me. I considered telling them the truth, just to watch bushy-brows' face, but it would have been pointless. Besides, in my business you don't give out that information; it's part of the job.

But in a day or two I could regain my strength and attempt to escape. If I failed, they'd kill me. It was nothing to be worried about. Scared spitless, yes, but not worried.

I did not want to die, you see. I'd died before and hadn't liked it, and this time, if it happened, there'd be no chance for revivification. I'd heard stories of escapes from imprisonment, but, looking around, I just didn't see any way to manage it, and, damn it all, it hadn't been such a bad life. I'd worked my way up from nothing to something and I wanted to see how things came out. I wanted to be around to watch for a while longer. I wanted to leave some changes behind me, to make things a bit different before I went on my way.

Different? Maybe even better, though that had never been high on my list before. Maybe, if I got out of this, I'd do that. Are you listening, Verra? Can you hear me? They've got me trapped and scared, so maybe it doesn't mean anything, but it would be nice if, before I died, I could think to myself that the world was a little better in some way for my having been here. Is that crazy, Demon Goddess? Is this what happened to Cawti, is this why I hardly recognize my wife anymore? I don't know how I'll feel if I get out of this, but I want to find out. Help me, Goddess. Get me out of here. Save my life.

But she'd said I couldn't reach her from here, so I would have to save myself, and that just didn't look likely.

I'd been thinking and dozing and hurting and recovering and sweating for a few more hours when another meal arrived—this time some dumplings with a sauce that meat had been waved at, accompanied by seaweed and more of the bread. I was going to have to escape soon for yet another reason: If I got tired of the bread, I'd have nothing to live for.

Scratch off another day, another visit from the local bone-tightener, and another couple of meals. I was beginning to feel like I could maybe move if I had to. The pain from the wounds was almost gone, but I still hurt from where I'd bruised myself in the fall. I expect that I'd have broken bones if my fall hadn't been "cushioned" by tree limbs, which had given me teeth-loosening love pats all the way down. If I had broken a bone, chances are you'd have heard this story, if at all, from a completely different viewpoint. And the end would have been different, too.

My questioner came back after letting me ponder for an entire two days, I suppose to see if I got nervous. He sat down a few feet away from me. I might have tried to jump him if I'd been in better shape and had my weapons and knew more about the layout of the place and the position of the guards and if he hadn't looked like he was ready for it.

"Well?" he said, trying to look stern and I guess succeeding.

"I would like to confess," I said.

"Good."

"I would like to confess that I wish very much to have a large dish of kethna, cubed and stir-fried with peppers and onions, seasoned with lemon and the rinds of clubfruit, with—"

"You obviously think this is funny," he said.

I shook my head. "Food is never funny. The meals I've been getting are tragic."

I noticed his hands kept trying to form fists, and decided that he was becoming impatient with me. Either they were serious about not beating prisoners, or he was saving up something good. He said, "Do you want to die?"

"Well, no," I said. "But it's bound to happen sooner or later."

"We want to know who sent you."

"I was following a vision."

He glared, then got up and walked out. I wondered what they'd throw at me next. I hoped it wasn't more seaweed.

I SPENT A FEW hours the next day remembering previous incarcerations. There had been one especially long one in the dungeons beneath the Imperial

Palace, as part of the affair that had gained me my exalted position in the Jhereg and had first brought my friend Aliera to the attention of the Empress. That had been a few weeks, and the worst thing had been the boredom. I'd dealt with it mostly by exercising and devising a communication system with my fellow inmates with which we could exchange rude comments about our various guards. This time I was in no condition to exercise, and I didn't know where the other inmates, if any, were. I'd about decided that maybe some gentle isometrics wouldn't hurt too much when the door opened again.

"Aibynn," I said. "Have you come to tend my poor afflicted body? Or minister to my spirit?"

He sat down on the other bunk, looking faintly surprised to see me. "Hey," he said. "I guess you aren't used to dreamgrass."

"I was in a weakened state," I said. "Try it on me again sometime."

He nodded thoughtfully and said, "I didn't think you'd be alive. I thought they were going to, you know—" He made a chopping motion at the back of his neck.

"Probably are," I said.

"Yeah. Me, too." He leaned back, not seeming at all disturbed. I got the impression that he carried fatalism maybe a bit too far. Of course, it was quite possible that he was working for them. It was also possible that he wasn't, that he'd been put in here so we could have conversations for them to overhear. The level of subtlety was about right for what I'd seen of these people.

I said, "Had any good meals?"

He considered this carefully. "Not really, no."

"Neither have I."

"I wouldn't mind—" He stopped, staring up at the window. I followed his gaze, but didn't see anything remarkable. I looked back at him.

"What is it?"

"There are bars on the window," he said.

"Yes?"

"The room I was in didn't have a window."

"What about it?"

He picked up the wooden spoon from the remainder of my last meal, went up next to the window, and tapped one of the bars.

I said, "You think you can knock it loose?"

"Huh? Oh, no, nothing like that. But listen." He tapped it again. It gave out the usual sound of thick iron when struck by thick wood. "Doesn't that sound great?"

I tried to decide if he was joking. "Ummm, I think it needs tuning," I said.

"That's true. I wonder if it would work to wrap a strip of cloth around part of it."

I sighed and settled back onto my bed, hoping they were, in fact, listening. A few hours later the door opened. A pair of guards held their short spears and looked like they knew how they functioned. My friend the Royal whatever was behind them. He nodded to me and said, "Please come with me."

I nodded to Aibynn and said, "Drum for me."

"I will," he said.

To bushy-brows I said, "I'm not certain I can walk very far."

"We can carry you if necessary."

"I'll try," I said. And I did. I was still a bit shaky on my feet, and my back hurt, but I could do it. I wobbled a bit more than I had to just on the principle that it couldn't hurt if they thought I was worse off than I was. We only went a few feet down the hall, though, to a room which had a pair of low backless stools and several windows. He took one of the stools, and I lowered myself onto the other, not enjoying it.

He said, "There has been considerable discussion about what to do with the two of you. Some are in favor of suspending the ancient laws against torture. Others think you should be publicly executed right away, which will prevent the riots that seem to be brewing."

He paused there, to see if I had anything to say. Since I didn't think he'd want to hear about how my back felt, I stayed mute.

"At the moment His Majesty Corcor'n, the son of the man you killed, has everyone convinced to wait until we hear from the mainland. We expect them to deny having sent you, but we want to give them the option. If they do the expected, we will probably execute you. If you're curious, most people are in favor of stoning you to death, though some think you should be bound and thrown to the orca."

"I'm not really curious," I said.

He nodded. "While we're waiting, you still have the chance to tell us about it. We will also be telling your comrade the same thing. If he talks before you do, he will most likely be exiled. If you talk, he will die and you might be allowed to leave. At least you will be allowed to take poison, a far more pleasant death than either of the other two."

"You know that from personal experience?" I said.

He sighed. "You don't want to tell us about it? Who sent you? Why?"

"I just came here for the fishing," I said.

He turned to the guards. "Return him to the cell and bring the other one." They did this. I could have said something clever to Aibynn as we passed, but nothing came to mind. I'd have given quite a bit to be able to hear what went on between the two of them, but I still had no connection to the Orb, and witchcraft, as I've said, wasn't working. Maybe they were just sitting around playing s'yang stones long enough to make it look good. Or maybe they really believed he was helping me. Or maybe there was something else entirely going on that I was completely missing. It wouldn't be the first time.

THEY LEFT US THERE for two more days, during which I learned the distinction between "popping" a beat and "rolling" a rhythm, between fish and animal skin heads, how to tell if there is a small crack in the jawbone one intends to use as a beater, and the training that goes into making a festival, or "hard-ground" or "groundy," drummer; a ritual, or "crashing surf" or "surfy," drummer; and a spiritual, or "deep water" or "watery," drummer. Aibynn had studied all three, but preferred surfy drumming.

I was less interested in all of this than I pretended to be, but it was the only entertainment around. I was interrogated twice more during this time, but you can probably fill in those conversations yourself. Conversation with Aibynn was more interesting than the interrogations, when he wasn't drumming, but he didn't say anything that helped me figure out if he was really working with them or not.

At one point he made a passing reference to the gods. I considered the differences between Dragaeran attitudes toward the divine and Eastern attitudes, and said, "What are gods?"

"A god," he said, "is someone who isn't bound by natural laws, and who can morally commit an action which would be immoral for someone who wasn't a god."

"Sounds like you memorized that."

"I have a friend who's a philosopher."

"Does he have any philosophy on escaping from cells?"

"He says that if you escape, you are required to bring your cellmate with you. Unless you're a god," he added.

"Right," I said. "Does he have a philosophy about drumming?"

He gave me a curious look. "We've talked about it," he said. "Sometimes, you know, when you're playing, you're in touch with something; there are things that flow through you, like you aren't playing at all, but something else is playing you. That's when it's best."

"Yeah," I agreed. "It's the same thing with assassination."

He pretended to laugh, but I don't think he really thought it was funny.

AFTER HE CAME BACK from his second session with the Royal Whootsi-doo, I said, "What did he ask you about?"

"He wanted to know how many sounds I could get out of my drum."

"Ah," I said. "Well?"

"Well what?"

"How many?"

"Thirty-nine, using the head and the shell, both sides of the beater, fingers, and muffling. And then there are variations."

"I see. Well, now I know."

"I wish I had my drum."

"I suppose so."

"Has it rained since you've been here? I didn't have a window at first."

"I'm not sure. I don't think so."

"Good. Rain would ruin the head."

A little later he said, "Why *did* we kill the King?"

I said, "We?"

"Well, that's what they asked me."

"Oh. He didn't like our drum."

"Good reason."

Silence fell, and, when we weren't talking, all I could think about was how badly I wanted to live, which got pretty depressing, so I said, "Those times you feel like you're in tune with something, do you think it might be a god?"

He shook his head. "No. It isn't anything like that. It's hard to describe."

"Try," I said, and he cooperated by keeping me distracted until I drifted off to sleep.

EARLY IN THE AFTERNOON on the second day after Aibynn had joined me, I was listening to an impromptu concert on iron bar (tuned with pieces of a towel), wooden spoon, and porcelain mug, when I felt a faint twinge in the back of my head. I almost jerked upright, but I held myself still, relaxed, and concentrated on making the link stronger.

"*Hello?*"

"*Boss?*"

"*Loiosh! Where are you?*"

"*I . . . coming . . . later . . . can't . . .*" and it faded out. Then there was connection with someone else, so strong it was like someone shouting in my ear. "*Hello, Vlad. I hope all is well with you.*"

It only took me a moment to recognize the psychic "voice." I almost shouted aloud. "*Daymar!*"

"*Himself.*"

"*Where are you?*"

"*Castle Black. We've just finished dinner.*"

"*If you tell me about your dinner I'll fry you.*"

"*Quite. We understand from Loiosh that you're in something of a predicament.*"

"*I think the word predicament is awfully well chosen.*"

"*Yes. He says that sorcery doesn't work there.*"

"*Seems not to. How did he get there?*"

"*He flew, apparently.*"

"*Flew? By the Orb! How many miles is that?*"

"*I don't know. He does seem rather tired. But don't worry. We'll be by for you as soon as we can.*"

"*How soon is that? They're planning to execute me, you know.*"

"*Really? For what?*"

"*A misunderstanding involving royal prerogatives.*"

"*I don't understand.*"

"*Yes. Well, never mind. When can you get here?*"

"*Since we can't telep—*" And the link broke. Daymar, a noble of the House of the Hawk and a fellow who has worked very hard at developing his psychic abilities, is capable of being arbitrary and unpredictable, but I didn't think he'd chop off a conversation in midsentence. Therefore, something else had. Therefore, I was worried.

I cursed and tried to reestablish the link, but got nothing. I kept trying until night had fallen and I had a headache, but I got nothing except morbid thoughts. I fell asleep hoping for rescue and vaguely wondering if I had dreamt it all. I woke up in the middle of the night with the half memory of a dream in which I was flying over the ocean, into a nasty wind, and my wings were very tired. I kept wanting to rest, and every time I did an orca with the face of a dragon would rise out of the water and snap at me.

If I'd've had half a minute to wake up, I would have figured out what the dream meant without any help, but I didn't have the half a minute, or any need for it.

"*Boss! Wake up.*" His voice in my head was very loud, and very welcome.

"*Loiosh!*"

"*We're coming in, boss. Get ready. Is anyone with you?*"

"*No. I mean, yes. A friend. Well, maybe a friend. He might be an enemy. I don't—*"

"*That's what I like about working with you, boss: your precision.*"

"*Don't be a wiseacre. Who's with you?*"

But there was no need for him to answer, because at that moment the wall next to me turned pale blue, twisted in on itself, and dissolved, and I was face-to-face with my wife, Cawti.

I stood up as my roommate stirred. "You and how many Dragonlords?" I said.

"Two," she said. "Why? Do you think we need more?"

She tossed me a dagger. I caught it hilt-first and said, "Thanks."

"No problem." She walked over to the door, played with it for a while, and I heard the iron bar outside hit the floor. I looked a question at her.

"There may be things in the building you want," she said. "Spellbreaker, for example."

"A point. Is, um, anyone still alive?"

"Probably."

Enter Aliera: very short for a Dragaeran, angular face, green eyes. She gave me a courtesy.

I nodded.

"I found this." She handed me a three-foot length of gold chain, which I took and wrapped around my wrist.

"Cawti had just mentioned it," I said. "Thanks."

My roommate, who didn't seem at all disturbed by these events, stood up. "Remember what we said about the philosophy of escaping from cells?"

Cawti looked at him, then back at me. I considered. He might really be just what he seemed, in which case I'd gotten him into a great deal of trouble for helping me. I glanced at the door to the cell. Aliera was now in the room, and there was no commotion to indicate anyone had noticed us escaping. Behind me was a roughly circular gap in the wall, eight feet in diameter, with nothing on the other side but island darkness, fresh with the smell of the ocean.

I said, "Okay, come on. But one thing. If you have any thoughts of betraying me—" I paused and held up the dagger. "In the Empire, we call this a *knife*."

"Knife," he said. "Got it."

Loiosh flew in and landed on my shoulder. We stepped through the wall and out into the night.

Lesson 5

Returning Home

CAWTI LED THE WAY, with Aliera bringing up the rear. We slipped past the single row of structures that represented the city. I realized that I'd been right next to the Palace, and that we were copying almost exactly the route I'd taken after the assassination. We entered the woods outside of the town and stopped there long enough to listen for sounds of pursuit. There were none. My feet were not enjoying the woods. I considered sending Loiosh back to find my boots, but I didn't consider it very seriously. I glanced back at Aibynn, who was also bootless. It didn't seem to be bothering him.

"It's good to have friends," I remarked as we started walking again.

Cawti said, "Are you all right?"

"Mostly. We'll have to take it slow."

"Were you, um, questioned?"

"Not the way you mean it. But I've managed to damage myself a bit."

"It's well past the middle of the night already. We're going to have to hurry to be there by morning, not to mention losing the tide."

"I'm not sure I can hurry."

"What happened?"

"I'm too old to be climbing trees."

"I could have told you that."

"Yes."

"Do the best you can," she said.

"I will." My back already hurt, and now my hand started throbbing. I said, "If we meet anyone drumming in the woods, let's not stop for conversation."

"You'll have to tell me about that," said Cawti. I heard Loiosh laughing inside my head. Aibynn, walking directly in front of me, either didn't hear the comment or chose to ignore it. Branches slapped against my face, just as they'd done last time. Last time I hadn't had Cawti and Aliera with me, so I had cause to be optimistic. On the other hand, the branches still stung. Cheap philosophy there, if you want it.

After an hour or so we stopped, as if by consensus, though no one said anything. I sat down with my back against a tree and said, "What's the plan?"

Aliera said, "We have a ship waiting for us in a cove a few miles from here."

"A ship? Can you drive one of those things?"

"It has a crew of Orca."

"Are you sure they'll be waiting for us?"

"Morrolan is there."

"Ah." And, "I'm flattered. Grateful, too."

Aliera smiled suddenly. "I enjoyed it," she said. Cawti didn't smile. After a few minutes' rest we stood up again. Loiosh left my shoulder to fly on ahead, and we made our way through the woods once more, now at a brisk walk. It was still very dark, but Aliera was making a small light that hung in the air a few paces ahead of us, bouncing in time to her steps.

As we walked, I said to Aibynn, "Is there anything we should be watching for?"

"Trees," he said. "Don't run into them. It hurts."

"Falling out of them isn't much fun, either, but I don't think that's a real danger just at the moment."

"Were you unconscious when you landed?"

"I expect so. I don't really remember anything about it. I was pretty much gone as I fell."

"Too bad," he said.

"Why?"

"The sound you made when you hit. It was a good one. A nice, deep thump. Resonance."

I couldn't decide if I should laugh or cut his throat, so I said, "I'm glad you didn't tune me, anyway."

I kept my eyes on the light, watching it bounce, and I wondered how Aliera had been able to produce it without sorcery to work with. For that matter, though—"Aliera?"

She turned her head without slowing down. "Yes, Vlad?"

"I was told sorcery doesn't work on this island."

"Yes. I lost my link to the Orb about ten miles from shore."

"Then how did you melt down that wall?"

"Pre-Empire sorcery."

"Oh. The rough stuff."

She agreed.

"Getting good, eh?"

She nodded.

"Isn't it illegal?"

She chuckled.

Cawti still hadn't said anything. About then Aibynn increased his speed and caught up with Aliera. "This way," he said.

I said, "Why?" at just the same moment Aliera did.

"Just want to see something."

"Loiosh, is anyone around?"

"I don't think so, boss. But you know I can't always tell with these guys."

"Eyeball it. Check out the way our friend is heading."

"Okay."

After a few minutes he said, *"Nothing I can see, boss. You're almost up to the clearing where they caught you."*

"Oh. That explains it, then."

"It does?"

We got there. The ashes in the fire were quite cold by now. Aibynn found his drum, looked it over, and nodded. If it had been destroyed, I'd have been convinced he was friendly to us. As it was, I still owed him something, but I had no way of knowing what sort of payment he deserved. Time would tell. He also hunted around some more, then gave a small sound of satisfaction and pulled a mass of fur from near the tree I'd fallen from. He shook it and put it on his head.

"What kind of animal was that?" I asked.

"A norska."

"Oh, yes, I see." It was dark brown and white, and still had the norska face in it, with the fangs showing. It didn't look nearly as absurd or disgusting as it ought to have. We resumed our walk.

I allowed myself to feel cautiously optimistic; the entire army of Greenaere, if there was one, would have a hard time keeping Aliera away from that boat, especially if Morrolan was on the other end.

"The sky is getting light in the east," said Aliera.

"We're not going to make it," said Cawti.

"Tell me where the bay is," said Aibynn. "I can probably get us there during flood tomorrow without being seen."

"In the daylight?" I said.

He nodded.

Cawti said, "What do you mean, probably?"

"It depends which bay you mean. If it's Chottmon's Bay, there's too much open ground."

We all studied him. "If Daymar were here," said Aliera, "he could mind-probe him and—"

"If Daymar were here," I said, "he'd still be back at the Palace studying the weave on the rugs while the army took potshots at his back."

"Does he like rugs?" inquired Aibynn.

"All right," said Aliera. "I'll inform Morrolan of the delay. The bay is marked by a high pinnacle, like a crown, on one side, and a stand of tall thin trees on the other. It is about a quarter of a mile across, and there is a small barren islet in the middle."

"Dark Woman's Cove," said Aibynn. "No problem."

"Remember," I said. "This is—"

"Yes. A knife."

He set out in the lead. We moved slowly, but steadily, and didn't run into anyone looking for us. Aibynn appeared to wander aimlessly, hardly looking where he was going and never stopping to look around. I stayed right behind him, ready to stick a knife in his kidney at the first sign that he'd betrayed us. If he knew this, he didn't give any indication, and it was the middle of the afternoon when we saw the little bay, with a lonely ship sitting in the middle of it.

We waited in the woods that came right up to the beach while they sent a boat for us. Cawti still had hardly spoken to me.

HE STOOD ON THE prow of the ship, tall, aloof, Dragaeran, and dry. The Orca on the ship assisted us without any questions, and a few of them gave him dark looks. I suspect these had to do with Blackwand, sheathed at his side. No one wants to be that close to any Morganti weapon, and Blackwand was the kind of blade that survivors write dirges about.

He and Aliera were cousins, both of the House of the Dragon, which meant they preferred a good battle to a good meal—practically my definition of madness. They were young as Dragaerans go, less than five hundred years old. I'd live out my entire life while they were both young, but no sense in dwelling on that. He wore the black and silver of the House of the Dragon with the emphasis on the black, she with the emphasis on the silver. She was short and quick; he was tall and just as quick. The three of us got acquainted one day in the Paths of the Dead. Well, that isn't strictly true, but never mind. There were things that made us friends in spite of differences in species, House, class, and how important we rated food, but never mind that, either. He was there, waiting, when the boat with two undistinguished Orca brought us to the ship.

He gave Aibynn a curious glance, but didn't mention him. He gave a crisp order, and the ship swung a little, shook, turned, settled, and began to move. We sailed neatly away from the island, as if the escape had been no major feat at all. Which, I suppose, it really hadn't, my nerves to the contrary.

I watched the splotch that was Greenaere begin to grow smaller against the reddish horizon, and a tightness in my chest of which I hadn't been aware began to ease. I glanced at the crew, and was a bit disappointed that they were strangers; for some reason I wouldn't have minded running into Yinta, or someone else from *Chorba's Pride*. On the other hand, I wasn't seasick, in spite of no longer having the charm I'd set out with.

Spray hit my face and stung my eyes as the sails above me snapped full, dragging the ship along. Morrolan stood next to me, Aliera next to him. Aibynn was near the front, the prow or the bow or whatever, doing something to his drum. Cawti was not in sight. I said, "I owe you one, Morrolan."

He said, "I'm disturbed."

"About my owing you something?"

"Daymar said he couldn't maintain the contact with you."

"Yes. I wondered about that."

"I feel something on that island."

Aliera said, "There's a reason why our links to the Orb were severed. It wasn't the distance."

"It mislikes me," said Morrolan.

I said, "Huh?"

"He doesn't like it," said Aliera.

"Oh."

Morrolan shifted slightly, keeping his eyes on the island. His long fingers rubbed the large ruby on his silver shirt. I looked back. The island was almost invisible now. Loiosh was on my shoulder. I said, *"Where's Rocza?"*

"She stayed home."

"Not the oceangoing type?"

"I guess not. She was worried about you, though."

"That's good to hear. You must have had quite a flight getting back to shore."

He didn't answer at once. Images came to mind that reminded me very much of a dream I'd just had. My imaginary wings still ached. He said, *"I was worried about you, boss."*

"Yeah. Me, too."

I left Morrolan and Aliera there and walked around the deck until I found Cawti. She was studying the ocean ahead as I'd been watching behind. There was even more spray here; heavy droplets instead of a fine mist. Night was sneaking up behind day, ready to strike.

"You seem not to trust your friend," she said.

"I don't."

"Then why did you bring him along?"

"If they aren't playing some kind of game, then I owe him."

"I see. You always pay your debts, don't you, Vlad?"

"I detect a note of irony in your voice."

She gave me no answer.

"You rescued me," I said after a while.

"Did you doubt we would?"

"I didn't know you could. I didn't know Loiosh would be able to cross that much water."

"It must have been hard for you."

"Not as hard as—" I stopped, studied my fingernails, and said, "It wasn't that bad."

She nodded, still not looking at me.

I said, "I'm glad the revolution could spare you for a few days."

"Don't be snide."

I bit my lip. "I hadn't actually intended that the way it sounded."

She nodded again. There was a splash off to the left. Probably more orca, but I'd missed them. She spoke softly, so I could hardly hear her over the creaking and wind.

> "I watch the passing hours dress
> Themselves in robes of twilight grey,
> And sit here, pale and powerless
> To halt the ending of the day.
>
> "A bitter tale it seemed to me
> Who thought my lesson fully learned
> To open wounds I deemed to be
> Unfairly dealt, not truly earned.
>
> "But tomorrow we begin again
> To open veins for words to say:
> Enlightenment through common pain,
> Dressed in robes of twilight grey."

After an interval of tossing ship and breaking waves I said, "Sounds Eastern."

"It's mine."

I looked at her. She didn't move. I said, "I didn't know you wrote poetry."

"There's a great deal that—no. Sorry. It came to me a few nights ago, as I was sitting there, worried about you. Or maybe wondering if I should be more worried about you; I don't know which."

"A bitter tale," I agreed. "What does it mean?"

She shrugged. "How should I know?"

"You wrote it."

"Yes. Well, if there was something buried in it that I was trying to say, I don't know what it is."

"Let me know if you get any ideas."

The corner of her mouth twitched.

I watched the ocean do its ocean stuff some more. Up and down, and across, going nowhere. That kind of thing.

"I'm trying," said Cawti, "to think of something deep and philosophical to say about waves, but I'm not having any luck."

"You'll find something."

She shook her head. "No, but I ought to. About how they start somewhere, and keep coming closer, then they move you around and keep going, but we don't know what causes them, or where they come from, or, well, something like that."

"Mmmm."

"You made a lot of waves, didn't you, Vlad?"

"Are you speaking in general or in specific?"

"Both, I guess. No, in specific."

"Do you mean the whole business of the last few months, with the Organization, and the Empire, and your friend Kelly?"

"Yes."

"Yeah, I guess I made a lot of waves. I didn't have much choice."

"I suppose not."

"I wonder what Herth is up to."

"Word is, he's happily retired on what you gave him for South Adrilankha."

"South Adrilankha," I repeated. "The Easterners' ghetto."

"Yes."

"And now I'm the one who runs it."

"Not all of it."

"No. Just the illegal parts."

"Going to clean it up?"

"Do I detect a note of irony in your voice?"

"A note? No. A symphony, perhaps."

"You don't think I can, or you don't think I will?"

"I don't think you can."

"Who's to stop me?"

After perhaps a minute she said, "What do you mean, clean it up? Just what illegal activities do you intend to continue?"

"The ones they want. I'll make sure the gambling is fair, that the whore-houses are clean and the tags are treated well, that the loans are at reasonable rates, that—"

"How can gambling be fair for people who can't afford to gamble at all? How much does it help to give fair treatment to people who are selling their bodies? What is a reasonable loan rate to someone who has gone into debt because he lost everything at one of your tables, and how will you collect from those who can't pay?"

I shrugged. "It's going to go on, anyway. I'll be better than anyone else."

"I think I've made my point."

"I can't solve all the problems of the whole world. And neither can your friend Kelly, however much he thinks he can."

"Have you been paying attention lately? Haven't you seen it?"

"Seen what? Parades of Teckla through the streets? People in parks shouting at each other about things they already agree with? Posters that say—"

"And now there are Phoenix Guards watching them, Vlad. And I mean Phoenix Guards—not Teckla put into cloaks and given spears. That means they're scared, Vlad, and it means they don't dare use conscripts. Do you think maybe they know something you don't? Three weeks ago, even two weeks ago, none of that was going on except in South Adrilankha. Now you even see some of it on Lower Kieron. At this rate, what's going to happen in another two weeks? Another two months?"

"In my opinion, not much."

"I'm aware that you think so. But perhaps—"

"No, I don't want to argue about your damned revolution."

She shrugged "You brought it up."

"Can we talk about us?"

"Yes," she said, but I found I didn't have anything clever to say after that. The ship plunged, the waves broke around it, to re-form in our wake as if we'd never been. I wanted to say something deep and philosophical about that, but nothing came to mind.

"I'm going to get some sleep," I said. "If Aibynn starts drumming, throw him overboard." I shifted with the waves until I found the tiny ladder that led to the area below the deck. I found a place to stretch out, located a blanket, and let the ship rock me to sleep.

It MUST HAVE BEEN about ten hours later that the same rocking woke me up. I stumbled up the ladder, banged my shoulder against something metal that some idiot had fastened to the wall (I think it was a hinge), scraped my shin when my feet slipped on the ladder, and made it onto the deck. Morrolan was still where I'd left him. The orange-red sky was hidden by low grey clouds, and the wind was vicious indeed. Morrolan's cloak whipped about him in a frenzy of romantic appeal. I was still wearing the shapeless robe I'd been given while imprisoned, or I'd have been romantic, too. Sure. I made my way along the railing until I was next to him.

"Rough sea," I said, almost shouting above the roar of water and wind and creaking wood. He nodded. I looked around, suddenly thinking how flimsy the ship was. I said, "Anything unnatural about the weather?"

He gave me a funny look. "Why do you ask?"

"Tell you the truth, I don't know. Is there?"

He shook his head.

Loiosh landed on my shoulder. *"Think we're in for a storm?"* I asked him. *"How should I know?"*

"I thought animals had instincts about that kind of thing."

"Heh."

"What do you make of friend Aibynn?"

"I don't know, boss. He's funny."

"Yeah."

I checked the time through my link to the Orb, found out it was well

before noon, but long past when I usually break my fast, and realized I was
hungry. I started to ask Morrolan about food when it hit me. "I have my
link to the Orb again."

He nodded. Talkative son of a bitch.

"When did it happen?"

"During the night sometime."

"Well, that's a relief."

"Yes."

"What about food?"

"There's bread and cheese and whitefruit and dried kethna below."

"That'll do. Couldn't we just teleport home from here?"

"Go ahead. I'm in no hurry."

"If we run into a storm—"

"I've decided that we won't."

"Ah. Never mind, then."

I went below again, found the food, and did appropriate things with it.

As THE NEXT DAY'S dawn spilled an orangish tint on the sea to our right,
the city of Adrilankha peered down from the Whitecrest Hills and spread her
port and docks like a lap to receive us. The sailors gave us, and Morrolan
in particular, ugly looks, because they knew he'd managed the winds that
had brought us home so quickly, and Orca, I've learned, believe that if one
conjures fair winds, nature will respond with a storm as soon as she can
manage it. Perhaps they're right. But Adrilankha, staring down at us like a
great white bird, the cliffs her wings and her head the great manor of the
Lyorn Daro, Countess of Whitecrest, didn't seem to care. Neither did I, for
that matter.

As we passed Beacon Rock, the crew raised a bucket of water from the
sea and spilled it on the deck, a ritual I've always wondered about, since I'm
told that Adrilankha is the only port at which it is performed. They went
through it mechanically, then prepared ropes and did other sailor things that
I understood no better than I had the last time I saw them.

But I wasn't really watching then. Aliera was next to me, Morrolan next
to her, with Aibynn on my other side, and Cawti a little further away. Loiosh

was on my right shoulder. I wondered what was passing through their minds as the city grew before us, one building at a time: the Old Castle, where the Three Barons had practiced their strange magics during an Athyra reign a few cycles ago; Michaagu's, perhaps the best restaurant in the Empire except for Valabar's; the Wine Exchange, fat and brown, built of stone that plunged deep into the hill.

And behind them, the city. Or, rather, the cities, for we had each our own: Aliera and Morrolan, who didn't live there, knew the Imperial Palace and her surrounding Great Houses; a perpetually trimmed garden below the slopes of the Saddle Hills. Aibynn, perhaps, saw a place as strange and wild and unknown as his island was to me. Cawti would see South Adrilankha, the Easterners' ghetto, with her slums and her stench and her open-air markets and Easterners who walked always lightly, ready to run from the Phoenix Guards, or the occasional young Dzur adventurer, or damn near anyone else. I saw the city that held my special place along Lower Kieron Road, where the bitter of violence mixed with the sweet of luxury, and you walked with your eyes open, either to grab at a passing opportunity or to prevent yourself from becoming one.

These cities loomed before us, one and many, growing larger and more present as we watched; they took my eyes and held them as the dock lieutenant signaled to our ship with the black and yellow flags of safe harbor, and guided us in.

I was home, and I was afraid, and I didn't know why.

PART TWO

Business Considerations

Lesson 6

Dealing With Middle Management I

"PEOPLE ARE STARTING TO ask about you, Vlad," said Kragar, two minutes before the door blew down in front of us.

I was three days back from Greenaere. Cawti was off seeing her old friend Kelly and his merry band of nut cases and I had returned to running my business and trying to clean up South Adrilankha without filing Surrender of Debts to the Empire. (This is a joke; the Empire would not accept Jhereg debts. Just thought I should clarify that.)

Progress on all fronts was nil. That is, Cawti and I kept trying to talk and it kept going around in circles. I still didn't have an office in South Adrilankha, and I had no reliable reports coming in. I had not heard from Verra. I didn't know what Aibynn thought of Adrilankha because he didn't talk much; in fact, he wasn't around much. I still wondered if he was a spy. I had explained the situation to Kragar, who had suggested getting Daymar to probe his mind. The idea made me uncomfortable, and I wasn't sure if it would even work. We were discussing various alternatives when Kragar suddenly said, "Never mind that. There are more pressing problems, anyway."

"Like what?" I said, which is when he said, "People are starting to ask about you, Vlad."

"What people?" I said.

"I don't know, but someone above you in the Organization."

"What's he asking about?"

"About that group of Easterners, and your relationship with them."

"Kelly's people?"

"Yeah. Someone's afraid that you're involved with them."

"Can you find out—what was that? Did you just hear something?"

"I think so."

"Melestav, what's going on?"

"Commotion of some sort downstairs, boss. Should I check it out?"

"No, hang tight for now."

"Okay. I'll let you know if—" He broke the connection, or it was broken for him. I caught a quick flash of pain, as if he'd been hit.

I took a dagger into my right hand and held it out of sight below the desk. Then came a rumble, and Loiosh yelled into my mind, and the door blew down. There were six Jhereg standing in the doorway, all of them armed. Melestav hung limp between two of them. There was blood on his forehead. His eyes flickered open like a candle uncertain if it should ignite, but then they focused. He caught my eye, turned his head to the enforcers supporting him, taking a good hard look at each one, then he looked back at me. He made a weak attempt at a smile and said, "Someone here to see you, boss."

I kept my hands under the desk as I studied the intruders. They had to assume I was armed, but there were more of them than there was of me. I was puzzled. I knew that they had not come in here specifically to kill me, because there were too many of them for that. On the other hand, I doubted their intentions were friendly.

One of them, a relatively short Jhereg with curly red hair and puffy eyes, said, "Bring your hands up where we can see them."

I let another dagger fall into my left hand and said, "I'd just as soon not, thanks."

He looked significantly at Melestav. I made a significant shrug. He said, "There's someone who wants to see you."

I said, "Tell him I don't appreciate how he sends his invitations."

Puff-eyes looked at me for a moment, then said, "We haven't killed any of your people—yet. And the gentleman who wants to see you is in a hurry.

It's probably in your best interest to let me see your hands." He sounded like he had something caught in his throat.

"All right," I said, and brought my hands up. I was still holding the daggers. I think they hadn't expected that.

Puff-eyes cleared his throat, which didn't help. He said, "You want to put those down, or should we settle things right now?"

Six of them, one of me. All right. I deliberately turned and threw the daggers, one at a time, into the center of the wall target. Then I turned back to them, folded my hands, and said, "Now what?"

"Come with us," he said, and nodded to a bony Jhereg who looked like he was made out of knotted rope. The latter made a few economical gestures with his hands, and I felt the teleport begin to take effect. I clenched my jaws against the nausea and wondered who could afford to casually hire a sorcerer who could teleport seven at once. Or maybe it wasn't as casual as it seemed. Maybe—but it was too late for that kind of speculation.

Body and mind went through the sieve and emerged, more or less unchanged, in a part of town I knew, in front of a lapidary's shop that I also knew. I said, "Toronnan." They didn't bother to answer, but then I hadn't really phrased it as a question.

We made a parade into the shop where a fellow with the looks and in the dress of the House of the Chreotha did long-fingered things with thin silvery wire and a pair of curved pliers. I had it on good authority that this "Chreotha" had at least three kills on his record; he played his role, however, and didn't give us a glance as we went by.

My stomach, which always flops around when I teleport, was settling down enough for me to be annoyed that Loiosh had been too far away when the teleport went into effect. On the other hand, what could he do? We came to a door at the end of a hallway of tan-colored wood paneling, and one of my escort clapped.

"Come ahead," came the muffled sound from inside, and he opened the door. Toronnan was my boss, if you will. That is, my area was inside of his, and he got a cut of everything I made. In exchange for this, I was rarely bothered by anyone trying to push his way into my area, and I got the benefits of the Jhereg connection inside the Imperial Palace. His office was neither terribly impressive nor revealing. He didn't have a knife target like I did, he didn't have any psiprints of his family or scenes of gently sloping hillsides with happy Teckla working the fields. Just a bookcase with a few folders neatly tucked into it, a wooden desk with a smooth top and a neat array of quill pens on one side, blotter, paper, and well on the other, a tray of sweetmeats on the right corner, a pitcher of water with a half-full glass next to it, a brandy decanter with six glasses near the pitcher. There was one other chair, although there would have been room for several. There were no windows, but that was hardly surprising. Jhereg custom forbids assassination in or around one's home; it says nothing about one's workplace.

Toronnan himself was a small, nervous-looking man, with almost invisible eyebrows and thin lips. His demeanor might make one think of him as weak and harmless, which he wasn't. As I walked in he stood up and put a folder into the bookshelf next to him and motioned me to sit. I did, he did, and he nodded to my escort. They closed the door behind them. I liked it that he put whatever he was working on away; sometimes people like to show how powerful they are by ignoring you for a while. I said, "You know, you could have wheels installed on that chair, so you could scoot over to the bookcase and not have to stand up. That's how I do it. Saves time, you know."

He said, "No, this is about the only exercise I get these days." His voice was smooth, like a minstrel's, and deep. It always made me want to hear him sing.

"I understand," I said.

He kept his eyes fastened on mine. I was uncomfortably aware that my back was to the door. Normally this doesn't bother me because most of the time Loiosh is there.

After a moment he shook his head. "How long has it been, Baronet? Three years that you've been working for me?"

"About that," I said.

He nodded. "You've been earning pretty good, and keeping your buttons polished, and not spilling anyone's wine. There were people in the Organization who were nervous about an Easterner trying to run a territory, but I told them, 'Give the lad a chance, see what he does,' and you've done all right."

This didn't seem to call for a response, so I waited.

"Of course," he continued, "there's been a bit of trouble from time to time, but as near as I can tell you haven't started it. You haven't been too greedy, and you haven't let anyone push you around. The money's been coming in, and your books have been balancing. I like that."

He paused again; I waited again.

"But now," he said, "I'm hearing things I don't like so much. Any idea what I've been hearing?"

"You've heard that I use paper flowers on my dining table? It's not true, boss. I—"

"Don't try to be funny, all right? I've heard that you've been associating with a group of Easterners who want to bring about the next Teckla reign early, or who maybe want to just throw the whole Cycle out, or something on this order. I don't care what the particulars are. But these people, their interests don't coincide with ours. Do you understand this?"

I stared at the ceiling, trying to sort things out. The fact was, I didn't really have anything to do with those people, except that my wife happened to be one of them. But, on the other hand, I didn't feel like explaining myself. I said, "To tell you the truth, I think these people are harmless nuts."

"The Empire doesn't think so," he said. "And there are some people above me in the Organization who don't think so, either. And there are some who want to know what you're doing with them."

I said, "I've just taken over Herth's interest in South Adrilankha. Why don't you relax for a while, see what the profits look like, and then decide?"

He shook his head. "We can't do that. Word's come down from our Imperial contacts that, well, you don't need to know the details. We have to make sure that no one in our organization is involved with those people."

"I see."

"Can I have your assurance that you won't be involved with them in the future?"

He was staring at me hard. I almost felt threatened. I said, "Tell me something: Why is that every time I talk to someone who's high up in the Organization, you always sound the same? Do you go to some special school or something?"

"I wouldn't say I'm high up," he said.

"Now you're just being modest. No, I take it back. The Demon doesn't sound like the rest of you."

"How do we sound?"

"Oh, you know. The same sort of short sentences, like you want to get in all the facts and nothing more."

"Does it work?"

"I guess so."

"Well, there you are."

"But if I ever get that high, am I going to sound like that, too? It worries me. I may have to change all my plans for the future."

"Baronet, I know you're a real funny guy, okay? You don't have to prove it to me. And I know you're tough, too, so you don't have to prove that, either. But the people I'm dealing with on this aren't interested in a jongleur, and they're a lot tougher than you are. Are we clear on that?"

I nodded.

"Good. Now, can you give me any assurances about these Easterners?"

"I can tell you they don't like me. I don't like them, either. I don't have any plans to have anything to do with them. But I control that area now, and I'm going to run it as I see fit. If that brings me into contact with them, I can't tell you how I'll handle it until it comes up. That's the best I can do."

He nodded slowly, looking at me. Then he said, "I'm not sure that's good enough."

I matched his gaze. I was armed and he knew it, but I was in his office, in the one chair he had. If he had done half the things in his office that I'd done in mine, he could kill me without moving a muscle. But sometimes it's safer not to back down. I said, "It's the best I can do."

A moment later he said, "All right. We'll leave it at that and see what happens. Leave the door open when you leave." He stood up as I did and gave me a bow of courtesy. As I was leaving the building, the sorcerer who'd brought me there offered to teleport me back. I declined. It was only a couple of miles.

"But my feet are already sore," said Kragar.

The sorcerer jumped about twenty feet straight up. I managed not to, though it was close.

"How long have you been here?" he said.

Kragar looked puzzled and said, "You teleported me yourself; you should know."

I said, "Sorry, it looks like a walk today," and we left before the sorcerer could decide if he ought to do anything. When we were safely away, we let ourselves laugh good and hard.

IT WAS WELL PAST midnight when Cawti returned. Rocza flew from her shoulder and greeted Loiosh, while Cawti threw her gloves at the hall stand, flopped onto an end of the couch, pulled her boots off, wriggled her toes, stretched like a cat, and said, "You're up late."

"Reading," I said, holding up the heavy volume as evidence.

"What is it?"

"A collection of essays by survivors of Adron's Disaster and the early years of the Interregnum."

"Any good?"

"Some of them are. Most of them don't have anything to do with the Adron's Disaster or the Interregnum, though."

"Dragaerans are like that."

"Yes," I said. "Mostly they want to talk about the inevitability of cataclysm after a Great Cycle, or the Real True Ultimate Meaning of the rebirth of the Phoenix."

"Sounds dull."

"Is, for the most part. There are a few good ones. There's an Athyra named Broinn who says that it was the effort to use sorcery during the Interregnum, when it was almost impossible, that forced sorcerers to develop the skill that makes sorcery so powerful now."

"Interesting. So he doesn't think the Orb was changed by going to the Halls of Judgment?"

I nodded. "It's sort of an attractive theory."

"Yes, it is. Funny that it never crossed my mind."

"Nor mine," I said. "Seen our houseguest?"

"Not lately. He's probably all right."

"I guess. He's not the type to get himself into trouble. I still wonder if he's a spy."

"Do you care?"

"I care if he made a dupe of me. Other than that, no. I don't feel any special loyalty to the Empire, if that's what you're asking."

She nodded and stretched again, arms over her head. Her hair, long and dark brown and curling just a bit at the end, was pleasantly disarrayed over her narrow face. Her warm eyes always seemed big for her face, and her dark complexion made it seem as if she was always half in shadow. I ached for her, but I was getting used to that. Maybe I'd get used to not seeing the little tic of her lip before she made an ironic remark, or the way she'd stare at the ceiling with her head tilted, her brow creased, and her wrists crossed on her lap when she was really thinking hard about something. Maybe I'd get used to that. Then again, maybe not.

She was looking at me, eyes big and inquiring, and I wondered if she guessed what I'd been thinking. I said, "Are your people up to anything that you can tell me about?"

Her expression didn't change. "Why?"

"I got called in today. The back room wants me to assure them I'm not cooperating with Kelly. I think something's going on with the Empire, and the Organization thinks something's going on in South Adrilankha."

Her gaze didn't leave mine. "There's nothing going on that I can tell you about."

"So you people *are* up to something."

She stared at me vacantly, a look that meant she was pondering something, probably how much to tell me, and didn't want the reflections of her thoughts careening across her face. At last she said, "Not the way you mean it. Yes, we're organizing. We're building. You've probably seen things in your own area."

"A few." I said. "But I can't tell how serious it is, and I need to know."

"We think things are going to break soon. I can't give you details of—"

"How soon?"

"How soon what? An uprising? No, nothing like that. Vlad, do you realize how easy it is for the Empire to find out what we're doing?"

"Spies?"

"No, although that's possible, too. I mean that the spells for listening through walls are far more readily available to the Empire than the spells to counteract them are to us."

"That's true, I guess." I didn't say that I had trouble imagining the Empire being concerned enough about them to bother; that wouldn't have gone over well. On reflection, what with the Phoenix Guards all over the place, it might not be true, either.

"All right," she continued. "That means that what we do can't really be secret. So it isn't. When we make plans, we assume the Empire could find out about them as they're made. So we don't hide anything. A question like 'How soon?' doesn't mean anything, because all we're doing is preparing. Who knows? Tomorrow? Next year? We're getting ready for it. Conditions there—"

"I know about conditions there."

"Yes," she said. "You do."

I stared at her for a moment and tried to come up with something to say. I couldn't, so I grunted, picked up my book, and pretended to read.

An hour or so later Aibynn clapped at the door and came in. He ducked his head like a Teckla, smiled shyly, and sat down. His drum was clutched under his arm, as was something that looked like a rolled-up piece of paper.

"Been playing?" I asked him.

He nodded. "I found this," he said, and unrolled the thing.

"Looks like a piece of leather," I said.

"It is," he said. "Calfskin." He seemed unreasonably excited.

"Don't you have cows on the island? I'm sure I saw—"

"But look how thin it is."

"Now that you mention it, it is pretty transparent. Are the cows different here?"

He shook his head impatiently. "It's the tanning and cutting. I've never seen calfskin this thin. It's as thin as fish skin, and warmer."

"Warmer?"

"That's how they make those big drums sound so good."

"What big drums?"

"The ones outside the Imperial Palace, that they play every day to announce the ceremonies and things."

"I've never noticed them."

"You haven't? They're huge, like this." He stuck his arms way out. "And they get about ten of them going at once and—"

"Now that you mention it, I have heard some of that, behind the horns, doing the Reckoning every day."

"Is that what it's called? But now I know how they get the drums to sound that way. Calfskin. I'd never have believed it. They work better in the air here, too."

"The air?"

"The air in the city is really dry. I haven't been able to make my drum sound right since I got here."

This was the first time I'd ever heard anyone suggest that Adrilankha, a city pushed flat against the southern coast, was too dry. "Oh," I said.

"Why do they wear masks?"

"Who?"

"The drummers."

"Oh. Hmmm. I've never thought about it."

He nodded and wandered off to the blue room. As he left, he was running his fingers across the piece of leather, still holding his drum under his arm.

I noticed Cawti looking at me, but I couldn't read her expression.

"Calfskin," I told her. "They make the drums out of calfskin."

"Nothing to it, when you know," she said.

"Maybe that's our problem, though. Maybe the air here is too dry for us."

She smiled gently. "I've suspected that for a long time."

I nodded and settled back in my chair. Rocza landed on her arm and stared up at me quizzically. "Calfskin," I told her. She flew off again.

I SAT IN THE lower east parlor of Castle Black and looked at the Lord Morrolan. He didn't look so tall sitting down.

After a while he said, "What is it, Vlad?"

"I want to talk about revolution."

He cocked his head and raised both eyebrows. "Please?"

"Revolution. Peasant uprising. Violence in the streets."

"What about it?"

"Could it happen?"

"Certainly. It has before."

"Successfully?"

"That depends upon the meaning you choose for success. There have been rulers slain by their own peasants. During the War of the Barons there was a case where an entire county—I believe Longgrass—was turned into—"

"I mean more long-term success. Could the peasants take and hold power?"

"In the Empire?"

"Yes."

"Impossible. Not until the Cycle points to the Teckla, in any case, which will be several thousand years from now. We'll both be safely dead by then."

"You're quite certain?"

"That we'll be dead?"

"No, that it couldn't happen."

"I'm certain. Why?"

"There's this group of revolutionaries that Cawti's gotten involved with."

"Ah, yes. Sethra mentioned something about them a few weeks ago."

"Sethra? How would she know?"

"Because she is Sethra."

"Mmmm. What did she say?"

Morrolan paused, looking up at the ceiling as he remembered. "Very little, actually. She seemed to be concerned, but I don't know why."

"Perhaps I should speak with her, then."

"Perhaps. She will be coming here later this evening to discuss the war."

I felt a frown settle around my lips. "What war?"

"Well, there isn't one yet. But surely you've heard the news."

"No," I said hesitantly. "What news?"

"An Imperial cargo vessel, the *Song of Clouds*, was rammed and sunk yesterday by raiders from Greenaere."

"Greenaere," I said, swallowing bile. "Oh."

Lesson 7

Matters of State I

MORROLAN, ALIERA, AND I lunched in the small den, with an opening onto a balcony that looked down at the ground a mile below. I did not partake of the view. Morrolan's cooks prepared a cold soup of duck with cinnamon, an assortment of chilled fruit, kethna with thyme and honey, various green vegetables with ginger and garlic, and wafers dipped in a strawberry glaze. As was his custom, he laid out several wines with the meal, rather than selecting one for each course. I had a dry white from the Tan Coast, and stayed with it for the whole meal, except for dessert, when I switched to what my grandfather would have called plum brandy, but the Dragaerans called plum wine.

The subject was war. Aliera's green eyes were bright as she speculated about landings on Greenaere, while Morrolan thoughtfully considered naval commissions. I kept trying to find out why it was happening. After shrugging off the question several times, Aliera said, "How can we know why they did it?"

"Well, hasn't there been any communication between the Empire and the island?"

"Perhaps," said Morrolan. "But we know nothing of it."

"You could ask Norathar—"

"There is no need," said Aliera. "She'll tell us as much as she can, when she can."

I glowered into my duck and tossed down more wine. I don't usually toss wine down; I tend to drink it in installments of two or three gulps at a time. Aliera, who holds her glass like she's holding a bird, bottom two fingers properly under the stem, takes tiny lady-like sips at dinner, but when she's out in the field, as I happen to know, she'll slug it down like anyone else. Morrolan always holds the glass by the bowl, as if it were a stemless tumbler, and takes long, slow sips, his eyes looking across at his dinner partner, or the person with whom he is speaking. Now he was looking at me. He replaced his glass, which contained something thick and purple, and said, "Why are you so interested?"

Aliera snorted before I had time to speak. "What do you think, cousin? He was just there, and everyone was after him. He wants to know if whatever he did caused this. I don't know why he should care, but that's what he's after."

I shrugged. Morrolan nodded slowly. "What did you do?"

"Nothing I can talk about."

"He probably killed someone," said Aliera.

Morrolan said, "Did you kill someone of sufficient importance to prompt anger at the Empire?"

"Let's change the subject," I said.

"As you wish," said Morrolan.

Ginger and cinnamon were the main scents of this meal. Loiosh sat on my left shoulder and received occasional scraps. He thought there was too much ginger in the vegetable dish. I told him that, in the first place, there was no such thing as too much ginger and, in the second, jhereg don't eat vegetables. He was saying something about jhereg in the wild versus civilized jhereg when one of Morrolan's servants, an elderly woman who moved like a Serioli water clock and had streaks of black in her grey hair, entered and announced, "Sethra Lavode."

We all stood. Sethra entered, bowed slightly, and seated herself between Aliera and me. She always preferred to be announced without titles; part of her mystique, I guess, though I couldn't say if it was sincere or contrived. You haven't met her yet, so picture if you will a tall Dragaeran wearing a

black blouse with big, puffy sleeves drawn tight around her wrists, black
trousers tucked into calf-high black boots, a silver chain from which hung a
pendant depicting a dragon's head with two yellow gems for eyes, and long
silver dangling-things on her ears that glittered when she moved. She had the
high, sharp cheekbones of a Dragonlord and the pointed Dzur hairline. Her
eyes, which slanted upward as a Dzurlord's, were dark and set deep in her
head, and looking into them one always felt the danger of being lost in the
thousands of years of undead memory she held. Iceflame, blue hilt against
the black, created echoes inside my mind. She was a vampire, a sorcerer, a
warrior, and a statesman. Her powers were legendary. Sometimes I thought
she was my friend.

"You are discussing the war, I presume?" she said.

"We have been," said Morrolan. "Have you news?"

"Yes. Greenaere has formed an alliance with Elde Island."

Aliera and Morrolan exchanged looks that I couldn't interpret, then Morrolan said, "That's rather surprising, considering their histories."

Sethra shook her head. "They haven't actually fought since before the
Interregnum."

"Last time we fought Elde," said Aliera, "Greenaere was on our side."

"Yes," said Sethra. "And they lost half their fleet for their trouble."

"Fleet?" said Morrolan. "Then they have a navy?"

"They have many fishing boats, and most of them are capable of long
voyages. The fishermen become their navy when they need one."

"Do they have a standing army?" asked Aliera.

"Not to speak of," I said.

They both looked at me. When I didn't elaborate, Morrolan cleared his
throat and said, "Elde does."

"It seems strange," I said, "that they think they can win against the
Empire."

"Perhaps," said Aliera, "they're hoping it won't come to war."

"In that case, they're stupid," said Morrolan.

"Not necessarily," said Aliera. "They haven't done so badly in the past.
There have been nine wars with Elde, and—"

"Eleven," said Sethra. "Twelve if you include the first invasion of Dragaerans, but I suppose we oughtn't to include that one."

"However many," said Aliera. "The Empire has never won decisively. If we had, they'd be part of us."

Morrolan made a dismissing gesture. "They've always been hurt worse than we have."

"Not always," said Aliera. "They attacked during the Ash Mountain uprising, and we had to negotiate a peace. A common ancestor of ours was beheaded for that fiasco, Morrolan."

"Ah, yes," he said. "I remember. But other than that—"

"And during the fifteenth Issola reign, they attacked again and we had to sue for peace."

"There was a war with the East at the time."

"All right, so as long as we're not distracted—"

"So," interrupted Sethra. "Just what *is* going on in South Adrilankha, Vlad?"

First Morrolan, then Aliera stopped and looked at me as the significance of what she'd said hit.

"Good question," I said. "I've been wondering about that myself."

AMONG MY ENFORCERS AND bodyguards was a guy called Sticks, named for his favorite weapon. I called him into my office and had him sit down. He did, his long legs stretched out in front of him, his demeanor relaxed. He always seemed relaxed. Even when he was in action, which I've seen close up during a recent incident I don't care to dwell on, he never seemed to be hurried or upset. I said to him, "You told me once that you used to work connecting musicians with inns that wanted music."

He nodded.

"Do you still have much connection with it?"

"Not really."

"Do you know the others in the business?"

"Oh, yeah. There are eight or ten who keep it pretty well locked up."

"Name some names."

"Sure. There's a woman named Aisse. I wouldn't work with her, though."

"Why not?"

He shrugged. "She never seems to know quite what she's doing. And when she does, she never lets the musicians know. Word is she lies a lot, especially when she screws up."

"Okay. Who else?"

"There's a fellow named Phent who doesn't lie quite as much, but he's about as incompetent and he charges twice what everyone else does. He's got a lock on the low-life places. They suit him."

"I might need him. Where can I find him?"

"Number fourteen Fishmonger Street."

"Okay, who else?"

"There's Greenbough. He's not too bad when he isn't drunk. D'Rai will keep you working, but she'll also get a hold on you and try to keep everything you play sounding the same. Most of the musicians I know don't like that."

"Blood of the goddess, Sticks, isn't there anyone good in the business?"

"Not really. The best of the lot is an outfit run by three Easterners named Tomas, Oscar, and Ramon. They have South Adrilankha and a few of the better inns north of town."

"How do I reach them?"

"About a mile and a half up Lower Kieron, behind the Wolves' Den, upstairs."

"I know the place. Okay, thanks."

"Mind if I ask why you're interested, boss?"

"I'd rather not say, at the moment."

"All right. That all?"

"Yeah. Have Melestav send Kragar in."

As he shut the door, Kragar said, "Mind if *I* ask why you're interested, Vlad?"

I jumped, stared at him, and said, "Were you here the whole time?"

"I didn't know it was private."

"It doesn't matter. I'm after a couple of things. One is to see if I can help Aibynn find work. The other is to get another source of information in South Adrilankha. Musicians hear almost as much gossip as whores."

"Makes sense."

"Since you've already got the information, why don't you go make contact with that group behind the Wolves' Den?"

"What, you want me to do something safe and easy for a change? Sure. What about this Aibynn? Will they need to hear him?"

"Maybe. I'll talk to him and send him by. But first see if they're interested in making a little money on the side, without needing to know who's paying them."

"Okay. Anything else?"

"No. Anything here?"

"Tevyar got excited again."

"Oh?"

"Some Iorich owed him money and started acting tough, and Tevyar tried to handle it on his own, got enthusiastic, and killed him. You know how he is."

"Yes. He's an idiot. Revivifiable?"

"No. Crushed his head."

"Double idiot. Is it likely to cause any trouble?"

"Not as far as I can tell. He didn't leave any traces."

"That's a relief."

"Should we do anything about it?"

I considered for a moment, then shook my head. "Not this time. Having to cover the loss ought to teach him something. If not . . ."

"Right."

Loiosh flew over to my shoulder from the coatrack. I scratched under his chin. "What about Kelly's people? Anything to report?"

Kragar shifted in his chair and his normally expressionless face fought with itself for a moment, as if uncertain how to settle down.

"The Empire has begun conscription in South Adrilankha."

"So soon?"

He nodded. "Only Easterners, too."

"Interesting. Have Kelly's people done anything about it?"

"They had some sort of parade. About a thousand people, give or take."

I whistled. "Anything happen?"

"No. It looked like they were going to send in press gangs, but they didn't."

"With a thousand crazed Easterners, I'm not surprised."

"There's supposed to be some sort of meeting or rally tomorrow evening."

"Okay. Anything else?"

"Routine stuff. It's on your desk."

"Fly, then, and let me know what happens."

When he was gone, I looked at the scribbled notes he and Melestav had left. I okayed credit for a couple of good customers, agreed that we needed some new furnishings in one of my gambling places, refused a request for additional manpower at another, and made a few notes on my calendar for business meetings.

None of which I really needed to attend.

In fact, I wasn't really needed for much of any of this.

Things had reached the point around the office where it would practically run itself. I suppose I could have been bothered by this, but actually I was pleased. I had worked very hard to get it to this point. The irony was that it came just when I had the additional problem of South Adrilankha to worry about, so I couldn't really enjoy it. It crossed my mind that I would probably never reach the point where I could just sit back and watch the money roll in, and only deal with major problems.

But, on the other hand, maybe if that ever happened, I'd have too much time on my hands.

Loiosh shifted on my shoulder and I scratched his chin. Conscription in South Adrilankha. Why? Was war with Greenaere really imminent? Was the war scare an excuse to harass Easterners? If the war was real, had I caused it? If so, why had Verra sent me to shine the King? Well, that part was easy: because she wanted the war. Why?

I called out to her, just to see if she felt like responding, but she didn't. I wished I could ask her directly. I'd like to be able to find out what was going on in the strange, non-human mind of hers.

I entertained sacrilegious thoughts for a while, but they got me nowhere, so instead I considered the war. If you looked at a map of the Empire, the notion of war with Greenaere would seem laughable—this huge monster of a landmass next to a little splotch shaped like a banana. It made no sense. They must know that. The Empire must know it. What was going on? Who was pushing whom, to try to do what? What sort of intrigues were being played out in the Imperial Palace? What sort of lunacies on Greenaere? What sort of machinations in the Halls of Judgment?

"*You know, boss, it might not matter. You might be out of it, now that you've done what you were hired for.*"

"*Do you really think so?*"

"*No.*"

"*Neither do I.*"

I SPOKE TO AIBYNN that evening while waiting for Cawti to come back home. I told him about that group behind the Wolves' Den. He nodded, his eyes focused on something else.

"Why don't you go in and see them?" I said.

"What? Oh. Yeah. I'll do that."

The conversation faltered, and he went back to the blue room. I chewed my lip, wondering. Loiosh stopped chasing Rocza around the flat long enough to echo my own thoughts: "*What a strange fellow, boss.*"

"*Indeed,*" I said. "*But just strange, or does he have a game of some sort?*"

Cawti hadn't come home when I went to sleep that night, and she still hadn't when I left the next morning. A year ago I'd have been frantic. Half a year ago I'd have attempted to reach her psionically. Things had changed.

When I got to the office, Melestav said, "Heard the news yet?"

I sighed. "No. Do I need to be sitting down?"

"I'm not sure. Word is out that Greenaere has made an alliance with Elde Island."

"Ah. Yes. I knew that."

"How?"

"Never mind. Has anyone actually declared war?"

"I've heard that the Empire has declared war, that the island has declared war, that the island has apologized, claiming it was all a mistake, that Elde has come over to our side, that they have some great new magic that will destroy us all, that the Empire is surrendering and the islanders will be occupying the mainland, that—"

"In other words, nothing official."

"Right."

"Okay, thanks."

I went into my office to consider. Presently Kragar arrived and said, "I spoke with Ramon and he went for it, Vlad. Jumped at it like a dzur after dinner."

I frowned. "Too eager?"

"I don't think so. I think they just need the money."

"All right. We can afford it, anyway. We'll need to set up someone to stay in touch with them, unless you want to do it yourself."

"No, thanks," he said. "I have enough to do as it is. I hardly have enough time to—"

"Yeah, yeah, yeah. How about Sticks?"

He nodded. "That makes sense. I'll talk to him. Any suggestions for the information exchange?"

"What do you mean?"

"I mean, do you want it all going through Sticks, or through Sticks and me, or Sticks and you, or what?"

"Oh." I considered. "Why don't we do the recognition symbol bit?"

"A ring or something?"

"Yeah. Go get a few rings made, and give me one, one to Sticks, and keep one yourself. And keep close track of what happens to them all."

"All right, I'll talk to Sticks and take care of it this afternoon."

"Good. Another thing: I want to know what happens at this big get-together they're supposed to be having today in South Adrilankha."

"Okay."

Within six hours my arrangements with the firm of Tomas, Oscar, and Ramon had paid off. First, they managed to find Aibynn a job with a musician of the House of the Issola who played Eastern instruments to accompany his singing of pre-Interregnum ballads. Second, they were the ones who, through Sticks, brought me word that most of Kelly's organization, including Cawti, had been arrested.

Lesson 8

Dealing with Middle Management II

One of the easiest and yet most effective offensive uses of sorcery involves simply grabbing as much energy from the Orb as you can handle without destroying yourself, channeling it through your body, and directing it at whomever or whatever you want to damage. The only defense is to grab as much energy as you can handle without destroying yourself and use it to block or deflect the attack.

It so happens that I've acquired a length of gold chain which, used properly, acts to interrupt any sort of spell sent against me, so I'm pretty safe from this kind of thing. But once, in the middle of a battle I should never have been in, I was hit from behind.

It felt like I was burning from the inside, and for what seemed like minutes I could feel veins, arteries, and even my internal organs burning. Every muscle in my body contracted, and I felt the muscles in my thighs attempt to break both of my legs and almost succeed. A Dragon warrior who was standing about fifteen feet in front of me was struck by an arrow at about that same time, and I spent minutes watching him fall over. I smelled smoke, and saw that it was coming from under my shirt, and realized with a horrible sick feeling that the hair on my chest and on the backs of my arms was burning. I knew that my heart had stopped, and my eyeballs felt hot and itchy. All sound vanished from the world, and returned only very slowly, beginning with a horrible buzzing, as if I'd been stuck in a bee's nest. It amazed me that there was no pain, and amazed me even more when I realized that my heart had started beating again. Even then it wasn't over, because for a while I couldn't stand up; efforts to move my legs only made them twitch. When, after several minutes, I was able to stand, I remember trying to pick up my sword and being unable to, because trying to take a step toward it led me off in a different direction, and efforts to extend my hand caused it to reach somewhere I had not intended. It was twenty or thirty minutes, I believe, before the effect wore off, during which time I was in the grip of a terror the like of which I'd never felt.

Since that time, the memory has come back at odd times, and always very strongly. It isn't like pain, which you don't really remember—the incident was burned, and I think I mean that literally, into my brain—so sometimes all the sensations wash over me, and I can't breathe and I wonder if I'm going to die.

This was one of those times.

The incident on Greenaere was the fourth time I'd been imprisoned. The first was the hardest, just because it was first, but none had been easy. By removing someone's freedom of movement, you remove some measure of his dignity, and the thought of this happening to Cawti, to the woman whose eyes crinkled when she grinned, and who threw her head back when she laughed so her dark, dark hair rippled across her shoulders, to the woman who had guarded my back, to the woman who—

—to the woman who didn't know if she loved me anymore, to the woman who was throwing away her happiness and mine for a pail full of slogans. It was almost more than I could stand.

"You all right, boss?" said Sticks, and I came back to an awareness of him, staring up at me and looking worried.

"After a fashion," I said. "Get Kragar."

I leaned back in the chair and closed my eyes. Presently I heard Kragar's voice. "What is it, Vlad?"

"Shut the door."

The latch, Kragar's footsteps, his body settling into the chair, the rustle of

Loiosh's wings, my own heartbeat. "Find me detailed plans of the dungeons of the Imperial Palace."

"What?"

"They're below the Iorich Wing."

"What's going on?"

"Cawti's been arrested."

A break in the conversation stretching out to the horizon, infinite, timeless.

"You can't be thinking of—"

"Get them."

"Vlad—"

"Just do it."

"No."

I opened my eyes, sat up, and looked at him. "What?"

"I said no."

I waited for him to continue. He said, "A few weeks ago you lost control and almost got yourself killed. If you lose control again you're on your own."

"I haven't asked you—"

"But I'm not going to cut wood for your barge."

I studied him carefully, my thoughts running quickly, although I don't recall the substance. At last I said, "Get out."

He left without another word.

I DON'T REMEMBER ANY nausea following the teleport to Castle Black, nor do I remember what Lady Teldra said in greeting when I came through the portals. I found Morrolan and Aliera in the front room of the library, where the chairs are the most comfortable and he most enjoys sitting. It is the largest of the rooms, but has fewer books than the others, with more room for browsing, sitting, or pacing.

Morrolan sat, Aliera stood, I paced.

"What is it, Vlad?" he said after I made a few trips past him.

"Cawti's been arrested. I want your help in breaking her out."

He marked his place with a thin strip of gold-inlaid ivory and set his book down. "I'm sorry she's been arrested," he said. "With what is she charged?"

"Conspiracy."

"Conspiracy to what?"

"It isn't specified."

"I see. Will you have wine?"

"No, thank you. Will you help?"

"What do you mean by breaking her out?"

"What does it sound like?"

"It sounds like what we did to get you off of Greenaere."

"Exactly."

"Why do you wish to do that?"

I stopped pacing long enough to look at his face, to see if this was some form of humor. I decided it wasn't. "She broke me out," I told him.

"It was the only way to free you."

"Well?"

"I would suggest, with the Empire, that we try other methods first. Her former partner is the Heir, after all."

I stopped. I hadn't thought of that. I allowed Morrolan to pour me some wine, which I drank and didn't taste. Then I said, "Well?"

"Well what?" said Morrolan, but Aliera understood and excused herself from the room. I sat down and waited. We didn't speak until Aliera returned, perhaps ten minutes later.

"Norathar," she said, "will do what she can."

"What is that?" I asked.

"I hope enough."

"Had she known?"

"That Cawti was arrested? No. It seems there has been quite a bit of trouble in the Easterners' quarter, though, and that group she's in has been in the middle of it."

"I know."

"There are several such groups, actually, all over South Adrilankha, and the Empress is worried about the potential for destruction."

"Yes."

"But Norathar has some influence. We shall see."

"Yes."

I brooded for a while, staring at the floor between my feet, until Loiosh said, "*Careful, boss,*" at the same time Aliera said, "Who is 'she' and who is 'he'?"

"Eh?"

"You just said something about why did she want him dead."

"Oh. I didn't realize I was speaking aloud."

"You weren't exactly, but you were broadcasting your thoughts so strongly you might as well have been."

"I guess I'm distracted."

"Well, who is she?"

I shook my head and went back to brooding, being a little more careful this time. Morrolan read, Aliera stroked a grey cat who had set up shop in the library. I finished the wine and refused a second glass.

"Tell me," I said aloud, "where the gods come from."

Morrolan and Aliera looked at me, then at each other. Morrolan cleared his throat and said, "It varies. Some are actually Jenoine who survived the creation of the Great Sea of Chaos. Others are servants of theirs who managed to adapt when it occurred and use its energy, either while it was happening or during the millennia that followed."

"Some," added Aliera, "are simply wizards who have become immortal, and acquired the power to exist on more than one plane at the same time."

"Well, then," I said, "how are they different from demons?"

"A matter of interpretation only," said Morrolan. "Demons can be summoned and controlled, gods cannot."

"Even by other gods?"

"Correct."

"So if a god were to control another god, that god would become a demon?"

"That is correct. If we were to learn of it, we would begin to refer to that god as a demon."

"It seems pretty arbitrary."

"It is," said Aliera. "But it's still significant. If a god is just a force with a personality, it makes a big difference whether it can be controlled, don't you think?"

"What about the Lords of Judgment?"

"What about them?"

"How do they get there?"

"War," said Morrolan, "or bribery, or from friendship with other gods."

"Why do they want to?"

"I don't know," said Morrolan. "Do you, Aliera?"

She shook her head. "Why all the questions?"

"Something to talk about," I lied.

"Do you wish to become a god?" asked Morrolan.

"Not particularly," I said. "Do you?"

"No. I don't care for the responsibility."

I snorted. "To whom are they responsible?"

"To themselves, to each other."

"Your Demon Goddess doesn't seem particularly responsible."

Aliera jerked upright, almost stood, and her hand almost went for Pathfinder. I drew back. "Sorry," I said. "I didn't think you'd take it personally."

She glowered at me for a moment, then shrugged, Morrolan looked at Aliera, then turned back to me and said, "She is responsible, though. She's unpredictable, and capricious, but she rewards loyalty, and she won't cause a servant to act in a way that will harm him."

"What if she makes a mistake?"

He looked at me closely. "There's always that danger, of course."

I said no more, but considered what I'd been told. It still felt just a bit scandalous to be speaking of my patron goddess this way, as if she were a mutual acquaintance whose strengths and weaknesses of character we might bandy about for amusement. But if what they'd told me was true, then either she had some sort of plot going which would, perhaps accidentally, make everything come out all right, or else something had screwed up at, let's say, a very high level.

Or Morrolan and Aliera were wrong, of course.

Lady Teldra appeared at the door and announced the Princess Norathar: Duchess of Ninerocks, Countess of Haewind, et cetera, et cetera, and Dragon Heir to the Throne. Not as tall as Morrolan, not as strong-looking as Sethra, yet she had a grace about her movements.

Ex-assassin was left out of the list, but as an assassin, she had worked with Cawti as part of one of the most sought-after teams of killers in the

Jhereg, hard as that was to believe listening to either one of them now. I knew something about her skills as a fighter; she'd killed me once.

Norathar walked over to the tray of strong liquors, found a brownish one that she liked, and poured herself a tumbler full. She took a good third of it off the top and stood facing us. She said, "The Empress has given leave for the Lady Taltos to be released. The Lady Taltos has refused." She sat down then and had some more of her drink. Loiosh, on my right shoulder, squeezed with his talons.

"Refused?" I said at last, in what I think was a steady voice.

"Yes," said Norathar. "She explained that she would wait with her companions until they were all free." I could now hear the strain of her voice, as she worked to speak clearly and calmly. She was a Dragonlord down to her toes, like Morrolan and Aliera, and in the time since she'd been made the Heir, she had changed, so these days she seemed more tightly controlled than either of them. But now this control was frightening, as if it only barely held in check a rage that could destroy Castle Black.

I noticed all of this with the back of my mind, as I concentrated on keeping my own temper in check, at least until I could decide at whom it should be directed.

Then, suddenly, I realized who that should be, and I said, "Lord Morrolan, you have a room, high up in a tower, with many windows in it. I would like to visit that place."

He looked at me for a long moment before he said, "Yes. Go, Vlad, with my blessing."

Left out the door, down the hallway to the wide, black marble stairway leading to the Front Hall. Down the stairs, out of the Hall toward the South Wing, then up, jog past the lower dining room, past the southern guest rooms, up a half-flight, turn around, around, through a heavy door that opens to my command, since I work for Morrolan and helped set up the spells that guard it.

"Are you sure this is a good idea, boss?"

"Of course not. Don't ask stupid questions."

"Sorry."

A room all in black, lit by candles made from tallow from fat rendered from the hindquarters of a virgin ram, with wicks made from the roots of the neverlost vine, the whole scented with cradleberry, so the room smelled like the last dregs of a sweet wine just starting to turn to vinegar. Four of them were lit, and they danced to celebrate my arrival.

Artifacts of Morrolan's experiments in witchcraft littered small and large tables, and his stone altar, black against black, was just barely discernible at the far end. Here I had lain helpless while Morrolan battled a demon that had taken his own sword from him. Here I had parlayed with spirits from my ancestral home for the release of the Necromancer's soul. Here I had battled with my own likeness, come to take me to that land from which none return.

But never mind, never mind. I stepped onto the narrow, metal stairway, which twisted around and brought me at last into the Tower of Windows, where I had once tortured a sorceress into releasing the spells that prevented Morrolan's revivification. That was pretty recent, and the taste of the experience was still in my mouth. But never mind that, either.

The surest way to achieve communion with Verra, the Demon Goddess, involves human sacrifice, which my grandfather had made me swear never to do. Yet I believe that if I had had the means at hand, I would have done so then. I looked about the tower, filled with windows which did not look upon the courtyard below, some of which did not look upon the world I knew, some of which did not look upon reality as I understood it. I tried to prepare my mind for what I was about to do.

I arbitrarily picked a window, a low wide one, and sat down before it. It looked out upon dense fog, swirling, through which I saw trees and tall shrubs, as well as quick movements that were probably small animals. I had no way of knowing if I was seeing my own world or some other, nor did it matter.

Loiosh settled onto my shoulder, and his mind merged more fully with my own. I went back to my earliest memories concerning the Demon Goddess, instructions from my grandfather in the proper rituals, tales of battles with other gods, especially Barlen, her enemy and lover. I remembered seeing her in the Paths of the Dead, her strange voice, and her multi-jointed fingers, and her eyes that seemed to see past me and into me at the same time. I remembered her when she had commissioned me to kill the King of Greenaere; was it only days ago?

As I remembered, and let myself be filled by the awe of the Easterner and the respect of the Dragaeren, it occurred to me that blood sacrifice may be carried out in more than one way. I took my dagger and sliced open my left palm, hardly noticing the pain. "Verra!" I cried. "Demon Goddess of my ancestors! I come to you!" I scattered droplets of blood through the window. They vanished into the fog, which swirled and lightened, until in a few short moments it was a pure featureless white. This, too, seemed to shift, until I saw once more the hallway through which I had walked, following mist and a black cat. There were a few drops of blood on the floor.

I stood and stepped through the window.

Same hallway, same confusion of distance and dimension due to the featureless white. This time there was no black cat to guide me, however. I wondered which way to go, and I wondered, too, if it mattered. There was no window behind me. Loiosh shifted on my shoulder and said, *"That way feels right, boss."* On reflection, it felt right to me, too, so I sheathed the dagger and began walking.

The mist never appeared, either, so perhaps that had been arranged for my benefit; the Demon Goddess seemed to me quite capable of theatrics. No mist, no cat, no sound, but the doors appeared much sooner than they had the last time. In a way, it would be oddest if that corridor really was just a corridor, of some fixed length, and it took however long to walk it depending on where one appeared.

This time, standing before the doors, I studied the carvings a bit. At first glance, they seemed to be abstract designs, yet as I looked I began to pick out or imagine shapes: trees, a mountain, a pair of wheels, what might have been a man with a hole in his chin, something else that might have been a fanciful four-legged beast with a tentacle where its nose ought to be and a pair of horns emerging from its mouth, perhaps an ocean below what I'd thought was a mountain but now seemed to be a stick supporting a circular blob.

I shook my head, looked again, and they were all abstract designs again. Who knows how much was there and how much I'd supplied?

For lack of anything else to do, I clapped at the doors and waited for one very, very long minute. I clapped once more and waited again. I still had my link to the Orb, and I thought of seeing if I could force or blow the doors open, but then I thought better of it.

"*Good thinking, boss.*"

"Shut up, Loiosh. Do you have any great ideas?"

"*Yes. Strike it with your fists, like Easterners are supposed to.*"

"And if there are defensive spells on it to destroy anyone who touches it?"

"*Good point. There's always Spellbreaker.*"

I nodded. That was an idea. I stood there like an idiot a little longer, then sighed and let the gold chain fall into my left hand. I swung it around, then stopped. "*Perhaps this isn't such a good idea.*"

"*You have to do something, boss. If you're worried about protections, hit it with Spellbreaker. If not, either strike it or just see if it will push open.*"

I considered for a while, then got mad at myself for standing there like an idiot. Before I could come to my senses, I whirled the chain around and lashed out at the door. It hit with a clank of metal against wood which instantly died out. There were no sensations, I felt no sorcery, and, fortunately, Spellbreaker left no mark on the door.

I pushed the right-hand door, and it creaked a bit but barely moved. However, when it swung back, there was a gap between the two doors sufficient for my fingers. I pulled the door, which was as heavy as it seemed, and it slowly opened enough for me to slip inside.

As I walked forward, I saw the shimmer and sparkle in the air that I'd seen before at Verra's appearance and disappearance. It occurred to me that perhaps that was how it would look to an observer when I stepped through to her realm.

In the time it took to form those thoughts, she had arrived. Her eyes followed me as I approached her throne, and when I got near, the cat, whom I hadn't noticed against the folds of her white gown, jumped down and inspected me. Loiosh tensed on my shoulder.

"*There's something about that cat, boss. . . .*"

"*That wouldn't surprise me a bit, Loiosh.*"

I stopped at a convenient distance before her throne and waited to see if she would speak first. Just when I was deciding that she wouldn't, she said, "You're getting blood on my floor."

I looked down. Yes, indeed, my palm was still bleeding, and the blood was running down Spellbreaker, which still hung from my left hand, and was slowly splattering onto the white tiles. I turned my palm over, and Spellbreaker came to life, as it has done every now and then before, to hold itself upright, like a yendi about to strike. There was a tingling in my hand then that ran up my arm, and as I watched, the cut stopped bleeding and closed up, leaving a faint pink scar.

I hadn't known Spellbreaker could do that.

I carefully wrapped it around my left arm again and said, "Shall I scrub the floor for you?"

"Perhaps later."

I looked for traces of humor on her long, strange face, but didn't see any. I did, however, identify what made her face seem so odd: Her eyes were set too high. Not by much, you understand, but the bridge of her nose was ever so slightly lower on her forehead than on a human or a Dragaeran. The more I studied it, the stranger it seemed. I turned away from her.

"Why have you come here?" she said.

Still looking away, I said, "To question you."

"Some might believe that presumptuous."

"Yeah, well, I'm just that kind of guy."

"Apparently. Ask, then."

I turned back to her. "Goddess, I asked before why you chose me to kill the King of Greenaere. Perhaps you answered me fully, perhaps not. Now I ask this: Why was it necessary that he die?"

Her eyes caught mine, and held them, and I trembled in spite of myself. If she was trying to intimidate me, she succeeded. If she was trying to convince me to withdraw the question, she failed. At last she said, "For the good of the people in the Empire, both Dragaerans and Easterners."

"Bully," I said. "Can you be more specific about that? So far, the results have been the death of the crew of a Dragaeran freighter and the arrest of several Easterners, including my wife."

"What?" she said, her eyebrows rising. I don't think I was really, truly frightened until then, until I realized that I had surprised her. That was when my stomach twisted itself into knots and my mouth went dry.

"The organization of which my wife is a member—"

"What of them? Were they all arrested?"

"The leaders, at least. This Kelly, my wife, several others."

"Why?"

"How should I know? I suppose because they refused conscription, and—"

"Refused conscription? That fool. The whole point was—" She cut herself off abruptly.

"Was what?"

"It doesn't matter. I underestimated this man's arrogance."

"Well, that's just great," I said. "You underestimated—"

"Quiet," she said, snapping the word out like an arrow past my ear. "I must consider what to do to rectify my error."

"Just what were you trying to do, anyway?"

She stared at me. "I do not choose to tell you at this time."

I said, "It was all directed at Kelly's people in the first place, wasn't it?"

"Kelly, as I've said, is a fool."

"Maybe, but judging by what happened before, he knows what he's doing."

"Certainly he does, in a narrow field. He is a social scientist, if you will, and a very skilled one in certain ways. He studied—it doesn't matter."

"Tell me." I don't know what got into me that caused me to start interrogating her like a button-man who'd been sloughing off, but I did it.

Her mouth twitched. "Very well. During the Interregnum, when your people—Easterners—roamed over the Empire like jhereg on a dragon's corpse—"

"*Yum.*"

"*Shut up.*"

"—many vaults were unearthed that had lain buried and forgotten for so long that you cannot conceive of the time. Some of these were records preserved by the House of the Lyorn, who have the skill to preserve things that ought to be allowed to crumble away. Or perhaps we should not blame them—it's been said that one cannot kill ideas."

"What ideas were unearthed?"

"Many, my dear assassin. It was an amazing time of growth, those four hundred and ninety-seven years of interregnum. Sorcery was all but impossible then, so that only the most skilled could perform even the simplest spells. Conversely, this skill was passed on and retained, and taught to those whose interest ran in that direction. What was the result? Now, when the Orb is back, sorcery has grown so strong from the new skills that what was inconceivable before the Interregnum, and impossible during it, is now commonplace. Teleportation on such a level that some fear it will replace trade by ship and road. War magics so strong that some believe the individual fighter will soon become a thing of the past. Even resurrection of the dead has become possib—"

"What has this to do with Kelly?"

"Eh? My apologies, impatient Easterner. Things were discovered by your people, during that time, things that go all the way back to those who first discovered this world."

"The Jenoine?"

"Before the Jenoine."

"Who—?"

"It doesn't matter. But ideas that have been preserved far too long, and from another place, lay dormant until then. And even when they were unearthed, no one understood them for nearly two hundred years, until this Kelly—"

"Goddess, I don't understand."

She sighed. "Kelly has his hands on the truth about the way a society works, about where the power is, and the cause of the injustice he sees. But it is truth for another time and another place. He has built an organization around these ideas, and because of their truth, his organization prospers. But the truth he has based his policies on, the fuel for this fire he is building, has no such strength in the Empire. Perhaps in ten thousand years, or a hundred thousand, but not now. And by proceeding as he has, he is setting up his people to be massacred. Do you understand? He is building a world of ideas with no foundation beneath them. When they collapse . . ." Her voice trailed off.

"Why don't you tell him so?"

"I have. He doesn't believe me."

"Why don't you kill him?"

"You don't kill ideas like that by killing the one who espouses them. As fertilizer aids the growth of the tree, so does blood—"

"So," I said, "you decided to start a war, thinking they'd march off and forget their grievances so they could fight for their homeland? That doesn't—"

"Kelly," she said, "is smarter than I thought he was, curse him. He's smart enough to destroy every Easterner, and most of the Teckla, in South Adrilankha."

"What are you going to do?"

"Consider the matter," she said.

"And what do you want me to do?"

"I'm sending you home at once. I need to consider this." She gestured with her right hand, and I found myself, once more, before a window in Morrolan's tower. The window looked upon the face of the Demon Goddess, who stared at me and said, "Try to stay out of trouble, will you?"

The window faded to black.

Lesson 9

Making Friends I

MORROLAN AND ALIERA WERE where I'd left them, Norathar had gone. I checked through the Orb and discovered that I'd been gone less than two hours, and most of that time had been taken up walking to and from the tower. I sat down and said, "I'll take that refill of wine now."

Morrolan poured it and said, "Well?"

"Well what?"

"What happened? I should judge that you have just had a moving experience of some sort."

"Yes. Well. I suppose. I haven't discovered anything that will help get Cawti out of the Imperial Dungeons."

Aliera shifted. "Did you see Verra?"

"Yes."

"What did she say, then?"

"Many things, Aliera. It doesn't matter."

Morrolan considered me, probably wondering whether he ought to push for more information. I guess he decided not to. Aliera was frowning.

"Well, then," said Aliera, after a moment. "We're back to planning another jailbreak. We've been doing quite a bit of that lately. I wonder if the Cards would have predicted it, had I thought to attempt a reading."

"I don't think a jailbreak is in order," I said.

Aliera turned her blue eyes on me. "Why not?"

"If Cawti won't accept an Imperial pardon, what makes you think she'll accept being broken out by force?"

Aliera shrugged. "We'll have to get the whole batch of them, that's all."

I shook my head. "I don't think they'll go. I think they want to stay in prison until they're all released together."

"What makes you think so?"

"I've spoken to them. That's how they think."

"They're nuts," said Aliera.

"That's more true than you know," I said. "Or less."

"And so," said Morrolan, who had never looked happy about the notion of breaking into the Imperial Dungeons, "what do you suggest?"

"I'm not certain. I'll have to think about it. But I know what I'm going to do first: find out just what, by the blood on Verra's floor, is going on in South Adrilankha."

"Blood on Verra's floor?" said Morrolan. "I don't think I've heard that oath before."

"No," I said. "You probably haven't."

THE NEXT DAY WAS going to be short. That is, it was the day before the Festival of the New Year, so most people quit working around noon. I kept all of my people working, since Holy Days are some of our best times, but I gave them all bonuses. I had no idea if either of the people I needed to see was going to be working all day, some of the day, or not at all, so I awoke much earlier than usual. I broke my fast and spent some time throwing things for the jhereg to snatch out of the air and fight over.

"Loiosh, Rocza seems funny. Is she pregnant?"

"Huh? No, boss. At least, I don't think so. I mean, the way things work—"

"Never mind. What is it, then?"

"Well, you know she's been a little closer to Cawti than I have, so, I mean—"

"Oh, I get it. All right."

I slugged down my klava, dressed, collected Loiosh and Rocza, and headed out for my first errand. Aibynn was in the blue room but hadn't stirred. I envied him.

Kelly's group had moved twice since the last time I'd visited their headquarters, and this last place was a great deal different from the others. Up until now they'd met in a flat that two or three of them lived in, but they'd recently found an empty storefront not too far from one of the farmer's markets that appeared irregularly all over South Adrilankha. Whatever windows it once had were boarded up, either as a painfully inadequate defensive gesture or because they couldn't afford oiled paper or window glass. I stood there for a while and considered. As always when visiting the Easterners' part of town, I felt a slight relaxation of tension, but this time it was hardly noticeable as I studied the low, wood-frame building.

It was pretty obvious, once you got near it, both for the banner hung across the front that read "Stop Press Gangs!" and for the troop of Phoenix Guards who stood across the street from it, silent and ominous, ignoring the dirty looks they got from passersby. As Cawti had said, they all seemed to be Dragonlords and Dzur. That is, they were professionals, not conscripted Teckla, which meant there'd be no reasoning with them, and they'd fight well.

But never mind that. I watched from down the street where I could keep an eye on both the Phoenix Guards and whoever went through the door of the storefront. Eventually someone I recognized went in. I left my place, waved cheerfully to the goldcloaks, and followed him in.

He greeted me with all the warmth I remembered from our previous encounters. "You," he said.

"My dear Paresh," I told him. "How is it that they didn't arrest you, too? No, no, let me guess. They only hauled in the Easterners. Either they decided that a Dragaeran, even if a Teckla, doesn't deserve prison, or they decided that a Teckla, even if a Dragaeran, must be harmless. Am I right?"

"What do you want?"

"My wife back. How do you propose to get her out of prison?"

"We will be giving a demonstration of our strength tomorrow. We expect five thousand Easterners and Teckla, all of them committed to fighting until conscription stops and our friends are released. Many of them are determined to fight until the Empire itself is run by us, and for us. Do you have all that, or shall I repeat it?"

"I'll read it back to you: You aren't doing anything except shouting at each other about how mad you are and hoping the Empress laughs herself to death."

"She didn't laugh much a few weeks ago, when she pulled the troops out of South Adrilankha."

"They are, however, back."

"For the moment. But if we have to shut down—"

"Shut down your mouth, Paresh. I came here to find out if you had any plans for getting my wife out of the Imperial Dungeons. It seems you don't. That's all I wanted to know. Good day."

As I turned away, he said, "Baronet Taltos," and put such scorn into my title that I almost dropped him right then and there. I didn't, but I did stop and turn back to face him. He said, "Consider how your wife will react if you find some way to yendi her out of prison, while everyone else stays there. Think it over."

I felt a sneer growing on my face, but I didn't give him the satisfaction of letting him see it. I walked out the door and headed back toward my own side of town, where everyone hated me for reasons I was more comfortable with.

ALL RIGHT, SO I couldn't count on them. I hadn't really thought I could, but they deserved to be asked. Where did that leave me? Nowhere, probably. I stopped my walk long enough to make contact with Kragar.

"*Any news?*"

"*Those minstrels sure hear things, Vlad. They're better than the street tags. They play the court, and they listen, and they gossip. That was a great idea.*"

"*Save the praise, Kragar. Have we learned anything?*"

"*We sure have. The big arrest of Easterners was—um, I'm not certain you're going to like this.*"

"*Let's have it.*"

"*Okay. It was by request of and based on information supplied by the Imperial representative of House Jhereg.*"

I took a deep breath and, for no reason I'm aware of, my hands went through the automatic gestures that check to make sure my various concealed weapons are in their proper places.

"Okay, Kragar. Thanks. Anything else?"

"Nothing out of the ordinary."

"I'll be in touch."

I was wearing my usual cloak, but it was clean. The grey tunic I'd put on was in good shape, and my trousers, while not really suitable for court, weren't bad. My boots were a bit scuffed and dirty, so I stopped when I was back in Dragaeran country and had a Teckla clean and polish them, for which I tipped him well. Then, to keep them clean, I carefully teleported to the vicinity of the Imperial Palace.

I leaned against the nearest wall and counted passersby until my stomach felt well again, then made my way around to the path which led to the Jhereg Wing. There were two old men standing outside it pretending to be guards (who in his right mind would break into the Jhereg Wing?), to whom I nodded as I went by. Inside, a cheerful young man in grey and black was sitting behind a short oak table. He asked my business.

"Count Soffta," I said.

"Have you an appointment, my lord?"

"Naturally."

"Very well. That door, up the stairs, all the way to the back."

"Quite."

"A pleasant afternoon, my lord."

"Yes."

Every inch the nobleman, that's what I am. Heh. The cheerful young man's identical twin was sitting behind the table's identical twin. He asked my business. The table remained mute.

"Count Soffta," I said.

"Have you an appointment, my lord?"

"No."

"What name shall I give?"

"Baronet Taltos."

There was a bit of a twinge to his eyebrows, as if maybe he'd heard the name, but that was all. "A moment, if you please," and he was silent for a few heartbeats. Then he said, "You may go in, my lord."

"Thank you."

There's a saying that goes, "Only Issola live in the Palace," and it may be true. That is, if it were possible for a Jhereg to look like an Issola, Soffta did. His build was a bit chest-heavy, his face was regular, with the narrow forehead and peaked crown, and his movements were smooth and slow, and seemed practiced. No, he didn't really look like an Issola, but about as close as a Jhereg can come. His office had four comfortable-looking chairs and a view of the courtyard. Each chair had its own round, three-legged table on which the guest could set his drink, made from the bar at the far end of the room. All very nice and non-threatening, it was.

He motioned me to a seat. "Baronet Taltos," he said. "A pleasure. Drink? I have some Fenarian wine."

Issola. "That would be nice," I said. I saw the bottle and realized he meant brandy. "Clear and clean," I said. The chair was as soft as it looked. Not very good for getting out of in a hurry. I wondered if that was deliberate. If I had designed the room, it would have been.

He poured me a drink, and the same thing for himself. I wondered if he really cared for it, at least served the right way, or if he was being polite. I'd probably never know. It was Tuzviz, probably the most commonly available Fenarian brandy; good if not remarkable. At least I could tell there were peaches in its ancestry.

When we were both sitting and enjoying the fire on our tongues he said, "How may I serve you, Baronet?"

"The Empire has mistakenly arrested my wife while clearing out some Eastern rabble from South Adrilankha. I'd like to see about obtaining her release."

He nodded sympathetically. "I see. Most unfortunate. Her name?"

"The Lady Cawti. Taltos of course. She's the Countess of, let me see . . . Lostguard Cleft, I think."

"Yes. Bide a moment, enjoy the wine. I'll see what I can do."

"Very well."

He left the room. I got up and stared out the window. Off to the side I could just make out the vast hall of the Iorich Wing, beneath which were the dungeons. It was completely walled in, dark and solemn, with their banner flying above it and Dragonlords in the gold cloaks of the Phoenix Guards walking along the walls. No, on reflection, it would have been damn hard to break her out.

Directly below me was a rock garden in blue and white, and strips of neatly manicured lawn dotted with stunted trees. Directly in front of me, on a tall, lone flagpole, flew the banner of the House, stylized jhereg, sinister, wings spread, claws outstretched, black on a field of grey. It filled me with no emotion whatsoever.

Presently Soffta returned and sat down behind his desk again. He was looking very grave indeed. "It seems," he said, "that someone has already intervened on behalf of the Lady Cawti, and she refused release. Do you know anything about this?"

"Mmmm," I said. "What would it take to procure her release in spite of her refusal?"

"Why, I'm not sure, Lord Taltos. Such a refusal is almost unheard-of, and forcing a release, well, I imagine an order of the Empress would do it."

"No doubt, no doubt," I said. I stood up and strolled back over to the window, looked out of it. I paced a bit, and my pacing took me behind Soffta's chair. He let me get behind him, but I saw the tension in his neck muscles. Court representative or not, he was a Jhereg, not an Issola. "A difficult situation," I said. "Perhaps there is nothing to be done."

"Perhaps not," he said, still not looking at me. "Although I'm certainly willing to help as much as I can."

"Good, good," I said. "Perhaps, then, you could tell me something." As I spoke, I placed my hand casually on his shoulder. There was tension there now, but he kept his hands relaxed, in plain sight on his desk. We were ten feet from the door. "Just out of curiosity, how long has it been since blood has been spilled here, in the Jhereg Wing?"

"Not since the Interregnum, Lord Taltos."

"It would be bad for the Organization interests to have any sort of violence take place here, wouldn't it?"

"Very bad. I hope you aren't suggesting any."

I leaned on his shoulder, very slightly. "I? No, no, not at all. I wouldn't think of such a thing. I was just making conversation."

"I see. What was it you wanted to know?"

"Who arranged to have those Easterners arrested?"

There was the faintest hint of a tightening of muscles, but no more. "Why, the Empress, Baronet Taltos."

"At your request, Count Soffta. And I'm very anxious to learn which of my colleagues asked you to make the request."

"I believe you have been misinformed, Baronet Taltos."

"Have you heard of me, Count Soffta?"

My hand didn't leave his shoulder, but neither did it tighten, nor did I make any other movement. He said nothing for two or three heartbeats, then he said, "It may take me some time to find out, and I'm expecting a rather large number of visitors very soon."

"Yes, I imagine you are. But under the circumstances, I'm willing to let it take as much time as necessary. I'm sure your visitors will understand."

"It could be very expensive."

"I'm prepared to pay. It is my wife, you know."

"Yes. . . ."

"So the cost is irrelevant."

"I guess it is."

"Perhaps it would be best if you could gather the information?"

I could almost feel him weighing the odds, attempting to select the best thing to say, the best thing to do. "There may be repercussions—"

"I have absolutely no doubt that there will be. I accept them."

"All of them?"

"Whatever may happen. But I hope your information is complete and accurate, or there could be consequences you don't foresee."

"Yes. Toronnan."

"I'm not surprised. Do you know why?"

"No."

"Very well. Will you do me the honor of accompanying me out to the street?"

"I should be glad to, Lord Taltos."

"Then let us walk together."

We did so, smiling, my hand resting gently on his back. When we reached the street, I made certain there was no one nearby and composed my mind for a teleport. I let Spellbreaker fall into my left hand, just in case. "Count Soffta, I wish to thank you for your help."

"The fruits of your inquiry will be my reward, Baronet Taltos."

"No doubt. One thing, though."

"Yes."

"The Tuzviz you served me. It was quite good, but it is brandy, not wine. You should remember that."

"Thank you, Lord Taltos. I shall."

I released him and let the teleport take effect.

AN UNUSUAL SIGHT, NOT explained by the celebrations prepared for the next couple of days, greeted me when I walked into my office: Sticks was there, holding his clubs lightly, as if tossing them around, and next to him, looking quite out of place in his bright island clothing and norska hat, was Aibynn. They were speaking quietly about something arcane, Aibynn pointing to the clubs, and Sticks gesturing with them. Perhaps they were comparing the arts of battery and drumming. On reflection, that isn't that strange an idea: Both require relaxation and tension in the right degree, speed and suppleness, and good understanding of timing, control of the body, and concentration of the mind. Interesting notion.

But at the time I wasn't thinking about that. I said, "Aibynn, what are you doing here?"

He spoke, as always, slowly, as if he were constantly being distracted by the ultimate rhythms of the universe. "To say thanks for lining up that job for me."

"Oh. Think nothing of it. It's going well, I take it."

"Well? We've played one night together and we've been summoned to play for the Empress tomorrow."

"For the Imperial New Year's celebration?"

"Yeah, I guess so. Odd time to call it New Year, though. On the island, the year begins in the winter."

"Spring makes more sense, doesn't it?"

He shrugged.

"In any case," I went on, "the New Year is a big deal at the Palace. I'm very impre—hmmm."

"What is it?"

"Eh? Nothing." It had suddenly occurred to me that I had slain his King, and here he was about to appear before my Empress. If he were, in fact, an assassin himself, I had just set her up as elegantly as if I'd planned it. I briefly considered whether to do anything about it, then decided that it was none of my business. It may be that if he was an assassin I'd have to clear out before they traced the connection between Aibynn and me, but other than that, so what?

I congratulated him again and went past into my office, asking Melestrav to send Kragar in. I forced myself to concentrate on the door, and so I noticed him when he entered. He took one look at me and said, "Who's the target?"

"Toronnan."

"Himself, eh? Is he after us, or are we after him? Not that it really matters."

"Neither one, exactly. Kelly's bunch were arrested by his orders. I want to find out what he's after."

"Sounds good. How?"

"Buy someone in his organization, of course."

"Oh, sure. Just like that."

"If it was easy, Kragar, I'd do it myself."

He blinked. "It's nice to hear you say that out loud after all this time of—"

"Kill it."

"Speaking of."

"Hmmm?"

"We going to shine him?"

"I hope not. I've done too much of that. Any more, and people are going to start getting nervous—people I don't want to make nervous. Besides, I have my hands full with South Adrilankha right now; I don't need more territory."

He nodded. "That's what I've been thinking. Okay, I'll see if anyone is for sale in his organization." He got up, stopped, and said, "Do you think he might have bought someone in ours?"

"No way to know," I said. "It's a possibility. But I'm not going to start getting paranoid about it."

"I guess not."

"Oh, bring me a full set of weapons. It's about that time."

"Okay. Back soon." He left, looking unusually thoughtful.

A couple of hours later, as I was finishing up the process of changing weapons, Melestav walked into my office.

"Message by courier, boss."

"Oh, really? Someone's being formal. Did he let you chop for it?"

"Yeah. Here it is."

I inspected the single folded and sealed sheet and learned nothing interesting. I didn't recognize the seal, but I don't think there are more than three or four seals I would recognize. I'm not certain I'd know my own. I opened it, read, and considered.

"What is it, boss?"

"What? Oh. The gentleman who invited me over a few days ago wants to see me again, but he's not in as much of a hurry."

"Toronnan?"

"That's the guy."

"Think it's a setup?"

"Hard to say. He wants me to name the time and place, today or tomorrow. It would be hard to rig that."

"Okay, Vlad," said Kragar. "Do you want me to set up protection?"

"Damn right."

"Good. I'll take care of it. Where?"

"I'm still thinking about it. I'll tell Melestav when I decide."

He left to make arrangements.

"What do you think it is, boss?"

"I don't know. I hope it's not the beginning of another war; I don't think I could handle it."

"You and me both."

"Maybe I should get out of this business, Loiosh."

"Maybe you should."

He fell silent and I considered. Maybe I should get out—out of the whole thing. Killing people for money, earning a living from Teckla and fools, maybe I'd had enough. Maybe I could—

Could what? What would I do? I tried to imagine myself living like Morrolan or Aliera, safe on a piece of land somewhere watching the Teckla work the fields—or not watching as the case may be. Sitting around, indulging whatever vague curiosities came my way. No, I couldn't see it. Perhaps my existence was pointless in any grand scheme of things, but it kept me entertained.

Yes, but was that sufficient justification for all the things I had to do, just to stay alive and in business? Well, why did I feel the need to justify myself in the first place? In part, I guessed, because of Cawti. She'd been just where I knew I didn't want to be, idle and frustrated, and she'd handled it by getting involved with a bunch of crazies with a noble cause. What else? Well, there was my grandfather, whom I respected more than I respected anyone else. He knew what I did and, when I asked him, had given me his opinion on it. More fool me for asking.

But this was silly. Perhaps, later, I could decide if I wanted to change the way I lived, but right now my wife was in prison and I had just stirred up a school of orca by oh-so-gently threatening the Organization representative in the Imperial Palace, someone who ought to be left alone if anyone should. No, the Organization wasn't about to let one lone Easterner get away with anything like that. I was going to have to either figure out a way to pacify them or figure out a way to escape. Maybe I'd relocate to Greenaere and learn to drum.

Or not.

"*Melestav.*"

"*Yeah, boss?*"

"*Find out where Aibynn is playing tonight and send a courier to Toronnan. Tell him we'll meet him there at the eighth hour.*"

"*Okay, boss.*"

"*And put the word out that we might get hit soon.*"

"*Again?*"

"*I guess it's just one of those years.*"

"*I guess so, boss.*"

Lesson 10

Making Friends II

THE LOQUACIOUS MADMAN IS on Czigarel Street near Undauntra, in a district with very little Organization activity. I arrived two or three minutes early with Sticks and an enforcer we called Glowbug. Kragar had said he'd be there, too, but I didn't notice him. It is unlikely, however, that I would have noticed Sethra Lavode in that crowd. The festivities were already beginning. There were trails of cold fire traveling along all the walls; bouncing globes throughout the room, changing colors as they swirled; and ribbon trails hanging from the ceiling.

The crowd was mostly Teckla, all decked out like the bouncing globes in reds and yellows and blues, and merchants and artisans proudly wearing whatever they worked in, and brazenly flaunting their lovers, but here and there you could see the masked aristocracy of the House of the Tiassa or the Lyorn, adding a gentle touch of light blue or brown, and inserting whatever particular flavor of loud troublemaking or quiet drunkenness pleased them the most.

Which is not to say the place was crowded—yet. It's a big place, and things were just starting to get going. It was loud, but not deafening. Either a very good or a very strange time and place to have a business meeting.

Toronnan arrived less than two minutes after I did, preceded (as was I,

by the way) by a couple of toughs who checked the place over for any sign
of this being a setup. It isn't easy to tell that sort of thing, even when there
isn't a celebration going on, but it can be done. You have to look at everyone
in the place, especially the waiters, and note how each one carries himself,
where he is placed, and if he seems to be carrying any concealed weapons,
or looks familiar, or doesn't seem to fit in.

I had done that a few times, and the one time it really had been a setup,
for a guy named Welok, I had almost missed it that one of the cooks wasn't
using his knife the way a real cook would—instead of gripping it between
thumb and forefinger on the blade with the pommel resting on the heel of
his hand, he was gripping the pommel like a knife-fighter. I mentioned this
to Kragar, with whom I was working, who looked closely and realized that
he knew the guy. The meeting was called off, and three months later I was
hired by Welok to kill an enforcer named Kynn who worked for Rolaan—
the man who'd called the meeting.

But I digress. I hadn't set up anything and neither had Toronnan. Indeed—
this was a very bad situation to kill someone in, because the large and unpredictable crowd is likely to surprise you, and assassins *hate* surprises. He
sat facing me, his back to the door. I started to signal a waiter over, but he
didn't let me. "This won't take that long," he said.

I kept my face expressionless. It is a major break in protocol to set up a
business dinner and not eat. I wasn't certain what it indicated, but it wasn't
good. I settled back in the chair and said, "Go ahead, then."

"This has gone up to the Council. You have powerful friends there, but I
don't think they can help you this time."

"I'm still listening."

"We're sorry your wife got involved in this, but business is business."

"I'm still listening."

He nodded. "I was up before the Council today. They asked if you could
be shined without a fight. I said not unless they could find Mario. That
doesn't mean they aren't going to try, but you probably have a reprieve. Do
you understand?"

"Not quite. Keep talking."

"We just had a big mess between you and this Herth character, and before
that you had an altercation with some teckla that ended up with the Empire

stepping in, and in between was a big, bloody mess in the Hills between Be'er and Fyrnaan."

"I heard about that. I wasn't involved."

"That's not the point. The Organization has been calling way too much attention to itself and the Council is tired of it. That's the only thing that's keeping you alive."

"I take it I've offended someone."

"You've offended everyone, idiot. You don't go around threatening the Organization representative in the imperial Palace. Can you understand that?"

"Threaten? I?"

"Don't play stupid, Whiskers. I'm telling you to lay off. I'm telling you—"

"Why did you arrange to have those Easterners arrested?"

"You don't ask me questions, Whiskers. I ask you questions, you answer them, then I tell you things and you do them. That is the nature of our relationship. Can you grasp that, or do I need to illustrate it?"

"Why did you arrange to have those Easterners arrested?"

A sneer began to appear on his face but he put it away. "Is there some reason I should answer you?"

"I'll kill you if you don't."

"You'd never make it out of here alive."

"I know."

He stared at me. At last he said, "You're lying."

I shook my head. "No. I don't lie. I'm cultivating a reputation for honesty so I can blow it when something big comes along. This ain't it."

He snorted. "Just how much bigger a thing do you want?"

"Wait and see."

His teeth worked inside his mouth. Then he said, "Orders came from the Council. I don't know who it was."

"You could probably make a good guess if you put your mind to it."

We matched stares, then he said, "My boss. Boralinoi."

"Boralinoi," I repeated slowly. "That would make sense. My area is your area is his area, and I now own South Adrilankha, so he's responsible."

"That's right. And if you think you can mess with him—"

I shook my head. "I want my wife back, Lord Toronnan. That's what it all comes down to, okay? There's no way I'm going to let her rot in the Imperial Dungeons, so you'd better figure out a way to help me, or stay out of my way, or try your best to put me down, because I'm going to be moving."

He stood up. "I'll remember that, Lord Taltos. I will remember it."

After he was gone, I moved to the other side of the table, so I could watch the musicians, who were just setting up. It took me a while to find a waiter, but I finally succeeded and ordered pasta with peppers and sausage. He seemed surprised that I actually wanted to eat; I suppose most people were just drinking. And then when he started to leave, Kragar called him back and ordered one of the same, which puzzled him even more although he tried not to show it.

"What happened?" he said.

"I seem to have made another enemy."

"Oh? Toronnan?"

"No. The Jhereg."

Kragar cocked his head to the side. "Tell me something, Vlad: Why do I keep sticking with you?"

"I don't know. Maybe you aren't. Maybe you're setting up to knife me."

"Don't start getting paranoid now."

"Well, if you aren't setting up to knife me, maybe you should be. This would be the right time."

He stared at me very hard, no sign of banter on his face. "You'd better give me the details," he said.

I did so, starting with my interview with Soffta, up to the conversation with Toronnan. The food arrived in the middle of it and, as I was concluding, the musicians started up. I was surprised at how well the crowd quieted down, but I was pretty sure they'd make up for it later. I hoped to be gone by then.

The food was edible, the wine quite dry but good. The singer was good. Albynn stayed pretty much in the background so I didn't notice him too much, though I might have if I'd known anything about music. I did note the dreamy smile on his face, which reminded me of how my grandfather looked when in the middle of a spell. For all I know I look the same way.

Eventually they stopped, and Aibynn came over and introduced his partner, a relatively short Tiassa named Thoddi. We discussed inanities for a while, then they played some more. Kragar said, "What's the plan?"

"I think I'm going to have to find this Boralinoi."

"That could be dangerous."

"Probably. Find out where he works."

"What? Now?"

"Now. I'll wait here."

"Look, Vlad, aside from the obvious stupidities of barging in to see this guy without setting things up, how do you know Toronnan hasn't just sent a team over here to shine you when you leave?"

"Let him try," I said. "Just let him try."

"Vlad—"

"Do it. Find out where he is. I'll wait here."

He sighed. "Okay. I'll see you soon."

My enjoyment of the music was dampened just a little by a need to keep an eye on the door, but not too much, because there were Loiosh, Sticks, and Glowbug. Presently Kragar got hold of me again and told me where to find Boralinoi when he was working.

"He isn't there now, Vlad. You'll have to wait until tomorrow."

"I guess."

"Why don't you think the whole thing over, then? Maybe you—"

"Thanks, Kragar. I'll see you tomorrow."

The crowd was just making it impossible to listen to the music when they stopped, and announced that they were finished and someone else would be playing next, which surprised me. I threw an Imperial into the jar, paid for the food and drink, and walked back home with Aibynn. We didn't speak for a while, then I ventured, "You sounded pretty good."

"Yeah," he said. "That was a good one. Did you notice those fake seventy-twos I was throwing into the seventeens?"

"Uh, well, no, not really."

He nodded. "They weren't really seventy-twos, because you have to punch the one, the six-seven-eight, the ten, and the sixteen-seventeen of every measure, but it kind of works if you pretend every third measure is . . ." He went on, with me nodding and making interested sounds. Sticks, who was in front, fell back a bit to listen and the two of them got into a discussion of arcane matters beyond the likes of me. I still wondered who Aibynn really was, and what he was doing here, and if he was going to assassinate the Empress.

Not that I cared.

"*What do you care about, boss?*" said Loiosh as we walked up the stairs to my flat.

"*Getting Cawti out of prison.*"

"*And then?*"

"*Don't ask difficult questions, Loiosh.*"

I asked Sticks and Glowbug if they wanted some wine before they took off. Glowbug didn't, but Sticks knows the kind of wine I keep around the house, so he was right behind me when I went through the door.

What impressed me the most, I think, was how quickly Toronnan had moved. It was, what, half an hour, maybe, since I'd left him. The assassin was waiting just inside the door of the flat, and neither Loiosh nor I had any inkling. But Sticks, as I said, was right behind me, and when the dagger came slicing toward the back of my neck, he acted, pushing me sideways and forward into the room. I rolled and came up in time to see Sticks holding his clubs, connecting with the guy's head, very hard. The guy went down. I felt a burn along my neck, touched my hand, and found blood. I hoped his blade hadn't been poisoned. I discovered I was trembling.

"Good work," I told Sticks. His only answer was to slump to the floor. It was only then that I noticed the stiletto that had gone completely through his throat and out the back of his neck.

Aibynn came into the room then and knelt next to Sticks, whose eyes were open and glassy. Loiosh landed on my shoulder and nuzzled my ear. I inspected the corpse of my enforcer and saw that his backbone had been neatly severed. What you call in the business a lucky shot.

AN HOUR OR SO later the bodies were gone, and Kragar was sitting in the living room with me while I gradually stopped trembling. "Right in my house, Kragar," I said for about the ninth time.

"I know, boss," he said.

"You don't do that."

Aibynn was in his room, drumming, he said, to pull himself back together.
Kragar said, "I know why they did, though."

"What do you mean?"

"Remember a few weeks ago? Didn't you go busting into someone's house
to get information from him?"

I took a very deep breath. "Yes," I said.

"There you have it. You broke the rules, they broke the rules. That's how
it works, Vlad."

"I should have known."

"Yeah."

Not more than a month before, Sticks had refused an offer for my head.
His refusal had made him a target, and I'd saved his life, just as he'd saved
mine before. And for what?

"I don't think you should stay here, Vlad."

"I'm not going to, Kragar. Thanks. I'm all right now."

"I'll wait until you leave, if you don't mind."

"Yeah, okay."

I suggested to Aibynn that this might not be a safe place to stay tonight.
He said, "No problem. I have a friend I can stay with."

"Good. I'll see you sometime."

Kragar escorted me down the stairs and left me when it looked safe.

"*Where are we going, boss?*"

"*An inn I know, on the other side of town.*"

"*Why there?*"

"*It's across the street from where Boralinoi works.*"

"*Ah. What about Toronnan? He was the one who—*"

"*Fuck Toronnan. Fuck revenge. I'm getting Cawti back.*"

It was a good three-hour walk, but I think it did me good.

I WAS UP EARLY the next morning, waiting just outside the inn where I'd
spent the night. I stood in the shadow of the doorway, waiting. Rocza flew
around looking harmless and terrorizing all the local, city-bred jhereg while
Loiosh waited with me. I had six good hours of sleep inside of me, followed
by three cups of klava and crumb-bread with goat cheese. A sharp, steady

wind came up the hill from my left, smacking me in the face and giving rise
to reflections on the passing away of the old and the unfathomable nature
of the new.

Not a bad day to kill, not a bad day to die, if either came to pass.

While I didn't know what Boralinoi looked like, I had no trouble spotting
him by the two enforcers who preceded him, the one on either side, and the
two who followed him. They were good, too. I idly went through possibilities
for nailing him as he walked down the street, and came to the conclusion
that I'd have to bribe at least two, perhaps three of those enforcers to have
a reasonable chance. They really were attending to business, and I had to do
some fast shifting to avoid being spotted. Boralinoi was dressed expensive
and walked like he knew it. I thought he'd look good in court, with his
perfect black curly hair, rings on all his fingers, and delicate precise steps.
He looked like he was probably perfumed, and doubtless had a scent-cloth
next to his collar, lest he meet with someone whose breath he didn't like.

He went into the leather shop that housed his offices in back. I gathered
Rocza to my other shoulder and followed him in. I've always loved the smell
of fresh leather, though here it was a bit overpowering, I suppose due to the
admixture of scents of various oils and unguents used by this mysterious
trade. In the front part of the store hung vests and jerkins, and when I slipped
past to the back, there was an old Vallista laboriously pushing a heavy needle
and thick thread into the seam of what looked like a leather flagon. Why
anyone would wish to drink from a leather flagon, I don't know.

Before he noticed me, I got past him and was facing a stairway leading
up. At its top were two Jhereg who didn't look friendly. They studied me
and seemed to be wondering if they should challenge me or just drop me
where I stood. I reached the top alive and said, "Vlad Taltos to see Lord
Boralinoi."

The shorter of the two said, "Appointment?"

"No."

"Wait there, then."

"Yes."

He concentrated for a moment, nodded as if to himself, and said, "What
do you want to see him about?" He had a voice like a metal file; it set my
teeth on edge.

"It's a personal matter."

"So make a sacrifice."

"Whom do you suggest?"

He smiled a little. I wondered if he kept his teeth crooked on purpose, just for the effect. He concentrated again, then said once more, "Wait."

After a minute or two of standing there regarding the toughs who were regarding me, he said, "Go on in, the boss will give you five minutes."

"Oh, happy day," I said, and went past them.

There were five more in the next room, one at a desk and four lounging around. I knew them all for killers at once. The one at the desk nodded to me, the others looked me over much the way I look over a game hen before I loosen its skin to fill it with mushrooms, garlic, and tarragon.

There were three doors. I pointed to the middle one, asked a question with my eyebrows, received a nod, and went through. His desk was big, and he sat behind it like he belonged there. There were two Jhereg in the room with him, one quiet-looking wisp of a man with a pinched-in face and a dimple who was either an accountant or a sorcerer, and another tough, this one with the cold look of someone who would kill anyone, anytime, for any reason at all. When I came in he shifted his shoulders and ran a hand down his chin, in a gesture I recognized as checking to make sure the surprises under his cloak were all in place and ready. I automatically ran a hand through my hair and adjusted the clasp of my cloak. All of mine were set.

There were no windows in the room, and, so far as I could tell from a quick glance, no other exits. I'd give odds that there was a hidden door somewhere, because that's how these people work, but I couldn't find it. Loiosh shifted uncomfortably on my shoulder; he didn't like the lack of an escape route, either. Rocza, on my other shoulder, picked up some of his nervousness. Boralinoi's eyes rested on each of the jhereg in turn, then he looked at me.

"I've heard of you, Lord Taltos," he said.

"And I, you, Your Lordship."

"You wanted to speak to me. Go ahead."

"It's a private matter, Your Lordship."

Without taking his eyes from me, he said, "Cor, N'vaan, don't speak of this to anyone."

That was the best I was going to get, then. I said, "I'm coming to you for advice about my marriage, Your Lordship."

"Sorry. I'm not married."

"A shame, Your Lordship. Marriage is bliss, you know. But I believe Your Lordship might be able to help me, anyway."

He took a scent-cloth from his collar and waved it in front of his face, dabbed it against the corners of his mouth, crumpled it up in his hand, and leaned back in the chair. "You're talking about the woman who's been working with those troublemakers in South Adrilankha."

"She's the only wife I have, Your Lordship. I'd sure hate to lose her."

"Why do you come to me?"

"It was by your orders that those people were arrested. I would think you could have one released."

"What makes you think I arranged it?"

"A dream I had last night, Your Lordship. We Easterners always believe our dreams."

"I see." He leaned forward and stared at me. "Listen to me, Baronet Taltos, so I don't have to repeat myself. Those troublemakers are making trouble, and not just in South Adrilankha. The trouble they're making affects what happens in the rest of the city and beyond its borders. We've already had noticeable cuts in our profit in several areas, traced directly to Teckla getting too smart for themselves. If a thing like that happens on its own, so be it; I wouldn't interfere. But it isn't happening on its own, these people are making it happen. And who's right in front of making it happen? Your wife, Taltos. A Jhereg. The Empire has come to us, through our representative, and complained. They've denied petitions of ours because of the trouble stirred up by this Jhereg Easterner wife of yours. We can't have that.

"Yes, I got them arrested. I'll even tell you how, Taltos. I had a sorcerer of mine blow up a watchstation in South Adrilankha, and leave messages all over it that looked like they'd done it. Does that shock you? It shouldn't. They needed to be put away, and I've put them away. If I haven't done it thoroughly enough, then I'll go back and do it again.

"I'm sorry it's your wife who's involved, Lord Taltos, I really am. But that's just your hard luck. Let her out? She was the one I most needed to get. So live with it. Go out and find someone else. If I have my way, she'll rot in the Imperial Dungeons until the Great Sea of Chaos floods the Empire. That's all I have to say. Happy New Year."

"*Easy, boss.*"

"*I know, Loiosh. I'm trying. Keep Rocza under control, will you?*" I didn't say anything for a moment, trying to check my temper, and to keep the effort off my face. Then I spoke very slowly and carefully, to make sure there was no mistake.

"So you arranged for my wife to be arrested by the Empire?"

"Yes."

"That is, my wife in particular?"

"Yes."

I looked him up and down once, and said, "You know, I believe I'm going to mess you up."

"No, you're not," he said, and concentrated very briefly. The door behind me opened, and, as I turned my head, five of them came through. They were all of them holding daggers; no doubt they'd been waiting for this. I turned back and saw that Boralinoi had pushed his chair back and the two who'd been standing there stepped between him and me. The tough one drew a shortsword. There was an awful stillness, as if the time between heartbeats had stretched across an ocean of movement, holding the world exactly as it was for just one instant that took forever.

"You're right," I said at last. "I'm going to kill you."

Interestingly enough, if there'd been fewer of them I might not have gotten out of there. But the room wasn't really big enough for all of them to work together, as long as I got the jump; and I did. Loiosh let me see what was behind me well enough for me to throw a pair of daggers into the stomachs of the two directly behind me, which slowed them down a great deal, and at the same time Rocza flew at the most dangerous of them, the sorcerer.

I spun away throwing a handful of darts randomly in the general direction of the three between me and the door, then pivoted away from whatever those behind me might be up to. I was through the door before they could recover. Loiosh went flying down the hall to find out what was up ahead while I turned back to the door.

I had just time to draw my rapier, which is sometimes a handicap against the huge Dragaeran longswords, but worked very nicely indeed against the

Jhereg with the dagger who charged out at me. I cut his knife hand and scored his neck in two quick movements of the wrist that would have made my grandfather proud, then backed up a few steps.

I took a throwing knife into my left hand as Rocza flew out the door and past me to help Loiosh in case he was in trouble. Verra, my goddess, what a team we were that day! The tough one with the shortsword appeared in the door and took my knife directly in his chest. He didn't go down, which was ideal, since he blocked the door quite effectively. Loiosh gave me the all-clear for the next room, and I was through it and down the stairs.

I'm not much of a sorcerer, but it doesn't take much of a sorcerer to fuse a door shut, and the few seconds that gained me made all the difference.

"Two toughs in here waiting for you, boss. We're distracting them, but—yikes!"

"You all right, Loiosh?"

"Near miss, boss."

"Tell me when."

"Wait . . . wait. . . ." I took Spellbreaker into my left hand, wishing I'd had a third hand to hold some darts. *"Now!"* and I charged through the door, point-first.

Loiosh and Rocza had, indeed, distracted them, and the point of my rapier through a throat distracted one of them more. The other, slashing desperately at Rocza, concentrated on me and gestured, but Spellbreaker, spinning wildly, handily stopped whatever it was. I slashed in his general direction just to give him something to think about, then I was through the door. Loiosh and Rocza beat him out of it, I shut it, did my little fusing thing again, and ran like hell down the stairs.

The leatherworker seemed to be just a leatherworker, because his only reaction to seeing me appear with a blooded sword was to squawk and cower, and then I was in the street, across the street, behind a building.

"We're teleporting, folks."

"What if they trace it?"

"Watch me." And I put forth my power and appeared in the courtyard of Castle Black, where a guest is always safe, as I've good reason to know. I didn't throw up, but the aftereffect of the teleport had me on my knees and the world spinning. Seeing the ground a mile below didn't help, either, but

knowing I was safe, if only for a moment, more than made up for the discomfort.

After a time, I got to my feet and headed for the great double doors, my knees vibrating like Aibynn's drum.

Lesson 11

Matters of State II

LADY TELDRA DIRECTED ME to the third-floor study in the South Wing, where I found Morrolan closeted with Daymar, whom I mentioned earlier. Daymar was thin and angular, with the sharp nose, chin, and jawline of the House of the Hawk, softened by a broad forehead and wide-set eyes. Loiosh flew over to greet Morrolan. Rocza, oddly enough, flew over to Daymar, whom she had never met, and stayed on his shoulder for the entire conversation.

Morrolan and Daymar were hunched over a table. Between them was something that looked to be a large black jewel. They were poking at it and staring at it as if it were a small animal and they wanted to see if it was alive. I went over to the table myself, and it took them a few moments to notice me. Then Daymar looked up and said, "Oh, hello, Vlad."

"Good morning. What is that?"

"That," said Morrolan, "is black Phoenix stone."

"Never heard of it," I said.

"It is similar to gold Phoenix stone," said Daymar helpfully.

"Yes," I said. "Only black instead of gold."

"Right," said Daymar, not noticing my sarcasm.

"What is gold Phoenix stone?"

"Well," said Daymar, "once we discovered the black, we started digging around in Morrolan's library and found a few references to it."

"Morrolan," I said, "would *you* care to enlighten me?"

"Do you recall," said Morrolan, "the difficulty we had with psionic contact on the island?"

"Yes. Daymar was cut off, as I recall."

He looked up from scratching Rocza's chin. "Not cut off," he said. "I collapsed from the effort of maintaining contact."

I stared at him. "You?"

"I."

"My goodness."

"Yes."

Morrolan said, "The only place Phoenix stone occurs is on the eastern and southern coast of Greenaere. Essentially, no psychic activity can pass through the effect of the stone, and the concentration around the island is sufficient to make it unreachable."

"Then why could Loiosh and I communicate?"

"Exactly," said Morrolan. "That is, indeed, the question. The only idea I've been able to come up with is that the connection between witch and familiar is fundamentally different from psionic communication. But how it is different, I don't know. I'd been planning to reach you, but since you are here, perhaps you'd be willing to assist us in a few experiments to determine exactly that."

"I'm not sure I like this, boss."

"You and me both, Loiosh." To Morrolan I said, "This may not be the best time."

His eyebrows focused on me. "Why? Has something happened?"

"Oh, nothing. Another close brush with death, but what's one more of those?"

For a moment he looked puzzled, trying to work out where the irony was, then he said, "Would you like some wine?"

"Love some. I'll help myself." I did so.

Morrolan said, "Tell me about it, Vlad."

"Jhereg troubles."

"Again?"

"Still."

"I see."

Daymar said, "Can I help?"

"No. Thanks."

"Say, boss, doesn't Aibynn have one of those things hanging around his neck?"

"Come to think of it, yes."

"So that's why I could never spot him."

"Or anyone else on Greenaere, probably. Yeah."

I turned back to Morrolan. "Where did you find this?"

A little Morrolan smile flitted across one side of his face. "Exploring," he said.

"Where?"

"In the Imperial Dungeons."

My heart started hammering. I said, "Cawti—"

"She's fine. We didn't actually speak much, but I saw her—"

"How did you—?"

"I was visiting the Palace, and I got lost, and about thirty Imperials got lost as well, and there I was."

My hands were getting tired where I was gripping the chair. I relaxed them. "Did you speak at all?"

"I said hello, she looked surprised and nodded to me, by which time my guide was too nervous about the whole thing to keep me there. But I kept noticing these crystals about the place, so I acquired one on my way out."

"But she seems well?"

"Yes. She seemed quite, um, spirited."

"Did—damn. Wait a moment." I grumbled, debated ignoring whoever it was, decided there was too much happening right now, and let my mental barriers down.

"Who is it?"

"Me, boss. Where are you? I can hardly maintain contact."

"Just a moment, Melestav." I moved to the far side of the room, well away from the crystal. *"Is that better?"*

"Some."

"Okay. What is it? Can it wait?"

"*Another messenger, boss.*" There was something odd in his tone. I said, "Not from Toronnan this time?"

"*No, boss. From the Empress. She wants to see you. Tomorrow.*"

"The Empress?"

"*Yeah.*"

"Tomorrow?"

"*That's what I said.*"

"Tomorrow is New Year's day."

"*I know.*"

"All right. I'll talk to you later."

I turned to Morrolan. "Can you think of any reason why the Empress would want to see me on New Year's day?"

He cocked his head to the side. "Do you sing?"

"No."

"In that case, it must be something important."

"Oh, grand," I said. "I can hardly wait."

"In the meantime," said Morrolan, "I just want to try a couple of things. I assure you there is no risk."

"*What the hell, boss? The worst that can happen is that it'll kill us, and then we don't have to worry about what the Empress is going to do.*"

"*A point,*" I said, and told Morrolan to go ahead.

THE NEXT DAY WAS the first day of the Month of the Phoenix, in the Year of the Dzur, during the Phase of the Yendi in the Reign of the Phoenix, Cycle of the Phoenix, Great Cycle of the Dragon, which is why most of us say the year 244 after the Interregnum.

I was off to the Imperial Palace. Happy New Year.

If you're sitting on the edge of your chair waiting to hear what the Imperial Palace was like, you're in for a disappointment; I don't remember. It was big and impressive and was built by people who know how to do things big and impressive, and that's all I remember. I was there just past noon, all dressed up in my Jhereg colors, with my boots brightly polished, my cloak freshly cleaned, and a jerkin that fairly glittered. I had found my pendant of office and put it around my neck; just about the first time I'd worn it since I'd inherited it. I had thought for a long time about leaving Loiosh behind, and he'd politely refrained from the conversation, but in the end I couldn't bring myself to do it, so he sat proudly on my right shoulder. Rocza, who *had* been left behind, wasn't very happy about it, but there are limits to how much of an outrage I wanted to be the first time I officially appeared before the Empress.

Appear before the Empress.

I was a Jhereg, the scum of society, and an Easterner, the scum of the world. She sat with the Orb revolving about her head, in the center of the Empire, and at her command was all the power of the Great Sea of Chaos, as well as all the military might of the Seventeen Houses. She had survived Adron's Disaster, and braved the Paths of the Dead, rebuilding, almost overnight, an Empire that had fallen to ruin. Now she wanted to see me, and you think I was in shape to take notes on architecture?

I'd seen her once before, but that was in the Iorich Wing, when I'd been questioned concerning the death of a high noble of the House of the Jhereg. It seems that a minor boss in the Organization, a certain Taishatinin or something, had bought himself a Dukedom in the House and then proceeded to get himself killed. I can't imagine why he wanted it except perhaps to feed his self-esteem, but there it was; he was a Duke, and when a Duke is murdered, the Empire investigates.

And somehow my name came up, and, after spending a couple of weeks in the Imperial Dungeons, I was ordered to testify "Under the Orb," with the Empress there to observe, and all these peers of House Jhereg who had no power at all in the running of the Organization. I was asked things like, "When did you last see him alive?" and I'd say, "Oh, I don't know; he was always pretty dead," and they'd rebuke me sternly. They asked my opinion as to who killed him and I said that I believed he had killed himself. The Orb showed that I was telling the truth, and I was; messing with me the way he'd been doing was like asking to die. The only time the Orb caught me lying was when I made some remark about how overwhelmed I was to be speaking before such an august assembly.

I remember catching a glimpse or two of the Empress, seated behind me to my left, and wondering what she thought of the whole thing. I thought she was pretty for a Dragaeran, but I don't remember any of the details, except for her eyes, which were gold.

This time I noticed a little more. After a vague period of feeling as if I were being handed from one polite functionary to another, and in which I gave my name and titles more times than I had in the last year put together, I was allowed into the Imperial throne room, and then I heard my name, stepped forward, and became aware of myself and my surroundings for the first time that day. Globes and candles were lit, and the place was full of aristocrats, all in a festive mood, or pretending to be in a festive mood.

I was aware of her, too. She wore a gown that was the color of her eyes and hair, and her face was heart-shaped, her brows high and fine. I stood before her in the Hall of the Phoenix. Her throne was carved of onyx and traced with gold in the representations of all Seventeen Houses. I instinctively looked for the Jhereg, and saw part of a wing near her right hand. I also discerned unobtrusive black cushions on the throne and didn't know whether to be amused or not.

The seneschal announced me and I stepped forward, giving her the best courtesy I knew how to give. Loiosh had to adjust himself to keep from falling off, but did so, I think, fairly gracefully.

"We give you welcome, Baronet Taltos," she said. Her voice was just a voice; I mean, I don't know what I expected, but I was surprised when she sounded like someone you'd meet at the market pricing coriander.

"Thank you, Your Majesty. I ask only to serve you."

"Indeed, Baronet?" She seemed amused. "I suspect the Orb would detect a falsehood there. You are usually more careful in your evasions."

She remembered.

"It is a pleasure not to have to dissemble before Your Majesty," I said. "I prefer to lie directly."

She chuckled, which didn't surprise me. What did surprise me was the lack of scandalized murmuring from the faceless courtiers behind me. Perhaps they knew their Empress. She said, "We must speak together. Please wait."

"I am at your service, Majesty."

As I'd been coached, I stepped backward seventeen steps, and then to the side. I wondered if watching an hour or so of Imperial business would be boring or if it would be interesting. In fact, it was startling, because I had momentarily forgotten the festivities, and the first thing I noticed was Aibynn holding his drum to the side and speaking with the singer I recognized, and someone I didn't know who was holding an instrument similar to the Eastern Hej'du.

I went over and said hello. Aibynn seemed faintly surprised to see me, but also distracted. Thoddi was more gregarious, and introduced me to the other musician, an Athyra whose name was Dav-Hoel.

"So, there are three of you now," I remarked to Thoddi.

"Actually there should be four of us, but Andler refused to play before the Empress."

"Refused?"

"He's an Iorich, and he's upset about, you know, the conscription in South Adrilankha, and the Phoenix Guards, and that kind of thing."

"I don't want to hear about it," I said. Thoddi nodded as if he understood, which I doubted. "Anyway," I said, "good luck."

Shortly after that, they were called on. Thoddi began to sing some old tavern song about making candles, full of innuendo and bad rhymes, but I watched Aibynn. He had the same dreamy smile as always, as if he were hearing something you couldn't hear, or seeing something through his half-shut eyes that you couldn't see.

Or knew something you didn't know.

Such as, for instance, that he was about to assassinate the Empress.

"He's going to do it, Loiosh."

"I think you're right, boss."

"I don't want to be here."

"Can you think of any way to leave?"

"Well, no."

"What do we do?"

"You come up with a plan. I'm fresh out."

I watched with a horrified fascination as Aibynn began to move, the drum cradled against his left side. He spun in place for a while, then began to dance out and back as the singing died and they just played. Was he moving closer to the Empress? I tore my eyes away from him and saw her having a low-voiced discussion with a lady of the House of the Tiassa. The Empress smiled, and though she spoke with the Tiassa, her eyes were on the musicians.

She had a good smile. I wondered if it was true, the tavern gossip about a lover who was an Easterner.

Aibynn was, yes, closer now. If he had concealed a knife, or a dart, or a blowgun, he could hardly miss, and no one was near him. I began to move forward. I glanced back at the Empress, and she was looking at me now. I stopped where I was, unable to move, my heart thundering. She smiled at me, just a little, and almost imperceptibly shook her head. What was she thinking? Did she think that *I* . . . ?

The song ended on a roll of the drum and a clatter of the lant-like instrument Thoddi played, and the musicians bowed. Aibynn returned to the side, and they started another song, an instrumental piece I didn't know. I stepped backward, shaking and confused. What had just happened? What had almost happened? How much had I imagined?

Dav-Hoel's instrument teased the melody the same way Aibynn's drum was teasing the rhythm. On the other hand, I wished they'd just play the song, but everyone else seemed very impressed, and the Empress looked positively excited. I've never been very knowledgeable about music.

After that they did a silly song about snuff, then an instrumental they introduced as the Madman's Dance, and then Loiosh said, "*Boss, wake up! The Empress!*"

"Huh? Oh." She was gesturing to me, still looking amused.

I came forward, bowed once more, and she said, "Come with me."

"Yes, Your Majesty."

She stood, stretched quite unselfconsciously, threw a purse to the musicians, and went behind the throne through a curtained doorway. I followed, feeling self-conscious enough to make up for both of us. She turned back to me and nodded that I was to catch up to her. I did, and the four of us, the Empress Zerika, the Orb, Loiosh, and I, walked together in silence. Was it stranger for her to be walking with a Jhereg, a jhereg, or an Easterner? On the other hand, if it was true that she had a human lover—

She caught me staring at her and I turned away, feeling myself blushing.

"You were thinking improper thoughts about your Empress?" she said in a voice that sounded more amused than offended.

"Just speculating on rumors, Your Majesty."

"Ah. About an Eastern lover?"

"Um, yeah."

"It's true," she said. "His name is Laszlo. He isn't my lover because he is an Easterner, nor despite it. He is my lover because I love him, and he is an Easterner because that is the house in which his soul resides."

I licked my lips. "How can you read my thoughts without my familiar catching you at it?"

She laughed, just a little. "By watching your face, and by guessing. I've gotten pretty good at it."

"That's all?"

"It is often enough. For example, I saw you try to foil an attempt on my life that was not going to take place. Had you forgotten the Orb, which protects the life of the Emperor?"

I blushed once more. I *had* forgotten. To cover, I said, "It hasn't always worked."

"You," she said, "are not Mario. And neither is your friend from Green-aere."

"Then I imagined the whole thing?"

"Yes."

"How did you know what I was thinking?"

"You were not troubling to keep your worries from your countenance, and you *are* an assassin."

"Who, me?"

"Yes," she said, "you."

There was nothing to say to that, so I said nothing. We went around a corner and through more plain white halls. She said, "For some reason, I do my best thinking when walking right here."

"Like a Tiassa," I said without thinking.

"What?"

"Excuse me, Your Majesty. Something I heard somewhere: Tiassa think walking, Dragons think standing, Lyorn think sitting, and Dzur think afterward."

She chuckled. "And when do you think, good Jhereg?"

"All the time, Your Majesty. I can't seem to help it."

"Ah. I know the feeling." We walked some more. She seemed very casual with me, but there was the Orb, circling her head slowly as we walked, and changing color occasionally; from the murky brown a few moments ago to a calm blue. I wondered if she was deliberately trying to confuse me.

"You are a very unusual man, Baronet Vladimir Taltos," she said suddenly. "You bring someone you think might be an assassin into the Empire and allow him to appear before me, and yet you were ready to act to protect me when you thought he might really do something."

"How did you know he is from Greenaere?"

"I suspected it when I found him psychically blank. I checked with the Orb, and there are memories recorded of the sort of clothes he wears and the type of drum he plays."

"I see. Your Majesty, why did you summon me?"

"To see what you looked like. Oh, I remembered you faintly, from your skillful dancing around the truth during a certain murder inquiry. But I wanted to know a little better the man who threatened his own House representative right on the Palace grounds, and whose wife is best friends with my Heir."

I chuckled at that, remembering the nature of that friendship.

"Yes," she said, smiling. "I know all about it."

"How?"

She shook her head. "Norathar has told me nothing. But I am, after all, the Empress. I suspect I have a better spy network even than you do, Lord Taltos."

Ouch. "I wouldn't doubt it, Your Majesty." What *didn't* she know? Did she know, for example, that I was the one who had started the war with Greenaere? Probably not, or I'd be in the cell next to Cawti. "Is this how you usually spend the New Year's festivities, Your Majesty?"

"It is when we are threatened with war, and simultaneously with rebellion. I worry about these things, Baronet, and decisions must be made—such as if I am to step down and let the House of the Dragon take the Orb. I will spend today seeing everyone who I think may have a role to play in all of this."

"What makes you think I will have a role to play in war and rebellion, Your Majesty?"

"I could give several answers to that, but the short one is, when I searched the Orb for names, yours was one that emerged. I don't know why. Can you tell me?"

"No," I said, keeping careful control of my features.

"Cannot, or will not?"

"Will not, Your Majesty."

"Very well," she said, and I breathed again.

I said, "Will there be war, Your Majesty?"

"Yes."

"I'm sorry to hear it."

"As am I. The alliance of Greenaere and Elde will be a difficult one to defeat. It is all but impossible to effect a landing in either place, whereas we have too many miles of coastline to protect. In the end, we may have to crush them with numbers, and that will be costly, in lives and everything else."

"What do they want, Your Majesty?"

"I don't know. They don't seem to want anything. Perhaps there is a madman behind it. Or a god."

We went around another turn, again to the left, and there was a slight rise to the floor. "Where are we now, Your Majesty?"

"Do you know, I'm not exactly certain. This is a route I walk often, but I've never known exactly where it goes. There are no doors or other paths that I've found or heard of. I sometimes wonder if it was put here just for this purpose."

"Then I suppose it would be pretty useless during the reign of a Dragon, Lyorn, or Dzur."

She chuckled. "I suppose it would."

The walk straightened out. "Your Majesty, why is my wife in your dungeons?"

She sighed. "First, let us be accurate. They are not dungeons. Dungeons are dank cells where Duke Curse-Me-Not keeps merchants he can't justify executing but whose goods he likes more than the prices. The Lady Cawti of Taltos, Countess of Lostguard Cleft and Environs, resides in the Imperial prison on suspicion of conspiring against the Orb."

I bit my lip. "Noted, Your Majesty."

"Good. Now, as to why she is there: because she wants to be. There was a petition to release her, it was granted, she refused."

"I know about that, Your Majesty. The Lady Norathar made this petition. What did she say upon refusing?"

"She didn't specifically say she wanted to stay, but she wouldn't sign the document we required for her release."

"Document? What sort of document, Your Majesty?"

"One that said she would not engage in any activities contrary to the interests of the Empire."

"Ah. That would account for it." The Empress didn't say anything. I said, "But, Your Majesty, why was she arrested in the first place?"

"I'm wondering," she said slowly, "how much you know, and how much I should tell you."

"I know that it was my own House that made the petition. But why was it granted?" In other words, since when did a Phoenix Empress care a teckla's squeal about the business workings of House Jhereg?

She said, "You seem to think I am at liberty to ignore whatever requests I wish to."

"In a word, Your Majesty, yes. You are Empress."

"That is true, Baronet Taltos, I am Empress." She frowned, and seemed to be thinking. The floor began to slope up and I began to feel fatigued. She said, "Being Empress has meant many things throughout our long, long history. Its meaning changes with each Cycle, with each House whose turn it is to rule, with each Emperor or Empress who sets the Orb spinning about his or her head. Now, at the dawn of the second Great Cycle, all of those with a bent toward history are looking back, studying how it is we have arrived at this pass, and this gives us the chance to see where we are.

"The Emperor, Baronet Taltos, has never, in all our long history, ruled the Empire, save now and again, for a few moments only, such as Korotta the Sixth between the destruction of the Barons of the North and the arrival of the Embassy of Duke Tinaan."

"I know only a little of these things, Your Majesty."

"Never mind. I'm getting at something. The peasants grow the food, the nobility distribute it, the craftsmen make the goods, the merchants distribute them. The Emperor sits apart and watches all that goes on to see that nothing disrupts this flow, and to fend off the disasters that our world tries to throw at us from time to time—disasters you can hardly conceive of. I assure you, for example, that stories of the ground shaking and fire spitting forth from it and winds that carried people off during the Interregnum are not myths, but things that would happen were it not for the Orb.

"But the Emperor sits and waits and studies and watches the Empire for those occasions when something, if not checked, might bring disaster. When such a thing does occur, he has three tools at his disposal. Do you know what they are?"

"I can guess at two of them," I said. "The Orb and the Warlord."

"You are correct, Baronet. The third is subtler. I refer to the mechanism of Imperium, through the Imperial Guards, the Justicers, the scryers, sorcerers, messengers, and spies.

"Those," she continued, "are the weapons I have at hand with which to make certain that wheat from the north gets south as needed, and iron from the west turns into swords needed in the east. I do not rule, I regulate. Yes, if I give an order, it will be obeyed. But no Emperor, with the Orb or without, can tell if every Vallista mine operator is making honest reports and sending every ton of ore where he says he is."

"Then who *does* rule, Your Majesty?"

"When there is famine in the north, the fishermen in the south rule. When the mines and forges in the west are producing, the transport barons rule. When the Easterners are threatening our borders, the armies in the east rule. Do you mean politically? Even that isn't as simple as you think. At the beginning of our history, no one ruled. Later, it was each House, through its Heir, which ruled each House. Then it became the nobles of all the Houses. For a brief time, at the end of the last Cycle, the Emperor did, indeed, rule, but that was short-lived, and he was brought down by assassination, conspiracy, and his own foolishness. Now, I think, more and more it is the merchants, especially the caravaneers who control the flow of food and supplies from one side of the Empire to the other. In the future, I suspect it will be the wizards, who are every day able to do things they could not do before."

"And you? What do you do?"

"I watch the markets, I watch the mines, I watch the fields, I watch the Dukes and the Counts, I guard against disasters, I cajole each House toward the direction I need, I—what is that look on your face for, Baronet?"

"Each House?" I repeated. "*Each* House?"

"Yes, Baronet, each House. You didn't know the Jhereg fits into this scheme? But it must; otherwise why would it be tolerated? The Jhereg feed off the Teckla. By doing so, they keep the Teckla happy by supplying them with those things that brighten their existence. I don't mean the peasants, I mean the Teckla who live in the cities and do the menial work none of the rest of us are willing to do. That is the rightful prey of your House, Baronet, for if they become unhappy, the city loses efficiency, and the nobility begins to complain, and the delicate balance of our society is threatened."

The slant of the floor was back down now; I decided my legs would probably survive. "And these people," I said, "are threatening the Jhereg, and so they must be removed. Is that it?"

"Your House thinks so, Lord Taltos."

"Then you don't really believe they are a threat to the Empire?"

She smiled. "No, not directly. But if the Teckla become unhappy, well, so will others. If there were no war looming over us, perhaps it wouldn't matter. But we may require more efficiency than ever, and to have our largest city disrupted, just at this moment, could have terrible consequences for the Empire."

I thought about a story I'd once been told by a Teckla, and almost said that if the Teckla were so damn happy, why didn't she just go become one, but I was afraid she might take it the way I meant it. So I said, "Is one Jhereg Easterner likely to make that much of a difference?"

"Will it matter to your House, Baronet?"

"I don't know, Your Majesty. But it won't matter to them as much as it will matter to me."

We passed through a curtain and were once more in the throne room. I heard the strings of Thoddi's instrument, the wail of Dav-Hoel's, and the clacking drone of Aibynn's drum. The courtiers bowed, and it was as if they were bowing to me, which was pretty funny. The Empress pointed to a woman in the colors of the House of the Iorich. The woman approached as Zerika sat herself in the throne. I backed away.

"I hereby order and require the release of and full freedom for the Countess of Lostguard Cleft and Environs," she said, and I damn near cried.

Lesson 12

Basic Survival Skills

Two stony-faced Dragons, each wearing the gold cloak of the Phoenix and a headband bearing an Iorich, delivered Cawti to the steps of the Iorich Wing of the Imperial Palace, a half hour's walk from where I had left the Empress. When they first appeared, each holding one of her arms, I almost put them down right there, but Loiosh spoke to me sharply. They released her on the bottom step, backed up, bowed to her once, turned together, and walked up again without a backward glance.

I stood three feet from her, looking in vain for signs of what she'd been through. Her eyes were clear and sharp, her expression grim, but she appeared unharmed. She stood for a moment, then her eyes focused on me. "Vlad," she said. "Are you responsible for this?" She held up her right hand, which contained a rolled-up parchment.

"I guess so," I said. "What's that? A pardon?"

"A release. It says we concede your innocence and don't do it again."

"At least you're out."

"I could have been out before, if I'd wanted to be."

"I'd say I'm sorry, but I'm not."

She smiled and nodded, being more understanding than I'd expected. "Perhaps it's for the best."

I shrugged. "I thought so, when you broke me out."

"Hardly the same thing," she said.

"Maybe not. How was it?"

"Tedious."

"I'm glad it wasn't worse than that. Would you like to come home?"

"Yes. Very much. I'd like to bathe, and eat something hot, and then—"

I waited. "And then what?" I asked after a moment.

"And then back to work."

"Ah. Of course. Shall we walk, or be sick?"

She considered. "Do you know, before the Interregnum, when teleportation was more difficult, there were Teckla who earned their livelihood driving people around the city behind horses and donkeys. Or sometimes they used only their feet, pulling small coaches. They wore harnesses like they were horses or donkeys themselves."

"I don't like horses. What are donkeys?"

"I'm not certain. A variety of horse, I think."

"Then I don't like them, either. You've been reading history, I see."

"Yes. Sorcery has changed our whole world and is still changing it."

"It has indeed."

"Let us walk."

"Very well."

And we did.

I FOUND SOME DRIED black mushrooms, poured boiling water over them, and let them soak. After about twenty minutes I cut them up with scallions, leeks, a little dill, various sorts of peppers, and thin strips of kethna. I quick-fried the whole thing with garlic and ginger while Cawti sat on the kitchen chair, watching me cook. Neither of us spoke until the food was done. We had it over some pasta my grandfather had made. I had a few strawberries that were still good, so I put them in a *palaczinta* with a paste made from finely ground rednuts, cinnamon, sugar, and a bit of lime juice. We had that with a rare strawberry liqueur Kiera had given me, having found it in a liquor store she was visiting after hours.

"How," I said, "can you stay away from a man who can cook like this?"

"Rigid self-control," she said.

"Ah."

I poured us each some more liqueur and set the plates on the floor for the jhereg. I leaned the chair back, sipped, and studied Cawti. Despite her bantering tone, there was no light of humor in her eyes. There hadn't been for some time. I said, "What would I have to do to keep you?"

She looked at the table. "I don't know, Vladimir. I'm not sure there's anything, anymore. I've changed."

"I know. Do you like what you've become?"

"I'm not certain. Whatever it is, it hasn't finished happening yet. I don't know if we can change together."

"You know I'm willing to try almost anything."

"Almost?"

"Almost."

"What won't you do?"

"Ask me and we'll see."

She shook her head. "I don't know. I just don't know."

This was another conversation we'd had before, with variations and embellishments. I went into the other room, next to the window so I could hear the street musicians outside. I had thrown them a bag of coins now and again, so they often played right below the window; it was one of the things I liked about the place. I threw them a bag of coins and listened for a while. I remembered how it felt to walk down the streets with her, feeling her shoulder touch mine. It had made me feel taller, somehow. I remembered meals at Valabar's, and klava in a little place where we made sculpture from empty cups and the sugar bowl. I made myself stop remembering, and just listened to the music.

A little later Aibynn returned, his drum carefully wrapped in thick, soft cloth. He set it against the wall and sat down.

I said, "How did it go in court today?"

"Great," he said. "The Empress wants us back."

"Congratulations."

"What were you doing there?"

"Recovering my wife."

"Oh." He looked over at her, sitting on the longchair and reading her paper. "Good thing you got her."

She smiled at him, stood up, and said, "I believe I will bathe now."

"Mind if I watch?" I said.

She turned the smile toward me. "Yes," she said, and walked into the bathroom. I heard the sound of wood being put into the stove and of water being put on to boil. Aibynn began playing his drum, so I couldn't hear the rustle of fabric and the splashing, which was just as well, I suppose. His fingers were a blur, the beater was another. The drum hummed, then moaned, then sang, with pops and clicks emerging as if they were part of the room. I fell into it and managed not to think for a while. Maybe I should learn to drum.

An hour later she came out in her red robe, Fenarian embroidery around the bottom, tied with a white cloth. The combination enhanced her dark eyes. She sat down again in the longchair. I spoke over the low moan of Aibynn's drum. "Are you going back to South Adrilankha tomorrow?"

"Yes. As long as I'm out, I'm going to work to force the Empire to release Kelly and the rest of our people."

"Do you think you can?"

"I don't see any other option."

I thought about the Empress, about being bound in cords of necessity, and said, "Do you know what they say about cornering a dzur?"

"Yes, I do. What do they say about killing thousands of people in a war that isn't any of our business? What do they say about incarcerating us in their dungeons? What do they say about starving us into submission? What do they say about their Phoenix Guards beating and killing us?"

"A point," I said.

"I'll be gone all day tomorrow."

"Yes, I suppose you will."

"Good night, Vlad."

"Good night, Cawti."

She went into the bedroom. I moved over to the long-chair and sat down on the soft darrskin, stretched over a hardwood frame. It was still warm where she'd sat in it. Aibynn stopped playing, looked at me, expressed a wish that I'd sleep without dreaming, then put his drum down and went into the blue room. I stared out at the night through the window and felt the warm breeze that smelled just a little of the sea. Loiosh and Rocza flew over and sat on my lap. I scratched their respective chins, and presently I fell asleep.

I HAD A DREAM I don't really remember, which is almost the same as not dreaming. I think the growing light in the room and the voice in my head were both worked into it. The ugly taste in my mouth was not. I hate talking to people, even psionically, before I've had a chance to rinse my mouth out.
"Who is it?"
"It's your trusty and true assistant."
"Joy. What is it, Kragar?"
"Glowbug just got offered six thousand for looking the other way while some nice fellow sends you on to your next life."
"Six thousand? Just for looking the other way? Verra! I've come up in the world."
"I get the impression that he was tempted."
"He'd be stupid if he wasn't. Why didn't he take it?"
"He thinks you're lucky. On the other hand, he's worried."
"Sensible guy. Let me wake up and I'll get back to you."
"Okay."
I rinsed out my mouth and gave myself a quick wash. *"I think we're in trouble this time, Loiosh."*
"It's a lot of money, boss. Someone's bound to go for it."
"Yep."
I started water for my morning klava and checked on the other occupants of the house. Cawti was gone, Aibynn was still sleeping. I put a log into the stove and used sorcery to light it, then set a couple of my rolls in it, got out butter and some ginger preserves. I poured the water over the ground klava, took the rolls out, prepared them, dumped heavy cream and honey in the klava, sat down, ate, drank, and thought.

Someone with the resources Boralinoi had could get me, eventually. Sooner or later, someone on my staff would give. Hell, with the kind of money he was throwing around, I might have sold out one of my own bosses at one time. Personal loyalty only gets you so far in this business; cash gets you further. There were three ways I could think of to prevent him from buying someone off and setting me up. The first, to kill Boralinoi before he could get to me, was a fine idea but impractical; it would take two or three days, at least, to even get all the information on him that I would need. For the second, outbidding him, I just didn't have the resources. That left the third, which would have several potential repercussions that needed serious consideration. I had another roll.

I took my time eating and thinking. When I was done, I put the plate into the bucket, drew some more water, and got sticky stuff off my face and hands.

"*Kragar. Kragar. Kragar.*"

"*Who is it?*"

"*Master Mustache himself. When can you have everyone in the office?*"

"*What does 'everyone' mean this time, Vlad?*"

"*All my enforcers, Melestav, you.*"

"*Is it urgent enough that they should break off whatever they're doing?*"

"*Might as well. There isn't any time of day or night when some of them won't be busy doing something.*"

"*I guess. How 'bout an hour?*"

"*I'll see you then.*"

"*Want an escort?*"

"*No. Just make sure there's no one around the office who might want to do me injury.*"

"*Okay, boss. We'll be there in an hour.*"

I finished dressing, made certain of all of my concealed weaponry, and collected both Loiosh and Rocza. Aibynn was up by then, but I was pretty distracted so we didn't converse much. I send Loiosh outside first to make sure the street was clear, then carefully teleported to a spot within a quick dash of my office, but that held possibilities for other escapes if that route was blocked. It turned out to be unnecessary; except for the usual wave of nausea, the teleport was uneventful. I ducked inside the psychedelics shop that was a front for the gambling room that was a front for my office, and there I waited until I felt a little better. I went back and into my office.

They were there, twelve enforcers, Kragar, and Melestav. We were crammed into the area outside of my office and Kragar's, in front of Melestav's desk. I sat on the edge of his desk and considered the fourteen killers here assembled. Glowbug squatted against the wall, looking intense. Melestav, whose desk I'd usurped, stood near me protectively, looking at the others as if he wasn't quite sure I was safe, which was possible. There was Chimov, in the middle, waiting patiently. And the others.

Sticks would have grabbed a chair in front, and his long legs would have been stretched out to the side, his arms folded, and he would have been looking curious and ironic. An anger began to build up inside of me, but I had no time for it now; I concentrated on those who were there. These were the men who kept my business going, who, just by existing, prevented Jhereg with hungry eyes from creeping into my area or trying to push me around. These were the men who took turns guarding my back when I'd walk around my area, and inspecting meeting places to make certain everything was safe. If I couldn't count on them, I might as well kill myself.

For the first time, as I studied them studying me, it seemed odd that there were no women among them. It has been Jhereg custom, as long as the Organization has existed, that most of the women were sorcerers, and worked in what was referred to as the Left Hand of the Jhereg, or, informally, the Bitch Patrol. When they didn't refer to us as the Right Hand of the Jhereg, they had many colorful names for us that I see no need to go into. The two organizations cooperate, but there is no love lost between them. Once, many years before, I'd been told by an Oracle that my own left hand would bring me to the brink of ruin, and I'd wondered if the Oracle referred to the Left Hand of the Jhereg.

But I digress.

"First of all," I said, "let me tell you what's going on, as far as I can tell. The gentleman who's after my head this time is much bigger than anyone who's been after it before. He has the resources to offer six thousand to anyone who will just move aside and let me get it, not to mention what he's willing to pay to the man with the knife. On the other hand, the last thing he wants is a war, so I don't think he's going to be going after any of you directly.

"This," I went on, "leaves each of you with several choices. You can, of course, sell me out. Pretty tempting, this time. I hope to make it less so in a moment. Two, you can continue business as usual and hope I can come out on top yet again, unlikely as that seems. Or, third, you can get out while you're still alive. That is what I wish to discourage."

I paused and looked about the room once more. No change in any expression, and—where was Kragar? Oh, there. Good. "This entire affair will run its course, I think, in a very few days. At the end of that time, if I win, you will all be doing at least as well as you do now, maybe better. If I lose, of course, things won't look so good.

"None of you will be protecting me, because I will not be going around with any protection." That caused a few eyes to widen. "In fact, I will not be going around at all. I will be hiding, and Kragar will run things, though I'll be in touch with him. This will remove the temptation to sell me out, because you won't be able to do so. It will remove the danger that you'll be taken down in an attempt on me, because, if there is such an attempt, you won't be there. This will begin at once, at the end of this meeting.

"So all I'm asking, gentlemen, is that you keep working for a few days and see how it all shakes out. I think the potential gains are worth the risks. Any questions?"

There were none. "Fair enough. Let Kragar know if you want out. That's all." I stood and walked into my office, moving abruptly just in case someone had been bought off and thought he could get out alive in the confusion. I sat behind my desk, feeling as if all my senses were sharpened, so I noticed Kragar as he came in. I said, "Well?"

"They're all sticking."

"Good. What do you think of the whole thing?"

"Nice of you to warn me in advance about my new responsibilities, Vlad."

"What new responsibilities? It's nothing more than you've been doing for most of the last year, anyway."

"I guess. Do you know where you're going?"

"I'm not certain. Probably Castle Black. We both know how hard it is to dig someone out of there."

"And we both know it can be done."

"True, true. I'm still thinking about it."

He nodded and looked thoughtful. "As far as I can tell, they're all taking it pretty well."

"That's good. Guess what your next set of orders is?"

He sighed. "Find out everything there is to know about dear Lord Boralinoi. And you want it yesterday."

"Good guess."

"It's lucky I started work on it yesterday, or it might have taken longer."

"You mean you've got it?"

"No, but I've started. Another day or two and I should have it."

"Good. Hurry."

"I know."

"Any news of the war?"

"You have better sources than I do. Last I heard they were getting the fleet together in Northport. There's lots of activity at the harbor, in any case."

"But no new disasters?"

"A couple more freighters sunk, and there's a rumor of a convoy being attacked by some ships from Elde, but I don't know if it's true."

I nodded. "How about South Adrilankha?"

He looked uncomfortable. "Not good, Vlad. While you were off having tea with the Empress, there were some nasty skirmishes between press gangs and Easterners. Word is two Phoenix Guards were killed and another eleven or so injured."

"And Easterners?"

"No idea. Thing is, it's spreading. Nothing around here, yet, but there have been signs of trouble on the docks and in Little Deathgate."

"What sort of trouble?"

"Placards going up, Teckla banding together and throwing things at Phoenix Guards. One or two barricades went up in Little Deathgate, but they didn't last long."

"Anyone hurt?"

"Not yet."

"That's something. What's the issue? Conscription?"

"No. Kelly's arrest."

"By the Phoenix!"

"That's what the word is."

I shook my head, wondering if I really knew half as much about this city as I thought I did. It was like there were invisible forces running through the streets, forces that controlled our lives and directed our actions, leaving us as helpless as a slave or an Empress. Things were happening that I couldn't understand, couldn't control, and might not survive. And whatever those things were, Cawti was right in the middle of them.

"I think I'd better be going, Kragar. I've just thought of an errand that won't wait."

"All right. Give the old man my regards."

"I will."

"And be careful, Vlad. Just because I can guess where you're going doesn't mean Boralinoi's people can, but it doesn't mean they can't, either."

"I'll be careful, Kragar. And good luck with your new job."

He snorted. "I'll need it," he said.

I followed him out, still thinking about Sticks. Something occurred to me, and I stopped and asked Melestav to find the names of the freighters that had gone down. It was unlikely *Chorba's Pride* was one, and I couldn't do anything about it, anyway, but I wanted to know. And I guess, somehow, I'd have felt better knowing that Trice and Yinta were still alive. He agreed to do so, and I sent Loiosh and Rocza out ahead of me, to make sure it was safe to go outside.

There was a thump behind me, and at first it didn't register that anything was wrong. Then I saw Melestav facedown on the floor and I moved away, drew a dagger, and looked around. I didn't see anything. Loiosh came back and landed on my shoulder, also looking anxiously around. I was not attacked.

Then I noticed that Melestav had a dagger in his hand and realized from his position what he'd been up to. It was only after that that I noticed Kragar, standing above my secretary's body.

"Shit," I said.

Kragar nodded. "You were set up perfectly, Vlad."

"But he didn't notice you."

I started shaking and cursing at the same time. That had been as close as I'd ever come. I looked down at his body. He had not only saved my life more than once, he had *died* doing it, and now this. Now he'd tried to shine me, and for what? Money? Power?

If you want to push it back, he'd tried to shine me because I'd had to go and threaten the Imperial representative, and then threaten someone on the Jhereg Council. I couldn't blame anyone but myself for this. I kept staring at the body until Kragar said, "No point in standing around here, Vlad. I'll take care of things. Get somewhere safe."

I did so without another word.

THE BELLS IN MY grandfather's shop went *tinga-ling* as I pushed aside the rug that he used as a door. "Come in, Vladimir. Tea?"

"Thank you, Noish-pa." I kissed his cheek and said hello to his familiar, a short-haired white cat named Ambrus. The tea had a distinct lemon tang and was very good. My grandfather's hands shook, just a little, as he poured. I sat in a canvas chair in his front room while Loiosh and Rocza, after greeting Noish-pa, settled down next to Ambrus for conversation on subjects I could only guess at.

"Where are your thoughts, Vladimir?"

"Noish-pa, what are they doing around here? I mean, the Empire, and these rebels."

"What are they doing? You come to an old man like me for this?" But he smiled with his few remaining yellowed teeth and settled back a little. "All right. The elfs want to go to war, for what reason they do not tell me. They want sailors for their ships, so they pull in young men and women for it. They send in gangs who grab people and take them, without even saying farewell to the family, and bring them to the ships, which sail away. Everyone is upset, some throw things at the elfs who want to take them. Now, these *forradalomartok*, they say that the war is a, what is the word? *Urugy*."

"Pretext?"

"Yes, a pretext, to bring in soldiers. The *forradalomartok* organize against this, and everyone says, 'Yes, yes, we fight,' and then they arrest this Kelly and now everyone says, 'Let him go or we will wreck your city.' "

"But it all happened so fast."

"That is how these things happen, Vladimir. You see all your peasants smile and look sleepy and they say, 'Oh, this is our lot in life,' and then something happens and they all say, 'We will die to keep them from doing this to our children.' All in a night it can happen, Vladimir."

"I guess so. But I'm frightened, Noish-pa. For them, and for Cawti."

"Yes, she still walks with these people. You are right to fear."

"Can they win?"

"Vladimir, why do you ask me? If soldiers come into my shop, I will show them how old I am. But I will not go looking for them, and so I know nothing of such things. Perhaps, yes, they can win. Perhaps the soldiers will crush them. Perhaps both at once. I don't know."

"I have to decide what to do, Noish-pa."

"Yes, Vladimir. But there is little help I can give you."

We sipped tea for a while. I said, "I don't know, maybe it's good to have this problem. It means I don't have to worry about what's going to happen afterward."

He didn't smile. "It is right not to worry now. But is it possible for you?"

"No," I said. I stared at my hands. "I know you don't approve of what I do. The trouble is, I'm not sure I approve of it anymore."

"As I told you once before, Vladimir, killing people for money is no way for a man to earn a living."

"But, Noish-pa, I hate them so much. I learned that I used to be one, and I thought that had changed things, but it hasn't. I still hate them. Every time I come to see you, and smell the garbage in the streets, and see people who have lost their sight, or who have diseases that could be cured by the simplest sorcery, or don't know how to write their own names, I just hate them. It doesn't make me want to fix everything, like Cawti; it just makes me want to kill them."

"Have you no friends, Vladimir?"

"Hmm? Well, yes, certainly. What has that to do with it?"

"Who are your friends?"

"Well, there's—oh. I see. Yes, they're all Dragaerans. But they're different."

"Are they?"

"I don't know, Noish-pa. I really don't. I know what you're saying, but why do I still feel this hate?"

"Hate is part of life, Vladimir. If you cannot hate, you cannot love. And if you hate these elfs, then that is what you feel and you cannot deny it. But more foolish than this hate of elfs you have never met is to let it rule you. That is no way to live."

"I know that, but I—" I broke off as Amrus jumped into Noish-pa's lap, mewing furiously. Noish-pa frowned and listened.

"What's wrong?" I said.

"Be still, Vladimir. I don't know."

Loiosh returned to my shoulder. Noish-pa got up and walked into the front of the shop. I was about to follow him when he returned, holding a sheet of white parchment. He took a quill pen from an inkwell, and with a few quick slashes drew a sideways rectangle. He dipped the pen again, not blotting it at all, and made sloppy signs in the corners. I didn't recognize the symbols.

"What is this?"

"Not now, Vladimir. Take this." He handed me a small silver dagger. "Cut your left palm." I did so, making a cut right next to the tiny white scar I'd made only two days before. It bled nicely. "Collect some blood in your right hand." I did that, too. "Scatter it onto the paper." He held the paper about three feet in front of me. I tossed the blood onto it, making an interesting pattern of red dots. Then he threw me a clean cloth to bind my hand up. I did, concentrating a little to stop the blood and begin the healing. I wished, not for the first time, that I'd troubled to learn basic sorcerous healing.

Noish-pa studied the red dots on the parchment and said, "There is a man outside, near the door. He is waiting for you to come out so he can kill you."

"Oh. Is that all? All right."

"You know how to find the back door."

"Yes, but Loiosh will be taking it. We'll handle this our way."

He looked at me through filmy eyes. "All right, Vladimir. But don't be distracted by shadows. Concentrate always on the target."

"I will," I said. I stood and drew my rapier. "I know how to make the shadows vanish."

Lesson 13

Advanced Survival Skills

"*O*KAY, LOIOSH. *YOU KNOW what to do.*"

"*What about Rocza?*"

"*She can wait with me, just in case.*"

We went into the back room, past the kitchen, and I let Loiosh out, then returned and stood waiting near the doorway, blade in hand. Rocza landed on my shoulder. She was heavier than Loiosh, but I was getting used to her.

"*I don't see him yet, boss.*"

"*No hurry, chum. Lots of places to hide out there the way things are packed togeth—*"

"*Got him!*"

"*Let me see. Hmmm. Don't recognize him.*"

"*How should we play it?*"

"*Has he seen you?*"

"*No.*"

"*Okay. Out the door, three steps, I'll take a left so we can get him away from the shop. I'll let him catch up a bit, you hit him when he starts to move, and I'll join you then.*"

"*Got it.*"

I put my sword away since I wouldn't be using it at once and kissed my grandfather good-bye. He suggested once more that I be careful, and I allowed as to how I would. I walked through the doorway, made a show of looking around, then headed to my left.

"He's following."

"Okay."

I scouted the area, looking for a place with enough people, but not too many. After about two hundred yards I found it. I slowed down, checked for an escape route or two, and finally stopped in front of a fruit stand and picked up an orange. I dug around in my purse for a coin.

"Here he comes, boss."

I paid for the orange, took my dagger from my belt, cut the orange in half, and palmed the blade while looking like I'd put it away. I started sucking on a half.

"He's behind you, walking between a pair of humans. They aren't with him, so don't worry. He's getting close. He's got a weapon out . . . now!"

I turned and threw the orange at him. At the same time, Loiosh struck at his knife hand and Rocza left my shoulder to attack his face with her talons. His knife hit the dirt of the street as he backed away. Loiosh got him turned around and I put my dagger in the middle of his back all the way to the hilt. He screamed and fell to his knees. I took another dagger out, grabbed his chin, slit his throat, and dropped the knife. Since he was now unable to scream, some local did it for him, and quite well, too.

I walked around the side of the fruit stall, careful not to make eye contact with anyone, and slipped between two buildings, where Loiosh and Rocza joined me. We zigzagged our way past a couple more streets, then went into a tavern, where I found water to clean orange and blood from my hands. I hate it when my hands are sticky.

We emerged into South Adrilankha midday, with gaggles of young men leaning against buildings surveying passersby, and tradesmen out in front of their shops eating. The standard meal seemed to be long loaves of bread which they dipped into something in a wooden bowl, while holding a bottle between their knees. As I relaxed a bit, since there seemed no sign of pursuit, I began to get the feeling that all was not normal here, but I couldn't for the life of me figure out how.

"Can you figure out what it is, Loiosh?"

"I'm not sure, boss. It's subtle."

I continued walking, heading generally toward the area where Kelly's people had their headquarters. I noticed a group of a dozen or so Easterners, men and women, trotting past me. On their faces was a strange mixture of determination, confidence, and fear. No, not fear, maybe nervousness. Two of them had homemade pikes, one had a large kitchen knife, the others were unarmed. I wondered where they were going. For some reason, my heart beat faster. It seemed to fit in with whatever else I was unconsciously noticing.

"They're waiting for something, boss. It's like everyone smells that something is going to happen."

"I think you're right, Loiosh. I wonder."

Not far from the new headquarters was a small park, shaped like a diamond with an arc cut out of one side. It was called the Exodus, which had something to do with the arrival of masses of Easterners to Adrilankha during the Interregnum. There were a few clumps of half-starved trees, a pond full of water and algae, and unkept grass and weeds with several paths cutting across them. I crossed the Exodus on a path that took me near the small rise by the arc. I stopped there for a while and watched.

There was a pack of about two dozen boys and girls, most of them nine to eleven years old, who were industriously turning trees into spears. They had a pile of perhaps fifty already, and the work was neatly divided up: Some cut down the saplings, others trimmed and shortened them, another group removed the bark, while others smoothed and polished them, and yet another group put points on them. They were all filthy, but most of them seemed to be enjoying themselves.

There were a few who seemed grimly intent on their jobs, as if they considered themselves to be involved in matters of high importance, and some, especially the ones cutting up the logs, just seemed tired.

I watched them for a while as the significance washed over me. It wasn't so much that they were making weapons, it was the systematic way in which they were going about it. Someone had put them up to this and explained exactly what to do. Yes. Someone.

I started walking again, faster now, but I didn't make it to the headquarters. I was still half a mile away when I came upon a guard station. There was no one there wearing the gold cloak, however; instead there were a score of men and women, mostly Easterners, but I picked out a few Teckla as well, all armed, and all wearing yellow headbands. They stood outside the guard-house, smiling and saluting everyone who came by.

They scowled at my Jhereg colors, but were willing to talk to me. I said, "What does the headband mean?"

"It means," said a willowy human woman of middle years, "that we are protectors. We have taken control."

"Of what?" I said.

"Of this part of the city."

"Can you tell me what happened?"

"Press gangs," she said, as if that explained everything.

"I don't understand."

"You will, Jhereg. You'd best move along now."

It was either that or start killing Easterners. I moved along.

"I don't like this, boss. We should get out of here."

"Not yet, Loiosh."

A breeze came up, and brought with it a smell that I couldn't place. I'd smelled it before; the associations were not pleasant. But what was it?

"Horses, boss."

"That's it. Where?"

"Left here. Not far."

It wasn't far. Just around a curve in the street, and there were more of the brutes than I'd ever seen at one place since the Eastern horse-army at the Wall of Baritt's Tomb. But this time, instead of being ridden, they were attached to large carts—six or seven carts, I think—and the carts were being loaded with boxes. I recognized them as the sort of farmers' transports that regularly came into South Adrilankha with deliveries, and left while it was still morning. What was most unusual was how many of them there were.

I approached, and asked one of the workmen what was going on. He, too, sneered at my colors, but said, "We have control of South Adrilankha; now we are issuing proclamations for the rest of the city."

"Proclamations? Let me see one."

He shrugged and pulled a piece of paper out of the box. It was neatly set in printer's type, and said, in distinctly unimaginative language, that the East-

erners and Teckla of South Adrilankha were refusing to admit press gangs
into the city, and were demanding the release of their imprisoned leaders,
and were rising as one to take the government from the hands of tyrants,
and so on and so on.

It was there, as these wagons began to drive off, that I began to get a
sense of unreality—a sense that became stronger as I wandered off and saw,
lying unattended and ignored in the street, the body of a Dragaeran, dead
from many wounds, wearing the gold cloak of the Phoenix Guards.

A LONG TIME LATER, in the cottage of an Eastern family where I spent a
night, I found Maria Parachezk's little pamphlet "Grey Hole in the City," a
description of those few days in Adrilankha. As I read it, I lived it again; but
more than that, I found myself nodding and saying, "Yes, that's true," and,
"I remember that," as she described the pikemen's stand at Smallmarket, the
Guardsmen walking twenty abreast down the Avenue of the Moneylenders,
the burning of the grain exchange, and other events that I actually witnessed.
If you find the pamphlet, read it, and, if you like, insert here descriptions of
any event that catches your imagination. Because until I read it, I didn't really
remember any of those things.

I remember laughs and screams, fading into each other as if they were
part of a single musical composition, although they were long hours apart.
I remember the smell of the burning grain, and looking down at my hands
to see the ashes there. I remember standing in an alley, out of the way of a
marching battalion of Phoenix Guards, tapping a broken axe handle against
the wall of a boardinghouse. There was blood on the axe handle, but I don't
know how I acquired the thing, much less if I was the one to blood it.

Maria Parachezk, whoever she is, was able to make sense out of the whole
thing, put events in order and connect them logically. I wasn't then, so I'm
not going to pretend to now. Apparently the insurgents, Easterners and
Teckla, were actually winning until late in the second day of the rebellion,
the third of the new year, when the sailors on the *Whitecrest* withdrew their
support of the rebels and allowed the landing of the Fourth Seaguard, who
broke the siege at the Imperial Palace. But, from where I was, I never saw
any difference between winning and losing, right up until the end, when the

Orca came through the streets, mowing down everyone they saw. I didn't even find out until afterward that the Imperial Palace had been attacked twice and was under siege for nine hours.

I remember that, at one point, I became aware that I'd been in South Adrilankha for an entire day, and I remember the early evening of that day, when it seemed that the whole city was screaming, but, as I go through my memories like a cedar chest I've lost something in, I don't think that I saw anything more than sporadic fighting even at the worst. There'd be silence, a few people running, then the sound of metal on metal or metal on wood, screams, the horrible smell of burnt human flesh, so like and so unlike the smell of cooking meat.

Did I actually strike a blow for "my people"? I don't remember. I've asked Loiosh, but he remembers even less; only that he kept asking me to go home and I kept saying not yet. I know that I tried to make contact with Cawti several times, but she wasn't receiving.

For some reason, it was only when the massacre started—and even then I wasn't conscious of it as a massacre—that I remembered my grandfather. I walked quickly through the streets, only dimly aware that I was hurrying past the bodies of Easterners, men, women, and children. I am grateful that I can bring to mind so little of what I must have seen. I know that I skidded on something and almost fell, and only later did I realize that it was blood, flowing from the lacerated body of an old woman who was still moving.

I came across some fighting, but mostly I skirted it. At one point I ran into a patrol of four Dragaerans wearing the gold cloaks. I stopped, they stopped. They saw I was an Easterner, and they saw I was a Jhereg, and I guess that puzzled them. They didn't know what to do with me. I was not then holding a weapon, but they looked at the two jhereg on my shoulders and the rapier at my side. I said, "Well?" and they shrugged and moved on.

I saw the fires while I was still a mile or more from my grandfather's shop. I began to run. The first thing I noticed when I got there was that the house across the street from his shop was burning, as was the little grocer's next to it. As I got close enough to smell burning vegetables, I saw that Noish-pa's shop was still standing, and I began to feel relief. Then I saw that the entire front was missing, and my heart sank.

I came up to it, and the first thing I saw was the bodies of three Phoenix

Guards. There was no doubt who had killed them; each bore a single small wound right over the place where a Dragaeran or a human keeps his heart. I dashed into the shop, and when I saw him, calmly cleaning his blade, I almost cried with relief.

He looked up and said, "You should leave, Vladimir."

"Eh?"

"You should leave here. At once."

"Why?"

"Quickly, Vladimir. Please."

I looked back at the bodies, looked at my grandfather, and said, "One got away, huh?"

He shrugged. "I've never been able to kill women. This is a weakness we have from being human."

"You're lucky she wasn't a sorcerer," I said.

"Perhaps. But there is little time. You must leave at once."

"If you'll come with me."

He shook his head. "I have nowhere to go. They will find you."

I chewed my lip. "There may be a place," I said. "Bide." *Morrolan. Funny-talking Dragonlord. Dragaeran witch. Wielder of Blackwand. Morrolan. Morrolan. . . ."*

"Who is—Vlad?"

"Himself."

"Where are you? Are you all right? The whole city—"

"I know. I'm in the thick of it, but I'm all right. I request sanctuary, Lord Morrolan. For myself and for my grandfather."

"Your grandfather? What happened?"

"Phoenix Guards tried to burn his shop down. He prevented them from doing so."

"I see."

"Where are you now?"

"The Imperial Palace, but I'll be leaving soon."

"What are you doing there?"

"I was preparing to defend the Empress, if necessary. But the siege was broken."

"Siege?"

"Your Easterners, Vlad."

"Oh. Who's with you?"

"Aliera, Sethra."

"Sethra? That must have made quite a stir."

He chuckled. *"I wish you could have seen it. What about you? Is everything all right?"*

"Yes, as far as the rebellion goes, but I've got Jhereg troubles. That's why I need sanctuary."

"I seem to recall another Jhereg—"

"Yeah, me, too. But we're in a hurry, Morrolan. There may be some goldcloaks coming back, and—"

"Very well, Vlad. You have sanctuary for at least seventeen days. Probably forever. And your grandfather as well, of course. I'll inform Teldra."

"Thanks. See you soon."

I turned to Noish-pa and said, "It's settled. We can stay at Castle Black."

He frowned. "What is that?"

"A floating castle, Noish-pa. It's really quite comfortable. You'll like Morrolan. He—"

"He is an elf?"

"Yes, but—"

"No. I will remain here."

I smiled. "Very well. I know I can't make you leave."

"Good."

I went over and sat down in one of his chairs. He frowned and said, "Vladimir, you should go now."

"No."

"What?"

"If you stay, so do I. You can't make me leave, either."

"They will return in force."

"Indeed. And with sorcerers. But I know some tricks."

"Vladimir—"

"Both of us or neither, Noish-pa."

He looked me in the eye, then a bit of a smile came over his face. "Very well, Vladimir. Bring me to the elf castle."

"Be prepared to be sick, Noish-pa."

"Why?"

"Teleport spells do that to humans. I don't know why."

"All right, then." He picked up Ambrus, his familiar, and took one last glance around the shop. "Let us leave at once, then."

I put one arm around my grandfather's shoulders and concentrated on the courtyard of Castle Black. When the image was clear, I drew on the power, shaped it, and felt the familiar twist in my bowels. South Adrilankha vanished, and the walls of the courtyard appeared in reality to match the picture in my mind.

Noish-pa looked queasy, but otherwise all right. I watched his face as he slowly recovered, even more slowly than I did, and became aware of the size of the courtyard, of the ground below us, and then of the symbols on the walls and the huge double doors some forty paces in front of us.

"How can this elf know the Art?" he asked.

"He's very unusual for a Dragaeran," I said.

When he was able to, we walked together up to the doors, which opened before us. Noish-pa looked at me but didn't comment. Lady Teldra gave us a courtesy and said, "Lord Vladimir, we are so relieved that you are safe, and delighted that you will be staying with us. And you, sir, your grandson has spoken so much and so highly of you that we were nearly afraid to hope for the honor of your presence here someday. We are delighted that you have come, though sorry for the hardship that forced the journey on you. Please be welcome. I am Teldra."

She is, after all, of the House of the Issola.

He stared at her, his mouth opening and closing, and then his face lit up in a big grin and he said, "I like you," and, for the first time, I think I saw Lady Teldra actually touched.

She showed us in. "The Lord Morrolan requested that you await him in the library," she said. "If you would follow me?"

Noish-pa seemed awed by the display of Castle Black as we made our way down the marble halls and up the wide stairways. Ambrus looked around as well, as if he were memorizing an escape route. I could almost see Noish-pa making notes to himself to study various of the sculpture, paintings, and psiprints we passed. Lady Teldra would have been willing to stop and let him examine them then, and would gladly have told all their histories and given brief biographies of the artists, but I badly wanted to sit down.

Morrolan's library is actually quite a complex of rooms, so it was helpful to have her show us which one. It says something either about him or about Dragaerans in general that his books were arranged neither by subject nor title, but, primarily, by the *House* of the author. We awaited him in the largest room, which was, quite naturally, filled with books written by Dragonlords.

We had hardly gotten seated, and Lady Teldra was just pouring the wine, when he entered. We both stood and bowed, but he motioned us to sit. He bowed deeply to my grandfather, rising in time for Loiosh to land on his shoulder. Rocza flew over to Ambrus, who hissed at her, and then allowed herself to be licked, which startled me.

We all sat down again, and Lady Teldra poured us all wine, giving the first glass to my grandfather. I said, "On behalf of my grandfather, Morrolan, thank you. We—"

"Never mind that," he said. "Of course you're welcome here as long as you want to stay. But do you know about Cawti?"

I stopped with the glass halfway to my lips, carefully set it down, and said, "Tell me."

"She's been arrested again. This time, under direct orders from the Empress. The charge is treason against the Empire. Vlad, she's facing execution."

Lesson 14

Fundamentals of Betrayal

I FELT MY GRANDFATHER'S eyes on me, but I didn't look at him. I said, "Has a trial been set?"

"No. Zerika says she's going to wait until the troubles are over."

"Troubles? Was that her word for it?"

"Yes."

"I see. Has Norathar done anything?"

"Not yet. She's been directing troops. She says—"

"Directing troops? In the city?"

"No, she's putting together an invasion force for Greenaere."

"Oh. That's a relief, anyway."

"Why?"

I shook my head. It would be too hard to explain. "How much have you heard about what's going on?"

He shrugged. "Disorders. I was at the Imperial Palace during the second attack, and throughout the siege, so I mostly know about activities there, but I heard at least some of the rest. Zerika says things should be under control by tomorrow morning."

"Under control," I repeated. I looked at Noish-pa, but this time he was looking away.

"Yes," continued Morrolan. "Sethra has established order in—"

"Sethra! Lavode?"

"Sethra the Younger."

"How did she end up in command?"

"The brigadier of the Phoenix Guards resigned yesterday over some dispute with the Empress. I don't know the details."

"Maybe he didn't like the idea of slaughtering thousands of helpless Easterners."

"Helpless? Vlad, weren't you listening? There were attacks on the Imperial Palace. They laid siege to it. They actually threatened the Empress—"

"Oh, come now. She could have teleported out anytime she wanted to."

"That isn't the point, Vlad. Threatening the sanctity of—"

"Can we change the subject?"

"You asked," he said stiffly.

"Yeah. Sorry." Loiosh flew back to my shoulder and nuzzled my ear. I said, "What about the war?"

"Are you sure you want to hear about it?"

"I'm trying to figure out how to get Cawti out of there. The first thing I need to know is what's going on with the Empress, so I can decide how to try to influence her. Does that make sense?"

He seemed startled; I guess that sort of thinking wasn't what he expected of me. Then he said, "Very well. The Empire is still trying to put together an invasion fleet to attack the Greenaere and Elde alliance."

"Trying?"

He looked grim. "A task force sailing from Adrilankha to Northport in preparation for an attack on Greenaere was itself attacked by several alliance warships, and three of them were sunk. I don't know how big they were, or how many were lost, or—why are you smiling?"

Why *was* I smiling?

I took a sip of wine without tasting it. I had never particularly cared about the Empire one way or the other; that is, it was there, I lived in it and ignored it. Even the onset of war hadn't inspired any particular feelings in the sense of who I hoped would win the conflict. But now, I realized, I wanted the Empire to be hurt. Very much I wanted them to be hurt. I would love it if the Empire was tumbled, inconceivable as that was. I wanted to see the Orb rolling, broken, on the ground. I wanted to see the mighty Palace, with all its pillars of silver, and its walls cut of black marble, rooms in which ten Eastern families could live, burned to the ground.

I remembered only flashes of the last two days in South Adrilankha, but there were looks on faces that I knew I'd remember as long as I lived, and if the only way to ease the pain was the destruction of the Empire, then that's what I wanted. In a life governed by hatreds, this hatred was a new one. Maybe it was what Cawti had felt all along. Maybe now I could understand her.

I tossed aside dreams of the Empire fallen; such dreams would not win my wife's release. In fact, the best would be if I could find a way to . . .

If I could . . .

"Nothing," I said. "I think I know how to save Cawti, though."

My grandfather looked at me sharply. Morrolan said, "Oh?"

"Do you think you'd be willing to help? I will also need Aliera's help, and, I think, Sethra's. And possibly Daymar's."

"What do you have in mind?"

"I'll explain when we're all together. Say, this evening. I should warn you, it will be dangerous."

He gave me a look of contempt. I'd only said it to annoy him, anyway. "I will help you," said Morrolan.

"Thank you," I said.

My grandfather spoke for the first time. He said, "Vladimir, will you travel again through the fairy-land?"

"Excuse me?"

"Travel through the fairy-land, the way we did to come here."

"Oh. Yes, I expect so."

He nodded thoughtfully and spoke to Morrolan. "I see that you practice the Art."

"Yes," said Morrolan. "I am a witch."

"Have you devices I might use? All of mine are lost."

"Certainly," said Morrolan. "I'll have Teldra bring you to my workshop."

"Thank you," said my grandfather.

Morrolan nodded and said, "Aliera is here. Shall I make contact with Sethra and Daymar?"

"Yes," I said. "Let's get started."

A few minutes later he reported that everyone would be assembled for dinner that evening, which gave me several hours to kill. I realized that I was desperately tired and asked Lady Teldra to show me to a room. I gave my grandfather a kiss, bowed to Morrolan, and stumbled to the chambers I'd been assigned.

Before I fell asleep, I got hold of Kragar and said, *"What's the news from Jhereg center?"*

"You are, Vlad."

"Do tell."

"Three more offers, all refused. Whether they'd have been refused if anyone knew where you were, I don't know."

"Okay. Do you have the information I wanted?"

"Yes, indeed. And someone knows I'm collecting it."

"Oh?"

"I was offered twenty thousand to convince you to collect it in person."

"Twenty thousand? Why didn't you take it?"

"I didn't think I could talk you into coming for it without getting you suspicious."

"Hmmm. You're probably right. Can you send it by messenger to Castle Black?"

"Easy."

"Good. Any, um, disturbances in the area?"

"Not to speak of. Everything pretty much passed us by. We were lucky."

"Yes," I said. Lucky. Images came bubbling up like Teckla to a feast, but I shoved them back down. No, now was not the time for thinking about that. Maybe there'd never be a time for thinking about that, but now I was tired.

"How are things on your end?" said Kragar.

"Working their way toward resolution."

"Good. Keep me informed."

"I will. Have the messenger ask them to wake me when he gets here."

"Okay. See you later, Vlad."

"Don't count on it, Kragar." Before he could ask what I meant by that, I was asleep.

* * *

KRAGAR'S MESSENGER WAS TOO quick for me to get enough sleep, but the two or so hours I got, along with the klava supplied by Lady Teldra when she woke me, put me in good enough shape for the moment. I sat up in bed, sipped klava, and studied the sheaf of documents giving all the significant details of Boralinoi's life and personal habits.

He was another of the Council members who got there by being in the right place when Zerika returned with the Orb ending the Interregnum. He was considered good at arranging compromises between rivals, but he was not, himself, a compromiser. He'd done a few very nasty things to secure his position, and since then his reputation had protected him. There had been no known attempts on his life, and his habits didn't indicate that he was terribly worried about such things. On the other hand, he knew I was after him, so it could be tough.

On yet a third hand, he had a mistress, so it could be pretty easy. Given a couple of weeks to set it up, it should be no problem. But, of course, I didn't have a couple of weeks to set it up. I wouldn't have an Organization in a couple of weeks. Still, it might be possible to do it more quickly. I could do what they'd done to me, set up outside his mistress's flat and wait for him to emerge. Not very professional, not the kind of sure thing I liked, but it might work.

I shook my head. The business with Cawti was more urgent, but I had a handle on that. It bothered me that it might not get Cawti released even if it worked, and it bothered me that if things went bad, the business with Boralinoi would remain unfinished. And I owed that son of a bitch one. I considered the matter and kept considering it as I dressed, then put it out of my mind. One thing at a time.

The front dining room, with its huge glass windows overlooking the courtyard, blackwood chairs and table, and hanging brass lamps, was just big enough for Morrolan, Aliera, Sethra, Daymar, Noish-pa, and me. Daymar was on his best behavior; that is, he sat in his chair, between Morrolan and Sethra, instead of floating cross-legged as was his wont. My grandfather was clearly uncomfortable; I doubt he had been so close to so many Dragaerans ever in his life, but he did his best to pretend he was at ease. When he tasted the Bazian pepper stew, he smiled in amazement and no longer had to pretend. Morrolan smiled at him. "Your grandson gave my cook the recipe," he said.

"I hope he left nothing out," said Noish-pa.

Aliera nibbled daintily and said, "What's the plan, then? My cousin"— she indicated Morrolan, perhaps for Noishpa's benefit—"said it would be exciting."

"Yes," I said. "We're going to end the war."

"That will be pleasant," said Daymar.

"You aren't in it, I'm afraid."

"Oh?"

"Except, of course, for getting us there."

"Where?"

"Greenaere."

"You wish to journey to Greenaere?" said Morrolan. "Explain."

"The Phoenix Stones prevent psionic communication, and they prevent sorcery. Daymar was able to temporarily punch through the one, and I suspect that with Sethra's help he could punch through the other long enough to get us in. Perhaps even to get us out again after."

"After what?"

"After we have forced a truce on them."

"How?"

"Leave that to me. Your job is to keep me alive long enough to get the truce into our hands."

There was considerable silence at this point, then Morrolan said, "Several things need to be discussed, I think."

"Go on."

"In the first place, I do not perform assassinations."

"No problem, I do. If you want to kill someone, you are welcome to challenge him to single combat, if that somehow pleases you more."

"Then you admit you are going to assassinate this King?"

"No. But neither do I deny it."

"Hmmm. In the second place, we cannot be sure Daymar and Sethra can succeed. The Empire has tried several times to break through and failed. What makes you think this time we can succeed?"

"Several things," I said. "First, we now know about the Phoenix Stones. Second, we know that Daymar has succeeded once already, in a limited way. Third, we have Sethra Lavode." She smiled and dipped her head by way of acknowledgment.

"It sounds chancy," said Morrolan.

I said, "Sethra?"

"It's worth a try," she said. "Just how well do you know Greenaere?"

"I have a spot marked well enough to teleport to, if that's what you mean."

"I don't know if that will be good enough. We're going to need a solid, detailed image of the place, memories of all five senses."

"Hmmm. I've got an idea for that. Let me think about it."

"Very well," said Sethra.

I said, "What next?"

Morrolan spoke up again. "How do you know that, if we succeed, the Empire will, in fact, release Cawti?"

I shrugged. "I don't. I'm working on that. I have some ideas. If they don't pan out, perhaps we'll scrap the whole plan. I'll know by noon tomorrow."

"It seems to me," said Morrolan, "that you are doing a great deal of hoping here. You hope we will be able to break through the Phoenix Stones. You hope you can force a treaty out of Greenaere. You hope we will be able to escape again. You hope the Empress will be sufficiently grateful to you to free Cawti."

"You've expressed it quite well."

I waited for about two breaths, then: "Count me in," said Morrolan.

"Sounds like fun," said Aliera.

Sethra nodded and Daymar shrugged. Noish-pa looked at me steadily for a moment, then resumed eating. I wondered what he was thinking. Perhaps he was remembering how I'd said I hated Dragaerans, and now, when I was in trouble, whom did I go running to for help? A good point, that. I'd known them a long time, and we'd been through so much together. I just never thought of them as Dragaerans; they were friends. How could I—

"When are we going to do it?" said Morrolan.

I asked Sethra, "How much time will you and Daymar need to prepare?"

"At least until tomorrow. We won't know until we start looking at the problem."

"All right. Tentatively, tomorrow afternoon. If you aren't ready by then, we'll see. In the meantime, I have to run home and get somebody."

"Who?"

"You'll meet him. He's a drummer."

"From Greenaere?" said Sethra.

"Yep."

"Think he'll help?"

"If he's a spy, which I think is possible, he'll be glad to. If he isn't, he might not."

"If he's a spy—"

"It won't matter for what I'm trying to do."

"Very well, then," said Morrolan, and called for dessert, which involved fresh berries of some kind and a sweet cream sauce. It arrived, and I ate it, but I don't remember how it tasted. After dinner I made sure my grandfather was settled in as well as possible, studied Kragar's notes a bit more, then walked out to the courtyard of Castle Black.

"Loiosh, you and Rocza stay real alert."

"I know, boss. I'm not happy about this at all. They were waiting for you once—"

"I know. How's your lady doing?"

Rocza shifted on my right shoulder and nuzzled me a little. I got my mind fixed on a place across the street from my flat and teleported there. Loiosh and Rocza left my shoulder as we arrived and buzzed about.

"No one here, boss."

"My compliments to Rocza. She's learning the business, I think."

"She's got a good teacher. You okay?"

"I didn't lose my dinner, anyway. Give me a minute and stay alert."

"Check."

When I felt better I walked up to the flat. I was in luck: Aibynn was there, and there were no assassins.

"Hey, how you doing?"

"Not bad. How'd you like to help me out?"

"Doing what?"

"Ending the war."

"That sounds fine. What do I have to do?"

"Come with me, and let someone read your mind while you remember everything you can about that spot on Greenaere where we met."

"I could do that."

"You'll have to take your pendant off while you do it."

"What? Oh, this?" He fingered the Phoenix Stone around his neck, then shrugged. "That's fine."

"Good. Come with me."

"Just a minute."

He collected his drum and stood next to me. I took a look around the flat, wondering if I'd ever see it again, then we teleported right from there, because I still didn't feel very safe.

Aibynn stared around Castle Black in amazement. "Where are we?"

"The home of Morrolan e'Drien, House of the Dragon."

"Nice place."

"Yeah."

Lady Teldra greeted him like an old friend; he grinned from ear to ear. I went back up to the library and performed introductions. He was pleasant, and either didn't know or didn't care who Sethra Lavode was, not to mention Aliera and Morrolan. They were polite to him, and then Lady Teldra showed him to a room. I found my own room and slept for about fourteen hours.

LATE THE NEXT MORNING I saw Morrolan in his workshop, where he was showing Noish-pa around. I found myself fascinated by the door that led to the tower that held the windows. Morrolan caught me staring at it, but asked no questions. Instead he mentioned something else: "I've had an official emissary from House Jhereg."

"Oh?"

"I've been asked to surrender you."

"Ah. Are you going to?"

He snorted. "What did you do to them, Vlad?"

"Actually, nothing. It's what they think I'm going to do."

"What is that?"

"Kill someone important."

"Are you?"

"Only if we escape Greenaere successfully. First things first, you know."

"Of course. What about the Empire?"

"I'm going to see to that in a few moments."

"Can I help?"

"Perhaps. Can you arrange for the Empress to see me?"

"Certainly. When?"

"Now."

He stared at me and his mouth worked for a moment. Then he concentrated, and was silent for about two minutes. It was interesting trying to piece together the conversation from the expressions that crossed Morrolan's face. He shook his head twice, shrugged once, and once his face twisted up into an expression I couldn't fathom. At last he opened his eyes and said, "She is expecting you."

"Excellent. Can you arrange a teleport?"

"In the courtyard."

"Thank you."

I took a last look at the door to the tower, smiled at Noish-pa, who was already absorbed in work of some sort, and made the long hike, down and around and up and through to the library. I gave Lady Teldra a big smile, which left her a bit puzzled, I think, then I went out into the courtyard where one of Morrolan's sorcerers greeted me respectfully and sent me to the square outside the Imperial Palace that is reserved for those arriving via teleportation.

My stomach had settled down by the time I entered the Palace proper, but I hardly noticed it in any case, my mind was racing so. I was led through hallways and past terraces and inconspicuous guard locations, and at last out into the throne room, with its massive seventeen-sided dome and windows of colored glass. As I approached, I noticed Count Soffta among the courtiers, and I gave him a big smile. His brows came together, but other than that he betrayed no expression.

I bowed to Her Majesty, my heart thumping with excitement, my brain pounding with ideas.

"I greet you, Baronet Taltos."

"And I, you, Your Majesty. Care to take a walk?"

Her eyes widened, and that time I heard the courtiers gasp. But she said, "Very well. Come with me." And she led the way behind her throne.

The walls were still white and featureless, but this time, in my excitement, I nearly outpaced her. For some reason, I no longer had such awe of her as I'd had before; whether it was the state of my mind, or the events of the past few days, or a combination, I don't know.

She said, "Are you here to plead for your wife, or to reprimand your Empress for her actions among the Easterners?"

"Both, Your Majesty."

"Neither will move me, Baronet. I'm sorry, because in all honesty I like you. But to threaten the Empire is unforgivable, which is my only answer to both entreaties."

"Your Majesty, I have, on the one hand, a proposal, and, on the other, information."

She glanced sideways at me, appearing both amused and curious. "Proceed," she said.

"Allow me, Your Majesty, to begin with some questions. May I?"

"You may."

"Do you know why the citizens rebelled?"

"There were many reasons, Baronet. The press gangs, a necessary evil in time of war. The measures, the _justified_ measures, taken against the irresponsible violence in which they engaged. Certain regrettable conditions under which they live."

"Yes," I said. "Let us consider the irresponsible violence. Would the massacres—and I use the word advisedly, Your Majesty, for that's what they were—would the massacres have been necessary had the citizens not engaged in what you called the 'irresponsible violence'?"

She considered. "Probably not," she said.

"Well, then, suppose it was not the citizens who destroyed the watchstation in South Adrilankha, and I suspect committed several similar acts, but was instead a certain Jhereg, who wanted these Easterners suppressed."

She stopped in her tracks and stared at me. "You have evidence of this?"

"His own words that he'd done it."

"Will you swear to this?"

"Under the Orb."

She resumed walking. "I see." I gave her time to consider things further. After a bit she said, "Are you aware that, if you do so swear, by the law, you must do so publicly?"

"Yes."

"So the Organiza—excuse me—your friends and your House will know that you have betrayed this person?"

"Yes."

"And you are prepared to do so?"

"Yes."

"When?"

"When we return to the throne room, Your Majesty."

"Very well. I must say that, moving as this is, and as angry as it makes me, it does not free your wife from the responsibility for leading rebellion."

"That, Your Majesty, is where my proposal fits in."

"Let's hear it, then."

"Your Majesty, I will, personally, bring about a peace with Elde and Greenaere, at no cost to the Empire and at no risk to you, if you will release my wife."

Once more, she stopped and stared at me. She resumed walking. "What makes you think you can do this?"

"I have an idea of what they want, and why they began the war, and I think I can fix it."

"Tell me."

"No, Your Majesty."

And again the sidelong look, followed by a low laugh. "Can you convince her to stop stirring up trouble in South Adrilankha, not to mention the rest of the city, or the rest of the country?"

"Probably not," I said.

She nodded and chewed on her lower lip—a most non-Imperial gesture. Then she said, "Very well, my lord Jhereg. Yes, if you can do what you say, I will release your wife."

"And her friends?"

She shrugged. "I can hardly release one without releasing them all. Yes, if you can publicly swear, under the Orb, that the violence was deliberately caused by a Jhereg, and if you personally conclude a peace with Greenaere and Elde Island that costs us nothing, I will release your wife and her associates."

"Good. Thank you, Your Majesty."

She stopped yet a third time and touched my shoulder. Above her, the Orb went white. She saw me looking at it and said, "What I am saying now is not being remembered."

"Oh."

"Lord Taltos, do you know the Organization will kill you if you betray them?"

"Perhaps," I said. "They will certainly try."

She shook her head. The Orb resumed its pinkish hue and the Empress led the way back to the throne room, where she announced a declaration under the Orb.

The court watched. The Orb floated over my head, and prepared, however it did so, to determine truth or falsehood. I phrased my accusation very carefully, so there could be no question of the truth, or of the guilt. All the time I spoke, my eyes were on Count Soffta, who was trying very hard to keep any expression from his face.

And I was smiling.

PART THREE

Aesthetic Considerations

Lesson 15

Basic Improvisation

I RETURNED TO CASTLE Black and considered consequences.

My life was worth rather less than the small change in my purse, and if things went as I more than half expected them to, I would only have the satisfaction of cheating the Organization of the pleasure of killing me themselves. I indulged myself in a few minutes of soul-searching as I returned to my chambers to rest for a while.

This was nothing like the fatalism that comes upon certain Lyorn who take too long a view of life, and it wasn't really the suicidal madness that had taken me for a short time after I'd been broken under torture. It was more that things had lined themselves up so that I had fewer and fewer options, so the one remaining had to be the right thing to do.

Which brought up the next question: When had I suddenly become enamored of doing the right thing, rather than the practical thing? Was it on the streets of South Adrilankha? Was it in my grandfather's shop, when he said, so simply and quietly, that what I did was wrong? Was it when I finally realized, once and for all, that the woman I'd married was gone forever, and that, whoever she had become, she had no use for me as I was? Or was it that I was finally faced with a problem that couldn't be solved by killing the right person; could only be solved, in fact, by performing a service to the Empire that I hated?

That, I suddenly realized, was what had happened to Cawti: She had transferred her hate from Dragaerans to the Empire. There are fools who pretend that one can get through life without hating, or that the emotion itself is somehow wrong, but I've never had that problem. But sometimes your own hate can fool you as much as your own love, with results that are just as disastrous. It had been silly, at best, to think that I hated Dragaerans when all of my close friends were of the race. Cawti's hatred of the Empire, which I now shared in my own way, was perhaps more reasonable, but ultimately frustrating. Noish-pa was right: Hatred is inevitable; allowing it to control your actions is foolish.

I didn't know where that left me now, and I admitted, as I stared at the ceiling and hid my thoughts from Loiosh, that none of it mattered, anyway. By surrendering to "right" as opposed to "practical," I had changed irrevocably. But once you allow yourself to recognize necessity, you find two things: One, you find your options so restricted that the only course of action is obvious, and, two, that a great sense of freedom comes with the decision.

By this time tomorrow, Vlad Taltos, Jhereg and assassin, would be dead, one way or the other. I made certain all of my documents were correct and decided that the time allotted for self-indulgent soul-searching had expired.

But I fervently hoped that I would have a chance to give my Demon Goddess a piece of my mind before all was said and done.

It WAS EARLY AFTERNOON when I was summoned to Morrolan's lower workshop, the place set aside for his experiments with sorcery. I was much calmer, and beginning to be nervous. Make that frightened.

I picked up Aibynn on the way. Sethra, Daymar, and Morrolan were there, staring at the black stone and speaking together. They looked up when I came in and Sethra said, "Here, Vlad, catch," and tossed me the stone. "Now, speak to me psionically." I attempted to do so, and it was like it was back on the island; no one was home. I shrugged. "Now," she said, "watch." She gestured with one hand, and my rapier began rising out of its sheath. She stopped, it slid back in.

"Well?" I said.

"The stone has no effect on sorcery whatsoever."

"All right. But then—"

She held up a hand. "Now, if you please, set Spellbreaker spinning."

"Eh? All right." I let the chain fall into my left hand, wondering what she was after. It was very cool in my hand, and alive like a Morganti weapon was alive, yet different. I did as she'd said. When it was going good, spinning between Sethra and me, she gestured again. This time, nothing happened, except perhaps the faintest tingling running up my arm.

"Well?" I said. "We knew Spellbreaker interfered with sorcery. That's why I gave it the name."

"Yes. And so does whatever else is on the island. Does the similarity strike you?"

"Yes. What's your point?"

"There is more to that chain than I know," she said. "But I think we are able to determine one thing now. It is not, in fact, made of gold. It is made of gold Phoenix stone."

"Is that what you call it?" put in Aibynn, who'd been so quiet I'd forgotten he was there.

"What do you call it?" asked Morrolan, in all innocence.

"In my land," said Aibynn, "we call it a rock."

I said hastily, "I'm not really surprised that Spellbreaker isn't just gold; I've never seen gold as hard as the links of this chain."

"Yes. Black disables psionic activity, gold prevents the working of sorcery."

I studied Spellbreaker. "It certainly looks like metal," I said. "And feels like it."

"As I said, there's more to that chain than I understand."

"Well, all right. Now, do you know how to use this information to get past it to the island?"

"Possibly. Set Spellbreaker spinning again." I did so. She looked at Daymar, nodded, and gestured. Once again, the sword began to rise from its sheath, only very slowly. She stopped, it returned.

"Looks good," I said. "How?"

"How did Aliera break through the wall the last time you were on the island?"

"Pre-Empire sorcery," I said.

"Yes."

"Can you control it well enough to teleport with it? I'd understood such fine control was impossible, which is why the Orb was invented in the first place."

"Yes and no," said Sethra. "I can create a disturbance in the field set up by the Phoenix Stone, which allows Daymar to direct his energy through the gold stone, ignoring the black, which allows me to channel mine through the black, ignoring the gold. It isn't easy," she added.

"It is similar," added Morrolan, "to the way you and Loiosh communicate. It isn't exactly psionically, it's more—"

"Never mind the details," I said, "as long as it will work."

"It should," said Sethra. "As long as we can get a solid enough image of the place."

She looked at Aibynn. He stared back, looking innocent.

"All right," I said. "Sethra, what about getting us back?"

"Daymar will have to try to break through to you."

"All right, when?"

"Let's talk about it."

We decided that they would give us a couple of hours, and, after that, Daymar would attempt to reach me psionically every half hour until we said we were ready to return.

Sethra said, "You know, don't you, that it is much more difficult to teleport something to you than from you?"

"Yeah," I said. "But I trust you."

"As you say."

"Then we can proceed."

"Yes," she said. "Are you ready?"

"I was born ready."

"Then let us call Aliera and be about it."

Aliera arrived almost at once. She was wearing the black and silver battle garb of a Dragonlord. She was barely taller than I, which was quite short for a Dragaeran. It used to bother her, I guess, since she was in the habit of

We came to the place where I'd fought my first four pursuers, and I didn't take the time to see if there were any signs of the struggle. Loiosh led me; I led Morrolan and Aliera, and in about an hour and a half we were outside the village. It was early evening. There was no one in sight.

"Where is everybody, boss?"

"Probably on ships preparing to attack the Dragaeran navy."

"Oh."

"Let's eat," I said aloud, and we took out the food that had been packed for us by Morrolan's cook. I had dried winneasaurous and some good bread. I took my time eating, so it was nearly full dark by the time we were done.

"Now what?" said Morrolan.

I looked at their dim faces, Morrolan e'Drien and Aliera e'Kieron, watching me patiently and expectantly. I said, "Now I lead us to the place that passes for a palace and negotiate as appropriate, and get out."

"In other words," said Aliera, "we're just going to improvise."

"You got it."

"Good plan," said Morrolan dryly.

"Thanks. It's one of my best."

I led the way, with Morrolan and Aliera behind me. Quite a sight we must have looked as we walked up the wide shallow steps to the small, pillared building that housed the government of Greenaere.

We flung the door open in front of two sleepy-looking guards, neither of them in uniform, both holding the short, feathered spears I remembered too well. They stopped looking sleepy almost at once. The three of us could have put the two of them down without working up a sweat, but I held my arm up for them to wait.

The guards stared at us. We stared back. I said, "Take me to your—"

"Who are you?" croaked one of them at last.

"Unofficial envoys from the Dragaeran Empire. We wish to open negotiations with—"

"I know you," said the other. "You're the one who—"

"Now, now," I said. "The past is past," and I smiled into his face. Behind me, I felt the troops prepare for battle. There is something reassuring about having Morrolan with Blackwand and Aliera with Pathfinder ready to jump to your defense. The guards looked very nervous; not without reason. "We

would like to see the King," I said. There was no one else in sight down the
narrow corridor; they really hadn't considered the possibility of an attack.

"I—I'll see if he, that is, I'll find out—"

"Excellent. Do that."

He swallowed and backed up a couple of steps. I followed, Morrolan and
Aliera behind me, forcing the other guard backward, too.

"No, you wait here."

"Not a chance," I said cheerfully.

He stopped. "I can't let you past."

"You can't stop us," I said reasonably.

"I'll raise the alarm."

"Do so."

He turned and yelled, "Help! Invaders!" at the top of his lungs. For some
reason, I still didn't want to cut them down, so I just led us past them. As
we went by, I patted the one who'd recognized me on the shoulder. They
both looked rather pitiful, and the other one actually drew steel as we went
by. Morrolan and Aliera drew as well then, and I heard the fellow make
sounds of awe under his breath. Yes, it was still possible to feel a Morganti
weapon here on the island, Phoenix Stone notwithstanding. I expected Morrolan was noting that to study when he got back.

"This way," I said, and directed us into the throne room.

There were two more guards, a pale man with an odd white streak in his
dark hair and a hook-nosed woman. They had apparently heard the warn-
ings, because they stood with their spears out and pointed at us. To the right
of the throne was an old woman with grey hair and deep eyes, and on the
left were two men. One seemed quite old and rather unkempt. The other
was the bushy-browed interrogator I knew so well. He was armed only with
a knife at his belt, the old man was unarmed. The King, who looked like he
couldn't be more than two or three hundred (in a human that would be
eighteen or nineteen, I suppose), stared at us in a mixture of fear and amazement. I recognized him, too; he'd been walking next to the King I'd assassinated, just as I'd suspected then. How long ago was that? It felt like years.

I led us up to the throne, stopping just out of range of those spears, and
said, "Your Majesty King Corcor'n, we wish you a pleasant evening. Um,
excuse me, is 'Your Majesty' the proper form of address?"

He swallowed twice and said, "It will do."

I said, "My name is Vladimir Taltos. My friends are called Morrolan e'Drien and Aliera e'Kieron. We've come to discuss peace."

The two guards with the spears looked very unhappy and kept glancing at the two Great Weapons. Well, hardly surprising. I said, "Perhaps, my friends, we should sheathe our weapons." They did so.

The King said, in a raspy whisper, "How did you get here?"

"Sorcery, Your Majesty."

"But—"

"Oh, yes, I know. We've solved that problem."

"Impossible."

I shrugged. "In that case, we're not here, and you can safely ignore us. I should tell you, Your Majesty, that we came here in order to kill you and as many important advisors and chiefs as we could find. We changed our minds when we saw how poorly protected you were."

"Messengers have gone out," he said. "Troops will be arriving in moments."

"In that case," I said, "it would be well if we had our business concluded before they arrive. Otherwise, well, things could get ugly."

His mouth worked in anger and fear. The grey-haired woman leaned over to him and started to say something. I gave silent orders to Loiosh and Rocza. They left my shoulders and flew to the two guards. As puppets controlled by a single string, the guards winced, began to panic, caught themselves, and held still as the jhereg landed on their shoulders. I was very impressed with the guards; they trembled, but didn't move. I smiled.

The King said, "You assassinated—"

"Yes," I said. "I did. And you will never know the reason. But you have sunk several of our ships, killing hundreds of our citizens. How many lives is a King worth, Your Majesty? We are willing to call the score even if you are."

"He was my father."

"I'm sorry."

"Sorry," he said scornfully.

"Yes. I am. For reasons I can no more explain than I can explain why I did it. But what's done is done. Your father was given a good blood price,

Your Majesty; the crews of—how many ships? Your Majesty, we want to
end it. Can you—?"

At that moment there was the sound of tramping feet. I broke off my
speech, but didn't turn around.

"How many, Loiosh?"

"About twenty, boss."

"Aliera, Morrolan, watch them."

"We're already doing it, Vlad," said Morrolan. I think it bothered him to
appear to be taking orders from me. Tough. At that moment I heard Daymar's voice in the back of my mind. I let the contact occur and said, *"All is
well. Check back later."* The contact faded.

There were, indeed, a good number of them, but we were between them
and the King. Moreover, each of the two guards who stood between us had
a poisonous jhereg on his shoulder. I said, "You must decide, Your Majesty.
Unless, that is, you would like us to slaughter your troops for you first, and
then continue the negotiations?"

"How do you know," he said at last, "that I will hold to an agreement
made under these circumstances?"

"I don't," I said. "Furthermore, you are most welcome to break it. If you
do, of course, we will be back. Perhaps with a few thousand troops."

He turned to the old woman at his side and they spoke together quietly.

"Loiosh, what are they saying?"

"She says Elde has no objection to peace if he can get a guarantee that—"

"Very well," said the King. "I agree. The ships we've sunk will be the
indemnity for the damage done to us. We—bide a moment."

He spoke quietly to the two men on the other side of the throne.

"Loiosh?"

"I can't hear them, boss."

*"All right. The old woman must be the ambassador or something from
Elde Island. Perhaps the others are advisors of some sort."*

We waited while they spoke together, then the King nodded and said, "But
we require two things. First, assurances that no reprisals will be taken either
against us or against our ally. Second, we want the assassin and his accomplice returned to us for punishment."

I turned to glance at Morrolan and Aliera. Aliera was still watching the armed men at the back of the room; Morrolan turned his head toward me and silently mouthed the word "assassin," with a lift to his eyebrows. I smiled and turned back to the King.

"As to your first condition," I said, "I give you my word. Isn't that sufficient?"

"No," said the King."

"You aren't really in much of a position to bargain."

"Maybe," he said, apparently beginning to recover now that he had troops handy. "But maybe it isn't all that easy for you to break through here. Maybe you cannot send troops to invade us. Maybe it was only a fluke that allowed the three of you to arrive here this way. Maybe you didn't break through the way you claim you did, but sneaked past our ships in a vessel of your own."

"Maybe," I agreed. "But do you think we could slip past you in your own waters? And do you want to chance it?"

"If you do not meet the conditions, yes."

"What sort of guarantees do you want?"

"The word of your Empress."

I said, "We are unofficial envoys. I cannot speak for her."

"We will write out a treaty that specifies the conditions. The Empress may sign it and return it to me, or not. We will allow a single small ship, bearing your Empire's standard, to land to return the document. We will cease our attacks for three days, which will give time to sign and return it. I warn you that, during those three days, our preparations for war, and the preparations of our ally, will continue."

"Fair enough," I said. "As to the second condition, it is impossible."

He looked at me, then spoke quietly to his advisors. The one I recognized kept glancing at me. The King looked up and said, "In that case, you may signal the slaughter to begin, for we will not allow you and your accomplice to go unpunished."

"Your Majesty, have your scribe prepare the document while I consider this matter. We may be able to work something out."

"Very well." The old man at his left hand, it seemed, was the scribe. He left for a moment, and returned with pen, blotter, ink, and parchment, and began writing.

I said, "May I approach you, Your Majesty?"

The two guards in front of him tensed, but he said, "Very well."

"Vlad, what are you doing?" asked Morrolan.

"Bide a moment," I said.

I spoke to the King quietly for a few minutes, with the advisor, the emissary, and bushy-brows listening in. Loiosh said, *"Boss, you—"*

"Shut up."

"But—"

"Shut up."

The King looked at me closely, then at the advisor, who nodded. Bushy-brows also nodded. The emissary said, "It is no concern of ours, Your Majesty."

The King said, "Very well. So be it," and the scribe continued writing. I backed up. Loiosh and Rocza returned to my shoulders, and the two guards relaxed.

Aliera said, "Vlad, what did you just do?"

"Worked a compromise," I said. "I'll explain when we're back home."

While the scribe was working, I felt Daymar's contact once more. *"Five minutes,"* I told him. *"We're almost done."*

"I'll have Seth—" His pseudo-voice faded away in midsentence. The scribe finished, the King signed it. I took it, read it, nodded, rolled it up, and handed it to Morrolan, who at once started unrolling it.

"No," I said. "Read it at home."

"Why?"

"We have to leave now."

And, indeed, at that moment I felt Daymar's presence again. *"Okay,"* I told him. *"Take us home."*

The spell came on very slowly; so slowly I was afraid for a moment it wasn't going to work. But a reddish glow began to surround us. It became stronger, and I felt it begin to grab and take hold, and I felt the beginnings of the disorientation I'd felt before.

It was no difficulty at all to take a step to my left so I was out of range of its effects. I saw Morrolan and Aliera slowly fade, not realizing, yet, that I had been left behind.

The King was staring in amazement at the evidence that sorcery had invaded his realm. I brought his attention back to me by saying, "So, Your Majesty, just out of curiosity, what are the island customs as regards execution of regicides?"

Lesson 16

Dealing With Upper Management I

THEY CAME AND TOOK hold of my arms, others took my rapier, my belt dagger, and my cloak, leaving me with only about nine weapons, and those they'd no doubt get to later. The King said, "It has never happened before, so we have no custom. We shall not be cruel."

"Thanks," I said. "I appreciate that."

"I will stand by my agreement, but tell me now: Is it true that Aibynn of Lowporch was not your accomplice?"

"It's true. Until you demanded he be turned over to you, I suspected he was a spy of yours. He helped me, however, so I feel a certain loyalty to him."

"Why did you conceal our agreement from your friends?"

"They wouldn't have allowed it."

"Then perhaps they will try to rescue you."

"I'm sure they will. I think you should get it done quickly, before they have time."

He whispered to the advisor, who nodded and scurried off. "Soon," he said, "we will have enough troops to—"

"To die," I told him. "You don't know what you're dealing with. Have you ever heard of a weapon the Serioli call Magical-Wand-for-Creating-

Death-in-the-Form-of-a-Black-Sword? We call it Blackwand, and my friend Morrolan wields it. How about Dagger-Shaped-Bearer-of-Fire-That-Burns-Like-Ice? Sethra Lavode of Dzur Mountain carries that. And then there's Artifact-in-Sword-Form-That-Searches-for-the-True-Path. We call it Pathfinder, and Aliera e'Kieron carries it. Your Majesty, you are making a mistake if you think you can bring in enough troops to keep them from rescuing me if I'm still alive when they get here."

He stared. "Is it your Empress who makes you so loyal that you will sacrifice your life for her? Or is it the Empire?"

"Neither," I said. "They are holding my wife captive, and I hope to win her release."

"Captive? For what?"

"Leading a rebellion."

He stared, then began to smile, and then he laughed. "So, you sacrifice your life in the interests of the Empire that is holding your wife captive for trying to overthrow it? And you do this to win her release, so she can try to overthrow it again?"

"Something like that." I didn't think it was all *that* funny.

"Is that why you murdered my father in the first place?"

"No."

"Then why?"

"Look, Your Majesty, my friends will probably be back as soon as they've figured out what happened. It will take them a while to perform the spell again, but I don't know how long a while that will be. If I'm still alive when they get here, things will get very bloody very fast. And, to be honest, I'm not enjoying standing around very much. Why don't we just get this over with?"

"My dear assassin," said the King. "We intend to execute you. We are not about to just cut you down on the spot."

"Then you're a fool," I snapped.

"Do you really think they can be back so quickly?"

"Probably not, but I have no way of knowing. Right now, they're probably arguing with each other about that very issue. By now they've already decided to do it, and are figuring out if they remember the place well enough. They are *not* just standing around; I know them."

He nodded. "What about those—those beasts of yours."

"They won't hurt you."

"You think not? Boss, I'm going to kill anyone who tries to touch you."

"You will not."

"How are you going to stop me?"

"Loiosh, this is for Cawti."

"Yeah? So?"

I cleared my throat. "Excuse me, Your Majesty, but there's a bit of a problem here, after all. Give me a moment to work this out."

"With those beasts?"

"They, um, they're friends, Your Majesty, and they don't want anyone harming me. Give me a moment to speak with them."

He shook his head. "How does someone like you inspire such loyalty?"

"Damned if I know," I said. "Basic integrity, I guess."

He cocked his head to the side. "You speak lightly, but perhaps it is true. You were hired, were you not? You kill for gold?" I shrugged. "If I paid you enough, would you kill the man who hired you?"

I thought about attempting to assassinate Verra and laughed. "Not likely in this case, I'm afraid."

"A shame," he said. "Because you are nothing more than a tool, and I would rather have the wielder of the tool. Yes, I will kill you, and your poisonous friends as well, if necessary, and I will hold with the bargain I made. But I would much rather know who gave the order, so I can strike him down instead. Come. I offer you your life. Will you tell me?"

Was I supposed to tell him it was a god? Would he believe me? What would he do if he did? It was laughable. I said, "Sorry, the rules don't permit it. Let's get this done, shall we? Here, hand me that pouch of mine." No one moved. "Oh, come now," I said, "if I'd been planning to kill you, I would have done so when I had all the odds on my side."

The King nodded, and they released me and handed me the pouch, still watching me closely. I removed a couple of powders and set them on the floor.

"Boss, that's not fair."

"Neither is life, chum." "There," I said aloud. "Mix those powders to-gether equally, dissolve them in water. If anyone is bit by one of my friends,

that will make sure they take no worse effect than a bit of illness. It's what I used while training them. I assume you have someone who doesn't mind a bite or two?"

The King turned to bushy-brows. "Let it be done, then."

My old interrogator nodded and said, "By what means?"

"Send for an axe, and let his head be struck off."

"You know," I said, "that you'll get blood all over the floor."

"It can be cleaned," said the King. Then, "Don't you even care?"

I looked at his young face, and wondered how close he had been to the King his father, whom I had killed. I wondered once more about Verra, who had set all this in motion, and I regretted that I wouldn't have a chance to tell her about it in detail. "What's the difference?" I said. "Sure, I care. When has that changed anything?"

They sent for an axe, and while they were waiting for it about forty more island warriors arrived. Then the axe came, and once more they took my arms. The two holding me glanced nervously at the jhereg, and at the vials of powder on the floor.

"Boss, you can't just let them—"

"Watch me."

I looked at the axe. It was a very ugly thing that was intended for chopping down trees, not people. I hoped they'd be able to strike off my head without too many tries—it isn't as easy as you might think. I winced. "I hope it's sharp," I said.

"It is sharp," said the King.

Bushy-brows took the axe, but just as he turned toward me, before they could put me into the proper position, there began a faint blue glow in the room. It grew brighter as we watched.

"Took too long," I said.

"Prepare to attack," said the King.

I wondered if I should help keep my friends from being slaughtered or try to talk them out of saving me. I still hadn't decided when Aliera was suddenly there, Pathfinder naked in her hand, and, of all people, Aibynn, drum in hand, looking innocent and foolish.

"Attack!" cried the King.

"Wait!" cried Aliera.

Somehow, her voice stopped them, and everyone stood there, the air filled with naked swords and the awful power of the Great Weapon, and as they stood I became aware of someone else, on the floor, right at Aliera's feet. When I saw who it was, bound and gagged, I almost started laughing.

"What is this?" cried the King.

"I am Aliera e'Kieron of the House of the Dragon. I will have words with you, or slaughter. Will you let me speak?"

If they'd been able to send all three of them, or even any two, the issue would never have been in doubt. As it was, with Aliera unable to use sorcery, it could get ugly. If they attacked her, there would be a great deal of death, and I realized that, promise or not, I could not stand there and let them kill her. I still had a few weapons on me, and there was my familiar, as well.

"*Loiosh, get ready. You and Rocza. If they start—*"

"*We're ready, boss.*"

The King was standing now in front of his raised throne, and he looked at me, back at the almost-conflict, and said, "Say what you have to say."

"I offer you a trade," she said, sheathing her blade. "Give us the assassin, and we will give you the man who hired him. What say you?"

The King stood. "Indeed? I'd just been saying . . . remove his gag. I want to hear what he has to say for himself."

They stood him up and did this, and you would not want to hear the things he called me. It was positively shameful. I kept my face impassive. The King interrupted him at last and said, "You need not hate the one you paid for evil you were too cowardly to commit yourself. He never gave your name."

He drew himself up as well as he could, with feet and hands still bound, and said, "I deny having anything to do with this or any other assassination."

The King tapped his front teeth with his fingernails and said to Aliera, "How am I to know this is the guilty one?"

She bowed, came forward, and handed him two large yellow parchments that had been getting crushed in her belt. One I recognized from the parchment as the treaty the King had just signed. The other—

"It bears your Imperial seal," he said. "I recognize it. And is signed by Zerika herself." He nodded. "That will do." He turned to Boralinoi. "Why did you want my father killed?" he demanded.

"I did not. It is all a lie. I never—"

"Kill him," said the King.

"I'll do it," I said.

"What?" said the King.

"Well," I said, "you heard what he said about me."

The King looked at me, then smiled. "Very well, do it. Give him the axe."

I wanted to laugh aloud, but held it in check. I said, "I don't know much about axes. May I use a knife?"

Boralinoi screamed his rage and began tugging furiously at the bonds and cursing me and everything else in sight. I still wanted to laugh. The King nodded. I took a knife from a sheath between my shoulder blades as they forced Boralinoi to his knees.

"Hold his head steady," I said, and two of them came forward to do this. He never stopped screeching his rage until they held his jaws shut.

Sometimes, over the course of my life, I've felt regret for killing someone. Other times, not. I said quite clearly, "Sorry, boss, a job's a job," and put my blade neatly into his left eye. He screamed, convulsed, twitched, and died. I stared down at his body and was not displeased.

I looked at the King and wondered idly what would happen next. *"Let's go boss,"* said Loiosh. I still hadn't quite accepted that I was going to get out of this. Aliera caught my eye and motioned me to her.

Bushy-brows said, "Your Majesty—"

"Yes," said the King. He turned toward Aliera. "You may go. The others will be staying."

Aliera stared at him. "Is that how you keep your word?"

"I never gave my word," said the King. "Even by implication."

"I'm beginning to take a dislike to you," I said.

He ignored me. "Go. You have your peace. I'll take the assassins."

I thought the idea that, after all of this, I was going to die here after all was rather silly. So did Aliera, apparently, for she drew Pathfinder and the sensation of it filled the room. That was enough of a distraction to give me time to grab Spellbreaker, my cloak, and my rapier. I swung it around so the sheath went flying in the general direction of the King. One of the guards bravely stepped in front of it and went down clutching at his chest; I'll tell you about my sheath sometime.

I stepped over to Aliera and we stood back-to-back, waiting for them to charge. This would have been a perfect time for Sethra and Daymar to have come through. Aliera whispered, "It's going to be a while yet; they're exhausted."

"Great," I said.

"Attack," said the King.

"The door," I said.

Aliera led the way with Pathfinder, followed by Aibynn, while I guarded their back and sides, jabbing wildly with my rapier and swinging just as wildly with my cloak. I think the cloak did more damage than my sword, but Pathfinder, well, there were screams. Loiosh and Rocza flew into everyone's face and added to the confusion.

Let's just say we reached the door and leave it at that, all right? Once there, there were a few more of them in the hall, but they seemed less inclined to tangle with Pathfinder than the others had been, and then we were outside.

"Now what?" said Aliera.

"Run," I suggested.

"Where?"

"Follow me," said Aibynn.

"Just a moment," said Aliera. She pointed her weapon at the door and muttered something under her breath while making arcane gestures with her free hand. The door collapsed, burying a few guards with it and leaving three of them between the door and us.

They looked at the door, looked at Pathfinder, looked at each other.

"Well?" I said.

They said nothing. We took off, following pretty much the same route I'd taken before.

"What was that?" said Aibynn.

"Pre-Empire sorcery," I said.

"What's that?"

"Pretty effective," I said. I looked back. The three guards had decided to help dig their friends out of the rubble of the ruins of the front hall rather than to follow us. Wise.

We kept our speed up until we were rather deep in the forest, then we paused to catch our breath.

"Thanks, Aliera."

"Think nothing of it. I hope I didn't upset a plan."

"You did. That's why I said thank you. How did you acquire Boralinoi?"

"Courtesy of the Empress."

"Does she know he isn't really guilty?"

"He's guilty. Maybe not of killing the King, but he's guilty."

"Is that what the Empress said?"

"Yes."

"Well, I'll be damned. How did you get here so fast?"

"Sethra. Daymar. Aibynn. The Orb."

"The Orb?"

"Yes."

"I see." I turned to Aibynn. "How did you happen to come along?"

He shrugged. "I thought I might be able to help you get out."

"How?"

"Well, I could drum."

I looked at him. *"Loiosh, do you trust him?"*

"I don't know."

"Yeah. Me neither. This could still be—"

"I know."

Rocza fluttered off my shoulder and landed on Aibynn's. He seemed startled, but handled it gracefully enough.

"She trusts him, boss."

I looked at Aibynn, then looked at Rocza. I sighed. "Drum away," I said.

"Let's sit down," said Aibynn.

We did so.

He began to drum.

Lesson 17

Dealing With Upper Management II

I STUDIED THE WHITE hallway and said, "Either the Imperial Palace or—"

"It's not the Imperial Palace," said Aliera.

Aibynn was still sitting down. He seemed rather drained and tired. He stopped drumming and smiled wanly.

"How," I said, "did *this* happen?"

"Ask him," said Aliera, indicating Aibynn.

"Well?" I said.

"Sometimes," he said, "when you drum, you . . . it's hard to describe. You reach places. Didn't you feel it?"

"No," I said quickly, just as Aliera was saying "Yes."

"Boss—"

"Well, okay, maybe," I amended. "But why this place?"

"It was what you two were both thinking about." That was true; I'd been thinking how pleasant it would be to give Verra a piece of my mind, but why would Aliera have been thinking about it?

I said, "Why you?" at just the same moment she said it to me. I shrugged, turned to Aibynn, and said, "So all this time, you've really been nothing more than a drummer?"

For the first time, he seemed really surprised. "You mean you didn't believe me?"

"Let's just say I wondered."

Aliera stood up and said, "Let's go."

She seemed to know her way, so I followed her. It was only a short walk, this time, until we reached the doors, which were standing open. There was no cat this time. I thought I saw something or someone disappear behind the throne, but I wasn't sure. In any case, the goddess was there.

She said, "Hello, Aliera, Vlad."

"Hello, Mother," said Aliera.

Mother?

"Who is your friend, and what brings you here?"

"His name is Aibynn," said Aliera. "He brought us here to save our lives."

Mother?

"I see. Shall I send you back, then, or is there something I can do for you?"

Mother?

"Send us back, Mother. We—"

"Excuse me," I said. "Do you mean that literally?"

"Mean what?" said Aliera.

"You're calling her 'Mother.' "

"Oh, yes. Why? You didn't know?"

"You never told me."

"You never asked."

"Of all the—never mind. Goddess, if you'd be kind enough to send them back, I would have words with you that they don't need to hear."

Aliera stared at me. "I don't like your tone, Vlad."

I started to snap at her, but the goddess said, "It's all right, Aliera. He has some cause."

She looked unhappy, but said, "Very well."

"We can't take long," said the Demon Goddess, "or you'll be late for your appointment."

"Appointment?"

"With the Empress."

"I have an appointment with the Empress?"

"Yes. Morrolan has the message waiting for you, but I may as well tell you myself."

I licked my lips. "In that case," I told Aibynn, "I'll meet you outside the Imperial Wing of the Palace."

"All right," he said, still appearing exhausted.

The goddess said, "You interest me, drummer. Perhaps, sometime, you'd care to play for me."

"Sure."

I could have warned him that accepting work from the Demon Goddess didn't always work out the way one would like, but I thought it might be tactless. Aliera walked up and kissed Verra on the cheek. Verra smiled maternally. It was very strange. Aliera stepped back and nodded; she and Aibynn vanished.

I was about to start in on the goddess when a small girl emerged from behind the throne. I caught myself and said, "Hello, Devera."

" 'Lo, Uncle Vlad."

"Why were you hiding?"

"I can't let Mama see me yet."

"Why not?"

"It might upset things."

"Oh. So she"—I indicated the Demon Goddess—"is your grandmother?"

Devera smiled and crawled up into her lap.

"Boss, is it just me, or is this really weird?"

"It's both of us."

Verra said, "I'm sorry all of this had to happen."

"You bloody well should be."

"I did help save your life."

"Yeah. People have been doing that a lot. Thanks, I suppose."

"Is there something you want to say to me?"

"Yes, Goddess, there is. You've gone a good way toward messing up my life, and, what's more, manipulated events such that, through my actions, hundreds of people have died. I don't care what your motivations were; I don't want to have anything more to do with you. Okay?"

Devera looked unhappy, but didn't say anything. Verra said, "I understand, Vlad. But I won't hold you to that. You don't even know who you are yet. You're beginning another life now. Wait until you know what sort of life it is before you make decisions like that."

I started to say something more, but Devera climbed down from her lap, came up to me, took my hand, squeezed. "Don't be mad, Uncle Vlad, she meant well."

"I—" I stopped and looked down at her. I shook my head.

"Come," said Verra, "they await you at the Imperial Palace."

"For what?"

"You'll see. And I think we'll meet again, Vlad Taltos, however you feel about it at the moment." The room swirled and went away before I could speak again.

L IFE, THY NAME IS irony, or something like that.

"And by his own actions, at risk of his life . . ." The voice of the seneschal rolled like thunder through the court. My eyes were down, and my thoughts were filled with two conflicting desires: First, I wanted to turn around and see how Count Soffta was taking the whole thing. Second, I very badly wanted to throw my head back and laugh aloud.

". . . which would certainly have cost the lives of thousands of Imperial citizens . . ."

Loiosh, of course, wasn't helping any. He sat on my shoulder, looking around, nuzzling Rocza, and generally carrying on as if he were personally being honored, and saying things like, *"Do they really take this stuff seriously, boss?"*

". . . all the lands around Lake Szurke, within the Duchy of Eastmanswatch, for a distance . . ."

They had even given me a pillow for my knee; a pillow with a stylized Jhereg in grey against a black background. In keeping my eyes to the ground I kept seeing pieces of embroidered wing and head, and this made it harder than ever to keep a straight face.

". . . all rights and privileges pertaining to this rank, to be granted to all descendants and heirs of his body, for as long as the Empire . . ."

I wondered how Cawti would react, were she here. Probably not very well, knowing how she felt about the Empire. Perhaps what I missed most about the new Cawti was that she seemed to have lost her sense of humor. And for what? The words of the Demon Goddess came back to me, and for a moment, bitterness overwhelmed irony.

".. . crest with the Imperial Phoenix above of the symbol of House Jhereg . . ." His voice almost faltered there, but didn't. Had an Imperial title ever before been granted a Jhereg? Certainly, none had ever been granted an Easterner. My sense of humor returned.

".. . crest shall be entered into the Imperial Registry for all time, and may not be removed save by unanimous vote of the Council of Heirs and the Emperor . . ."

Just what I needed. I bit my lip. I was becoming anxious for this to end, because when it was over, I'd meet my wife once more. Would I have to say something at the end of the ceremony? No, a deep bow would do.

".. . shall be known as Count Szurke, and shall have the right of high and low justice upon his lands, and bear responsibility for . . ."

I wondered if this would make the Jhereg any slower to go after my head. Considering that I just implicated a Council member before the Empire, and then played a part in his murder, it wasn't very likely. How soon would they move? Soon. Very soon. If I was going to save my life, which I really should do after all the work Aliera and others had gone through to preserve it, I couldn't waste any time.

".. . stand now, before the Empress and the Heirs of the court, and receive . . ."

I had that rarest of positions, an Imperial title, which was worth exactly nothing. I wondered if the Empress saw the humor in it. The ceremony came to an end at last. As soon as was decent, I got out of there, intending to go back to the Iorich Wing. But as I was leaving the Imperial Wing, I found Aibynn, his drum at his feet, watching passersby and tapping out rhythms with coins on the marble railing against the wide stairway that led down into the antechamber.

"Here in the Empire," I said, "we call that a *banister*."

"Where are you going?" he said.

"Now? To meet my wife. After that, well, I'd like a favor from you."

"What's that?"

"The Phoenix Stone you carry; I want it."

He frowned, then said, "All right. It's still at that castle. You can just take it."

"Are you sure you won't need it?"

He shrugged.

"Your mind is made up, isn't it, boss?"

"Yeah."

"Thanks, Aibynn."

"You're welcome. What's that you're wearing?"

"This? I wear it so I don't get sick when—"

"No, that."

"Oh. It represents an imperial title. It doesn't really mean anything. Want it? In exchange for the one you're giving me?"

"No, thanks. Where are you going?"

I shook my head. "It doesn't matter. What about you? You can't go back home."

"Not now, anyway. That's all right. I like it here. The drumming is much more primitive."

Primitive? I chuckled, thinking of some musicians I'd met who'd have hated to be told that. "Whatever," I said. "Maybe I'll run into you again."

"Yes."

"And Aibynn . . ."

"Yes?"

"I think you were wrong about the gods."

"Oh?"

"I think when a god does something reprehensible, it's still reprehensible."

"Then what is a god?"

"I don't know."

"Maybe you can find out."

"Yes." I said. "Maybe I can. Maybe I will. Thanks."

He nodded an acknowledgment and went back to playing the banister. I walked around to the Iorich Wing, and found that I'd have to wait an hour or so while they finished the paperwork involved in releasing Cawti. That was all right; I had things to do. I walked away from the Palace, and, still taking delight in the lack of nausea, I teleported.

* * *

"YOU CAN'T DO THIS to me," said Kragar.

"I just did," I told him.

"I won't last five minutes."

"You've already lasted longer than that, and this isn't the first time."

"That was temporary. Vlad, I became a Jhereg because I couldn't be a Dragon. I was born a Dragon, you know that. And I'd try to give an order in battle, and no one would notice. I *can't*—"

"People change, Kragar. You've already changed."

"But—"

"Think of the money."

He stopped. "A point," he admitted.

"You also have the loyalty of everyone who works here. They know you and they trust you. Besides, what choice do I have? How much is the Organization offering for my head right now?"

He told me, and I was impressed in spite of myself. "The rumor is," he added, "that they want it Morganti."

"That would make sense," I said evenly, though I shuddered as I spoke. I looked around the office. It was still filled with all of my things—target on the wall, coat-rack where Loiosh and Rocza were perched, dark rings on the desk from where I habitually put my klava cup, the wheeled swivel chair I'd had specially designed, and more. It was more like home than home was.

"Will it ever be possible for you to come back?"

"Maybe. But even if it is, I'm not certain I'm ever going to want to. And what if I do? We can work something out, or I can start over somewhere else."

He sighed. "It's going to be hard to work around here without Melestav."

"Yeah. And Sticks."

We were silent for a few moments, out of respect for the dead. I still couldn't hate Melestav, and Sticks had meant a lot to me. I hate it when friends die.

Kragar said, "Will I be able to reach you?"

"No."

"Where are you going?"

"I don't know. I've been east, the sea is south. That leaves north and west. Probably one of those directions."

He considered carefully. Then he said, "What are you going to do about South Adrilankha?"

"You don't have to worry about it," I said. "I'm making other arrangements for that territory."

"Well, that's something, anyway."

I took another look around the office. So much of my life had filled that room. Loiosh flew over to Kragar, nuzzled his ear for a moment, and landed on my right shoulder. Rocza landed on my left. I stood up. "Oh, and Kragar, say good-bye to Kiera the Thief for me. Tell her I still owe her. On the other hand, I expect she can find me when she wants to."

"I'll tell her," said Kragar.

"Thanks. Good luck." I teleported.

I⊤ WAS LIKE REHEARSING a play; as if the director had said, "Do the bit over where you meet on the steps of the Iorich Wing, only this time make it more intense." This time she put her arms around me and held me like she meant it. I put my arms around her and wondered why I wasn't reacting more strongly. Loiosh and Rocza kept careful watch around us.

"Tell me about it," she said.

Standing there, alone on the deserted steps as the slow, thorough evening tucked itself into the corners of the Palace, I did. I told her everything, and as I did, I wondered at the calm voice of this speaker, relating the tale of revolution, assassination, and intrigue as if he had no part in it. What is he feeling now? I wondered. I wished they'd found someone for the part more able to convey emotion. Or perhaps that was the effect desired by the director, if not the playwright.

When I finished, she pulled back and stared at me. "They'll kill you," she said.

"I don't think so."

"What will stop them?"

"I have a plan."

"Tell me."

"First you tell me—are you coming back to me?"

She didn't look away, as I'd expected. Instead she studied me carefully, as one studies a stranger whose mood and meaning one is trying to read from his face. She didn't say anything, which I think was an answer. But I put it into words. "Too much has happened. Too much murder, too much change. Whatever we had, we don't have it. Can we create something else? I don't know. But you're going one way and I'm going another. For now, that's all there is."

Her eyes were so big. "You're going away, aren't you?"

"Yes."

"Are you ever coming back?" She asked it with an odd, detached air, as if she wasn't certain how much she cared, or was afraid she cared too much, or afraid she cared too little.

"I don't know," I said.

She nodded. "When are you leaving?"

"Right away."

"I'm sorry things have worked out this way."

"Me, too."

"You've left the business to Kragar?"

"Most of it. Except for South Adrilankha."

"What are you doing with that?"

I thought about the courtyard of Castle Black, until the image was strong and clear. I strengthened my connection to the Orb, drew energy, and began the teleport. "All Organization interests in South Adrilankha are yours," I said. "My people will be seeing you in the morning. Enjoy," I added, and I was gone.

ALIERA AND I SAT alone in the library of Castle Black, waiting for Sethra and Morrolan to join us. This place, like my office, held more than a few memories. I'd sat here with my friends—yes, they were certainly that—and held war-councils, consoled each other, and celebrated. Much wine had flowed in this room along with tears and laughter, as well as promises of aid and threats of dismemberment; many of these things within minutes of each other.

I noticed that Aliera was looking at me. "I met your daughter," I said.

"What daughter?"

"You'll find out."

"What are you talking about?"

"Ask your mother. Time does funny things around her, I guess."

She didn't answer directly. "I'll miss you," she said.

"I might be back; who knows?"

"The Jhereg carries a grudge."

"Don't I know it. But still—"

"What will you do?"

"I don't know. I want to be alone for a while."

"I can't imagine that."

"Me wanting to be alone? I suppose you're right. I'll have Loiosh and Rocza, anyway."

"Still—"

"Yeah. I'll probably find some place with people around. Probably Dragaerans, so I can go back to hating them in general and loving them in particular. But right now, I don't want to see anyone."

"I understand," she said.

"I owe you a lot."

"I owe you my life," she said.

"And I owe you mine, several times. I sometimes wish I could remember that previous life, back in the beginning."

"Sethra could arrange that," said Aliera.

"Not now."

"It might help you come to terms with who you are."

"I'll find my own way."

"Yes. You always do."

Morrolan and Sethra joined us before I could ask how she meant that. I said, "This is good-bye, for a while."

"So I had gathered," said Morrolan. "I wish you well on your travels. I shall watch over your grandfather for you."

"Thanks."

Sethra said, "I expect we will meet again, in this life or the next."

"The next," I said. "One way or another, it will be a different life."

Steven Brust

"Yes," said Sethra. "You're right."

I took my leave without another word.

Last of all I spoke with my grandfather. "You look well," he said.

"Thanks."

For the first time in my adult life, I was looking like an Easterner, not a Jhereg. I still had the same cloak, but it was now dyed green. I wore loose darrskin boots, green pants, and a light blue tunic.

"It's necessary, under the circumstances," I said.

"What circumstances are these, Vladimir?"

I explained what had happened, what I was doing about it, and what I thought he should do. He shook his head. "To be a ruler, Vladimir, even of a small place, it is a skill that I have not."

"Noish-pa, you don't have to rule. You don't have to do anything. There are about a hundred families of Teckla there, and a few Easterners, and they've been getting on quite well without anyone ruling them. You need not change anything. A stipend from the Empire goes with the title, and it is sufficient for you to live on. All you have to do is go to Lake Szurke and live in the manor, or castle, or whatever it is. If the peasants come to you with problems, I have no doubt you can suggest solutions, but they probably won't. You can continue your work there with no one to bother you. Where else will you go? And it is just west of Pepperfields, which is in the mountains west of Fenario, so you will be close to our homeland. What could be better?"

He frowned, and at last he nodded. "But what about you?" he said.

"I don't know. I am running for my life now. If things change, and I feel it safe to return, I will."

"And your wife?"

"That's over," I said.

"Is it?"

I tried to meet his eyes, but couldn't. "For now, it is. Maybe later, maybe after time has passed, but not now."

"I threw the sands last night, Vladimir. For the first time in twenty years, I threw the sands and asked what would become of me. I felt the power, and

I read the symbols, and they said I would live to hold a great-grandchild in my arms. Do you think the sands were wrong?"

"I don't know," I said. "I hope they were not. But if you are to see a grandchild, I must be alive to conceive one."

He nodded. "Very well, Vladimir. Do what you must. I will go to this place, and I will live there, so you will know where to find me when you can."

"When I can," I said. "When I can."

Epilogue

THERE WAS A PLACE I remembered well, that meant nothing to anyone else, but a great deal to me. It was engraved forever in my memory, from the isolated patches of bright blue safe-weed among the tall grasses to the bent oak that loomed over the clearing as if to keep it safe from predators above; from the thorns of the wild winesage to the even slope of the wallbush, pointing away from the nearest water. Though barely more than a child when I'd been there before, I knew it; it had etched itself into my memory with a fine detail that I usually saved for the locations of hidden weapons on enemies or the daily habits of targets. Nature, in all its varied beauties and horrors, had hitherto been lost on me, save for this place. Perhaps now that would change.

Somewhere to my left came the sniggering laugh of a chreotha, spitting out its weaving to trap a norska or a squirrel. A bring-me-home, growing from the oak, whipped back and forth in the chilly breeze like a lazy whip: *woosh-snap, woosh-snap*. A daythief, somewhere above me, sobbed in counterpoint to the chreotha. The breeze made the hair on the back of my neck stand up, and I shivered pleasantly. It was just time for lilacs to bloom; they were plentiful here and the scent mixed well with the blossoming of a stonefruit tree that hid itself behind the wallbush, outside the clearing.

It came to mind that it was spring, and that I'd never had much cause to notice the seasons before.

If my life as an assassin had a beginning, perhaps it was here, where I'd found the egg that would grow to become my familiar. If my life as an assassin had an end, it would be here as well. If it turned out to be only an interruption, well, so be it.

Loiosh and Rocza were quiet. Save for them, I was alone. Adrilankha was far away, and there were no cities for miles in any direction.

Alone.

Except for the two jhereg, no one was here to see me, or to speak with me, and the Phoenix Stone guarded my thoughts from any who would seek me that way. I had rendered myself invisible to sorcery. The hardware I carried, dozens of knives, darts, and other nasty things, seemed absurd here. I had no doubt that, as time went on, I'd gradually diminish their number, perhaps to nothing. On my back I carried what clothing I'd need for the changing of the seasons, a spare pair of boots, and a few odds and ends that might come in useful.

Just the three of us now.

It would be easy to give in to self-pity, but I would only have been lying to myself. It was a time of change, a time of growth, as exciting, in its own way, as the moment just before the target would walk up to the spot I'd selected for his execution.

What would happen? Who would I become? Would the Jhereg find a way to track me down? Would love, somehow, emerge from the ashes to which we'd reduced it? Or even spring up elsewhere, unexpected?

I felt a smile on my face, and didn't try to second-guess it.

I began walking west.